"THA...
GAMES AT ALL,"

said Faith. "Dangerous games are military pastimes, not mine."

Uttering this final declaration, she turned determinedly on her heel as if to go. Unexpectedly, Fletcher's hands seized her and spun her back around.

"No," he said.

"Lieutenant! You are hurting me."

There was a dangerous, unfathomable look in his eye. Faith took several short, rapid breaths. My own enemy, she thought.

And then his mouth pressed down, strangely warm and open, onto Faith's parted lips. For a moment, he held her hands still, and then he released them, so that he could embrace her, feel her slender form beneath his touch. Her arms lifted and wrapped about his neck, her fingers tangling in his hair. His lips moved along her skin to her throat and the tender pulse there. He ran his tongue against it, tasting the sweetness of her skin. She moved against him, toward him, the heavy skirt she wore pinned between them, and she felt a heady rush of warmth, in her heart—and in her flesh . . .

FAITH
AND
HONOR

ATTENTION: SCHOOLS AND CORPORATIONS

POPULAR LIBRARY books are available at quantity discounts with bulk purchase for educational, business, or sales promotional use. For information, please write to SPECIAL SALES DEPARTMENT, POPULAR LIBRARY, 666 FIFTH AVENUE, NEW YORK, N Y 10103

ARE THERE POPULAR LIBRARY BOOKS
YOU WANT BUT CANNOT FIND IN YOUR LOCAL STORES?

You can get any POPULAR LIBRARY title in print. Simply send title and retail price, plus 50¢ per order and 50¢ per copy to cover mailing and handling costs for each book desired. New York State and California residents add applicable sales tax. Enclose check or money order only, no cash please, to POPULAR LIBRARY, P. O. BOX 690, NEW YORK, N Y 10019

FAITH AND HONOR

Robin Maderich

POPULAR LIBRARY

An Imprint of Warner Books, Inc.

A Warner Communications Company

POPULAR LIBRARY EDITION

Copyright © 1989 by Robin Maderich
All rights reserved.

Popular Library® and the fanciful P design are registered trademarks
of Warner Books, Inc.

Cover illustration by John Ennis

Popular Library books are published by
Warner Books, Inc.
666 Fifth Avenue
New York, N.Y. 10103

 A Warner Communications Company

Printed in the United States of America

First Printing: October, 1989

10 9 8 7 6 5 4 3 2 1

To my mother,
from whom I learned
to respect
the written word

Acknowledgements

There are, naturally, those family members and friends to whom I am grateful. There are too many of them to mention by name, yet I thank them for their enthusiasm and faithful encouragement.

More specifically, however, I extend my deepest gratitude to my husband, Joe, and our three boys, for their tolerance of my state of mind as I immerse myself in my other worlds. Thank you, now, and forever.

To Denise—my especial gratitude.

To Jeanne, also; and Marie, for coming through when the library was not accessible to me.

To Donald Johnson, for the use of his computer, and the generous gift of his time and interest.

Thank you, one and all.

Robin Maderich

Author's Note

I should like to point out that I have used the Colton family of Longmeadow only for the sake of authenticity; it was my desire to attach the heroine to a place of true existence and real people. However, there was not, to my knowledge, a John Colton residing in the town during that time period, nor a daughter by the name of Faith Mary. Certain events of that revolutionary era are documented, and I have used them, yet otherwise there have been no intentional likenesses to any family members, now or then. I received my information from a very informative book entitled *After the Revolution*, by Barbara Clark Smith.

In addition, I must state that though Lord Percy is most assuredly an accurate historical figure, there was not a Lieutenant Irons under his command.

Finally, I beg forgiveness for an intentional inaccuracy, as the speech presented by Dr. Joseph Warren at the Commemorative of the so-called massacre was, in actuality, bits and pieces removed from a speech of his performance at a similar occasion three years earlier, on the second anniversary in the year of 1772.

FAITH AND HONOR

Chapter One

Boston
January, 1775

In the dim interior of a rattling, hired carriage, the young widow of William Ashley shivered, and woke. Bleary-eyed, she took stock of the inside of the vehicle, momentarily startled to find that, contrary to her uneasy dreaming, she was quite alone.

Faith Mary Ashley looked rumpled in her hunter green travelling attire with her flame red hair flying from beneath a beribboned black bonnet and wisping about her small face. She attempted to shift her body on the hard wooden seat in order to dispel the discomfort of her weary limbs. The jolting of the carriage over ill-kept roads had made her stiff in the most impossible places. With a slender, gloved hand, she massaged the sleep out from her eyes, then retrieved the lap-rug that had fallen from her knees. She closed her eyes again, leaning her head against the top edge of the seat.

Once the pain of a sharp rap against the base of her skull had subsided sufficiently for her to unclamp her teeth and draw breath, Faith called out to the driver to slow his rate of speed. He appeared not to hear.

"Oh, for goodness' sake!"

Sliding across the uncushioned bench, Faith lifted the thick, cloth-panelled curtain that covered the opening to the lacquered door. She opened her mouth to speak, then quickly shut it. She had not realized that they were so near to Boston. At the unfortunate expense of her battered form, the driver had, indeed, made good time.

Outside, the mud flats of the Neck which connected the harbor town to the mainland were hoary with frost; the ice along each blade of grass glittered in the sun. In long shadows the frost lay thickest, as if the touch of an artist's heavy hand had painted it so. Faith could see the chestnut, oak, and elm trees stark against an opalescent morning sky. Raucous crows fled the branches to fly in the warmth of the sun. Turning her head in hope of viewing the lofty spires and sharply angled roofs of Boston, Faith saw instead the dark silhouette of the British fort on the horizon. The heat of anger reached her chilled cheeks. She withdrew her upper body into the carriage, allowing the curtain on its rings to jangle into place.

Inhaling deeply, the young woman removed her gloves and made careful adjustments to her hair, tucking loose tendrils beneath the ruched edging of her bonnet. She retied the dark ribbon beneath her chin, then twisted and tugged the folds of her cloak until she was covered, tentlike, beneath the peat brown woolen garment. Slipping her gloves on once again, Faith tugged at each wrist, and used the forefinger of each hand to push the leather down between consecutive fingers. She tended to these matters with deliberate concentration, avoiding the thought of the ordeal that awaited her at the gate of the fort. It was far better and wiser not to anticipate trouble, as was her usual habit. Rather, she determined to keep her mind on other things, allowing her thoughts to return to the four months she had just spent with her family one hundred miles away in the village of Longmeadow, which was beside the Connecticut River.

But all she could recall was the vivid picture of her father, John Colton, and his expression of bewildered rage when he realized that he could no longer command his twenty-six-year-old daughter. He demanded to know how she dared to defy him by returning to Boston; he belittled her as a soft-headed female who could not possibly comprehend the dangers there.

Longmeadow was far more respectable than the bustling town that was the metropolis of North America and the capital of dissent and mob activity. Faith's reply had been cold and succinct. Boston had become her home.

She had spoken harsh, cruel words in her anger. She had hurt her father, and she regretted it. Yet she had told the truth.

The hooves of the mismatched pair of horses, the large bay and the scrawny sorrel, thudded into the hard-packed earth as they slowed. Groaning as if it would collapse, the carriage dipped first to one side and then the other as the narrow wheels caught in old ruts of passage. Faith clutched the seat for support. When that position proved insufficient, she extended both arms to the vehicle walls and locked them in a very unfeminine manner. She retained this position unconsciously, even when it became unnecessary, until the small panel beneath the coachman's box was opened without warning, and she heard the driver's booming voice. Flustered, she let her arms fall, smoothing down the tiny bows on her bodice.

"Fort's just ahead m'am. A bit of a hold-up, there. Farm carts, and the like, but we should be through soon enough."

"Very well," Faith answered softly, leaning forward in order that the driver should hear her. "I am quite ready."

"Yes, m'am."

Faith had a brief, obstructed view of the line of carts ahead, and then the coachman reached down between his woolen-clothed legs and quietly closed the oak panel. Sighing, Faith reclined in the seat and waited. She could hear her driver, a dark and surly man, cajoling the restless horses as sweetly as if they were his own fractious children. The conveyance inched slowly forward, the wheels creaking as they turned. Someone, at a distance, was bellowing orders. Faith felt her impatience mounting. Be calm, she instructed herself fiercely, knowing that any agitation witnessed by the guard would be construed as a reason for mistrust. And, as she was pondering in annoyance at the course those same guards would take under the circumstances, the carriage rumbled forward in an unprecipitated burst of speed, and then halted. With both hands, Faith prevented a fall to the floor.

"Sweet Jesus," she murmured in prayerful appeal.

Within moments of the brisk command to halt, the stiff suspension of the coach began bobbing as the vehicle was boarded by soldiers performing a cursory inspection of the packages above. There followed a peremptory knock on wood, and the door was opened.

Sunlight and chill air rushed in like water, dispelling all warmth from the confinement. Faith's breath plumed out before her. She felt a tickling in her nose as the tiny hair follicles shrank in the cold.

"If you would step out, please, m'am."

"Naturally," replied Faith, not without irony despite the deep authority with which the request was issued. "In all due haste."

Resting her hand on the door frame, Faith extended a daintily booted foot to the wooden runner. Unintentionally, a well-formed, white-stockinged calf was revealed nearly to the knee beneath the hemline of a pale, striped petticoat and the hunter green skirt. Hastily, Faith flicked the skirt down, dropping gracefully onto the frosty earth. She was a diminutive woman, long-legged despite her stature, but she found herself head-to-head with the middle-aged Captain of the Guard. The fellow's eyes were downcast, staring with pleasured shock at that part of her garment that had so recently ridden up to expose her limb. His face was ruddy as a brick.

"Sir?" Faith prompted him sharply. "You required to speak with me?"

With a good deal of coughing and blustering, the man collected himself, taking charge of his vagrant thoughts long enough to recall the nature of the situation.

"What is your name," he said, "and your business in town?"

"Mrs. William Ashley," said Faith, "and I live here in Boston, sir."

"Indeed?" The captain smiled hopefully, but Faith declined to return the gesture. Inhaling cold air bitterly through his nose, he went on. "Have you been away, then?"

Arching her brows, Faith felt her patience, which had been tenuous at best, slip away. She regarded the man with a strongly defiant gaze. "I have been away four months, and I am now, if you will permit me, returning to my home. Is there anything else which you need to know, Captain? Where I have been and what I did there, perhaps?"

The captain's look was severe and disgusted. He straightened his spine. "You have a waspish tongue," he said. "I suggest that you keep it in check." He regarded her angrily. "Where, pray, do you live, Mrs. Ashley? Exactly, I mean to say."

Bristling, the woman responded to the small man's query with undaunted iciness. "As if," she said coldly, "it is any true concern of yours, sir, I have a home in the North End, left to me, by my husband."

"Quartered?" he said, referring to the billeting of the British.

"Of course not," Faith retorted.

The captain looked at the red-haired Mrs. Ashley, his gimlet eyes angry. He recognized the emotion leaping in her own green gaze: it was the irresponsible, overzealous, self-righteous fervor of a patriot. Drawing himself up in an attempt to stand to his full height of five-foot-three, he said, "The North End is an area particularly rife in rebel dissidence, is it not, Mrs. Ashley? Where is your pass? I should like to see that paper, please."

Faith's hands clenched into fists beneath the heavy folds of her cloak, and she stamped her foot lightly onto the soil. Why had she not kept her temper under control? Biting her lip, she searched blindly through the pocket at her waist for the document which all travelers were required to obtain from Province House before journeying. Pulling the paper free of the narrow drawstring opening, she pushed it out from beneath her cloak, snapping it flat. "Sir," she said.

"Thank you."

His dark eyes were shiny as he perused the document rigidly, searching for flaw or forgery, but the seal of Governor General Gage was legitimate. He spoke with impatience. "Mrs. Ashley, your pass appears to be in order. However," and here he turned pointedly away on the heels of his black shoes to address the soldier still leaning over the top of the hired carriage who was watching the confrontation below with patent amusement, "Private! Search this vehicle. Get Randall to help you."

In dismay, Faith envisioned the hands of the British redcoats rifling through her belongings, through her most private articles of feminine attire and toiletry. Her cheeks burned. She stared, vexed, at the back of the captain's white-wigged head, frantic for words that would make him rescind his order. She took a step closer to him, and halted, glancing toward the coachman. He was staring, stone-faced, at the reins in his hands. Turning her head, Faith scanned the growing crowd beside the gate, and realized that there would be no aid from that quarter. She looked away.

"Captain," she said, "you may search my belongings if you so desire; there is nothing I can, or may, do to prevent that. I am not worried, for I have nothing to hide. But might I not point out, sir, that you should be more concerned with what I might try to smuggle *out* of Boston, rather than *into* it?" Breathing deeply, she lifted her shoulders and squared them, regarding the officer as he pivoted slowly around, his arms folded grimly across his chest. He regarded her with a newfound hostility.

"Madam," he stated stressfully, "I can only wonder at your knowledge of such matters. It does not bode well for your claim of innocence."

Faith frowned in annoyance. He was a wretched man.

He turned away from her, then, and moved to oversee the discharging of the carriage. Bunching her skirt in both hands, Faith lifted the hem of the garment above the top of her boots and started after him. The first item to be tossed down was her hatbox.

"Sir," said Faith, as the hatbox was unceremoniously opened and the protective layering of cream-colored cloth ripped away, "the smuggling of arms and stolen British munitions into the countryside is common knowledge, as I know you must realize. It is doubtful that anything of import could, or would, be brought into the town. Do you not agree?"

The captain grunted wordlessly. "What," Faith demanded sarcastically, giving in to her anger, "do you expect to find in there, Captain? Another missing cannon? Even were I to wear all of my hats upon my head, of which there are not many, mind you, I do not believe there would be the room. Or a pistol, mayhaps? If so, the weight of the box should have told your men differently. And why would I be troubling to return, either? Pray, enlighten me, sir.''

Among the crowd closest to the unfolding scene she heard a general tittering. The captain turned around, his entire countenance as ruddy as the dirty coat of his uniform. He advanced quickly, quivering with wrath. Faith wondered whether the man was going to strike her, or clap her in irons. She took a small step backward, an action less of fear than of avoidance, and came solidly up against a form of strong resistance; a form that was undeniably male in character, and which, upon the instant, took hold of her arm through the thick material of her cloak. She heard a voice above her head, remarkable in resonance and authority.

"Captain," the man spoke, his voice revealing the mother country in its accents. "I believe that the lady has made a valid point."

Faith gasped, attempting to remove her elbow from the stranger's grasp, but the man would not relinquish it. "Captain," he continued, quite calmly, as if there were no struggle going on beneath him, "am I not correct?"

To continue to struggle would be undignified. Rather, Faith decided, a well-placed heel, advantageous both in its minimal effort and in the effect of surprise, would work as well. Unfortunately, the stranger was acute in anticipating such an action, and sidestepped her descending foot. Afterward, he gave her arm a little shake, much as one might to a child misbehaving in public.

Though furious, Faith subsided.

"Captain?" prodded the stranger. "Until you give the order, your men will continue to tear through the private possessions of one of Boston's citizens. If you pause to reconsider, you will realize that your suspicions are unwarranted, and unfair."

From a distance of a half-dozen feet or so, the officer met the stranger's gaze above the woman's head. He obviously recognized the man. Briskly, he grunted his assent, then turned

to his men with a command to return the contents of the hatbox
and allow the vehicle to pass through the barricade without
further disruption.

"Thank you, Captain," said the stranger.

Growling a reply, the officer raised his hand in something
resembling half of a salute, and stalked away to oversee the
inspection of a loaded cart leaving Boston. The stranger released his hold on Faith's arm. Gathering her dignity on a
drawn breath, she pivoted to face him.

She stared at her benefactor. She had expected someone
British, and his features were, indeed, aristocratic, though de-
fined by strength rather than the characteristic weakness typical
to such beautiful structuring. Beneath an elegant, but dusty,
tricorne hat, his hair was dark; it swept away from a peak at
his forehead and was tied carelessly with taffeta at the nape of
his neck. His jaw was firm, clearly in need of a razor's application; his eyes were gray-blue, and as deeply set as those
of the Celts. He gazed at her in open assessment upon seeing
her startled expression.

"I—forgive me," she said, extending her gloved hand from
beneath her cloak. Shrugging in his tan greatcoat, he raised
his hand to take her fingers in a quick grasp, then let them
drop. "I am deeply grateful for the trouble which you have
taken in pleading my defense," she continued, staring in fascination at the slow smile that lifted the corners of his mouth.
"If I may return the kindness someday, sir, I will gladly do
so, Mr. . . . may I know your name?"

"Irons," said the man, in a well-modulated tone.

"Mr. Irons," repeated Faith, shifting her weight from one
foot to another in impatience. Grateful for a distraction, she
received her hatbox into her arms from a young footsoldier.
"Thank you once again," she said to Mr. Irons, and then
turned away, making the awkward ascent into the carriage
unaided. Once inside, she settled the hatbox onto the floor and
reached for the door. Mr. Irons was there ahead of her, grasping
the handle.

"I beg your pardon," he said, moving into a position that
shadowed the interior of the vehicle, "I am not normally one

to call in favors, but if you would not mind, I am rather weary and would be greatly disposed to call the account even if you would allow me to share your coach into town.''

For an instant, Faith was silent, thinking rapidly, but there seemed no excuse that she could reasonably offer him for refusal. Her hesitation did not go unnoticed.

Mr. Irons stepped back. Sunlight filtered in around his tall form, revealing the outline of his clothes and the rumpled, muddied condition of his dark breeches. ''I understand,'' he said. ''I should not have been so bold as to ask.''

His face was in shadow, concealed from Faith's view. But she clearly imagined the expression of annoyance that his tone betrayed.

''Mr. Irons, I am sorry,'' she apologized. ''Please come in. You are certainly welcome.'' To lend credence to her words, Faith slid the hatbox to the opposite wall with her foot. ''Come in and sit down, sir.'' She swept her skirts aside.

Wordlessly, the man bent and entered, settling himself on the bench facing her, stretching out his long limbs with an audible sigh. Extending his arm, he took hold of the window edge and swung the door shut heavily. Then, quite at his ease, he rapped on the coachman's box from beneath and ordered the driver to move on.

As the vehicle jolted into motion, Faith sat with eyes downcast, nervously regretting her decision. Her apprehension was not feigned, fluttering timidity. It was quite real; and totally unlike her.

After a moment, she risked an upward glance, surprising a look on the gentleman's face that nearly justified her feminine trepidation, yet immediately upon perceiving it, the expression vanished, and the man folded his arms across his chest, smiled benevolently, and closed his eyes. Licking her lips with a quick slip of her tongue, Faith looked away.

Through the slightly lifted curtain, she observed their passage along the barricade and the formidable line of soldiers, three men deep, who were dressed in their scarlet coats and white webbing. Progress was slow, and she found many pairs of eyes staring back at her own. Wearily, she rubbed suede-covered fingers across her brow, blotting out the sight. She hated the color of those uniforms. They were as red as freshly spilt blood.

Under cover of her curved and slender fingers, Faith peered once again at her companion. Incredibly, he appeared to be sleeping. At her leisure, she studied the disheveled state of his clothing. Somehow, it did not match the quality of his bearing, which suggested greater wealth or position. Perhaps, as with so many, this man had fallen upon hard times since the mandated closing of the harbor. Was he a British merchant? She would not care for that. The British merchants were adamant Tories, all.

She gazed at his face, at the relaxed planes, the high angles. He was clearly an Englishman, of extraordinary good looks, even in exhausted sleep. His jaw was strong and angular; his nose distinct, with a fine bridge and structure, his brows swept from it like the wings of an eagle.

Sighing, she stared at her own hands. Outside of normal curiosity, she had no interest in the man. What did it matter who he was, or what his political views were? He was a fleeting traveling companion, nothing more. He was not even a companion by choice.

Faith turned her eyes again to the parted curtain and the slowly passing vista of Orange Street. It had been only three years since her husband had been gone. That was not long enough, she thought, to forgive herself such idle musings about a stranger.

Leaning against the open window with one hand hooked in support over the casing, Faith welcomed the freshening breeze upon her cheeks. The wind was cool, damp, and scented with the salt of the sea. It tugged at her bonnet, at the ribbons, loosening wispy locks of hair to fly about her forehead and over her eyes. Home, the wind said to her, in its smells and its sounds. She had chosen a home far away from family and the familiar places of childhood.

Withdrawing her head, Faith pressed her spine against the uncushioned bench, removing her gloves in order to subdue the hair flying about her face, but her fingers were numb with cold. She lowered them with careful deliberation, then she raised her eyes in the same manner to view the male occupant of the bench opposite. Beneath thick, dark lashes, his gray eyes were narrowed and watchful.

Faith started, mantling to her hairline. "I woke you," she said. "I did not mean to."

"No harm done," replied the gentleman, cordially, shifting about to massage the back of one knee with a slow, circular pressure of his fingers. "I was not asleep, I am afraid."

Recalling her rude curiosity, Faith felt a renewed heat flush her fair skin. "Oh," she said, "were you not?"

"No."

Faith coughed delicately.

"You have me at a disadvantage," the man continued, resuming an erect position. "You know my name, but we have not been properly introduced."

Faith hesitated. "Mrs. Ashley," she said. "Mrs. William Ashley."

"Ah," said Irons quietly, embodying a certain disappointment in his tone. "The name is familiar. Would I be acquainted with your husband's craft, or place of business?"

Faith blinked. "My husband is deceased, sir."

"I am sorry, Mrs. Ashley."

In silence, Faith regarded the flaccid, stitched fingers of her fawn-colored gloves. Beyond them, over a soft swirl and fall of hunter green wool, the stranger's knee was two inches from her own. Defiantly, she avoided thinking of it. She held her leg very still.

"Mrs. Ashley?"

Faith looked up quickly. "Mr. Irons?"

"As you are aware," he said, "I could not help but overhear your . . . conversation with the guard captain. In particular, the latter part. Are you always so outspoken on such matters?"

"What matters?" Faith countered archly. She twisted the gloves in her hands. The scent of leather was sweet.

"Matters," replied Mr. Irons, "which one might consider more than a lady's business. Military matters," he qualified, "or treasonous."

Faith's lovely head lifted sharply at the unexpected edge to his words. She sat back, chin tilted in a posture which she unconsciously assumed whenever discussing the topic of her patriotism. "Which," she said, pulling her knees suddenly and firmly together, "do you believe, sir? Have I not the right to pass, unmolested, to my home? I am not a common criminal . . . no matter what I speak."

"Have I said so?" asked the stranger. "I have not, Mrs. Ashley. Not at all, although I would be remiss if I did not remind you that there are many who entertain no notions of leniency. You spoke of 'another cannon,' which might suggest that you have some personal knowledge of that which was smuggled out of Boston before. I am not inclined to believe that, but you must admit that such an acid comment could not sit lightly on the shoulders of a member of the British military, and of the troop whose duty it is to prevent such occurrences."

"What are you suggesting, Mr. Irons?"

"Only that you exercise caution in the future. Otherwise, you may find every one of your personal belongings in the hands of the military."

"Commandeered?" demanded Faith coldly.

"I beg your pardon?" said the man, and began to chuckle. "I should hardly think so. Not, at any rate, over such a trifling incident. I meant, Mrs. Ashley, another search-and-seizure, should the occasion arise that you desire to leave Boston."

"I see," said Faith, declining stiffly. He had made his point.

After a moment of consideration, Faith laughed self-consciously, lifting her eyebrows at Mr. Irons' expression. "Forgive me," she said contritely. "You have been very kind, and this, I suppose, is only a further warning."

"Indeed."

"Then it seems," she stated, "that I must thank you."

"You are quite welcome, Mrs. Ashley, I assure you." Smiling in amusement, he turned his body into the corner of the carriage, swinging one leg up onto the bench. Faith could see the long, curving muscles of his thigh through the fabric of his breeches. She averted her eyes, but too late to prevent the warmth that prickled along her skin.

"I must confess," the man went on, as if he had not noticed her gaze, or her distress, "that I had not expected an apology from you."

Faith frowned. "Oh?" she said. "Why not?"

"I have received the impression that you are very firm in your beliefs; possibly narrow in your sight of them."

"Stubborn?" assisted Faith, dryly.

"Yes," said the man.

"Opinionated?"

"Possibly," he agreed, appreciatively.

"And wicked, too, I would guess."

"In all probability."

By this time, Faith had developed an enthusiasm for their bantering, and had all she could do to keep from laughing outright. "Oh, come now, Mr. Irons, you know that I am none of those things, sir," she cried, nearly overcome by her unaccountable humor.

"Do I?" the man retorted.

"Not all of them, surely?" Faith rejoined, sobering slightly.

He looked at her, and a smile came to his face. "Perhaps not," he said.

She gazed at the man, at the smile that revealed well-kept teeth and an odd little dimple. Merriment was reflected in his dark eyes. He was enjoying the moment as much as she was. Faith smiled back, reserving nothing, and it lit her eyes in the dimness of the carriage. For so long, she had turned from the attentions of any man. Yet she welcomed the attention of this stranger. Alone with him, she risked flirtation, an open smile, laughter.

Without meaning to, she allowed the small silence to stretch between them. The smile left her face gradually. Across from her, the stranger's smile dropped with less subtlety. He grew very still. The gaze of his smoky gray eyes was direct and sober. Faith felt herself caught by it, as if in his hands. She was suddenly conscious of the breadth of his shoulders, in that confined space. Her lips parted slightly, in surprise. She wondered how his mouth would feel on her own, and there was such intensity in that one desire that she was left shaken, breathless.

And ashamed. She felt weak for allowing herself to lose control of her thoughts. Surely it was a betrayal of happy times past.

Faith jerked away, against the seat. Her blood pounded in her ears, and in her breast. Her cheeks felt hot. She pressed her hands to them, attempting to regain her composure.

"Mr. Irons, you must excuse me. I am as giddy as a child. It has been a long journey, and I am very tired."

It was some time before he replied. He removed his tricorne, brushing the dust from it as he placed it on the seat beside his leg. "I understand," said he. "Where have you been?"

Faith shrugged, toying with her gloves. "Longmeadow. I doubt if you have heard of it. It is a small village, more than one hundred miles from Boston, and a circuitous route, at best."

"I have never heard of the place, no. Is it your home, Mrs. Ashley?"

"It was," answered the widow. "Once."

Mr. Irons nodded. Grimacing, he reached a hand to his unshaven jawline, rubbing the stubble of hair beneath his extended fingers. "I have been abroad myself," he said, "in the countryside."

"What were you doing?" Faith asked, carelessly, her mind elsewhere.

The stranger paused, eyes narrowing. He ran his fingers through the coal black hair peaking at his forehead. "That," he said, "must remain no business of yours, Mrs. Ashley. I am sorry."

Rebuffed, Faith sat wordlessly. Annoyed with herself and her companion, she turned her attention outside to the street, which had grown more congested. Belatedly, Faith realized the carriage had slowed. In the same instant, Mr. Irons leaned across the seat and jerked the curtain closed.

Faith jumped in alarm.

"Mr. Irons, why did you—"

"A precaution," he interjected hastily. "You are a widow, traveling alone, and I do not suppose that it would be wise to be found, unexpectedly, in my company." He shifted about on the uncomfortable bench once again, unwinding the greatcoat from about his legs. The garment gapped in front, exposing a crisp white shirt, conspicuously clean compared to his breeches, with the ugly exception of an irregularly crusting stain of drying blood.

"Mr. Irons! You are hurt!"

"Am I?" the man countered. With a swiftness that was startling, he caught her hand as it appeared from beneath her cloak to reach out across the aisle to him. Her green eyes opened wide as she attempted to free her gloved fingers from his grasp. He resisted, rather firmly.

"Mr. Irons!"

"Mrs. Ashley," he said.

Slowly, he turned her hand over, caressing her palm with the ball of his thumb in a strong, sensual gesture. He closed her fingers, pressing them down within the curve of his hand. Faith felt a shortening of her breath in the close atmosphere of the coach as the simplicity of his touch revived sensations that had been long lost. He held her hand, and the strength of his grip and the gentleness, which spoke without words of further pleasures, caused her to shiver. With a tiny cry, she bit her lip, and pulled away.

"No," she said.

"Mrs. Ashley?"

Faith shook her head.

"I can see that I have upset you. I am sorry for that."

Faith did not reply. She gazed down at her hand, curled in her lap, and relived the tender thrill of a stranger's touch. How could she? Ah, how could she?

"I—I merely thought that you were hurt," she said.

"I am," he answered her, "but not seriously."

Faith said nothing. She kept her eyes averted.

After a moment, Mr. Irons turned to open the small panel beneath the coachman's box.

"Halt here, driver. As soon as the way is clear."

Gathering his coat close, he addressed Faith:

"We will be parting company shortly, Mrs. Ashley. I must thank you now for your hospitality. You are free from debt, should we meet again." He smiled, openly amused. Faith bristled.

"You are welcome, of course," she said.

"Will we meet again, Mrs. Ashley?" he persisted.

Faith raised her eyes to his, speechlessly. She saw a handsome man, a seemingly generous man, who was asking her a simple question. How easy it would have been, she supposed, to be careless and indulgent and say yes. The inclination was there, as well as the desire. But she told herself that she was tired, and long settled in her life, and that there was no place in it for a man such as he. There could not be.

"No," said Faith, more sharply than she had intended. "I think not."

The man answered in silence, rising from his seat as the carriage creaked to a halt. He swung the door open and stepped down. He turned without speaking to gaze into the vehicle's shadowed interior, patting the dust from his coat sleeves. His eyes were disquieting, rainwashed slate. Abruptly, he rapped on the coachman's high-box. The driver called to the horses. The carriage lurched into motion as the stranger swung closed the door without a word.

Faith settled back against the seat. She touched her cheeks.

As if there were someone nearby in need of convincing, she said aloud, "Thank goodness he is gone."

Chapter Two

Soldiers walked the street, singly and in pairs, occasionally looking for trouble, usually looking for work to supplement their meagre incomes. There had been a time when even Whig families had willingly provided for these red-coated boys who were far from home. They had prided themselves on their compassion.

But no more.

Sighing, Ezra Briggs allowed the sheer curtain to slip from his fingers over the mullioned window, shutting out the street-scene outside. He scratched the nape of his heavy neck just below the corona of frizzed white hair that was all which remained to him of a thick, dark head of fine locks, the man's gaze roved about his small law office. His littered desk held the stoppered ink-well and quill; his own split-tailed velvet coat hung on a chair back; and two stuffed armchairs were angled toward each other in front of the small, but ornate, firewell. Expensive carpet on pine planking and landscape paintings hanging on papered walls were evidence of his hard work in that office. He had made something of himself at a time before the upstart created by Adams and the admirable Mr. John Hancock. Then, a lawyer's profession had still been frowned upon as an unsavory occupation.

Removing his spectacles from his waistcoat pocket, Ezra slipped them onto his nose, then crossed the room to peer intently at the eight-day clock on the mantelpiece.

"My word," he muttered to himself, "it is later than I thought." Limping to the chair, he lifted the coat and put it on over the embroidered waistcoat and matching knee breeches, making certain that the cuffs of the coat were unbuttoned to allow the fullness of the gathered sleeves to show through. Such was the fashion; and he fancied it, though he had no taste for the long trousers which some men were sporting.

Suddenly, he recalled the state of his nearly bald head. "Mrs. Hart!" he cried, directing his voice toward the closed door that led to the back of the house and his living quarters.

"Mrs. Hart!"

The woman appeared posthaste, almost as if she had been standing just before the other side of the door. The housekeeper poked a white-capped head around the door frame, her one hand clutching the knob in support. She was bent over.

"Yes, sir?"

Briggs appeared puzzled. "What are you doing there?"

"Here, sir?"

"In that position, is my meaning," snapped the lawyer.

"Mr. Briggs," the woman said, in her softly rounded accents, "I do not appreciate being spoken to like that, sir. For nigh on twenty years, I have been working for you, sir, and you should know that by now."

Ezra pretended his usual annoyance at her response, glaring at the spare, feisty woman over the rim of his spectacles.

"You have not answered me, Mrs. Hart," he said.

"Aye, and that I have not. I were picking up me dust rag, if you don't mind, sir."

"Were you?" Ezra countered, his pale blue eyes twinkling with silent amusement. "Well, I have summoned you concerning my wig. Have you done with it, then? It is getting late, and I should like to be wearing it."

"Ah," grunted the woman, straightening her curving spine. "Been wonderin' when you'd get 'round to asking for it. I suppose you'll be wanting the mirror, too, eh?"

"Naturally," puffed the lawyer.

The housekeeper, tidy in brown homespun and cotton lace, waved the dust rag airily. "Naturally," she echoed, exiting with the sound of a crisp petticoat. Waiting, Ezra removed his spectacles for polishing. He worked them over carefully with his lawn handkerchief, first one oblong lens, and then the other, until they were spotless, and put them back on. The cleaning of his spectacles had become a morning ritual, a habit developed over the years. Without the polishing of the spectacles, the day should not begin.

Taking a turn about the chamber, Ezra settled into the chair before the fire, gazing at the rough pyramid of flaming timber. Where was Faith Ashley? he wondered. He really had expected her sooner. It was for precisely that reason he had sent the hired carriage after her, rather than have her spend most of the day on the back of a farm-cart, making her way down from Lexington. Well, doubtless the young woman would be arriving soon enough. After all, she could not possibly return home without collecting the key that she had left in his charge. And, he suspected, the lady's affection for him would naturally involve a personal visit to announce her arrival within Boston, and to thank him.

It was a course of events for which he had planned very carefully.

Tapping once on the oak-panelled door, Mrs. Hart returned, bearing Ezra's powdered wig on a wooden stand, and a silver-embossed looking glass. With remarkably few words, she held the mirror in the proper position while he donned the white wig, adjusted the curls over his ears and then assured himself that the taffeta tying the pony tail was of a shade to match his coat. Mrs. Hart had performed this duty for him countless times, and he knew that he would find no fault with her keeping of the hairpiece, but nonetheless he made a great show of concern.

"Somethin' wrong, Mr. Briggs?" drawled the housekeeper.

"Never," replied the lawyer.

Mrs. Hart nodded in satisfaction, pivoting on a trim heel to leave, but abruptly she looked beyond the man to the window with a curious expression. "Sir," she began, "there be a carriage pulling out front. Do you suppose that it could be—Mrs. Ashley?"

Following the housekeeper's gaze, Ezra Briggs' sallow complexion grew pink with pleasure. At last, he thought. These four months have seemed like a year.

"Open the door at once, Mrs. Hart. At once!"

The hired carriage had trundled to a noisy halt at curbside on Queen Street, narrowly avoiding a run-in with the open gutter that ran the length of the curving street to the wharf and harbor. The flowing refuse steamed. Inside the carriage, Faith wrinkled her nose at the stench. She had forgotten it, in the fresh air of the countryside. Extracting a silk-embroidered, lace-edged square of linen from the pocket about her waist, Faith pressed it to her nostrils gently.

Leaning forward with a frown, Faith pushed the dark curtain fully across the length of the bar with such force that the rings jangled. Revealed in the open frame of the window was the painted doorway of Number Twenty-nine, the mullioned windows with open shutters were of the same tint, and the sign hanging above the sidewalk bore the words: *Solicitor, Ezra Briggs*. Above the words was a comical little caricature of a man, who was dressed in a white wig and a fading dark robe, to indicate to the illiterate that this was the home of a lawyer.

As she was studying the familiar scene in a moment of self-indulgence, the door of the frame-house opened inward to reveal the rounded figure of the solicitor, impeccably attired as usual, bewigged and bespectacled, his pale blue eyes twinkling merrily.

Faith threw open the carriage door. "Ezra!" she exclaimed in delight.

"My dear," responded Briggs. "Come out, come out! Here, allow me your hand."

Faith rested her gloved hand in the soft palm of the man, and, standing at an extreme angle, with her skirt lifted to provide the necessary freedom of movement, she stepped lightly out of the vehicle and across the running gutter. Smiling at the elderly lawyer, Faith promptly bussed his chilled cheek.

"My dear!" he cried as if mortified, though secretly he was quite pleased, "mind the neighbors."

"Oh," said Faith, "fie on the neighbors! I may kiss, if I choose, the man who has been as an uncle to me, and friend to both my father and my mother since before I was birthed."

Ezra cleared his throat, dwelling for a fleeting instant on the term uncle. "Why, yes," he agreed, "of course."

Cheerily, Faith tucked her hand into the old man's velvet elbow. "Tell me how you have been," she insisted as they moved toward the open doorway and the creased, welcoming countenance of the housekeeper.

"Well enough," replied Ezra shortly.

"Indeed? How splendid to hear that! I have been worried, you must know. And your leg? You are still limping."

Ezra rolled his eyes behind their magnifying lenses. "There is not much to be done for that, I am afraid."

"What is it, then?"

"Inflammation of the joints," declared Mrs. Hart firmly, ensconced on the threshold with arms akimbo. Her eyes brimmed with tears as Faith spoke in greeting, and embraced her gently.

"Mrs. Hart," Ezra admonished in a soft voice, "contain yourself. Take the driver into the kitchen, and feed him something; tell him that I have said so, and he must wait for Mrs. Ashley. Faith, dear, come inside."

"Thank you," said Faith. "I am very much in need of a soft cushion to sit upon."

The lawyer laughed in appreciation of the jest that, in varied company, might have been considered too bold. Ushering Faith through the door past the dew-eyed housekeeper, he urged her into one of the chairs beside the hearth and sat down opposite. He crossed his silk-clothed knees, with difficulty. The buckles on his shoes winked with reflected firelight. During an interval of silence in which Mrs. Hart exited to do as she was bade and Faith removed her gloves and stretched her hands to the fire to warm them, Ezra watched the young woman with open fondness.

"I cannot imagine," he spoke after a time, "that your father would allow you to return to Boston once he had you beneath his roof, my dear. Do you not think that you would have been better in Longmeadow with your family?"

Faith made a small sound. "One can see why the two of you have remained friends, Ezra. Your thoughts run the same." Smoothing the fawn gloves upon her lap, she added, "He wanted me to stay, but I would not. My father no longer has control of my affairs. You must understand that."

Ezra shrugged his heavy shoulders. "I will do my best to see that you remain safe."

"Of course you will," Faith answered, tossing the gloves onto the polished top of the circular table nearby. Ezra Briggs was a Tory. He suffered from Loyalist politics, and Loyalist ideals. And he had no idea, she felt certain, of the true state of affairs within Boston, or of her own part therein.

"Mrs. Hart is preparing a little something for us, I believe. I know it's quite early in the day, but you will take tea with me, won't you?"

Faith looked up, studying the round, wizened face, the pale, ageing eyes beyond the pair of glass lenses. No, she thought, he does not really comprehend the rebellion in its entirety. Gently, she reminded him that she did not drink tea.

"But I do drink it, Faith, dear," Ezra chided. "If it is any consolation to you, the tea is Dutch black-market. There is no good English tea to be had, these days, with the harbor closed, and no one willing to import it anyway, after that criminal display on the Dartmouth. Indians, indeed! You may have cider, if you would prefer."

"I would, Ezra. I am sorry."

In an impulse toward uncustomary anger, the lawyer said, "Do not apologize to me. I am not the sovereign whom you rebels offend so wrongfully."

"Offend? Do you truly believe that all which is desired is offense, like children who do wrong to gain parental attention? I suppose it is that, yes, and much more."

Ezra waved his hand, catching the sunlight through the window in a small ruby on his pinkie. "I will not preach to you; I know how stubborn you are, and have been, since the very day that you insisted on crawling from your cradle." Faith's bright laughter was a balm. The lawyer smiled. "Oh, Faith," he said, "we must not quarrel, you and I. You have been gone four months, and I have missed you."

"And I you, Ezra! You shall have your tea, and I my cider, and not another word shall be said, agreed?"

Briggs sighed. "Agreed," he said.

Mrs. Hart served their small tea in the parlor a short time later, once Faith had taken the time to freshen up, washing her face and hands in scented water, and repinning her red-gold hair before the silvered surface of a gilt-edged mirror. Returning to the parlor with all wrinkles smoothed and gathers fluffed, she looked refreshed and as lovely as ever as she sat down to pour. Leaning across the table, she lifted the floral creamware teapot, tilting the elegant spout over Ezra's cup. The steaming dark brew gave off an earthy aroma.

Ezra closed his eyes, inhaling the scent. Faith was offering him brown lump-sugar or honey for his tea, but as always he refused both, reaching inside of his coat for the flask of intricately worked silver. Opening it, he let a goodly amount of the amber liquid run into his cup. The odor of colonial rum was heady, sweet, and dark. Ezra noted that Faith looked away, studiously observing the tip of her black boot peeking out from beneath the hem of her heavy skirt.

She has fine English features, he thought, though she may rebel against them. But the soft red hair and green eyes are of her mother's Irish ancestry. Her mother had that same pale scattering of freckles across the bridge of her nose just like

Faith's, but where her chin was both pointed and delicate, Faith's was founded on the determination of paternal kin, and of her own strong personality.

"You look like your mother, Faith, God rest her soul."

Faith smiled. "You have said that before."

"Have I?" Ezra responded. "Perhaps, I am forgetful."

"Only indulgent," said Faith.

"That also," he agreed, picking up a pumpkin tart from a pretty salt-glazed stoneware plate. He bit into it with relish, chewing in noisy contentment. He followed the pumpkin with an apple, turning the pastry over once before biting into the browned crust. The filling was fragrant with cinnamon. Faith tucked a stray lock of hair behind her ear, sipping at her cup of hot, spiced cider.

"Have you been to see Elizabeth, Ezra?"

The lawyer started, as if from a waking dream, or at the prod of some sharp object. "Elizabeth?" he echoed. "Why, yes, I have been. I went down to Salt Lane only two or three days ago. She is well, my dear, and anxious for your return."

Nodding, Faith reflected on the wisdom of having taken in the sixteen-year-old Elizabeth Watts to board after William's death. Not only was the child's company rewarding, the girl was a hard worker as well. But during Faith's stay in Longmeadow, Elizabeth had gone to her own home on Salt Lane where her six siblings lived.

"I must say," Ezra continued, "I was not made very welcome in that household, and I only went for your sake."

"Oh?"

"Yes," said Ezra. "One of the youngest babes, I do not know its name, had the temerity to stand in the middle of the floor chanting 'Tory! Tory!' to my face, and no one bothered very hard to correct it."

"Oh, Ezra, not really? Please, take into consideration the—"

Ezra interrupted. "Why you choose to acquaint yourself with seditious rebels is truly beyond my understanding! You, a gently bred woman, Faith! These rowdies who call themselves patriots, Sons of Liberty, even Masons, for goodness' sake!

They will bring trouble onto all of our heads, mark my words. The day is coming when our good King George will tolerate their behavior no more.''

Faith sat up, reassessing her earliest opinion that Ezra knew very little of the rebellion's extent. Yet, she felt a heat of anger suffuse her skin. She had tried, in the past, to enlighten the man, but he was as stubborn as she, admittedly, was herself. She drew a deep breath. "Ezra," she said, "am I not one of those seditious rebels you speak of?"

The lawyer was silent.

"You have no tolerance for Whig policies, it is true, Ezra, but if I may speak honestly, I love you no less because of that. I should hope that I am a person who is able to separate a man from his politics. Or, I should say, a particular man, for I have known you all of my life.''

"But you resort to violence in order to make a political point," Ezra said.

Eyebrows lifting, Faith countered, "Not I, personally?"

"Of course not," Ezra replied testily.

"Nor many others," said Faith.

Heaving a rummy breath, Ezra swivelled in his chair, tossing another log onto the fire. The wood, well seasoned, smoked and caught, sending brilliant sparks fleeing into the draft of the chimney. He loosened his waistcoat and stretched his legs to the hearthstone, the heat penetrating the soles of his silver-buckled shoes.

"Where," Faith went on, "is the line drawn between politics and friendship, affectation and conscience?"

Frowning, Ezra removed his spectacles, wiping the lenses with an edge of a cloth napkin. The lashes fringing his pale eyes were nearly white. He blinked them rapidly as he tried to collect himself.

"What about your attitude toward the British troops, Faith?" he asked suddenly. "I cannot but fail to point out your prejudicial anger toward them."

Quickly, Faith replied, "Ezra, they are an occupying force, sent to assure a denial of our individual rights, and those of the Body of the People."

"The Body of the People!" Ezra exclaimed with vehe-

mence. "I am heartily sick of the phrase!" He tapped a quiet
log with the iron poker so that it spat and fizzed, then he poured
himself another cup of tea, laced it liberally with a second dose
of rum, and muttered, "You speak far too fluently for a
woman."

In actuality, however, he found her intellect admirable,
though too often horribly infuriating. Faith was a headstrong,
iron-willed young woman. This fact was never made more
evident than when she had, with quiet insistence, wed the
smuggler William Ashley, against the wishes of her parents.
No matter how respected the profession was among the colonists in need of it, smuggling was still beyond the limits of
the law. But she had wed the man, even asking Ezra to stand
by, and had moved to Boston where her rebellious soul had
found its true wings.

The corners of Ezra's mouth turned down, but they could
not disguise the light that had come into his faded blue eyes.
He loved Faith, in a way that no longer had much to do with
his adoptive relationship of long-standing within her family.
Her frankness, her vitality, the invigorating stimulation of her
company, made him feel youthful in her presence; not as a
child, but as a man in his prime.

In the midst of Ezra Briggs' silence, Faith sipped at her
cider, looking here and there about the parlor to avoid any
impression of anger. She was not angry with the man, only
with his lack of vision. She had known him too long, and too
well, to be moved to ill feelings.

Slowly, she looked about the room that had become very
familiar and dear to her over the passage of years. It was
showing signs of maturity in the seasoned glow of the heavy
panelling; in the mellowed shade of the plastered ceiling, like
the gentle brown of eggshells; in the worn planking of the floor;
and in the great darkened well of the fireplace. Above the
mitered mantelpiece was a portrait of Ezra's wife, gone thirty
years and more. Kathleen Donovan Briggs had posed for the
portrait while still a bride-to-be in voluminous folds of rose-
colored silk and white tulle. Kathleen's eyes had apparently
been of such a rich, deep blue as to be nearly black, and the
ageing of the painted surface had done little to dispel the mys-

tery of her dark gaze. Faith recognized in the rendering the signs of a young woman in love. It was there in the eyes, in the carriage of the head, and in the contented slope of ivory shoulders; there, in the precious curve of the mouth.

Faith glanced sidelong at Ezra, who was toying with the idea of consuming another apple tart. He looked so comfortable and contained seated in the deeply cushioned chair which had so long been his favorite, and which had been in that exact place since before Faith had wed and come to Boston. One day, Faith would have a room such as this, full of her life's memories and possessions, many of them bearing William's mark upon them. She, like Ezra, would be tired, widowed for a multitude of empty days. She closed her eyes, and sighed. Did she really want a multitude of empty days? and objects in a room which would give comfort?

She was not alone. She had Elizabeth and Ezra, and her family, though they were far from Boston. She had acquaintances within the circle of her daily activity; and the jobs, meagre though they might be, that aided the patriot cause and kept her busy. Faith had settled into her life with independence and fortitude. She did not think she could reasonably ask for more.

Yet, for a few moments, she felt uncertain. And in her uncertainty, she was afraid.

Bending the wire frames of his spectacles to better suit the tilt of his ears, Ezra repositioned them in front of his eyes, swallowing the last mouthful of his second apple pastry. He searched his teeth with his tongue for a sliver of peel that had escaped the knife. "My dear," he said, as if continuing a conversation rather than speaking into the silence that had grown between them, "the years have mounted more swiftly than I have realized."

Startled by the similarity of their thoughts, Faith looked closely at the man.

"Ezra, what do you mean to say?"

Questioned with such directness, the lawyer hesitated. He coughed. He wiped his fingers on the white napkin, refolding the square of linen carefully. He rebuttoned his waistcoat. At his feet, the fire shivered, whistling. Outside, a brisk gusting

wind rattled the shutters against the clapboard. Faith rose and
went to the window. Clouds, which had been hovering threateningly over the mainland to the northwest since early evening
the day before, were rolling pearly gray across the Charles
River.

"This has been the mildest winter in many a year," Faith
commented when the man still had not spoken.

"Yes," concurred Ezra quietly, "the mildest in years."

"But I believe it will snow," Faith continued, eyeing the
lowering sky. She heard the scrape of wood on wood, and
knew that Ezra had risen from his chair. She waited, feeling
an odd chill of apprehension. She shook it off, chiding herself
for her foolishness.

"My dear," Ezra began, behind her elbow, then paused.
He was respiring heavily. The air was scented with stale rum
and earthy Dutch tea.

"Yes?"

"Faith," he said, faltering again.

William Ashley's young widow waited without speaking.
Outside the window, autumn's forgotten leaves tumbled past
like brown kittens chasing the winds. A newspaper impaled
itself on someone's rusted bootscraper, flapping erratically. In
the rear of the house, far away it seemed, Ezra's housekeeper
was conversing with the coachman, and laughing.

Faith turned her green eyes toward the lawyer. His sallow
cheeks were ruddy, his eyes hidden from her, behind the twin
reflection of the mullioned windows. She looked away again,
and up, at the fine, lacy edge of the curtains.

"Ezra," she said, "what is it?"

For a moment, Ezra stared at her profile, still breathing
forcefully, and then he did an odd thing. Something so startling
that Faith drew back in amazement, and then fear, for he was
dropping to his swollen, silk-covered knee. "Faith," he repeated again, short of wind, "will you—I wish to say—to
ask—"

Dismayed, Faith stooped, slipping her hands beneath the
lawyer's elbows to assist him to his feet. "Please, Ezra, stand
up. Are you unwell? Shall I call Mrs. Hart?"

"Damnation, no!" Ezra sputtered, scrambling upright. He

cleared his throat, adjusted his spectacles, tugged at the frilly ends of his sleeves. His wig was slightly askew. Faith set it to rights tenderly.

"Very well," said the lawyer enigmatically. "Very well."

Turning smartly on his heel, he stumped over to the fire and stood before it, hands hanging at his sides, and made a protracted study of his deceased wife's portrait. Faith followed to stand beside him, arms crossed, fingers tucked into the folded cuffs at her elbow, above the lace. She, too, stared at the portrait again, at the lovely features portrayed in cracking oils.

"Three years," Ezra said, his voice barely exceeding a whisper. "Three years since Ashley's passing. Is that not long enough for a woman such as yourself, Faith, to be alone?"

"Alone?" Faith echoed softly. How odd, that he should speak of this now, she thought. "Ezra, what do you mean?"

"You are young," he went on, "and healthy, and though you may be barren, I am too old to think of conceiving an heir . . ."

In shock, Faith's hands flew to her abdomen and rested there. She closed her eyes. "Ezra."

Abruptly, the man swung about and gaped at her, seeming to realize at last what he had just said to her. He had not meant to mention that yet. With an exclamation of impatience, of self-torment, he yanked at the turned hemline of his coat and stumped over to his chair, where he sat, as if his strength had left him. "Oh, my dear," he said, "I am so sorry. I should not have mentioned that which is neither tactful, nor kind."

Faith's gaze was riveted to the flames licking the length of the burning logs anew. "Ezra," she said sadly, "do not distress yourself so. How could you hurt me deliberately when you have loved me since my infancy? I used to call you Uncle Ezra, do you recall? When did I stop, I wonder?" Lifting her chin in a restoration of dignity, she took in the sight of the man in the chair, huddled, round-shouldered, with his wig slightly askance, and pictured him as once he had been, in his youth: dark-haired, slimmer, with a strength to his back that had certainly diminished in recent years.

Ezra looked down, at Faith's slim and lovely fingers resting suddenly in his own, and felt pain. In his chest, beneath his ribs. After a brief period, it subsided. He inhaled, just to be certain. With the forefinger of his other hand, he pushed on the slim piece of wire bridging his nose. It was a nervous habit, this toying with his spectacles, and one he was unable to forsake.

"Faith. Faith Mary, would you consent to marry me?"

Standing very still, Faith felt herself moved by a mild desperation. She had known that he was leading to the question, and had been unable to ward it off. Unconsciously, she released his hand. "I do not know what to say, Ezra. I—"

Ezra grunted, turned away.

"Why, after all, would you want to marry a man of my age, my dear? Naturally, I am hopeful for companionship, and yours is so vital, so stimulating." He poured himself a cup of cold tea. "What have I to offer you? An inheritance, when I pass on."

"Do not speak that way, Ezra," she said.

"I merely state the truth," he replied.

Faith sat down, slowly, smoothing her skirt along her thighs. "Is there—" she began, then faltered, and began again. "Is there something you are keeping hidden from me, Ezra? Are you ill?" Her heart had begun to beat unevenly within her breast, and her blood against her temples. "M-mortally so?"

"No," he said wearily. "I am not ill. Not mortally so, at any rate. I am merely tired. Tired of living my life alone. Do you not love me, Faith Ashley?"

"All of my life," Faith answered, without hesitation. "Why should I not? When I was a child, you—oh, Ezra, I am sorry. I am not a child, anymore, and the affection which you reserve for me is changed."

"Yes."

"And you are in need of a wife."

"Yes."

"To end your loneliness."

"Yes," said Ezra, his voice barely audible over the spitting of the fire and the rising wind sweeping across the chimney top.

"I am not the one you seek. I have no desire for marriage, Ezra; no longing for it, like a girl just out of short dresses. I

have my independence now, and I have grown into it, used to
it. I claim that right,'' she further stated, softly, ''as a widow.''

Ezra lowered his head. The firelight winked in merry duo
before his eyes. Velvet and silk, he thought bitterly, silver
buckles on imported shoes, the finest embroidery to ever flow
from a needle: of what use was it to dress in a manner that
swayed men's opinions, when it did naught to impress a
woman?

''Were I a younger man, would you consider me then,
Faith?''

''A younger man? Youth makes small difference.''

''Not always,'' said Ezra.

Faith colored hotly. ''Ezra!'' Her hands fluttered uneasily,
like birds startled from their roost. What he said was true, she
knew it. If she were so inclined to remarry, a younger man
would naturally be the most suited. Shamed, she recalled Mr.
Irons in every detail of his person: the shiny coal of his hair,
the strength of his features, the beauty, the shade of his eyes,
the feel of his hands, the power in their touch, and his breath,
featherlight, across her cheek . . . No! No, it was not worth
remembering. It was wrong; a weakness; a betrayal.

''Ezra, I understand what it is that you are saying,'' she
confided in a husky tumble of words. ''And it does not matter.
I beg of you, do not speak of it again.'' Her pulse was erratic.
A stranger, she thought. A stranger.

''Ezra,'' Faith said, bolting upright from the caned seating
as if she had been prodded by the honed point of a British
bayonet. ''You are a dear man, for whom I possess an enor-
mous affection. I suppose that you have counted on that, have
you not? And I find that I must treat your proposal with the
honor it deserves.'' She turned on the heel of her dainty, black-
laced boot to stare into the fire. Behind her, Ezra sat in silence.
His hands were always cold. They held no warmth, no strength,
though Faith saw in them safety and an inability to burn. She
lowered her lids, tightly, over her green eyes and said, in a
voice only mildly betraying her turmoil, ''Give me time, Ezra,
to consider my answer. I promise that I will, with care.''

In the deep cushion of his chair, Ezra stirred. He stared at the woman, at the narrow breadth of her shoulders held so stiffly, at the tumble of her hair, flame-bright, from beneath a white pinner. Unstoppering the rum flask, he took a long, quiet pull. His faded, ageing eyes were bright with animation.

"One week, my dear," he said. "You should need no more time than that."

Chapter Three

Faith glanced up at the sky. Softly gray clouds had amassed from the mainland to the seaward horizon, threatening a snow that seemed reluctant to come. A wind gusted out of the northwest, but it was not persistent. Halfheartedly, it pulled at her clothing and hair with damp, chill fingers, only to relinquish both with a flip of disgust. The afternoon spent at market was wearing on toward evening; the stalls were closing down with the final cries of the vendors; shopkeepers and craftsmen were standing about their doors, eyeing the hanging clouds and discussing the impending weather. Faith shifted the hanging net bag from one arm to the other, to ease the discomfort its fullness dragged across her muscles. The produce within the bag swung roughly against her hip.

She stepped out into the street, crossed the pavement of crushed shell-and-stone, and headed homeward. Elizabeth was tending the fire, waiting for her return with the vegetables for the stew. Faith had left the larder empty before her journey, to keep it free from rodents. But the house itself had seemed more empty upon her return. The parlor furniture was draped and the rugs were rolled into corners. It looked like a house abandoned, and her heels had echoed on the hardwood floor.

Faith's step lagged. The wind caught her full in the face, causing her eyes to water. It tugged at her bonnet, loosening it so that it fell about her shoulders, secured by salmon-colored ribbons around her throat. She retied the ribbons close beneath her chin once the wind calmed.

Oh, Ezra, she thought, in less than a week, you will demand my answer. She knew that was not entirely true. He was too gentle a man to insist. Rather, he would merely ask her again.

Picking up her purchases, she silently cautioned herself against hurting him. Ezra deserved better from her. If she were to remarry at all, why not to a man who had been as a mainstay in her life, who was, in essence, both family and friend? It would be the sensible, the responsible, the kindly thing to do. Ezra was not a young man, anymore, but did not wisdom come with age?

With a small sound of desperation, she hurried on. Unbidden, the image of the stranger, Mr. Irons, appeared in her mind. She stopped in the street. As though she had lost something of the courage upon which she prided herself, she stood motionless and uncertain. All about her, people returning to their homes parted around her still form. The wind whipped at her cloak, then let it fall, swirling over her dark skirt.

She felt foolishly immodest for thinking of the stranger. Shame overtook her and, with her heart pounding, she went forth again, determined to keep her wandering thoughts under control. She was not a child or an unmarried girl, but a woman—a widow—in full command of her feminine sensibilities.

As she increased her pace, the square bricks beneath her shoes grated roughly on her heels. She vaguely heard the sound of one man's voice, raised above the others, in vehement monologue, but she was too immersed in her own thoughts to pay him any heed. Gradually, the voice ceased, and she heard instead a murmur all around her, and a deeply shouted order.

Startled, Faith looked around, disconcerted to find that while she had been lost in her musings, a crowd had assembled in the street she had just crossed, effectively barring her way. A line made up mostly of men and several soldiers, who were conspicuous in their vivid red-and-white uniforms, stretched from the bakery to a small shop opposite it. Faith rose on tiptoe in an attempt to gain a better view of what was happening.

She was able to glimpse the scarlet of another uniform and a man who stood on a platform, or perhaps it was the back of a cart.

"What is happening here?" she inquired of a fellow standing before her. "Who is demanding dispersal of this assembly?"

The man turned, glancing over his shoulder, and down; then he shrugged indifferently.

"Is that fellow speaking on something of import?" she continued in curiosity.

"He's a Whig," said the man, as if that explained everything. And to Faith, it did. The situation clarified itself very quickly. She frowned.

"What is he saying?" she asked.

"Don't know," said the man, moving away.

Faith pushed her way closer, through the press of men still demanding to hear what the young Whig had to say. The British corporal beside the cart was insisting that they disperse and, by the time Faith arrived out in front, so was the speaker. They were eager to avoid confrontation between the citizens and the group of impatient soldiers nearby. When the speaker got down from the cart, waving his arms, and moving through the gathering, the assembly shifted with her, breaking up into small groups of twos and threes as everyone went back to the routine of the day. A group of children who had somehow been caught up in the midst of it gamboled past Faith with a triumphant crowing. One, the smallest, stumbled against Faith's legs. She caught him beneath the arm before he fell, but as she did, the bag slipped from her grasp and fell, splitting open on the pavement. Saved by the amount of cord encasing the packaging, the slab of lard remained intact, but the vegetables contained within rolled away in all directions, tumbling beneath passing feet and up against doorstones. With a cry of dismay, Faith dropped to her knees, scrambling for the produce before it eluded her.

Beside her, the child broke into tears.

"Oh, no," said Faith, turning to him, "don't weep. I don't mind. You did not mean to upset the bag. Look," she said, taking his hands. "Look there, most of my things have not gone far. Help me pick them up, won't you?"

Hesitantly, the child smiled, and Faith noticed that one tooth was missing in the front, giving him a mischievous expression. His face was smudged with dirt from play. Faith thought him to be five or possibly six years old. She smiled back.

"Go on," she said.

Kneeling on the ground with her skirt spread out about her, she began to retrieve those items which were closest to her, trying to make some use of the bag. One by one, the child returned the vegetables as if he had discovered a new game. Faith found herself laughing, her head tucked close as she scooped his offerings into the soft material of her lap. A wistful thought came to her then, as it sometimes did, that this child, any child, might have been one of her own, although she knew differently. The physician who had examined her after she had failed for so long to conceive had told her so. The word was barren, and she hated it, for it made her think of something dry and dusty and empty. No, there was no hope of a child; as Ezra had so recently reminded her.

Even after the child had gone, she kept her head bent, tying the ends of the bag together. The old sadness had come upon her swiftly, but she dismissed it just as quickly. She was even smiling again as she looked up to receive the potato a passerby handed her. He had sober blue-gray eyes.

"Mr. Irons," she said, a bit confused.

She suddenly felt unsettled and bewildered. Mr. Irons extended his hand to assist her. He had cleaned himself up somewhat, changed his breeches, and brushed his coat.

"Let me help you up," he said. "Give me the bag."

Faith did so, then placed her hand in his and allowed him to pull her to her feet. She quickly shook out her skirt, and pulled her cloak closed.

"What are you doing here?" she demanded. It was foolish of her to demand anything of him; a fact which she recognized immediately.

He looked unprepared for her question. Nevertheless, his answer came smoothly. "I came to listen to the speech. Why do you ask, Mrs. Ashley?"

Faith bit her lip, and looked away.

"Did you hear it?"

"No," said Faith. "I am afraid I did not."

Mr. Irons nodded. His expression was guarded, wary. "Mrs. Ashley," he said, "are you angry?"

"At what, sir?" asked Faith uneasily. From the corner of her eye, she could see him watching her. She was acutely aware of his proximity. It was as if they were alone again in the carriage. She could feel the warmth of him, even though he had not touched her, nor moved any nearer.

"Because I am here, Mrs. Ashley. You had no wish that we should meet again," he reminded her. "But I assure you, our meeting is entirely accidental. You can not condemn me for coincidence."

"I am not angry, Mr. Irons."

Standing very straight and still, she clutched the bag he had returned to her like a shield. His breath was a vapor before his nostrils, his eyes reflecting the leaden color of the clouds overhead. The wind tugged at his hair, lifting it from his temples. How beautiful he is, she thought. But when he smiled, she stepped away.

"Mrs. Ashley—"

Faith forestalled him, quickly. "I have no need of your aid."

He appeared startled. "I was not offering it," he said. "But," he added, "I might perhaps walk you home?"

Faith drew a quick breath. There was that in his tone which might have been mocking, but for the sincerity that shone in his eyes and in his smile. And it was that which made her afraid, which sent a slight tremor through her body. Vexed by her reaction, she balled her slender hand into a tight fist against her thigh. The leather of her glove stretched tautly across her knuckles.

"Need I remind you, sir," she said coldly, "of what I have said before? I have no desire to see you, Mr. Irons, or to spend time in your company. There is no reason to assume that a woman to whom you offered assistance is forever in your debt—"

"I told you that your debt had been paid, did I not?" he said, but it was as though she had not heard.

"—and a gentleman would not call in a lady's debt, at any rate. You, sir, are inclined to take personal liberties, I can see."

Faith lifted her head to him, chin up, and met his gaze fully for the first time since he had assisted her to her feet. Her green eyes sparkled, and beneath her heavy cloak, her bosom rose and fell with the strength of her emotion. She knew that it was not anger which drove her to speak to him so caustically. The fear of her attraction to him prompted it. She turned away quickly, leaving him without the opportunity for further speech.

When only a short distance from him, she glanced back, curious to know whether he looked after her. The wind caught her bonnet, and pulled it once again from her head, giving her pale red hair a sudden, unfettered freedom to fly out becomingly about her face. Though she had no reason to suspect it, at that moment Mr. Irons, who had not moved at all, wanted nothing more than to push his fingers into her hair, draw it away from her face, and kiss her without distraction.

With a tiny shiver, Faith turned away again. Fine flakes of snow fell onto her cheeks and over her shoulders. Her eyes wide, she kept her gaze on the path ahead and her feet moving in a simple pattern toward her home.

Chapter Four

The mattress sagged beneath the weight of Fletcher Irons' masculine, half-naked form as he perched on the edge of his bed, stretching and rolling the stiff muscles across his back before bending to fasten black gaiters over the tops of his shoes. First the left leg, then the right, and then he stood with a fiercely physical grace of curbed impatience, buttoning the white knee breeches of his officer's uniform as he strode to the window. Curving the fingers of both hands around the woodwork of the window ledge, Irons leaned forward, supporting his body weight on his palms. The dark hair on his chest curled damply from his bath. He stared out over the inn's yard some twenty feet below.

There was an expanse of churned mud outside of the stables: a morass caused by the tramping of booted feet and the prancing of military mounts eager for exercise. Bright morning sun reflected on the dubious snow of the prior evening; icicles that had formed in the night along the roof's edge were now steadily dripping moisture onto the ground below, making little pockets in the white crust. Straightening, Lieutenant Irons turned away in search of his cleaned and pressed shirt.

Finding it where the laundress had left it, on the back of the chair by the door, he held the garment aloft, slipping it carefully over the bandage on his collarbone, then tucking the long ends into the waistband of his breeches. This he followed with the white waistcoat, which he buttoned and belted; then he stood back in front of the small oval mirror and tied on the black cravat. Finally, he donned the scarlet coat of a British Lieutenant of Infantry, with its black lapel, collar, and cuffs. He buttoned back the coattail corners to expose the white underlining.

Dressing in full uniform for one's breakfast, he mused, was boring. Had he been one of his own men, encamped upon the Common, he would have been breakfasting at his ease, in his shirttails and blanket if he so chose, instead of dressing to impress a handful of Loyalist Americans in the dining room; and worse, to attempt through display to cow the rebel element. It was a ridiculous notion. He knew, and had even said as much to his superiors, that these men and women who called themselves "patriots" in their rebellion against the Crown and Parliament could not be bullied into submission. He did not believe that a single British officer, perhaps himself included, fully understood the extent of the colonists' concept of personal liberty. There was far more to their cause than a desire not to pay taxes.

Lifting his arms, Fletcher brushed the coal-black hair he had inherited from his Welsh mother, rolled it over each ear, plaited it over his collar, and secured the end with a brief length of white taffeta ribbon. His hair was thick and well kept, and he did not trouble himself with the use of stylish wigs as did many of his peers. Dropping the brush, he took up his officer's headgear from the stand on the dressing table and tucked it beneath his arm, then he turned on his heel to exit the room. At the door he paused, glancing once about the room to assure himself that all was in order before turning the brass latch and stepping out into the narrow corridor.

As he bent his buttoned knees, descending each step at an efficient military pace, he wondered whom, if any, of Boston's citizens he would meet in the dining room. There were always a few about, Loyalists mostly, although a number of Whigs were apt to show their heads as an act of defiance. But there happened to be one fellow in particular often breaking his fast at the inn, and in whose company the lieutenant found much pleasure. He was an elderly, affable gentleman, a Tory lawyer by the name of Ezra Briggs. The man's venerable age had embodied him with a good and definite character, and in such times of unrest it was a relief to find a settled conscience.

At a point of architectural convenience and whim, the stair opened onto a wide landing, meeting another descending from the other side. From the landing to the hall below, the staircase ran squat and deep with a fancy, carved balustrade that was somewhat out of place against the brick flooring of the entrance foyer, dining room, and parlor. Fletcher stepped down onto the gritty surface, crossing into the dining room. Lingering for a moment just inside the threshold, his gaze swept the crowded room.

"Irons!"

Fletcher's eyes snapped toward the dark-haired officer calling his name, and then his head followed, with a caution to which he had schooled himself. He grinned. The grin made him look less than his thirty-two years and more like the impetuous and rebellious boy he had been, not so very long ago, in Tunbridge Wells.

"Upton," he said quietly, but the special quality of his voice enabled it to be heard at the full distance of fifteen feet away where the other lieutenant sat, in the company of two other officers. "You have started without me, I see."

Lieutenant Upton choked a little on his strong black coffee. "I had thought you'd forgotten us, Irons," he said amiably.

"Am I that late?"

"Of course not. Sit down, man. We are not nearly finished, as you may have noticed." The lieutenant slid his chair to one side, pushing back the coffee pot and serving platter. One of his table-mates speared a slab of ham from the glazed platter, transporting it to his own plate, and proceeded to slice it into small, mouthsize pieces.

"Excellent fare this morning, Fletcher. Sit down, won't you?"

Irons arched one of his eyebrows at Lieutenant Upton. The younger officer was one of the few men in Boston with whom he felt the comfort of friendship. "As excellent as that which we remember of home, Brian?"

"Never!" admonished Upton with a smile.

At that exact moment, Fletcher became aware of a familiar face, straining to attract his attention from a table by the windows. "If you will excuse me, gentlemen, I believe that I will be breaking my fast in other company this morning."

Upton made a pretense at offense, then waved his heavily soiled and wrinkled napkin. "We will see you at the drilling then, Irons. If you are late to that, I shall have to call the physician to tend to you, my most punctual of friends. I should worry if you, Fletcher, should begin to make a habit of tardiness!"

Laughing, Fletcher turned away, striding through a dining room ablaze with scarlet to a table that stood in the corner near one of the tall windows facing the street. He greeted Ezra Briggs with a warm handclasp. The elder gentleman was dressed in an admirable brocade jacket, velvet waistcoat, and breeches. Fletcher complimented him on his attire.

"Join me, Lieutenant. I've been looking forward to seeing you again."

As Fletcher lowered himself into a chair opposite, Ezra unconsciously straightened his curving spine. He shifted his velvet rump on the cushioned seat, pushing the bridge of his spectacles with a swollen forefinger. "I've done with the newspaper, Lieutenant," he remarked. "Would you care to read it?"

Fletcher took the copy of *Draper's News Letter* and laid it on the table at his elbow. "Thank you, sir." He dropped his hat beside the paper, stretching his long legs beneath the table, easing a tightness at the back of his left knee, the result of an old injury: the slash of an Irish sword had left a wound that had not healed well. Explaining his order to the serving girl who appeared at his elbow, he then turned to Ezra. He noticed that the man did not look to have slept well. Behind the spectacles, his pale blue eyes were shadowed and the flesh beneath was puffed.

"Are you unwell, sir?"

Ezra started, hesitating fractionally before replying. "Why do you ask, Lieutenant?"

"Perhaps it is none of my business, but you do look tired, Mr. Briggs," said Fletcher.

"Ezra, call me Ezra, Lieutenant. And I am tired. Do not fret over my health. At my age, you will find that it is more trouble than it is worth."

"Is it indeed?" retorted Fletcher in appreciation of the lawyer's candid retort. "I will try to keep that in mind, sir."

Chuckling, Ezra shook out his napkin, tucking it into the front of his collar. With a steaming platter making its way to the table, he refrained from further comment. The lieutenant received the serving dish into his hands, politely serving Ezra before himself. A prayer was uttered softly, and in quiet efficiency Fletcher consumed his morning meal. After the first few mouthfuls, Ezra pricked the contents of his plate with his fork, repeatedly. He ate no more.

"Mr. Briggs," said Fletcher, lowering from his mouth a slice of toasted bread that was laden with gooseberry jam before he had bitten into it, "you are unwell, I fear. Is there nothing I can do to help you?"

Expelling through pursed lips, Ezra shook his head. "I am afraid not."

"Then it is something serious."

"Oh, no, Lieutenant," Ezra hastened, dropping his fork with a clatter against his plate. "I'm not ill. It is a personal matter. I—"

Fletcher waited.

"May I speak freely?" Ezra asked.

Fletcher gave the lawyer his full attention, his handsome face intent. "Naturally, sir."

Ezra leaned forward. He removed his spectacles, wiped them quickly with the edge of the tablecloth, and replaced them on his round, aged features. "Lieutenant Irons," he said, beginning slowly. "I have asked a female of my acquaintance to be my wife."

"Splendid!" said Fletcher.

"Perhaps not," countered Briggs.

"Ah," said Fletcher, wrinkling his brow. He wasn't certain that he understood the situation. "She has refused you."

"No, no!" cried Ezra, startling a fellow at a neighboring table who was obviously attempting to overhear their conversation. The lawyer lowered his voice. "She has not denied me. Although her initial reaction was to do so. She has asked for time to consider her answer, and I have granted it."

"That is often the way with women," Fletcher reminded him. "There is nothing unusual about that."

"I suppose that you are right," said Ezra. "I even believe that in the end, she will consent."

Fletcher's eyes narrowed. He lifted his coffee cup, sipping at the hot, black brew. "And you have changed your mind, Ezra?" he suggested gently.

"Oh, never, Lieutenant!"

"Fletcher."

"Fletcher. No, rather, it is the reason for the lady's consent which troubles me. No, no, that is not entirely true, either. I do not care about that. I only care that she will consent."

Fletcher sighed, lowering the porcelain cup. "You have lost me along the way, Ezra. Is it that you are concerned your lady friend will consent to wed you for the wrong reasons?" In his mind, he pictured a well-bred woman with powdered hair who was stout, yet retained the prettiness she had possessed in youth, and who was seriously in debt.

"Not wrong, precisely. Nor suspect, in any way. Don't misunderstand me, Irons. I have known her many years, many years." Frowning, he lapsed into silence.

Fletcher leaned back into his chair, regarding the lawyer steadily through his gray eyes. Without conscious connection of mind to deed, he moved his left leg to a position where he could massage the cramp that still nagged his knee. Pondering the lawyer's confession, he turned his head to the glazed window. Suddenly the pressure of his fingers began an irregular rhythm and though his countenance displayed nothing more than incidental interest, beneath the downward tilt of his black lashes his eyes were lucidly focused.

"I should not have burdened you with my woes."

"It is no burden," answered Fletcher reflexively, still staring out of the window.

Mrs. Ashley.

He had not expected the pleasure of seeing her again, and even now, unless he were to behave like a madman and rush wordlessly from the table out into the sun to stand beside her, he could not hope for anything so casual and specific as speech. But he could take in the sight of her, through the glass, watching the blowing of her titian hair in the gentle breeze, the intelligent animation of her features, the curve of her smile, the vitality of her posture.

Ezra Briggs, noting the lieutenant's preoccupation, glanced over his shoulder to the busy street outside. He started coughing. Blinking behind his spectacles, he found that he had no need to look again at the officer to recall the expression of the young man's countenance. Swallowing painfully, he asked the obvious question, dreading the reply, "Is it the lady who has caught your interest, Lieutenant?"

Fletcher had the grace to appear abashed. "Yes," he murmured huskily. "It is Mrs. Ashley."

After a perceptible pause, Ezra said, "Are the two of you acquainted, Fletcher?"

"Briefly," said Fletcher. "We met, in a manner of speaking, yesterday."

"Oh."

Ezra sat quite still, unwilling to volunteer further informa-

tion. He peered again through the window glass, frowning at
the exchange occurring between Faith and one of the stable
boys. It was Jimmy Watts, the younger brother to Elizabeth.
Ezra pressed two fingers to an ache in the center of his forehead.
"Mrs. Ashley is a widow," he said, with reluctance.

"So I was made aware. It is a shame to be widowed so
young. Was the husband considerably older than she?"

Ezra flinched, inhaling raggedly. "No, Lieutenant, he was
not. William was twenty-two when they met, and all of twenty-
eight when he died, sir."

"Disease?"

"Dysentery. He contracted it while in the West Indies, pur-
suing his, ah, profession. There were complications, I was
told. He died on shipboard, making his way home."

"A tragic tale, that." Fletcher lowered his brow pensively,
returning his gaze to the woman less than a dozen feet away
and the high window of glass which separated them.

Ezra spoke again, suddenly compelled to go on. "Naturally,
Ashley was buried at sea. That made his death more difficult
for poor Faith to comprehend. For months she refused to believe that he had gone."

Fletcher stared with increasing intensity at Faith, then deliberately turned away. Curiosity was not a noble thing, nor
was idle lust.

"Ah," said Ezra, with unparalleled relief, "here is another
pot of coffee. Would you care for another cup?"

The lieutenant looked up quickly as the steaming glazed pot
moved unsteadily across his line of vision, settling onto the
table before him. He sat up.

"Do you care for another cup, Briggs?"

"Thank you," answered Ezra, "no."

Upending the oily dregs from the bottom of his cup into a
saucer, Fletcher reached for the pot and poured the fresh
coffee into the empty cup. Sipping at the black brew, he
became pensive once more, his eyes straying again to Faith
Ashley.

He released his captive breath slowly. "Ezra," he said, "if
it is at all possible, sir, I should wish for a proper introduction
to Mrs. Ashley, one day."

For some time nothing was said, which was in itself a reply. Then Ezra frowned, and whispered:

"Lieutenant, the lady is a patriot."

Fletcher remained silent. He had surmised as much, of course.

"I confess to you now, Irons," Ezra continued, "her husband was a smuggler, and she bears a firm prejudice against the British military. I am not certain that I see the wisdom in such an introduction."

"Nevertheless," said the lieutenant, brow furrowed, "I would desire it, should an opportunity present itself. Would you mind?"

"No, Fletcher . . . naturally not."

Pulling one corner of his mouth inward with his teeth, Fletcher nodded in gratitude, then settled back in his chair to partake of his coffee.

Ezra's aged blue eyes observed the lieutenant; the way the fellow draped himself with easy confidence in the dining chair; the way he took his coffee, one steaming mouthful at a time. In silence, he watched the young man slide back his chair and rise and stretch his limbs discreetly. The strength of his masculine form was in the supple exactness of his movements.

"If you will excuse me, Briggs, I am expected out on the Common. In all probability," he added, "I am late."

"I understand," Ezra said, quietly. He stood, extending his hand for the lieutenant's brisk, firm clasp. "Irons," he said, forestalling the man's departure, "I have missed you these last several days."

Fletcher scarcely faltered in his reply. "I have been abroad in the countryside."

"Holiday?" Ezra responded in some surprise.

"No, sir. In the process of my duty to the Crown."

"I see," said Ezra uncertainly. "Lieutenant!" he called, as the officer would have turned away again, "would you consider dinner at my home? This Friday evening?"

Fletcher bent, reaching for his hat. "I will come, yes. I will be pleased to come."

"Oh, very good. My home is on Queen Street; my sign is above the door."

"What time then?" Fletcher straightened, adjusting his black cravat.

"Six o'clock?" the lawyer suggested.

"Fine," replied the lieutenant.

Ezra had the impression that the man was waiting for something more to be said. And Ezra said it, regretting the indelible spark of interest that leapt into the man's gray-blue eyes, but knowing that there was a purpose to his own self-apparent madness. How quickly the idea had come to him, and perhaps, how cruelly. His regret increased, and yet he spoke.

"It is possible that I can arrange for you to meet my friend, Mrs. Ashley, at that time," he said, and felt a sharp pain, below his heart. Ah, he should have spoken the entire truth; explained the significance of his confession in relation to Faith.

But it was too late. Without another word, Lieutenant Irons took his leave, crossing the floor with his lanky, yet enviously erect, military stride. His black hair was highlighted by the many candles of the chandelier which he passed so closely underneath. And even as he passed, a young lad with a chair climbed up, snuffing the flames with a brass instrument. Irons went on, through the doorway that barely contained his height, and was gone down the poorly illuminated corridor that ran beside the stairway.

At the table, Ezra Briggs removed the lenses from his face, holding them in infirm white hands webbed with the blue lines which were always prominent when the weather was chill. Soon he would be sixty-two, or was it three? It was not an ancient age, but he was old enough to recognize his limitations in life.

He pictured the young lieutenant in his mind. Irons was a man in his prime, a man of conviction and determination, a man of bold strength. He moved with lion-like grace and certainty. Why, then, had he all but promised the man an introduction to the woman that he, himself, so loved?

He knew the answer to that, of course. And it did not make him proud, nor content. Since his proposal to Faith, he had wondered if a younger man was, indeed, what she wanted, and the lieutenant was an attractive enough trial to discern her preference. Yet, his uniform would assure her scorn, and the realization, at week's end, that he, himself, had the most to offer. He would give her a few companionable years, until Death called him, and an inheritance afterwards, so that she need not worry again. It was not as though she did not care for him. She had, for years. And he would not give her cause to lament her marriage.

Did the type of love which he sought from her make that much difference, in the end? He thought not.

Once more, an image of the lieutenant came into his mind; an image of a proud, handsome face, and the expression upon it, as the young man gazed out of the window at Faith, at *his* Faith, in the street.

Ezra sighed. He removed the flask of rum from the inside of his coat, feeling the need for just a little bit of its bracing warmth.

Chapter Five

The mirrored glass caught the smoky light of the descending sun in a distressed and dusty haze. Faith turned on her toes in questionable admiration of her filtered reflection. The gown, she knew, was lovely, fashioned some years before from a bulk of imported leaf green silk traced with floral designs in gold and beige and rose. It had been bought in the time of her life when she had not been so quick to refuse the temptation of imported goods. Her hair, too, was dressed becomingly, twisted into a loose topknot while the remainder of her curling locks flowed, unchecked, over her shoulders. She wore no powder upon it, nor on her face, though she had lightly dusted her bosom where it rounded, by design of corset rather than nature, over the ruffled lacy edge of her chemise. Her lower arms and hands were without adornment with the exception of a rose ribbon about one wrist to which she had attached a white fan. But though she presented an attractive figure, her eyes quite plainly revealed the turmoil of her emotion.

Tonight she would have to give Ezra her answer.

Closing her eyes, she turned away from the mirror, flouncing in hooped skirt to the dressing table where she began a blind and panicked search for her silver-backed brush. Finding it, she furiously stroked the length of hair hanging over her left breast, holding the brush by its long fluted handle.

William had always admired her hair. He'd thought it very pretty, and soft. It was the color that had first called his attention to her, beside the Charles River. A warm spring it had been then, and she had been all of seventeen—which, perhaps, excused her for tying up her skirts above the knee and wading into the cool water beneath the riverbank in a lighthearted attempt to catch eels for her parents' supper. Faith had not known that she was being watched by a young man atop his horse beneath the shade of a nearby tree . . . or had she? Had she not stepped out of the water and seen him, and just for an instant lifted her skirts, in the progress of untying them, to midthigh before letting them collapse wetly about her legs?

She remembered his laughter, and his warm gaze.

Carefully, she set the brush down. Her lower lip trembled and she stilled it. That part of her life was over. William was gone.

And what of Ezra? she thought. Or, more specifically, what of a woman who is capable of an intense attraction for a perfect stranger? She had not forgotten those moments in the carriage, nor in the street. She could not. That was the reason why she could not refuse Ezra, in the end. His was an honorable offer, and possibly the most altruistic one she could ever hope to receive. Her affection for him went back to her days of toddling about in short skirts, demanding attention and receiving it in the person of Ezra Briggs. She did, indeed, love him, but her love was still that of a child. It would never be that of a woman toward her husband.

Could she bear the hurt inflicted upon him, she wondered, if she did, after all, deny him?

Confused by her circling thoughts, Faith pivoted on her stockinged heel, and strode across the room to gaze, distracted, from the bedchamber window. Across the cobbled street a woman stepped outside of her door, wrapped in a print shawl that scarcely concealed the roundness of her receding abdomen beneath her brown homespun. Rachel Revere had recently been delivered of her first child. And not for the first time, Faith was reminded of her own untested womb.

It had been God's will, she told herself sharply. She had no children, not even the hope of them. I should be grateful for Ezra, for a man who does not care for the begetting of heirs, she thought. He is a man upon whom I can rely, who can keep me well, and to whom I can offer comfort in his waning years.

And he is a man, she thought without bitterness, who will not rekindle that fire which once I knew so well. That can truly never be again.

"Mrs. Ashley?"

Faith turned from the window, pressing her palms to her hips and thighs, unusually cognizant of the sensation of silk against her skin.

"Yes, Elizabeth?"

Standing on the threshold, the blonde girl fluffed the yellow bangs over her forehead with nervous fingers. "Ain't it time to be on your way?"

"Is it?" said Faith.

"Yes, m'am. That's a real pretty dress you're wearing."

Faith smiled, a slight curve of her mouth, gentle and fond. "Thank you."

Elizabeth blinked her blonde lashes. With a lively, skipping step, she went to the bed and lifted Mrs. Ashley's cloak from the mattress. Giving it a shake to clear the wrinkles, she held it out.

"I sure 'ud like to go. Don't Mrs. Hart need help with the dinner? No one t'would need know I was around."

Faith crossed the floor, accepting Elizabeth's assistance into the cloak. With her own hands, she settled it carefully to avoid creasing the dress beneath. She shook her head, gently.

"Not tonight, Elizabeth," she said. "Not this night."

Elizabeth stepped back against the dressing table, turning to watch as her mistress walked down the corridor and descended the stair.

Lieutenant Fletcher Irons turned his back on the window and the strangely barren scene of last year's fallen leaves scuttling over the bare, dry ground like an advancing army, shadowed by the clapboard of a neighboring house. Above the rooftops, the night had swiftly overpowered the stubborn, rosy streaks of the setting sun. With his arms folded in their scarlet sleeves across the white expanse of his chest, Fletcher continued a careful, nonmilitary appraisal of his fellow guests.

Beside him a man of unremarked age, dressed fashionably and elegantly in brocade, velvet, and silk, sat perched passionately erect on the edge of a chair. As Fletcher watched, Mr. Charles Johnston, with flamboyance, and in the presence of a lady, took snuff, sneezing indelicately into a lace-edged lawn handkerchief. Refusing the proffered box, Fletcher concluded, probably correctly, that Charles Johnston was a man inclined to take liberties.

Next, he turned his gaze to the globular countenance of Edith Gillian, by far the better half of Mr. and Mrs. Francis Gillian. In the brief period since introduction, the husband had already shown himself to be obstinate, opinionated, and ill-mannered. His wife, conversely, was as kin to the angels, if only for the fact that she tolerated her husband's abusive temperament.

And Ezra, poor Ezra, seemed quite distracted as he slouched in his comfortable chair before the fire, attempting to maintain a conversation between himself and his guests. Fletcher could not help but wonder if the lawyer's nervousness was the result of a lack of conclusion between the man and the woman to whom he had proposed marriage. Briggs had not mentioned the subject, and the lieutenant had not supposed that he would. It was possible that the fellow regretted opening up to him. At any rate, Fletcher was not inclined to bring the matter up. It would have been inconsiderate to do so.

Yet, the member of the company who concerned Fletcher most of all had not yet arrived. Faith Ashley, with her pale red hair like flame, her eyes of summer green, and her enticing mouth, was late. Her visage had taken to pervading his dreams. Her wit, when they had met, had been as sharp as it was true, as had been her tongue, but this he enjoyed, having no use for a vacuous woman, or for those who pretended at it; and even less for one of waspish tongue who had not the intelligence with which to back it up. Admittedly, his experience with the fairer sex was not overly extensive, but he was able to recognize and delineate both his desires and needs very clearly. And his image of Faith Ashley, filled both to an overwhelming capacity.

In this, he thought, I am as my father.

Jonathan Winfield Irons had, forty years before, taken a dowerless, black-haired Welsh beauty to be his wife after an acquaintance of only one snowbound night and three weeks of deliberation against the judgment of his parents. Of course, he had been a good deal younger than his son's current age of thirty-two, and Fletcher supposed that fiery youth was just cause for the impetuosity of such behavior. He, of course, having had one serious adult relationship behind him—one that had been pressed upon him by the wishes of his own parents, and hers, and which had seemed, at the conclusion of his education, to be the proper course of his life—and nine years of fairly active duty in the British military, could not rely on a similar excuse for being so thoroughly smitten by a woman whom he hardly knew.

As he was musing thus, he observed the person of Ezra's housekeeper, Mrs. Hart, hurrying across the parlor and on into the small front-room that the lawyer utilized as an office. Belatedly, and annoyed with himself for having been so inattentive, he heard the sound of someone rapping on the sturdy wood of the street door. Slowly, he drew himself up, unfolding his arms and tugging on the lines of his scarlet coat. Across the room, Ezra had risen from his chair to stare with a look of expectancy at the shadowed rectangle of the open door. In a sudden gust of chill air, the two candles on the mantle guttered and the strong flame of an oil lamp flickered within its glass shade. And then Fletcher heard the voices: first, that of Mrs. Hart, and then, as he remembered them, the soft, husky, gently bred syllables of Faith Ashley in reply. He marvelled at the quickening of his pulse.

Drawing a deep breath of air, he steadied nerves that had not, even in the most unsettling of predicaments, tended to waver.

"Faith."

It was Ezra Briggs who had spoken, although in his mind the lieutenant had uttered the same name. The lawyer stepped forward to help Mrs. Ashley from her cloak. Beneath, she wore a silk print gown that took captive Fletcher's breath. Even old Ezra, he thought, appeared to falter. The man turned her about, took her hands, and began hasty introductions while she apologized for her tardiness. Apparently, she was already acquainted with the Gillians; and Johnston, who had leapt from his chair for the distinct pleasure of drooling over her hand, was blissfully unaware of the fact that she scarcely noticed his attentions, for her eyes upon entry into the room had been firmly fixed upon one source: the person of Lieutenant Irons.

"Ezra?"

Her voice quavered.

"My dear," answered the lawyer, "this is—"

"A British officer, Ezra?" she whispered hurriedly. "I don't understand. I never expected that you—"

It was then that Fletcher realized the woman had not yet seen him at all, not as a man, but merely as the uniform he wore—scarlet and black and white. How could it fail but catch her eye? He should have anticipated this reaction; Ezra had spoken of her strong dislike for the British troops. He took a step forward, out of the shadow by the window, putting himself closer to her vision just as Ezra was appealing to her sensibilities.

"Please, my dear, he is a friend of mine, and a guest in my home. Beside which, I believe the two of you have already met. Faith . . . Mrs. Ashley, Lieutenant Irons."

She turned her head then, slowly, regarding him with a certain bewilderment. In her green eyes, the lamplight was a faceted reflection. She looked at his face, studying it carefully with a small frown. And then her color heightened, a blush on her momentarily pale cheeks. Her expression grew cold.

"Lieutenant Irons?" she said, stressing his title. "You did not trouble to inform me of your rank when we met, sir."

"It would have been awkward," Fletcher replied.

"Nor did you trouble yourself to mention your standing within the British Military Service, at all. I took you to be a British merchant."

"Did you now?" said Fletcher, brows arched, cognizant of the confused manner in which his host was looking from one of them to the other, and of the curiosity of Ezra's guests. "I do not recall saying as much, nor did you ask otherwise."

"It did not come up," insisted Faith softly, wide eyes meeting his defiantly, "although you departed the carriage too quickly, and conveniently, for me to pursue that line of questioning."

Fletcher smiled. He could not resist. "Indeed?" he retorted. "My departure seemed a proper course of action, after you had allowed me to—"

"Lieutenant Irons! Kindly refrain from further mention of the subject, please. I do not see the necessity of discussion of either of our meetings. You are Ezra's guest, and I shall not be rude, if you think that you can help yourself from being so."

At this, Fletcher laughed, startling Mr. Johnston who had moved nearer for a better ear to their lowered conversation. Ezra took a step backward, turning in desperate search for Mrs. Hart and her announcement of dinner. Fortune being kind, the woman appeared in the doorway, wiping her hands on an apron and then signaling to Briggs that the meal could commence. Fletcher witnessed the undisguised relief on the fellow's face. He felt a similar relief of his own.

Chapter Six

Toying with the fork between his fingers, Lieutenant Irons pierced the slice of warm, tender goose. The meat released amber juices which puddled beside the beets on his plate. The fowl's natural oils rose to the surface in glistening circles. Discreetly, Fletcher lifted his gaze from his dinner to look across the lace-covered dining table to where Charles Johnston indulged himself in directing an excessive amount of flattery and attention toward the red-cheeked Mrs. Ashley. Ezra was seated to Faith's right, at the table's head, watching his guests with a deepening frown. Fletcher looked away, only to find the indomitable Mr. Gillian turning a sardonic eye upon his person. Ignoring the man, the lieutenant returned his concentration to his meal, attacking the succulent, spiced pale flesh with the cutting edge of his knife.

"A delightful meal, Ezra," said Edith Gillian suddenly, her globular countenance aglow with pleasure. "My compliments to Mrs. Hart. The goose is a special treat. Do you not think so, Lieutenant?"

Fletcher halted the fork before his mouth. Slowly, he lowered the utensil to his plate, smiling at the woman politely. "Yes," he agreed.

"I must get the recipe for the sauce," Mrs. Gillian added, addressing the remark to Faith. "I have a vast collection of recipes, Mrs. Ashley. I gather them wherever I may."

"Truly?" responded Faith. "What an interesting diversion. Every meal at your home must be delightful."

"Certainly, you must be an excellent cook yourself, Mrs. Ashley," Johnston interjected.

Faith declined to answer. Her cheeks flushed in the candlelight. Above the ruffled edge of her chemise, her bosom lifted in a sigh of impatience. Fletcher watched, suppressing a smile. He held a strong suspicion that Faith Ashley was more than capable of handling a man such as Johnston, and that if the fellow pushed himself at her any harder, he would find out the same for himself.

In fact, as he recalled her words to the guard captain and the way she had tried ever so ungently to tromp on his own foot in an effort to shake him off, he was certain of it. He could almost pity Johnston, for the man seemed rather pleased with himself.

Across the table, Faith shifted uncomfortably in her chair. The bone-stays of her bustle were beginning to chafe, though not nearly so much as the attentions of Mr. Johnston. After a moment she lifted her head and briefly, angrily, contemplated another source of irritation. Now that she was viewing him in the uniform of the British army, she had nearly expected to find that the erstwhile "Mr. Irons' " features were no longer so handsome and well set. But this was not so. His eyes, in the candlelight, were as dark and steady as she remembered them to be; his smile as attractive and openly friendly. She did not know how he dared smile at her. He had mislead her when dressed as a colonial. What could he have been about? Against her will, she recalled the sensual caress of his hand on her own. Biting her lip, she looked away hastily, and made to take up her wine glass in distraction. Tipping it, she spilled a small quantity of the ruby liquid onto the tablecloth.

"Oh!"

"My dear," said Ezra, reaching across to dab at the spreading liquid with his napkin. "No harm done." And then, quietly, "Is all well, Faith? You appear disturbed."

"Everything is well, Ezra," Faith assured the lawyer softly. "I am only a trifle clumsy tonight."

"Nerves?" supplied Ezra, smiling at her in a secretive manner that wrinkled up the corners of his eyes and his round cheeks, and did little to alleviate the confusion which had begun to creep into her thoughts. "We will speak later, when dinner is completed. I would perhaps like to share some news with my guests . . . ?"

"Of course," said Faith. She bowed her head, staring at the intricate pattern of the tablecloth. Beneath the table, she felt a slight nudge against her knee from Mr. Johnston, yet when she glanced his way he looked wholly innocent. She concluded, for his sake, that it was an accidental touch.

At that moment, Edith Gillian spoke up, totally disregarding her husband's scowling glances. "Ezra mentions that you are newly come from your home in Longmeadow, Mrs. Ashley."

"Yes," said Faith, bemused to find that she had been the topic of discussion at some earlier time. "I was visiting with my family."

"I fancy," continued the woman in an attempt at conversation as she pushed a beet in an uneven pattern over her nearly empty plate, "that you had more snow there this season than have we?"

"I suppose that is so," answered Faith, noting with some discomfort that at least three pairs of male eyes seemed incapable of turning away from her face, even though the conversation was of Edith Gillian's instigation.

"Christmas?"

"I beg your pardon?"

"Had you snow for Christmas, Mrs. Ashley? I always find it so—so—"

"Romantic?" suggested the woman's husband cuttingly.

"Why yes," said Edith, "that is the term I was searching for."

Faith cleared her throat in delicate embarrassment. "There was a wet snow, about a week or so prior, and it clung to the branches and froze there for days. Why, there was eventually a crust of ice so thick on the snow that we slid the Yule log over the ground."

Edith sighed in contentment. Fletcher sat forward, neglecting his sustenance in the pleasure of candid memory playing across Faith's features. At the end of the table, Mr. Gillian tapped his glass thoughtfully.

"A Yule log, Mrs. Ashley?" he said. "Is that not an English custom? I seem to know it as such."

Faith turned her head to view the man, hiding her irritation behind lowered lashes. "You are correct, sir, although there is some suspicion that it may be French. However, I prefer to view it as a family custom; indeed, a custom of the people."

Gillian moved forward in his chair. "I understand," he said. "It is a matter of convenience, then. After all, it is in keeping with the spirit of Christmas. Were it something else, as, say, the taking of tea, you would condemn it wholeheartedly. True?"

Before Ezra could speak up and forestall a reply from Faith, a slow smile turned up the corners of her shapely mouth.

"I suppose, Mr. Gillian," she replied, "that when we are taxed by the Crown for that wood which we remove from our own properties, to burn upon our own hearths, or when we are told that we must import that wood from English soil despite the fact that it is so plentiful here, then perhaps I will condemn the practice of burning the Yule log as vehemently as that of taking tea. Or perhaps, I will continue to do as I please, illegally, sir."

"Faith!" cried Ezra, aghast.

"Mrs. Ashley!" Gillian echoed.

Fletcher stepped in, seeking to alter the course of dissension. "At home, Mrs. Ashley, I would pull my youngest brother through the forest on the log. He was always undersized, was George."

Faith turned to the lieutenant, regarding him with only a little less than animosity. Beside her, Charles Johnston leaned forward, wreathing her in a vaporous cloud of wine-soaked breath. She blinked, and pulled away. "Your brother must be several years younger than you, then, Mr.—I mean to say, Lieutenant Irons," said Faith.

"Yes," answered Fletcher, cautious of the manner in which she had stressed his rank. "Six or seven years younger, I suppose. It is difficult to recall, now."

"Have you a large family?"

Her voice was cool, emotionless. Fletcher felt a wariness like a tingling in his spine. "Four brothers," he said. "I am the second oldest."

"And you miss them, Lieutenant?"

"Yes."

Faith's lips parted slightly. She had been preparing to suggest that he go home to them, but something in the artlessness of his single-worded response and in the manner of his expression made her hesitate. Instead, she found herself informing him, with civility, "I have a younger brother, Lieutenant. He is a cabinet maker, in Springfield."

"A worthy profession," said Fletcher. "A very worthy profession. I—"

"A cabinet maker?" interrupted Francis Gillian, stretching his neck forward, much like a turkey on a chopping block. "I suggest to you, Mrs. Ashley, that he should consider a new trade, and learn to make coffins. They are going to be needed before long, if you and your fellow 'patriots,' or whatever you call yourselves, continue on your path to destruction. Is that not true, Lieutenant?"

Fletcher, who had been taking careful stock of every aspect of Faith Ashley's countenance, swung protractedly to face the antagonistic Mr. Gillian. He kept his voice level, calm.

"I am not quite certain that I take your meaning, sir. I would be obliged if you would explain yourself."

"Come now, Lieutenant," scoffed the man, straightening against the high curve of the chair back. His sharp eyes gleamed in the flickering illumination of the candles overhead. They were like coals, with a burning heart. "How tolerant are we expected to be? It will not last. Day after day the troops are drilled over the Common. You, Irons, as one of Lord Percy's trusted officers, are there; you know what I am talking about. Is the time not coming to crush the rebellion by force?"

Fletcher inhaled deeply, controlling a growing anger. "There is no reason to expect that, Gillian. We should all hope and pray that violence will never be a necessary course of action." He glanced at Faith, and then away. The friendly animation she had displayed when she had thought him no more than a merchant, and which she had begun to display again in their brief, but pleasant, discussion of family, had vanished. He stared hard at the eyes to either side of Gillian's raptorlike nose.

"Oh, Lieutenant," Gillian continued, warming to his subject, "I am a personal friend of General Gage. You, sir, must know as well as I that the General has been writing letters all winter petitioning—"

"Sir!" Fletcher's tone, though not raised, resounded with authority. "I cannot imagine how you have come by this information, but if it is indeed the truth—and I call to your attention that one little word, *if*—then I question the wisdom of those who allowed you that knowledge. Matters such as these are not discussed lightly. They are of military importance, and to insure success and safety, would not be bandied about as if they were of no more influence than yesterday's weather."

Sitting forward once again, Francis Gillian tossed his napkin onto the table. "I take it," he replied with sarcasm, "that your caution at this table is on account of our dear Mrs. Ashley." His wife started in dismay, clutching his dark sleeve imploringly.

"Dear, do not take on so, I pray you."

He snorted in derision, but lapsed into silence. Edith Gillian turned to look at Faith across the table. "I am truly sorry," she said, and then to Ezra, "We have disrupted your table, I fear. It would perhaps be for the best if we were to leave."

"Leave? Us?" whispered Gillian harshly, insuring that he was heard by all.

Ezra frowned, wrinkling his forehead. Removing his spectacles, he began to polish them in earnest. "There is no need for haste," he said. "Poor Faith," he added, for her ear alone, "I should have known better, I think. How uncomfortable for you."

Shaking her head, Faith reached for his hand and squeezed it gently on the table top. "For you, Ezra, dear. I suppose I must grow accustomed to it."

"Do you believe that you may?" Ezra answered with hope. Faith did not reply.

"It is, of course, Mrs. Ashley's rebel inclinations that are at fault," said Gillian suddenly.

Beside Faith, Charles Johnston stirred. It was evident from his movement that he had been thinking hard on what he was about to say, and that too much consumption of wine had unsteadied him.

"No, no, let us all stay. One apology from Gillian and all will be well, do you not agree, Mrs. Ashley?" As he was speaking, his hand came up from beneath the table and, seemingly of its own free will, as the man was looking at everyone other than Faith, he began to caress her lower arm beneath the ruffled sleeve of her chemise.

With a small cry of indignation, Faith tossed Johnston's hand aside. The man reared back in amazement, almost toppling out of his chair. Fletcher hid a grim smile behind curved fingers.

"I would not consider an apology to Mrs. Ashley, I am afraid. She is a traitor against king and country," said Gillian.

Slowly, Faith stood up. She put her napkin down beside her plate carefully.

"This," she said, "is my country. Can you not understand that concept? Furthermore, Mr. Gillian, you will pardon me, I daresay, being the civilized man that you are, but I would not in my life accept an apology from you, even if I were foolish enough to trust you to offer one. It is exactly your type of thinking which has created the situation that prevails in the community today. I have long been aware of that fact. In addition," she hastened, forestalling interruption, "you should be ashamed. It is highly possible that you have, in your arrogance, supplied me with information that I will find useful."

Gillian flung himself, sputtering, against the table, turning angrily to Lieutenant Irons. "Arrest the woman! She speaks treason!"

"Treason?" replied Fletcher archly. "It was yourself, sir, who spoke out of turn. Mrs. Ashley has said nothing for which she may be legally condemned."

"I demand—"

But the lieutenant had pivoted away from the man, ignoring any further protest, and leaned across the lace tablecloth in a deliberate act of cool rage, pushing aside his plate and utensils as he did so. Coldly, he whispered to the recovering Johnston, "You will do well to keep your hands to yourself from now on, I assure you, sir."

Warily, Charles drew away, eyeing the lieutenant in a pretense at disdain.

Faith, unaware of the minute exchange between Fletcher and Charles, was apologizing contritely to Ezra. "Forgive me. You know how outspoken I can be." She attempted to smile at him, then shook her head. "I will be the one to leave, Ezra. It is only right."

"No!" Briggs' protest was vehement. "Have—have you forgotten?"

Faith hesitated, staring down into the lawyer's faded eyes, feeling suddenly very still and distant. It was as if, for an instant, time and life had stopped, and she was balanced on the edge of a strange and poorly built fence. On one side, Ezra peered up at her, on the other, a stranger, an unknown, waited for her. Gradually, she became aware of the lieutenant's gaze across the table and she turned her head to meet the dark promise there. It was filled with danger. Swiftly, she looked away.

"No," she said, "I have not forgotten. But this is no longer the proper time for discussion."

"Then," whispered Ezra, "the answer is no?"

"I have not said that," Faith insisted gently.

"What hope is there?"

Faith closed her eyes momentarily, as if staving off tears, then opened them again. "We will talk tomorrow. I will come here, to you."

Ezra replaced his spectacles with a vicious shove, pushing himself away from the table. His eyes betrayed the agony he felt. Faith felt a strong urge to take his hand, to kiss it and hold it to her face, as if by so doing she could ease the pain she was causing him—the pain she was causing herself. "Very well," he said. "Very well."

"It is for the best if I go now."

"Of course."

Abruptly, Johnston spoke up again.

"If you will permit me, Mrs. Ashley, I will see you safely home."

Faith looked over at the man with his lovely royal blue coat, at his drunken eyes, at his mouth that was moist, like a woman's. She turned away. "No thank you, sir."

"You will not, Charles," said Ezra, firmly. He would send for someone; perhaps Mrs. Hart's son. He rose to stand beside her on inflamed knees. "I will come with you to the door. Let me get your cloak, my dear."

Faith waited wordlessly as the man retrieved it from the hook beside the open door. Observing the exchange, Lieutenant Irons lifted his chair and slid away from the table. He stood. "Ezra," he said, "thank you for the delightful meal, but it is time that I was leaving myself. Mrs. Ashley, I would accompany you part of the way, if you will permit me. We follow the same route, I believe.''

Clasping the cloak to her rounded breast, Faith spun about. Her skirt swirled on its hoop, rustling with the sound of bird's wings rising to the air. She looked startled. ''No, Lieutenant, I—I rather that you did not. I shall have no trouble on my own.''

Fletcher laughed outright. ''I trust that to be the truth,'' he said. ''Nevertheless, as we will be taking the same streets for a time, there is no reason why we may not go side by side.''

''There are a number of reasons,'' Faith began, but something in his dark eyes caused her own to drop uncomfortably, and her words died on her lips.

''Please,'' Ezra implored suddenly, watching them both. ''I should feel more at ease if you did not go alone.''

Faith drew and expelled a quick breath. She stared intently at Ezra's face. He looked weary, resigned, without hope.

''Ezra?'' she queried softly.

The elderly lawyer shook his bewigged head. ''Please,'' he said again.

''As you will,'' Faith agreed with unintentional curtness. Draping her cloak about her shoulders, she tied the drawstring firmly beneath her chin. She kept her gloves in her left hand, crushing the soft leather in her fist. She had avoided looking again at the lieutenant, but she knew he was there, waiting behind her.

''Mrs. Gillian,'' she called, turning once more to the table, ''Good night.''

Still seated, and looking wretched, the woman nodded. Faith felt another pang of guilt. ''Good night, Mrs. Ashley,'' she said. Her husband stared speechlessly, arms folded across his narrow chest. Mr. Johnston had managed to stagger to the window and was leaning against the sill, gazing blindly out. He did not bother to acknowledge her.

At the street door, Faith took her leave of Ezra. She embraced him. He pulled free of her arms quickly, murmuring that he was cold.

''Go inside, Ezra dear. It would not do to catch a chill.''

"No," he agreed listlessly, "I suppose not."

"You must take care of yourself. I will be around, tomorrow, early."

The lawyer nodded, backing into the darkened office, one hand to the latch. He waved his hand in dismissal. "Good night, Irons," he said.

"Good evening, Ezra."

Quietly, Ezra shut the door.

For a brief space, Faith gazed blankly at the painted surface, faded to white in the moonlight, and then she turned to face the lieutenant. He was holding something out to her, something white, across the palm of his hand.

"I believe this is your fan, Mrs. Ashley. You left it on the table, and I took the liberty of picking it up for you."

"Thank you." She took it from him, opened it once, absently, then snapped it shut again and tucked it away, the rose ribbon trailing from it. Fletcher marvelled that the simple movement could emote such sadness, and he wondered why this should be so. The moonlight flickered in her green eyes and splintered like stars. Fletcher raised his hand, touching her very gently behind the elbow.

"Are you with me, Mrs. Ashley?"

Faith shook herself, as though from a dream. An odd choice of words, she thought. "Yes" she said, quietly. "Yes, I suppose that I am."

Without waiting for Lieutenant Irons, she lifted her silk skirt clear of the damp pavement and started off into the night.

Chapter Seven

Lieutenant Irons allowed Faith a brief lead, then casually proceeded to close the distance between them with his long-limbed stride. The round moon revealed the street in sharp-edged clarity and fell upon the widow's hair and cloaked shoulders like a hoary frost. "Mrs. Ashley," he said, drawing even with her on heavy soles, "just where are you going?"

"Lieutenant," Faith answered, without breaking stride or revealing any more to him than a profile limned in white, "I thought that you knew."

He chuckled, low in his throat, sounding like a friendly dog. "What I mean to say is this. Will you be taking Harrow's Alley, or Brattles Street? At this hour of the evening, I would prefer the latter, were I you."

"Indeed?" countered Faith. "Well, you are not I, sir, but I must advise you that the only danger on the street comes from drunken soldiers, and there are far more of those on Brattles than in Harrow's Alley." She paused on the edge of the rough curbing for effect, then prepared to leap over the steaming gutter to cross to the opposite side.

"Soldiers, yes," agreed Fletcher affably, "but surely not drunken. Here, give me your arm. I will assist you." Much to the lieutenant's amusement, Faith ignored the proffered arm and leaped over the narrow channel unassisted. He observed the unaffected and angry sway of her hips from beneath lowered lashes.

"By the way, Lieutenant Irons," said Faith, continuing on her way, "how is it that you maintain the knowledge of the route which I take from the home of Ezra Briggs to my own residence? Did you obtain this information as a matter of habitual curiosity, or do you receive pay for spying on Boston's private citizens, sir?"

The lieutenant faltered in his stride, recovering quickly.

"Do you not recall giving the information to that—to Mr. Johnston in the course of your conversation with him at dinner, Mrs. Ashley? I should be more careful, I think. He is not the sort of man to be trusted."

Frowning, he stared down at his shadow, stretched out beside that of Mrs. Ashley.

"Isn't he?" Faith tossed off the question in a careless manner, then abruptly began to laugh. She raised her hand to stifle the sound. "He nearly toppled out of his chair, didn't he, Lieutenant?" she asked when she had regained control of herself. "Oh, la, what a sight he was! How dare he touch me like that! And it was not the first time, Lieutenant," she added confidentially. "Earlier in the evening I felt him brush against my . . . leg . . . but I thought it was an accident."

"Is that so?" said Fletcher, slowly.

"Yes. The man must be short on common sense, and decency."

"And well into his cups besides," Fletcher concurred grimly. "It is possible that he consumed more wine before and during dinner, I would say, than I do in the course of an entire year."

Faith's smile was still evident in her tone. "Then, you are a temperate man, Lieutenant?"

"Yes," he admitted, "I suppose that I am."

For several minutes, they walked on in silence, Faith slowing her irritated pace and Fletcher adjusting his stride to match her own. The full moon rode high overhead on the outthrust palm of a dark-fingered cloud, which filled the sky beyond the cornices and chimneys like a nimbus. Below the overhung structures, the path was in shadow. He could hear the sound of her heels, and her slow, even, respiration. She was walking so near that he could have merely raised his hand to stop her, there, under cover of the darkness. To his amazement, he found himself doing so, without speaking, in a place where the moonlight fell in a knife's edge between two buildings, widening in diffused radiance across the pavement. Faith turned to face him, displaying no apprehension, only curiosity.

"What is it?" she asked him quietly.

He watched her face in the pale light, controlling an impassioned urge to discover how it would feel to have her in his arms, to touch and taste her mouth. In the moonlight he could count each freckle that spanned the bridge of her nose, and estimated the possibility of kissing them all.

"What is it?" she repeated uncertainly.

He waited overlong. Faith began to move away, and he was forced to call her by name, hardly recognizing the sound of his voice.

"Mrs. Ashley."

Faith glanced back over her shoulder, halting again. The

sound of her name, no, not her name, but the voice that had uttered it, caused her skin to shiver as if with cold. Yet a heated flush followed. Flustered, she looked away, then back again, her eyes focused carefully on the lieutenant's shoes and black gaiters. The intensity of her response to his voice appalled her. How could she react so to the sound of a man's voice? To *this* man's voice, especially? A man who was a commissioned officer in the British military. A man who had deceived her.

"Yes, Lieutenant?" she said, her soft tones subdued still further. "What did you wish to say?"

Fletcher cleared his throat. He took a step forward. Faith risked an upward glance, to the expanse of his comfortably broad chest and his scarlet coat muddied to rust in the moonlight. The brass buttons were so laboriously polished that they had a mirrored rim.

"Your constancy," said Fletcher, "is admirable. But a bit extreme. Must the uniform that I wear matter so very much to you?"

"I don't understand," she answered. "Why do you ask me this now?"

As if she had not spoken, he went on. "When you walked into Ezra's parlor, the sight of this uniform was hateful to you, and the man within it did not exist. Mrs. Ashley, I am the man within the uniform. Look at me."

Faith lifted her head. Her eyes in the night were wide, and clear as glass. "I see a British officer," she said.

"No. That is the uniform which you see. What of the man?" he persisted.

"That is the man," Faith retorted with such little force that he could barely hear her. "There is no separating the two. Please, I do not want to discuss this."

"Why not, Mrs. Ashley?"

Shaking her head, Faith strode away.

"Mrs. Ashley," said Fletcher, following closely, "the situation in the Colonies is dangerous. I do what is required of me."

"I see," Faith said, without turning. At a tangent, and against her will, she recalled the strength of the lieutenant's hands and, oddly, the smell of blood in his shirt. He had deceived her. She shivered, resorting to anger to steer her from the emotions overwhelming her. "Perhaps if it were I infringing on your private and public liberties you might better understand the way I feel."

"Exactly what," he said, "are you implying?"

"That the military has done just that. A maintenance army, indeed! What are you maintaining besides those rules and regulations that deny us our rights and an individual government to set our own rules and regulate our own taxation? Parliament serves nothing but itself, and as for our good King George—" Abruptly, she ceased, realizing that she had probably gone too far. Her breasts rose and fell rapidly within the confines of her silk corset.

With his ideas of romance sufficiently cooled, Fletcher stared at the back of Faith's head in irritation. "Gillian was right. I should arrest you. Except, my dear Mrs. Ashley, concerning matters of treason, there are none among us who possess that power. Haven't you realized that yet? A slap on the wrist, and a warning, is all that your 'organizations' receive, even though they run rampant, mobbing Loyalist citizens, destroying their homes, their property."

"Lieutenant Irons," Faith interjected, flouncing about in her hooped skirt to address him. "That is not entirely true."

"No," Fletcher was forced to agree. "Not entirely." Ah, but her eyes were filled with fire! Vexed, he continued, "General Gage, who, by-the-by, happens also to be your Royal Governor—"

"Imposed upon the citizens of Massachusetts, in particular those in Boston, by the British army, Lieutenant—"

"—has been lenient in regard to various matters which I am certain that you cannot possibly fail to bring to mind."

"Why do you say that, Lieutenant? Can it be that your general has found proof to issue warrants of arrest and yet has not done so?"

Slowly, Fletcher's mouth twisted into an ironic grin. "I would not answer that, even if that information was within the realm of my knowledge," he said.

"Oh, yes," replied Faith, "I seem to recall something similar from a conversation between yourself and that dreadful

Mr. Gillian. Concerning letters that had, or perhaps had not, been written by General Gage. Am I correct?''

In exasperation, and without further consideration for the sentiments and reactions of Mrs. William Ashley, Fletcher took her by the arm, though not ungently, and spun her about in the direction of an illuminated Brattles Street. He was gratified to hear her emit a small gasp.

''I had not expected to spend an entire evening conducting you on your way, Mrs. Ashley, or if I had, I had at least thought that it might be pleasurable. Let us waste no more time in futile argument over points of political delicacy, but walk as quickly as possible. Do you agree?''

Faith was silent, concentrating on the abundance of sensations that had been released by the firm, yet still remarkably gentle, grasp of his hand on the upper portion of her arm. She felt shamed by her arousal at such a small thing as the touch of a strong hand. It was a minute physical contact, from a man who was her enemy, or most certainly should have been. And a man who was very nearly a stranger to her still.

''Please, Lieutenant Irons,'' she whispered, ''release me.''

''Release you,'' growled Fletcher, ''I have half a mind to—''

Directly beneath the lantern hanging on the corner house on Brattles Street, Faith turned on the lieutenant, tossing the flaming mass of her red-gold hair over her shoulder so that it settled within the folds of her cloak like gleaming spun metal. The face she lifted to his was streaked with tears.

''Now, please, Lieutenant.''

Fletcher complied, immediately.

''I have hurt you.''

''No.''

''Then I have offended you,'' he said.

''No.''

She stood before him, trembling. How handsome he is, she thought, and kind, and arresting. And how afraid he makes me.

''Why should you possibly believe that it matters what I think of you as a man, Lieutenant?'' she asked him. Her bosom rose and fell, quickly, heavily, as if she had been hurrying, away. ''Or that I should be made to see any difference between

a man and the uniform that he wears? You have chosen your
life as a soldier; it is what you are, who you are, in your heart,
whether you wear the uniform or not.''

Fletcher looked down at her, his eyes half-closed. ''Still,
you must not hate the man, merely because you despise his
occupation,'' he said.

''Why not?'' Faith demanded, unable to bear the liberty he
was taking, in speaking so tenderly to her. He had no right.
Her voice quavered.

''I ask it of you, Mrs. Ashley.''

''Please,'' she said, ''don't.''

''I ask it of you, honorably.''

''No,'' said Faith, shaking her head in little movements of
denial that touched Fletcher with their desperation. He reached
out his hand, turning it palm up against her cheek, tracing the
line of tears with his thumb. His flesh was warm. Faith pressed
her cheek into the curve of his palm, closing her eyes. *What
am I doing? Why am I allowing this?* She felt the pressure of
his fingers, then, sliding downward, to the side of her throat,
caressing, burning, tilting her chin up and back. The feather-
light touch of his breath brushed her skin, and his mouth moved
over hers with tormenting leisure.

His other arm slipped beneath her cloak, across her back,
drawing her nearer, stepping backward into the shadows. His
fingers were open, on her rib cage, holding her close. She felt
a shiver run the course of his lean form. He released her mouth.
Breathing rapidly into the circle of his hands, she leaned her
forehead against his chest.

''I . . . I have never . . . Lieutenant, I am ashamed . . .''

''Do not be,'' said Fletcher.

''We are hardly acquainted,'' Faith whispered.

''It matters not.''

''It should.''

Wordlessly, Fletcher pressed his lips into her hair. It smelled
as sweet as flowers. He felt, rather than heard, her sigh against
his hands.

''What can you possibly think of me?''

''Only,'' he replied, stroking her waist wonderingly, marvelling at how small it was, aware of the cool feel of silk and

the raised pattern, "that you astonish me, in many ways. And I do not believe, even if we were of ten years acquainted, that you could ever fail to do so, my dear Mrs. Ashley."

"But you . . . you are—"

"A redcoat?" Fletcher supplied the word with a swift, grim laugh. "Can we not dispense with that anger?"

"No. No." But her fingers clutched at the black lapels of his uniform. The pulse of her bloodbeat was a rapid hammering in her temples.

"May I call on you?"

"You mustn't, Lieutenant."

"In secret?" Fletcher persisted calmly, with quiet insistence. His subdued voice rumbled through his chest beneath Faith's ear. She pulled away, pushing the edge of her teeth into her lower lip.

Suddenly, and from not so very far behind them, a voice called along the street. It was somewhat drunken and overloud; it was Mr. Charles Johnston.

"Hail! Lieutenant Irons! Is that you, sir?"

Fletcher swore under his breath. Gasping, Faith took a step backward, rustling in the shadow. "You have not answered me," Fletcher whispered slowly.

"No," said Faith breathlessly, one eye to the besotted man approaching. "We must not meet, either in public, or in secret, Lieutenant Irons. Please. I . . . I cannot." She made to turn away, but the officer grabbed her arm, holding her fast.

"Do not go. I have said that I will see you on your way, and I shall. I promise," he added, dropping his hand, "to behave in a gentlemanly manner. At any rate, it looks as if we will have the genial Mr. Johnston as chaperon. Good evening, Charles."

Smiling crookedly, Johnston paused on the bricked walk beside them. "Hadn't expected to catch you up. Came to make my amends. Could we not both see the lady home?"

Fletcher sighed, barely concealing his irritation. "Naturally, that is up to Mrs. Ashley to decide. Mrs. Ashley?"

Faith looked away from the lieutenant, to the street ahead. "Why not?" she agreed reluctantly. Johnston was immensely pleased.

"Wonderful!" he cried. "Will you take my arm, Mrs. Ashley?"

"That is hardly necessary," said Fletcher. "The path is well lit."

Rebuffed, Johnston swayed in confusion. "Naturally," he said.

Faith shivered in the absence of warmth of the lieutenant's arms. "May we go now?"

Fletcher resisted an impulse to caress her hair reassuringly. He hung back, observing her as she moved into the illumination of the lamp above the street. The light gleamed like a bright flame in her hair. She turned to look back at him, once, and the flame was in her eyes also, refracted as in water, gentled into a multitude of blunted sparks. Fletcher felt his chest tighten. Surely his mother had inspired in his father the same passion, created the same obsessive dreams that he now felt. Only such tumultuous emotions could have caused him to wed almost upon the moment of seeing the dowerless Jane, against the desire of his own parents.

Fletcher had not forgotten the special smile often shared by his parents in all the years that had passed since last it had greeted his eyes when he had turned his head from the comforting warmth of the fire, curled there, beside his brothers. He had thought himself capable of understanding it, back then, when he felt himself a worldly young man. But now he realized it had had naught to do with worldliness, but rather with the strength of determination and love.

Faith stood very still at the base of the stair, one gloved hand on the newel post, staring into the parlor where Elizabeth sat, head turned against the chair back, one lamp burning low and the fire nearly out, asleep over her needlework. Quietly, she went to her, removed the loop and cloth and thread from the girl's lap and gently woke her, urging her to go upstairs to her bed. The child was full of questions which she mumbled sleepily. With a finger to her lips, Faith silenced her and sent her off, then she sat down in the vacated chair. She extinguished the lamp.

In the darkened well of the fireplace embers broke free from the hissing logs and fell, crumbling, to the stone flooring, scattering like the final remnants of her resolve. How can I marry Ezra now? she thought, crossing her arms and rubbing them with her hands, from elbow to shoulder. How could she marry the man whom she had known for so many years, and loved, and hoped would provide her with safety from the burning touch of a stranger, when she had been in the arms of that stranger, and felt the touch of his mouth upon her own? It was a shattering, delightful, shaming touch that had irreparably breached the wall she had erected about herself.

Oh, Ezra, I cannot marry you, she thought, not even for your own sake. I am selfish, and a fool, and I will tell you as much. In my heart, I will long for another, and there is no honor in that.

She would not see the lieutenant again, of course. He was a British officer, an enemy to the people, to herself. There could be no honor between them.

With a flurry of motion, Faith lifted the iron poker in her right hand and swung it viciously onto the declining pyramid of flames, causing sparks to fly, and tongues of ochre and gold to leap high above the blackened wood. She watched them waver, and run, like a scene witnessed through a pane of glass beset by rain, not realizing until much later, when the fire had gone out, that she had been crying, quietly, all alone.

Chapter Eight

March, 1775

Fletcher Irons raised his cleanly shaven jaw to the penetrating warmth of the morning sun as he stood in the open cellar-doorway with his legs slightly spread. His arms in unfastened shirtsleeves were lifted at right angles to his body, his forearms were propped against the doorframe, his head was tilted back over his shoulders. He was the picture of comfortable relaxation. Behind him, the darkened corridor of the subterraneous passageway was empty and cool, echoing irresolutely with the activity of the inn above; sounds that, temporarily, held no meaning for him. Beyond his silhouetted form a brief stone-stair attained ground level, exposing to view an expanse of greening grass and warm, shafted, sunlight.

Fletcher ascended into full sunshine, breathing deeply as he fastened the cuffs of his white shirt over each wrist. He stepped out into the grass, turning to study the brick face of the back of the inn. He looked at his own window, curtain still drawn as if he had not yet risen. He still had time to return and finish dressing before breakfast. Lately—in fact, since the lawyer's disastrous dinner party—he had not had the pleasure of Ezra Briggs' company at breakfast. Having sent a polite note of inquiry around to the man, Fletcher had received a brief, and equally polite, note in return. Nothing more.

Slowly, his lanky stride subdued, the lieutenant strolled toward the front of the building, upsetting the dew on the grass. He questioned in his mind his concern for Ezra's nonappearance. Was it real, or did he hope to contrive a means to the elusive Faith Ashley? Since that night, he had not seen her. Not that he had expected to, nor that he had pursued her, for she had, if only verbally, expressed her opinion on that matter. Indeed, he thought about her considerably less now than he had during those first few weeks after he had escorted her home in the company of that obnoxious fellow, Johnston; he was far too busy, and his responsibilities too great, to be mooning about through the days like a stricken schoolboy. Yet those times, at night especially, when he had the leisure to dwell on the intelligent, lovely, and often sharp-tongued Mrs. Ashley, he realized that she obsessed him, body and soul, much in the manner in which a virus invades the blood. The symptoms, however, were not entirely disagreeable, nor debilitating. And, as with a virus, there was no cure, he supposed, but time.

Entering the inn through the double doors that had been thrown wide to the street, Fletcher crossed the foyer. He paused at the sound of his own name.

"Irons? My word, what are you doing up and about half-dressed, man?"

A suppressed smile caused the muscle in Fletcher's jaw to dance from cheekbone to chin. He pivoted from the waist, turning to face the officer addressing him.

"Good morning, Brian. If you are referring to the fact that I am not in uniform, I am on my way to amend that oversight."

"Are you, then?" said Upton. "I should be highly embarrassed to be caught dining with an officer who was not in full garb. What would old Percy have to say, eh? I should not like to find out." The younger lieutenant's muddy-colored eyes crinkled with a juvenile sense of mischief. "I suppose I must wait breakfast for you, Irons. Actually, I have just come down myself."

"Have you?" countered Fletcher dryly. "It must be later than I thought."

"You do have a peculiar humor, don't you, Irons? It is not late at all. Though I would hasten a bit, if I were you."

Fletcher turned fully about. "Why is that?" he asked.

"Surely you have not forgotten! Live volleys on the Common, first thing. Wake this town up with a show of arms; that's the way to do it!"

Fletcher frowned. Of course, he had not forgotten. With the unexpected generosity of the climate, drilling periods had increased as the time for decisive action approached. The colonial stores of arms outside of Boston were growing weekly, a fact which he knew to be true. And only last week, a second British cannon had been added to these supplies, dismantled and smuggled out right beneath the very noses of the guard on the Neck. It was only a matter of time now, for Governor Gage awaited the response to his winter letters with the opening of the seas; it would give him permission to either move against the rebels or treat with them. Many, as with Upton, seemed to prefer the former. Even so, desertions were multiplying, usually by enticement into patriot politics, and it was known that at least a dozen British soldiers were instructing farmers and militia in the proper use of firearms in secret meetings scattered throughout the countryside. Captured deserters were in dire risk of losing more than their freedom; as in wartime, the execution

of deserters was being seriously considered. As of yet, all of
Fletcher's own men remained true. But the strain was making
him short-tempered. He shook his head at Upton.

"You do not approve?" Brian demanded. "What would
you have us do, pray? Take thousands of seditious traitors and
line them up over our collective knee to issue a nasty little
spanking? Oh," he said, "that might be enjoyable after a
fashion, particularly with the women I have met, but hardly
effective."

Fletcher's winged brows lowered over his gray-blue eyes.
"Don't strain yourself with glee, Brian," he admonished the
laughing lieutenant. "The situation is hardly so amusing."

Upton sobered. "I realize that. But it looks as if there will
be some action before long," he continued, his voice lowered.
"Something more than those feints and forays with which we
have been exercising ourselves. Is that worrying you, Irons?
Any decisive move that is made should not be much more than
a lark, against these untrained rebels."

"Not entirely untrained," Fletcher reminded him.

"What? You mean those deserting bastards who are out there
instructing a mob of bumbling farmers? Come now. I do not
imagine there to be any real threat in that. Do you? Do you,
Fletcher?"

"I have not said so, but remember: overconfidence is a
burden to a military man, especially an officer. Have you
forgotten who said that?"

"Lord Percy, of course. I haven't forgotten."

"I hope not," said Irons, dropping his hand onto the lieutenant's scarlet shoulder and offering it an affectionate shake.
"Very well, I am on my way up now, to get dressed. I shan't
be long, I promise."

With that, he turned away, but once again Lieutenant Upton
interrupted his progress. He backed down the two steps he had
climbed, gazing down with his right eyebrow arched at his
friend and fellow officer. "What is it now, Upton?"

Grinning, the man folded his arms across his chest, matching
Fletcher's expression, eye to eye. "There is someone in your
room, Irons. An elderly gentleman that said he wanted to speak

to you. I didn't catch the name, but I sent him up. Thought you were still in there." He waited for a minute before asking, "Where were you, might I ask?"

"No," said Fletcher shortly in response to the lieutenant's questioning, "you may not." Then he turned, taking the steps two at a time. Ezra? he wondered, and felt guilt at the surge of hopeful elation.

From the base of the incongruous staircase, Lieutenant Brian Upton considered what had facilitated his friend's vigorous departure. What was the old fellow to Irons? Well dressed and elderly, the man had seemed vaguely familiar, but Brian was certain he did not know him. He wished now that he had paid closer attention to the stranger, for he might have provided some clue to Fletcher's reticence concerning his personal life. Not, of course, that anything Lieutenant Irons might or might not choose to do on his own time was any business of the younger lieutenant's. He was merely curious.

He knew, naturally, that in military matters Fletcher Irons was efficient, sensible, and often innovative, earning himself an enviable reputation for his levelheadedness and courage— two paired virtues that did not often travel hand in hand. Yet, conversely, in the rare, unguarded moment, the lieutenant revealed the faculties of a dreamer, a romantic, perhaps. It stood to reason that the man would suffer discontent from such a dichotomy, but he showed no inconsistency to his fellow officers, nor to his men. And it seemed to Brian suddenly that the time had come to draw the older lieutenant into a discussion that did not purely concern the military, into a revelation of his personal life.

Brian recalled the bottle of cognac in his room, still sealed. But he did not even know if Irons was a drinking man.

Balanced on the threshold, Fletcher hesitated, searching the tiny, dim chamber with a practiced glance for the form of his visitor. The curtains, still drawn, had a heavy backing that effectively blocked the light. Yet, having performed for duty in fog and storm and the blackest of moonless nights, the lieutenant had no difficulty in discerning the glint of twin ovals perched at head-level upon a molded shadow seated on the only chair in the room, which was angled into the corner.

"Ezra?" Fletcher called gently. "Mr. Briggs?" The tilt of the man's head suggested that he might be dozing. Not receiving a reply, Fletcher crossed the room, took the ruffled edges of the curtain in each hand and parted them. The morning light flooded the room brilliantly. In the chair, the man started and sat up, blinking his pale eyes. His wig had fallen to one side, revealing the yellow, frizzed ends of his natural hair rather than the usual shaven head of a man who sported a wig.

"Good morning, Briggs," said Fletcher, moving about the room to gather his waistcoat from the foot of the bed and his coat off the hook on the back of the door. "Have you been waiting long?" he asked as he donned both garments. "I am afraid Lieutenant Upton was unaware that I had gone out." Pushing buttons through buttonholes with the edge of his thumb, he puzzled over Ezra's lack of response. The lawyer sat with an unusual stillness, head slightly turned away so that he appeared to be gazing out of the window, but Fletcher suspected that he was not actually doing so. He looked frail, in that position, without defenses, an impression that startled the lieutenant, for the lawyer had seemed quite hale when last they had parted company.

Lifting his brush, Fletcher ran the bristles through his black hair, tying the healthy length of it at the nape of his neck with a fresh taffeta ribbon. When he spoke again, it was in a deceptively casual tone.

"I am very pleased to be seeing you again, Ezra. I've missed our breakfasts together. You have been well, I pray?"

At this, Ezra stirred, gathering himself in the chair. He cleared his throat dryly. "Yes, fine. I have been well enough, I suppose. And you, sir?"

"Very well, thank you," Fletcher said, and went to stand beside the window, leaning his shoulder against the frame, arms folded over his chest. He decided to address the lawyer frankly.

"Is there something wrong, Briggs? I must say, you do look

as if there might be." Without warning, an image of Faith flashed before his mind's eye, and was gone, coincidental in its timing, but causing an unconscious clenching of his fist over his biceps. He wanted immediately to ask after her, but with effort, he held his tongue. He turned, pressing the back of his head against the cream-colored edge of wood, and waited.

Heaving a decisive sigh, Ezra clapped his hands over the lower part of his thighs and pushed up from the chair. He began to pace, limping, ranging the small area between the bed frame and the opposite wall before he finally came to a rest before the window. He stood there, looking down into the yard, and the backs of his hands were behind him, against his coattails, the fingers intertwined. His lower lip worked, back and forth, against his long incisors. His skin in the sunlight had the texture and translucence of cambric cloth, lifted from the bone and muscle beneath in fine ridges and loose pockets. Beneath his eyes, the tiny tracing of veins stood out sharply; he had not slept well.

"I do not much care for the acceleration of events, Irons, do you?" he said, but not as if he expected or wanted a reply. Unclasping his hands, he brought his arms forward, extending a finger to the casement where a thin-legged spider was weaving its web. Following a brief study of the beautiful intricacies of a construction he could scarcely see anymore, even with the aid of magnifying lenses, he detached a supporting strand with his fingernail and then looked away with nothing but a passing interest in the damage he had caused. In the yard below, he saw vague crimson figures moving about on a background of emerald.

"Do you see her, Lieutenant?" he asked suddenly.

Fletcher glanced down into the yard. Observing nothing but soldiers and the washerwoman, a Negress nearly as black as coal, he began to question, "Who do you—" and then caught himself as the elderly lawyer turned to meet his eye.

"Am I keeping you from something, Lieutenant?"

"No."

It was a small lie, but he spoke it well, without the slightest inflection or false movement.

"Do you speak of Mrs. Ashley, Ezra?" he asked after a moment had passed.

"Yes," replied Briggs. "Yes. Have you . . . have you seen much of her lately, Irons?"

Fletcher's expression barely altered, but his respiration quickened fractionally, as did the beating of his heart. "Sir?" he hedged, "I beg your pardon, but there is not much chance of that. You and I both know of her tendencies to discriminate against those who wear this particular shade of red," he said, tugging on the folds at the bend of his elbow between thumb and forefinger. "I have not seen Mrs. Ashley since the night that I escorted her from your home."

Ezra opened his mouth, drawing breath to speak, then shut it again. Wordlessly, he withdrew the rum flask from the inner pocket of his coat and held it up so that it caught the rays through the glass panes. "Do you mind?"

"No, sir," said Fletcher.

"Do you have a cup about?"

"No cup. Sorry."

Fletcher watched Ezra unstopper the flask, positioning the neck against his lips to take a long, fragrant pull. The smell of rum at such an early hour was uncomfortable. Politely, the lieutenant refused the offered flask.

"Irons," said the lawyer, balancing the flask on the window ledge so that he could remove his spectacles. From somewhere, he produced a fine lawn handkerchief and began his usual vigorous wiping of the lenses. He repeated the lieutenant's name again before settling the spectacles into place on his nose. "Irons, did I ever mention that it was Faith Ashley whom I had asked to wed me?"

For the entire space of a heartbeat, Fletcher was silent, and then he answered gruffly, "No. You did not."

"Hmm," mumbled Ezra. "That much is obvious from your tone, sir." Retreating from the window, he sat down heavily in the lieutenant's only chair, drumming gnarled fingers on a velvet-clad knee. Fletcher straightened and dropped his arms.

"I can see, young man," continued Ezra, "that you are too mannerly to ask whether or not she refused me. She has. Very gently, of course, as is her way with me. You may have noticed that, at dinner. I am as a favored uncle to her."

Moving to the bed, Fletcher lowered himself, sitting, onto the worn mattress. "Why are you telling me, this, Briggs?" he asked, leaning forward, hands folded between his knees. He made every effort to appear normal.

"Why? I believe you know, Irons. I have had years to come to know the woman whom you have fallen in love with in a matter of weeks. Weeks? Hours. Oh, do keep still, sir; it was evident in your face that night at dinner, and it is revealed in your reaction every time her name is spoken, here, now. I pity you, Lieutenant. You are a man with many admirable qualities, and young—younger than I, at any rate—and you are possibly what Faith needs to build a happy life. But you wear that red coat and are committed to its purpose; there is no way of getting around that. Your love, if indeed at such short notice it is love, is more futile than mine, sir."

Fletcher rolled his eyes upward in a face angled to meet his hands. He felt the pressure of his molars, upper against lower, clenching in his mouth. He wanted not to feel anger toward that old man, but he could not help it.

"Is that all you have come to say, Ezra?" he retorted in a strained voice. "You need not have bothered."

"Oh, dear," said Ezra plaintively, "I have made you angry. That was not my intent. Or perhaps it was," he confessed abruptly. "Ever since I saw you, from the parlor window, walking from my house with Faith at your side, knowing that you are far more capable than I . . . younger than I . . . the sort of man who can contain her . . ."

"I have no desire to 'contain' her," Fletcher informed him. "And as to our walking together, though it was at my suggestion, it was at your insistence. Surely, you recall that. Why," he demanded further, "did you arrange our meeting at dinner, Mrs. Ashley and I? As you had asked the lady to be your wife, it makes very little sense to me. If nothing else, my attraction to her was evident from the beginning. It is a cruel sport which you have played with me."

Ezra sighed, and shook his head. "No, Lieutenant, do not

think ill of me, I beg of you. I am fond of you, Fletcher, though I have misused you, gravely. I thought, perhaps, to flaunt Faith before you, a virile, young man in uniform, knowing your interest, and knowing that she would turn it aside; if not for her love of me, then for her hate of what you represent. I'd hoped, I suppose, to win her to me because of it. You are correct, of course; it was a cruel game I played, and a reckless gamble. And it has not worked. I could not count on her consent merely because of the years of our acquaintance, and meant to tip the balance.''

The lawyer continued, "She loves me, it is true, but not in the way I long for. She would rather be alone. She has told me as much, clearly, and carefully. In spite of everything, or perhaps because of it, she is always careful with me.'' Once again, he sighed, an action that shuddered the loose skin about his mouth.

The lieutenant stared at him, seeming to be caught between anger and pity. Ezra's tongue slipped out to moisten dry lips. He recalled the moment during that disastrous dinner party when he had seen a certain something revealed in Faith's eyes when she had looked at the lieutenant without anger; he had known then the mistake he had made in bringing them together. Afterwards, he wondered if his own selfishness provided him with the right to keep her, whom he dearly loved, from happiness. It grieved him to think that he would try, and yet, he had deliberated long and hard before coming to this man, whom he had hoped to use in an attempt to assure Faith's consent. Even now, he wondered if he could speak . . .

"Would you mind fetching my flask for me?" he asked breathlessly. "I don't feel quite able to get up myself.''

Without unbending fully, Fletcher leaned forward, stretching to the ledge. His fingers encircled the flask and he dropped back, extending the container to Briggs, bottom first. "Are you ill?" he asked brusquely.

"Ill in spirit," he claimed, "if that does not sound overly dramatic. After all that I have just admitted, I have been torn between hope and dread, not knowing if Faith has spent these last weeks in your company.''

"But why? There was very little chance that she had, for

whatever reason, and if she had not, what would it matter? I am beginning to lose my understanding of this conversation, Briggs.'' Beginning to lose his patience as well, he kept himself admirably under control. It would have been foolish to vent his anger on a man who, in the end, did not deserve it.

"Forgive me, Irons. I have not seen Faith since she returned to refuse me, and I have been used to her companionship. But I have heard—rumors—that the activity in the North End has increased. Have you heard the same?''

A line creased Fletcher's brow in frowning. ''Yes,'' he admitted reluctantly. ''Why?''

Ezra sighed, pushing on the wired bridge spanning his nose with three fingers. ''Faith is involved, somehow. I have heard that, also.''

Fletcher shot to his feet. ''What?''

"I had hoped it wasn't true; this information was brought to me through a very private channel, it is not common knowledge, but I would measure it as true. If she had been with you, there might have been reason for hoping otherwise.''

"Where? Where did you hear this?''

"She is a headstrong woman—'' Ezra began.

"And in this case, foolish! This is no game!''

"I could not agree with you more, Lieutenant. But I am certain that Faith understands the risks. Even you, Lieutenant, on such short acquaintance should realize that.''

"Where did you hear this?'' Fletcher repeated.

"From my housekeeper, Mrs. Hart. There is good cause to believe it is truth. She would never have opened up to a Loyalist citizen, but she fears for Mrs. Ashley. And to think, all of these years I thought Mrs. Hart to be a staunch Tory! Things are moving too swiftly, Lieutenant Irons. In the wisdom of my years, I am afraid, sir.''

Pivoting on his heel, Fletcher skirted the bed, striding to the open door. He stepped out into the hallway. Then he swung about, returning to his starting point. In the small mirror, he could see the black edge of his sleeve; the brass buttons; the cochineal-dyed fabric: red as spilled blood.

"So am I, Ezra,'' he said.

"What exactly is it that has been done?''

"I don't know that, Lieutenant."

His anger toward Ezra was forgotten, directed instead toward Faith and the stupidity of her self-righteous conscience. In spite of all that he had said to her on that night that now seemed so long ago, patriot activities were treasonous. The time was coming when arrests would be made, and although it was unlikely that any but the most vital and public Whig leaders would be taken into custody, there was still the danger of mistreatment and the very distinct possibility that all her possessions would be commandeered for British use, were she found out. Worse, she could be hurt, physically, in the course of her actions. With a violent turn toward the window, Fletcher hooked his arm above the frame and leaned his forehead against the cool glass.

Suddenly, he espied a familiar figure striding across the yard: that of Lieutenant Upton. Had he been so long that the officer had eaten without him, and was now leaving for the Common? Spinning about with a whispered expletive of frustration, Fletcher thanked Ezra for the information.

"I will do whatever is in my power, Briggs," he promised.

Rising, Ezra limped forward. "I thank you, Fletcher. And I would be grateful if you would accept my apology for anything I said earlier that may have offended you, and anything which I have done."

Fletcher exhaled in one deep, forgiving breath. He nodded. "I must hurry off, Ezra. We will speak again on this matter. Come around for breakfast another day, will you?"

"Certainly."

"Good day, Ezra."

"Irons . . . Irons, one moment."

Crossing the threshold, Fletcher paused, looking back. At the opposite side of the bed the lawyer stood leaning heavily on his cane, a recently acquired tool wrought in dark wood. He looked smaller, although he was still a large man, and weak, tired. "Yes?" said Fletcher. "What is it?"

"Irons, I—" and he hesitated, wishing that he could see the lieutenant's expression more clearly, for in that could he gauge the truth behind the man's answer. But Ezra's eyesight had been deteriorating, markedly, and now, when it was imperative that he judge the honesty of a man's reply in his eyes, he could not see them but through a discolored, murky haze. He moved closer, adjusting the spectacles, sliding them up and down over his nose until Fletcher's countenance was focused. "Irons," he said, "what I am about to ask you is of paramount importance to me. The years of close association with Faith, with her family, leave me with some responsibility. I have a duty of assured kinship; I am the favored uncle."

"Yes," said Fletcher. "Go on, please."

"I would ask that you always treat Faith in an honorable fashion. I do not care if she despises you; in your contact with her, I ask that you treat her well, and with respect. For I know, instinctively in these old bones, that you will not be able to leave her be. Unless the flame of your passion is snuffed out now, you will not, no matter how she discriminates against you." He laughed, and the bitterness was undisguised. "It seems, by coming here this morning, that I have arranged a sane cause for your pursuit, would you not agree? Nonetheless, Fletcher, I need your assurance that you will do as I have asked."

"You speak," pronounced Fletcher carefully, "as if you do not expect to be around."

"Oh, not at all. Someday, I shall be gone from this earth, but not soon, God willing. If for anything, I should like to live to see the close of this rebellion, and order restored in the name of King George!" Ezra declared vehemently.

"I pray that day comes soon, Briggs. And with no blood shed," amended Fletcher.

"Amen to that, Lieutenant," Ezra agreed. "But you have not answered me."

Fletcher's stormy blue gaze regarded the lawyer's pale one thoughtfully. "I suspect," he said slowly, "that our Mrs. Ashley is a stubborn woman, who will have neither need nor tolerance of me. I suspect, also, that I could not give her happiness, contrary to your claim. There is no reason to believe that. I do not think that her politics alone would keep us from a comfortable relationship. The lady has a mind and a will of her own, and a life that does not include the likes of me, sir." Somehow, he could not bring himself to add that Faith herself had requested that he remain separate from her life, for then he would be forced to admit the circumstances of that request.

"But I do say this," he continued, standing ramrod-straight in the open doorway, the cadence of his voice huskily sincere, expressive, marked by an attractive tonal quality that made Ezra flinch. "I will do as you have asked, for I am fond in supposing that we are responsible for those we love. And, if it is possible to love 'at such short notice,' to quote you, Ezra, as my father before me has done, then I do love her. What good may come of it, I do not know, but I do not seem, thus far, to be able to help myself. Are you content to accept that reply?"

"Yes, Fletcher," said Ezra softly, tugging on the top three buttons of his waistcoat. How torn he was, between wanting to welcome the lieutenant to what neither he himself, nor the officer, could possess, and wanting on the other hand to cast him out of what was becoming a peculiar little triangle; wanting, very much, to dislike him. It was not possible.

"You had better hurry, then, Irons. I have kept you overlong."

"My horse is swift when pushed, Ezra. Don't you worry." Striding away down the narrow, low-ceilinged corridor, he called back, "Pull the door to when you are ready to leave, won't you?"

"Of course, of course," Ezra murmured, knowing that the young man was already beyond earshot. He heard the lieutenant's voice again, distantly, on the stair, and then his quick tread. Recognizing that he was not being spoken to, he stepped wearily out into the hallway with its worn runner and cracked plaster, and pulled the door closed behind.

Ezra inhaled raggedly, his expression marked by his soul's pain. Yet, in his conscience, he had no choice but to use Faith's activities as a contrivance for Fletcher's interference. And his love for her left him with no choice but to offer her the happiness that she would otherwise deny. A younger man, and a companionship that would not end, God willing, after only a few years' time.

Beneath his hand, the curved head of his cane was warm,

already familiar, fitting into his palm and fingers. Favoring his better leg, he followed Fletcher's resounding footsteps. Even if such had been his desire, Ezra understood that it was beyond his ability to keep up. He might have, once. But he had found, not unexpectedly, that in the passing of the winter had risen the herald of his own.

Chapter Nine

"Ladies. We may begin without them. I am afraid our hostess is much occupied."

Seated in one of the many chairs that had been brought in to form a large square in the center of Faith's parlor, the widow Constance Winter looked about imperiously at the gathering of women; the angular features of her face were pinched, her brown eyes were probing. Her peppered hair was pinned up beneath a white mobcap, her dress was severe. Indeed she had worn no other color than black since Mr. Winter had passed on. About her shoulders, however, she wore a bright yellow shawl. Suddenly, she smiled, softening every angle of her expression excepting the sharp point of her nose. Bending forward, she reached down with a theatrical gesture and took hold of the unfinished quilt that was lying, stretched flat, at her feet. Every other woman did the same, without the dramatic flair of Mrs. Winter, draping the material across laps that were nearly all clothed in home-dyed colors. This was more than a meeting to complete the quilt: it was an assembly of women in quiet protest. For the quilt itself had a rebellious motif, commemorating the dreadful Boston Massacre, the anniversary of which was only two days away, on the fifth of March.

Before beginning, the women bowed their heads in a brief prayer, following Constance's lead.

"Dear Jesus, we implore Thy blessing of our small endeavor, that our stitches may be as steadfast as our men in this just and rightful cause. Praise be to the Lord. Amen."

The seven seated females raised their heads in murmuring unison. For a moment, there was silence, and then came the snip of shears, the clatter of great spools of spun-cotton thread unwinding over the plank floor, the tip-tip of needles against thimbles, the fluttering of a hum of conversation afresh, and from the rear of Faith's home, in the warmth of the kitchen, the squalling of an infant.

"Poor Rachel," sympathized one of the women, a young mother herself. "That babe of hers gives her no peace. Colicky, it is."

"Aye, it is that," agreed another. "I told Mrs. Revere just what she could do to help that poor child ailing, but I don't reckon she paid me any heed. Modern ideas!"

"Oh, hush. Perhaps she has tried it, and it didn't work. Diluted dandelion tea, I say."

At the head of the quilt, Constance nodded her head and smiled. She glanced sidelong at Paul Revere's youngest daughter, to see what she thought of the topic of discussion, but the girl was intently bent over a square of linen, the tip of her pink tongue poking between her teeth, working her needle with careful deliberation. At that moment, a rosy-cheeked, dark-haired Rachel Revere entered the room, supporting her infant son on her shoulder and massaging his lower back with her right hand.

"Dandelion tea, diluted," insisted the woman who had just spoken once again.

Mrs. Revere smiled, and was silent, catching the eye of her beloved husband's daughter as she began to stroll slowly along the borders of the room, whispering soothingly to her child. She glanced at her empty chair, and those of Faith Ashley and Elizabeth Watts.

Following the woman's glance, Constance's daughter-in-law Eugenie twisted her lips smugly. A dark light glittered in her brown eyes. No matter what the others thought of Mrs. Ashley, she had never been fond of the woman. And now, it seemed, she had been supplied with legitimate cause to vent her feelings.

She looked, once, over her shoulder, to assure herself that the young widow still remained in the kitchen, then she said, as if it were no more than a natural direction the conversation had taken, "I'm quite rightly surprised that Mrs. Ashley is continuing this sewing circle at her home, after what I heard tell," and then waited for the effect.

Rachel paused, turning. The flow of colored threads stilled as Eugenie Winter leaned forward in a conspiratorial manner. "Why is that?" she asked, steadily, all the while hushing the babe with a hand to its tiny back.

"I don't know that I like to say," Eugenie began, looking about again, needle in hand. With no need for prompting, she continued. "I heard . . . I heard," and now her voice was little more than a whisper, bringing all the women to the edge of their seats except Rachel Revere, who narrowed her eyes where she stood, and Constance, whose nose became even more pinched with impatience. "I heard that she was escorted home, quite late in the evening, by a British colonel."

The response was nearly immediate.

"No! A British colonel? Who? Oh, my."

"I do not believe it! How long ago?"

"Several weeks ago, from what I'm told," declared the younger Mrs. Winter, with relish.

"What a bold woman! To come to our meetings, and to go on with her own, here—"

"Are you saying that she is a turncoat?"

"Or worse, dear me."

Having listened to enough, Rachel pronounced with quiet deliberation, "It was a British lieutenant, not a colonel." She was rewarded with the satisfaction of Eugenie Winter's gaping mouth. Rachel hated gossip, especially vindictive gossip and tales that, in this case particularly, could do more than damage a person's reputation. "If you are worried that Mrs. Ashley is a traitor to our cause, I suggest that you allay your fears." Pausing to brush her lips against her son's soft cheek and to rock him gently, she took breath before continuing. "Mrs. Ashley relayed information to my husband which, though it was of no surprise to him, was still useful and sincere. And that, please ladies, does not go beyond this room. I do not

know the circumstances of Mrs. Ashley's stroll with the lieutenant. I do not care to know, except in that she saw fit to
increase the knowledge of those who are sorely in need of that
advantage. Do not, I pray, belittle Mrs. Ashley. She is, after
all, our hostess. And furthermore, she does not deserve it.''

With the baby now asleep on her lace-kerchiefed shoulder,
Rachel rocked him from side to side in the fresh air of the
open window, turning him to the warmth of the sun.

Backed with haste into the short corridor beneath the stairs,
Elizabeth stared down in dismay, her eyes wide but seeing
nothing. Her blonde hair fell about a face gone chalk-pale. She
felt herself tremble a little, and stop. She had, by misfortune,
come upon the tail end of Mrs. Revere's monologue in which
she chastised another, or all, of the women for being unkind
to Mrs. Ashley. Staring with blank shock, she wondered what
fault they had possibly found with Mrs. Ashley, and how they
dared speak about her in her own home. She did not know the
lieutenant mentioned and that frightened her.

Raising her head, she pushed her hair back off her forehead.
She swallowed, glancing back toward the rear of the house.
She was glad that Mrs. Ashley had stayed in the kitchen to
clean up the baby's spilled posset. Still puzzled, Elizabeth
frowned in confusion.

"What is it, Elizabeth?"

The girl started at Faith's voice, then inhaled with a small,
quick gasp. Her smile for Faith was quick, uncertain, false.
"Nothing, ma'am."

"You look upset, Elizabeth. Are you certain nothing is
amiss?" Faith swept past the girl, skirts in hand, looking
sharply about as if for some culprit. The expression made
Elizabeth giggle, involuntarily. She shook her head. "The
ladies are waiting, then," said Faith. "Let's do hurry."

Pressing her lips together, Elizabeth followed the woman
into the parlor. In the archway she paused behind Faith, peering
in wondering accusation at the women with the colorful quilt
stretched from lap to lap. She found them caught in a pose of

anticipation that was both unnatural and uncomfortable as they observed Faith's entry.

"Good morning, ladies," said Faith. "I am sorry that you had to begin without us, but I think that the pastries which Elizabeth baked for us will be worth the trouble." Her smile was returned nervously by several of the group, as was her salutation. Puzzled, Faith felt the muscles curving her mouth tighten and hold as her gaze moved from that of one woman to another. Only Constance Winter appeared undaunted, grinning at her, exhibiting her remarkably fine teeth.

With a sense of caution that might have been entirely out of keeping with a possibly imagined tension, Faith moved to take her seat beside a normally garrulous Miss Maddie Owens. Elizabeth flounced into the chair immediately to her left with her eyes downcast. Faith bent her head into the silence, arranging the quilt on her gray lap and studiously marking the pattern before bending to remove a needle from the pincushion on the floor. While in that position, doubled over in her chair and searching about with splayed fingers for the spooled, dyed thread, she observed the others surreptitiously, noting their every expression and attitude. Most had returned to their work and had even renewed a conversation of sorts, but Faith found both the younger Mrs. Winter and another woman, whom she scarcely knew, watching her openly. Annoyed and curious, Faith sat up and threaded her needle. When next she glanced in that direction, both women had turned away. Inhaling, Faith dutifully began to stitch.

Faith enjoyed needlework, whether it was routine mending or the manufacturing of something as significant as the quilt which the ladies hoped to display in Old South Meeting House on the anniversary of the massacre, to which an open assembly had been declared. Dr. Joseph Warren was to speak; Faith was looking forward to being there. Needlework was calming, conducive to the sorting and following of particular thought. By the time she had formed two hundred careful, perfect stitches, Faith was ready to address the group on a certain issue of importance, whether they cared to hear it or not. Folding her slender hands into her lap, she straightened her spine, clearing her throat in advance of speech.

Out of the corner of her eye, she saw Rachel Revere turn, the baby suckling at her breast beneath the cover of a light shawl, and start, her eyes widening with an avid interest. Constance, also, looked up, her expression one of sober expectancy.

"Yes, Faith?" she said.

Odd, Faith thought, how promptly they all responded to that brief query with their attention. She nodded gratefully in Constance's direction, impaling the quilt with her needle so not to lose it, and began to speak.

"Ladies," she said, pushing a tendril of red-gold hair from her cheek, "I assume that you are all aware of the orders recently issued by Provincial Congress to collect and store as many weapons as possible?" Taking the silence as agreement, she went on. "Because of this, our good blacksmiths are kept busy repairing old weapons and, when possible, making new ones. In the countryside, farmers are manufacturing saltpeter. There are, of course, caches of arms in towns all about, not to mention the public supplies. The seizure by the British of the gunpowder at Charlestown and the cannon at Cambridge is a setback, but not a devastation. Yet, here in Boston—yes, Mrs. Winter?"

Eugenie shook her head, declining to speak. She despised knowledgeable females, especially those who had recently been seen in the company of a British officer.

"Go on, Faith," said Constance quietly.

"Yes, thank you. Now, where did I leave off? Well, no matter. I will come directly to the point. It makes no difference if we have the gunpowder, or the weapons, for we have not the metal needed for the manufacture of shot." Faith faltered at the scowl of disapproval that appeared without restraint on the heavily handsome face of Eugenie Winter. Beside Faith, Maddie Owens sucked in her breath sharply, as if she had just swallowed something that had not appealed to her.

"Oh," moaned that woman, "must we speak of this? It is such a worrisome topic."

Faith turned, opening her mouth to speak, but Constance, dark brown eyes sparkling in irritation, forestalled her.

"Yes, Maddie," she said, punctuating each word with a jab of her needle into the air. "It is worrisome, and rightly so. Do not be addle-headed, and hold your tongue while Faith speaks. All of you!—do the same. I, for one, am obliged to hear what she has to tell us."

After a moment, Faith continued. "I am sorry if the topic either annoys or frightens you, ladies. There is not much to be done about that, I am afraid. I have been asked—"

"You?" interrupted Mrs. Winter. "Why you, and by whom, I reckon we all might be interested in knowing."

"Eugenie!" admonished Constance severely.

"The question is an understandable one," said Faith to the older widow. She had thought that Eugenie Winter's previous reaction had been due to a lack of loyalty but realized now that it was due merely to the woman's dislike for her. Well, that was only an opinion and no worry to Faith, although she could not recall what she might have done to incur the disfavor.

"I wish that I could answer you, Mrs. Winter," Faith added, a fact which infuriated the other woman. "But if you give the matter proper consideration, you will understand why I cannot, of course. Suffice it to say that certain arrangements have been made, and I am now doing more for the cause than merely losing my temper."

Sitting back, she felt a pulse in her throat as she recalled what had prompted her to make a more definitive move. It was a way of fleeing the emotions overwhelming her concerning Lieutenant Irons, a decision toward which she had been heading prior to that night in January, facilitated after by need. She was doing it for the common good, she told herself. Deep down, she knew that it was for her own. She would create a distance that would, in time, be beyond bridging. "I am certain," said Faith, after the brief but turgid interval, "that we all desire to do everything of which we are capable in order to comply with the orders of the Provincial Congress."

From her seat by the window, Mrs. Revere spoke. "Elizabeth, you may come take the baby now, if you will. Stand near to the open window and alert us to anyone who may be passing near enough to overhear our discussion, please.''

The two exchanged places, Elizabeth nearly overcome with delight at being allowed to coddle the young infant, and Rachel lowering herself into Elizabeth's vacant seat. By this time, all needlework had ceased.

"Pray tell, Mrs. Revere,'' drawled Eugenie Winter, "do you happen to know what it be that Mrs. Ashley is taking so long to utter?''

"Yes,'' replied Rachel with her unflappable calm, "I do. It is important that as many of us as possible be apprised of this situation, with normal caution naturally, so that we may act upon it.''

"It is our patriotic duty,'' Faith added, "to accept the necessity of sacrifice.''

There were murmurs of agreement.

"Most of us,'' said Faith, "are in possession of pewter which—''

"Pewter for gunshot,'' announced Constance triumphantly, wrinkling into a pleased grin. "Makes sense. T'wouldn't do to cast them from silver, and never from brass nor pure tin. So, pewter it is, then.''

"Yes,'' Faith said.

A stunned silence followed. Faith drew quiet breath and waited, her hands folded in black lace upon the colorful quilt. The only sound within the house was that of the baby, gurgling with surprising pleasure at the faces Elizabeth was offering.

"My . . . my pewter service has been in the family for more than one hundred years . . .''

All heads turned to face the woman in brown seated opposite Constance Winter. No one spoke, yet there was no doubt in Faith's mind that all thoughts were dwelling similarly.

"Ladies,'' Faith reminded them, "the choice is yours. You may decide as your conscience dictates.''

The noise that escaped from Eugenie's lips was both rude and unexpected. "You dare to speak of conscience?'' she demanded hotly.

"I beg your pardon?''

"Conscience,'' Mrs. Winter repeated, but she was unable

to offer an explanation for her statement before the woman in brown, married for five years to one of the town selectmen, spoke again.

"Will you do it, Mrs. Ashley? Will you give up your pewter to be melted down for gunshot?"

"I will," she said, firmly.

After a moment, she went on. "I would not ask of you that which I am not prepared to do myself. But if you do not care to make this sacrifice, whatever the reason, it will be understood. As a Christian woman, I have very real fears that should there be a major confrontation one of these balls may maim or kill a man, even though that man is our enemy."

"Sentimentality?" said Eugenie Winter, dryly.

"Do keep still," said Rachel, losing her patience.

By the window, Elizabeth made a small noise.

Frowning, Faith came back into the center of the room, skirting the square slowly until she was standing behind her own chair. She put her palms on the convex back, curling her fingers tightly around the painted wood. Her look was severe, passing over Eugenie before assessing the remainder of the group. "But," she said, and her tone had changed again, restraining several unpleasant urges and the taint of other emotions, "if the gunshot is not cast, there is the possibility that men we cherish, men we honor, will be killed."

"Are—are you suggesting that there will be—war?" asked Maddie Owens in frightened hesitation.

"No!" The vehemence of her declaration and the abruptness of her movement made the crisp petticoat beneath Faith's gray skirt turn, swinging, against her knees. "No," she repeated. "We should all pray, diligently, that such a thing will never come to pass. The Congress awaits a reply to their demands, which hopefully will be met. In the meantime, it is our duty to perform as we are bade."

"Oh, yes," agreed Maddie in a sudden turnabout. "Yes, yes." Her affirmative reply was echoed about the room.

"Where are we to bring the pewter?"

"It will be collected," said Faith. "If you agree now, then someone will come to your home, asking if there is anything about the house that needs repairing. If you have changed your mind, or must refuse for other reasons, then turn him away. Otherwise, allow him entry, and give him the pewter. You will know these men by the green coats they will wear.''

"And when," said one, "can we expect that they will come?"

"Tomorrow."

"T-tomorrow?"

"Do you object? You must decide now," Faith said.

"No. No, I do not object."

"Do not lose heart, ladies," Faith urged them. "We are strong." This last, she uttered for her own sake, as well as theirs, for once the pewter was melted and cast, the majority of the balls were to be smuggled out of town. She had convinced those who had doubted her that there was a safe way this could be done. But as the day approached, her heart had quailed.

There had been such stealth in Faith's speech, and the conversation that followed it, that when Elizabeth began to speak in a loud, panicked whisper nearly everyone jumped in alarm. Faith spun about.

"What is it, Elizabeth?"

Rising with the infant clutched desperately to her small bosom, the blonde girl hurried away from the window. Her blue irises were ringed about in white, in fright. "Oh, oh, forgive me! I ain't been paying attention like I should have! I didn't know anyone t'was there 'til I heard him on the path! He's coming to the door! A lobsterback! Right here!"

Fearing the child would swoon, Faith took the baby from her and returned him to his mother. "Ladies, start folding the quilt. I will answer my own door. Anything that a redcoat has to say, he may say to me."

"Yes. I am certain of that," muttered Eugenie.

Faith glanced around the room, suddenly anxious. Eugenie Winter appeared nothing less than smug in countenance. At last, Faith understood the woman's enmity. She bent to take the edge of the quilt into her hands to hasten the other women in the task. But at the sound of a fist on the door, she dropped the quilt and turned. Unaccountably, her hands had begun to shake.

Hiding her disturbance in a show of annoyance, she walked briskly to the door and yanked it open, but at the last moment she caught the edge of sturdy wood with her shoe, so those inside remained unseen. Her heart was pounding furiously. Her shoulders jerked back as if from the force of a blow. In disbelief, she stared at the man before her, knowing that her credibility among these women would be ruined.

He seemed too big for the small space of the doorway, yet his demeanor was not awkward. She stood firm, her head held high, and waited. There seemed no point in speaking.

"Mrs. Ashley," said the lieutenant.

"Yes?" She had to clear her throat, quietly, to get the one word out of it.

"May I come in?"

"I have company, Lieutenant. Our ladies' sewing circle is meeting here today." Deliberately, she delivered the statement coldly.

"Indeed? Then perhaps you should come with me, Mrs. Ashley."

"Are you arresting me, sir?" Faith countered with a return of strength.

"No."

"Am I in some manner of trouble then, Lieutenant?"

His look seemed to change then, to lose some of its hardness; his eyes reflected something that might have been pain. "Possibly," he replied, flatly.

Faith quickly looked away. It was the expression of torment that made her heart ache so. Behind her, she could hear Constance and Rachel urging the women to action, telling them to pack up their things, that the meeting was, of necessity, concluded.

"Lieutenant Irons," she said, "you may address your business to me, here, on the doorstone. What is it?"

"I do not think so, Mrs. Ashley," said Fletcher. "What I have to say is not something you would care for your friends to hear, I am certain."

"Are you so sure, Lieutenant?" said Faith.

"Yes," he said.

Faith drew breath, crumpling the material of her skirt beneath her fingers. Rachel appeared at her side, quietly.

"Elizabeth has my son," she said. "Is all well?" The question was directed both to Faith and the redcoated officer in the doorway. Faith nodded wordlessly, seeking encouragement in the woman's gaze and, gratefully, finding it there. Heartened somewhat, she touched the quilt in the woman's arms, and implored, "Do not let it come apart."

Rachel Revere understood that the widow was not referring to the quilt at all, but to all they had attempted to accomplish that day.

"I won't," she promised. "All will be well."

"Thank you. And now, will you see that everyone remains here, enjoying the cakes which Elizabeth has worked so preciously hard to bake? I must leave, just for a short time."

Rachel's eyes went from Faith to the lieutenant and back again in open appraisal. "And you are certain," she said, "that all is well?"

"I am in no danger, if that is what you mean," replied Faith with strange bitterness. She turned back to Lieutenant Irons, surprising a look upon his face that caught her breath. She could only hope that Rachel had not seen it.

"Lieutenant," she said, "I will come with you."

Lieutenant, thought Rachel. He is the one. And behind her, as she gently closed the door for Faith, she heard Eugenie remarking rudely over the same fact.

Chapter Ten

"Are you not the least bit alarmed, Mrs. Ashley?"

Faith, who had been scrutinizing a particular pattern in the woven rug, her fingers folded demurely together in a lap where a trim pair of knees were pressed together as securely as could be managed, feigned a calm she did not feel and smiled, glancing up in response to the lieutenant's question.

"Whose place is this, Lieutenant Irons?"

Taken aback, Fletcher looked from side to side, giving the sparsely furnished room a cursory search, almost as if he did not know the answer to that question himself. "As if it makes any difference," he said after a time, "these rooms are properly let to an acquaintance of mine."

Lies, he thought. A bad beginning.

"And he allows you the use of them often, I imagine?" continued Faith, with high sarcasm.

"I resent your insinuation," said Fletcher.

"I'd supposed that you might, sir."

"Mrs. Ashley!" Fletcher's tone was fierce. He had planned a calm, direct interview and a firm warning, but already she was distracting him from his intentions with her quick tongue. "Look at me," he said. "I have practically abducted you and yet you sit there, smugly I might add, and bandy words with me as if you thought them effective weapons."

"Aren't they?" Faith countered.

Taking a turn before her, Fletcher lowered himself into the chair opposite, leaning with his elbows on his thighs, and his hands folded between his knees. "Are you not frightened at all? I find that truly remarkable."

"How so?" replied Faith, coldly. "Would you harm me, Lieutenant?"

"The thought," he said, "has crossed my mind."

Impatiently, Faith rose from the chair. Fletcher followed her movements with his own, standing as she did. "How very interesting," said Faith, and turned her back on him. She strolled the perimeter of the room with a sway to her hips that showed more anger than seductiveness. Her skirts whispered over the floor in quiet response to the sound of her heels. Casually, as she passed the hearth, she ran her fingers over the top of the mantelpiece. They came up greyed by dust marring the black lace of her mitt. Wrinkling her nose, she brushed both clean with a snapping slap of her hands.

"Your friend, it seems, is in need of a housekeeper."

"Perhaps," grunted Fletcher, "he is only in need of a wife."

"To clean for him?" replied Faith archly. "How very boring."

"And for other reasons, I would suppose," said Fletcher, to irk her. She ignored him, continuing her stroll in expanding irritation until she had come full circle and was standing once again before her chair, in the warmth of the mote-filled sunshine. "Lieutenant Irons," she said, "if it would not be too much trouble for you to explain, I should like to know why you have brought me here. What is your reason? I had presumed that you were a man of your word, and that a bargain struck with you would be well kept."

"Bargain?" echoed Fletcher.

"Yes. You assured me that we would not meet again."

Fletcher's expression was of grim amusement. "I made no such assurances, Mrs. Ashley. If you will recall correctly, I had not the opportunity to respond to your plea. Yet, I have followed your wishes out of—" and here, he faltered, his expression no longer grim, nor so amused, "sympathy for you." He meant love, but could not confess it because he could not be certain that such an offer would not drive her away. His mouth felt dry.

Faith straightened her spine in embarrassment. *Sympathy*? Did he think her no more than a love-starved widow? Recalling the way she had clung to him, trembling in his arms, her cheeks flushed. He was as much as confessing that he had only taken advantage of the moment; that he had kissed her because she had been willing.

"Then, Lieutenant," said Faith, choking on her next breath, "why am I here?"

For a moment, Fletcher said nothing. A muscle in his jaw moved up and back. Faith had no cause to recognize it for what it was, and so she waited, eyes wide and insolent.

"I needed to speak with you," he said at last.

"Could we not have spoken on the street, as we walked? Was there cause to drag me along the road like a strumpet, to this . . . place?"

"I am sorry," he said. "Privacy seemed best. I wish to divert you from your present course that will lead only to trouble."

"Trouble?" said Faith, suppressing a withering uncertainty. Her voice quavered. She hoped he had not noticed; she must proceed with caution. "Whatever do you mean, Lieutenant?" she questioned, testing him. There was no way that he could know about her recent activities unless . . . "If you are referring to the motif of our needlecraft," she went on, trying to draw him off course, "the quilt upon which we were working before your interruption, sir, will be on prominent display at Old South Meeting House two days hence. You may study it as dearly as you wish at that time; the meeting is open to all."

Fletcher sighed. If nothing else, the sudden change of Faith's nonchalant tone alerted him to the truth of the situation. She was afraid. "You know that my reference has naught to do with this quilt of yours. I knew nothing of it, prior to this mention. Mrs. Ashley, whether you are aware of it or not, you are playing a very dangerous game." Slowly, he turned to face her. The sun was at his back, outlining his form, highlighting the uniform that he wore.

"I had no idea that I was playing games at all," said Faith, pretending a diligent search for lint on her black, fingerless gloves. "And I have no inkling as to the reason for your ramblings. Dangerous games are military pastimes, not mine."

Uttering this final declaration, she turned determinedly on her heel as if to go, in the hopes of dashing his thoughts. Unexpectedly, his hand seized her forcefully by the arm and spun her back around.

"No," he said.

Instantly, Faith lifted her hand in preparation to strike a violent, unthinking blow to the lieutenant's jaw. He prevented it deftly, by seizing that hand also, and bringing it down beside the other, caging them within his own.

"Lieutenant! This is most unseemly! Let go of my hands. You are hurting me."

"Be still," he said. "I am not."

"You are!"

"I am not."

There was a dangerous, unfathomable look to his eye; the danger being in the mystery, the uncertainty of what lay behind.

Faith took several short, rapid breaths. He is my own enemy, she thought.

And then his mouth pressed, cool and open, upon Faith's parted lips. For a moment, he held her hands still, and then he released them, so that he could embrace her, feel her slender form beneath his touch, the deceptively fragile array of her bones and the tensile strength of her movement. She willingly lifted her arms and wrapped them about his neck, her fingers tangling, caressing his hair. His lips moved along her skin to her throat, to the tender pulse there. He ran his tongue against it, tasting the sweetness of her skin. She moved against him, toward him, the heavy skirt she wore pinned between them, and she felt a heady rush of warmth, to her flesh, to her heart.

"My love, my love . . ." he murmured.

Faith made a small cry, and pushed away from him. "No. Please, you must stop. Let me sit down. I want to sit down."

With utmost solicitude, Fletcher assisted Faith to the nearest chair, then crouched on one knee beside her on the floor. Tenderly, he toyed with a wisp of hair that had fallen over her ear. She moved her head away, but not in haste.

"Lieutenant," she said, "I do not even know your Christian name."

He smiled, an arch to his winged brows. Somehow, the idea amused him. "It is Fletcher," he said. "Fletcher Jonathan . . ."

"Fletcher," Faith repeated, allowing the sound to hang in the air, wonderingly.

"Yes. Will it do?"

Faith shrugged, blinking. She felt tears, stinging her lids. "What am I to do now, Fletcher?"

"Do nothing," he said, simply.

"Nothing," said Faith, and turned her head away, to avoid his gaze, but she could feel it, the weight of it, open, and seemingly without deceit. She looked down, to her hands that were clenched tightly together upon the soft folds of her lap. "You do not understand. Not only have I behaved boldly, shamefully, in allowing you to kiss me in that fashion—"

"You returned that kiss in a most satisfying manner, Mrs. Ashley," he informed her.

"No. Hush. I must think."

"Think of what, my lovely little one? That you are, to put it lightly, fraternizing with your self-declared enemy? Or rather, how you have come 'on such short notice' to love me?" The smile he offered her was marked by irony.

"Love you?" Faith's fingers, intertwined, lifted once from her lap, and fell again. "How can you say so? What makes you believe so?"

Extending his hand to hers, Fletcher encircled her wrist, very gently. The pulse-beat of her blood throbbed there, like the rapid heart of a bird.

"I love you, Faith," he said. "It is that which makes me so certain. When you are in my arms, I have no doubt at all."

Faith detached her hand from his, opening her own, palm up, on her gray skirt. "No," she said. "No, I do not believe it possible to care so much, so suddenly." She rose; then, slowly, she strode to the window and stopped just short of it, lest she be seen in that place by someone passing in the street outside. She drew a deep breath, tilting her head back slightly with closed eyes. It is possible, she thought. It *is* possible.

"I must reiterate, Fletcher: why have you brought me here?"

Behind her, the lieutenant unfolded, stretching his cramped knee. He dusted off his white breeches with a quick swipe of his hand. "I have told you," he said.

Faith lowered her head, opening her eyes. "To speak with me. Of what? Love?" Deliberately, she edged her voice like a knife. "Or merely to take advantage of my femininity?"

"To take advantage—? Faith, Faith, do you not realize the truth? I am an honorable man, and I am in love." Foregoing anger, he came forward, placing himself at her side. In the sunshine her hair was flaming gold, and her eyes a translucent green, like deep, still water. The freckles that so became her paled to nothing. On her face was an expression of torment. "Would you rather that I kept silent concerning the matters of my heart, Faith, and spake only of those things which were my original intent? For I had no plans to confess my love to you."

"Did you not?"

"No."

"Then I beg of you, please, be still."

"Very well."

He took a turn away from her, then circled back to stand beside the window, leaning his shoulder against the frame, folding his arms.

"Faith," said Fletcher gravely, unsettled by the way in which events were running. "I do not believe you understand in what position you place yourself. And myself, by the way."

"How so?" whispered Faith, uncertain if he had returned to the topic she wished to avoid, or had begun another. "Explain yourself, please."

"In the pursuit of your activities, and my knowledge of them. Under normal circumstances, it would be my responsibility to act upon that knowledge. I could find myself in a goodly amount of trouble, for your sake. Do not misunderstand me. I will protect you, because I care for you, and the trouble is of no consequence."

"I do not take your meaning," said Faith, still whispering, still avoiding his eye. "What are my activities which could endanger you?"

Fletcher inhaled, deeply, through his nose. He was impatient, now, and not much caring for it. "Do you know that arrests have been made in Salem?" he asked her, seemingly at a tangent. Faith looked up, startled.

"Why, yes," she said. "But a court of jurors could not be found to try those men. Have you some clear reason for bringing this to my attention? Do you plan, after all, to arrest me? And on what charges?"

"I? Arrest you?" Fletcher said, and threw back his head suddenly to laugh, heartily amused. "I have not yet been commanded to do so," he said.

"You are infuriating," declared Faith.

"No more than are you," countered Fletcher.

Faith went on hotly. "What have I done, pray, that obliges you to go from declarations of love, to threats upon my liberty?"

Sobering, Fletcher regarded her with severity. "I do not exactly know. Yet, I will, with perseverence, unearth your secrets. Mark me. Mr. Briggs paid me a visit this morning before I had breakfasted, which should be an indication to you of his concern. He is a gentleman, and would not readily cause a man to forego his morning meal.''

"Ezra?" Faith repeated, brow furrowed. At the sound of his name, more from her lips than his, the guilt began afresh. Too many days had passed since last she had seen him, and for all her self-made excuses, she knew the true reason lay in that guilt, and its cause.

"Yes. He fears that you have become involved in active sedition."

"Does he?" She had hoped that Ezra would never come to know the full extent of it! "Where does he hear his information?"

"From his housekeeper, I am told, though he was quick to assure me that the woman would not have betrayed you had she not been deeply concerned."

Faith stood in silence. Mrs. Hart, Ezra, and Fletcher Irons. They were a plausible, but unlooked for, chain of involuntary espionage. Yet it was ineffectual, for Mrs. Hart most certainly received her information from the voluble Elizabeth, who was, of necessity, kept nearly in the dark. That realization brought her relief. "I am innocent—" she began, but was interrupted by the lieutenant.

"Hardly that," he commented dryly. "I do not expect you to admit your guilt to me, but I know that there is not a patriot woman in all of Boston who hasn't her own means of dissidence, and you, my dear, are overzealous. I have suffered the lash of your tongue, as you surely must recall. And have tolerated it, perhaps because it entertains me. Though not much.''

Floundering for a means to escape the accusation of his tone, Faith resorted to offense. "I resent your insinuation. Were I you, I do not think that I would care to cover the charges you have made with proof.''

"I have set no charges against you," Fletcher reminded her. "There are none. If you will not accept my other reason for wanting to stop you before you find yourself too deeply embroiled in something you cannot understand fully, then accept this: I am attempting to aid a man for whom we both care, Faith. That is all.''

Faith's hands fluttered to the kerchief about her shoulders. The lieutenant's last statement made her feel rather ill. "I've not meant to cause him worry," she said. "You must assure him there is no cause."

"I can't do that. I am not certain of that, myself."

Faith lifted her foot impatiently, then lowered it without a sound. "Is he well?" she asked. "How does he look?"

"Mr. Briggs?"

"Yes."

Fletcher sighed. "I do not think he is well. He looked tired, drawn. And, to be truthful, considerably older than when I saw him last. Are you aware that he is losing his sight? I noticed it, today."

Faith gasped in no small alarm. "No, I did not know."

There was an unfeigned vulnerability in the distress she displayed; Fletcher's anger seeped away as he thought to comfort her. Yet, he kept his distance and remained by the window.

"I was wrong, to stay away for so long. Will he forgive me?"

She was speaking as to herself, in total disregard of his presence. Fletcher watched her, opening a knowledge in himself like a wound. "You do love him," he stated, calmly.

"Of course," said Faith.

"Then why do you not marry him?"

"I—I beg your pardon?"

"Why do you not marry him?"

Faith frowned, deeply. "How do you know of this?"

"Ezra told me."

"He has?" She felt suddenly very breathless. "Were you bargaining for me, Lieutenant?" Her eyes glinted in their anger. "I do love him, but not in the espoused manner you are suggesting. I do not, nor will I, love any other man in that way, save my deceased husband. I am through," she said, "with love. I have had enough of it."

"I do not countenance that as the truth, Faith. I believe I know better."

"Mrs. Ashley to you, Lieutenant Irons. I would be obliged, sir, if you would not attempt insult again by contact with my person, physical or otherwise. And as for any activity of mine, there, too, you would be wise in minding your own counsel. Do not take advantage of our association with betrayal.''

"Then, my dear, you do admit to having something to hide?'' he retorted.

"I have not said so!''

"There are many things which you have not said, but I am not a stupid man, nor a blind man, no matter what you may think of me. And there, too, I can see beyond your anger. There are not many things of which you are afraid, but it happens that I am one of them.''

"How dare you?'' she tossed off disdainfully, lifting her head. "I, frightened of you, Lieutenant? A ridiculous notion, if ever I have heard one.''

"Indeed?'' he said, pushing off from the window and closing the gap between them in a single stride, commanding her, with his closeness, to meet his gaze. She did so, her narrow shoulders squared defiantly. "Kiss me again, Faith. Tell me then that you do not care for me at all.''

"No!''

"Are you afraid?''

"No.''

"Then kiss me.''

Faith shook her head in small movements of denial. Tendrils of hair fell across her brow and cheeks, so that she had to push them back with her hand. With an amused caution, Fletcher drew back slightly. "Do not be melodramatic, Lieutenant,'' she said, coldly.

"I have never been accused of that before,'' he said.

"I cannot imagine why not,'' answered Faith.

Fletcher frowned. Her heated retorts were beginning to irritate him, and he wondered how he could love a woman who seemed outwardly so vicious. He knew, in truth, that she was not; that she was afraid of loving him and therefore she could be rude and insolent. It was a strange defense, unwitting and automatic, that hurt him all the more because he loved her. He extended his hand to her own, observing her flinch, with a pain in his soul. Sighing, he let his hand fall.

"Faith.''

"Leave me be, Fletcher,'' whispered the widow, covering

her ears with her slender fingers. "If you care for me as you say you do, then leave me be!"

She fled his presence. He made no move to stop her. He stood, very still, listening to the sound of her retreat on the treadless stair. After a moment, Fletcher returned to the window, hooking his arm above the frame, and leaned his head against the cool glass. The sun cast long shadows in the street. Already, Faith's was not among them.

Straightening, Fletcher smoothed the scarlet-and-black lines of his uniform with an absent precision of practice and strode from the room. He walked out onto the cobbled street, the inn door slamming behind him like a crisp cannon blast. It drowned out the expletive that followed.

Chapter Eleven

Two days later, Faith stood just within the doors of Old South Meeting House, directing the hanging of the quilt. She had sewn rings into it along one edge, so that it could be suspended from a wooden dowel, like a banner, for all who passed through to appreciate. The Ladies Club had made a marvelous work of it.

Wiping her hand across her brow, Faith thanked the men assisting her and stood back to view the finished work. Satisfied, she moved inside to sit down.

The air inside Old South Meeting was coarsely scented from the press of bodies, warm, and humid. The wooden pews were filled to capacity, and the aisles were blocked by men standing shoulder to shoulder. Faith excused herself, forcing a passage through with the touch of her hand on an elbow, or a word, until she was close to the pulpit. Several of the town's leaders were seated there, including Sam Adams and the gentle, educated physician, Joseph Warren. Faith was eager to witness both of their oratory powers.

Beyond the wall of the meeting house, dark clouds rolled like heavy fleece under the shearer's hand, driven by a brisk, whipping wind coming in from the sea. Rain fell in a sheer, feather-light mist, glossing clapboard, shingle, and stone. Window-glazing fogged and dripped. Against the failure of the sun's appearance, several lamps had been lit inside the large hall of worship, three near the pulpit, and two more beneath the gallery just inside the massive doors. The quilt fluttered and snapped with every entrance. Voices were raised above the wind in a disharmonious thunder. And high overhead, a bird flew in, unnoticed, to seek shelter from the weather in the ceiling and rafter beams.

As Faith stared, Mr. Adams rose, calling for order with his resonant baritone. Conversation ceased, with the exception of a word or two here and there. Dr. Warren smiled in his kindly manner, waiting.

For Faith, this patient, reassuring smile brought rushing in the memory of a cold, brilliant, hard-edged day, when there had been a leaping fire upon the hearth. She remembered the sensation of the churn moving sluggishly through salt and thickening cream as she stood, preparing butter; she remembered the way the handle had stilled in her grasp when the captain of her husband's ship had entered, unannounced, his blue coat hanging about his shoulders. Behind him had stood Dr. Warren, smiling very gently, very compassionately. It was his smile which had forewarned her of the worst.

"William?" she had asked, but there had truly been no need to question.

She remembered the tears balanced on Captain Eller's sun-bleached lashes in the light of morning streaming through the window, and Joseph Warren's capable arms as she swayed on her feet, and broke down.

Faith observed the physician from over the edge of her silk fan. There had been many changes since that day, some relatively unimportant, and others not. For one thing, she thought with a wistful smile, she no longer churned her own butter, but purchased it locally at market. She also kept the street door locked, as if that could alter anything, and only the door leading to the kitchen yard remained unbolted. William's ship was gone, sold to Captain Eller himself before the mandated closing of the harbor. The sense of grieving, of having been abandoned, which had been with her for three years was suddenly renewed with vigor.

Long after the earnest opening recitation was completed, Faith's head remained bent. Only when she heard Adams' booming voice did she look up, expecting the onset of the man's speech. Instead, she was startled to observe that the fanatical patriot was addressing someone in particular, apparently at the rear of the building.

"Pray come forward! Come forward, please! Good citizens, I beg ye move aside for these officers of the Royal Garrison!" he implored with open arms, indicating that the men and women seated in the front row should rearrange their seating. Surprised, but obedient, the townspeople rose, making room for the British officers who were self-consciously moving to the fore from the shadowed area beneath the gallery. Pausing before the vacated pew, the officers glanced about uncertainly, then sat down with stiff restraint.

He is not among them, Faith thought. Thank God, he is not among them.

At the pulpit, Sam Adams nodded, the smug curve of his full lips increasing. By calling attention to the British officers, he had drawn them out into the open, to the fore in an effective strategy. The meeting was open to all, and most likely the redcoats had come to mock and jeer, but that would scarcely be possible now, seated so closely to the pulpit and the speakers themselves, with the whole of the congregation at their backs.

He began his speech then, a convincing oration to renew feelings of martyrdom and self-righteous anger. Below him, the British resorted to rudeness nonetheless, conversing loudly among themselves, with many gestures of hands. Adams concluded his speech, angrily.

When at last Joseph Warren stood to speak, he turned a dramatic profile to the audience. The snow-white folds of his toga undulated bizarrely to his movements, catching the radiance of the lamps hung to either side of the pulpit. He bade the crowd a good morning in a hushed voice. His demeanor ensured silence.

Faith straightened in anticipation. The men beside her had thoroughly stilled their conversation. It seemed that every eye was upon the man in the white robe, every ear waiting upon his word.

"The ruinous consequences of standing armies to free communities may be seen in the histories of Syracuse, Rome, and many other once-flourishing states; some of which have now scarce a name!" the physician began, much as he had similar speeches made during the five years since the Massacre itself. "Soldiers," he continued after a moment of deliberation, "are also taught to consider arms as the only arbiters by which every dispute is to be decided between contending states; they are instructed implicitly to obey their commanders, without enquiring into the justice of the cause they are engaged to support."

Not only is Fletcher a soldier, Faith thought, he is a commander of soldiers. She allowed her fan to fall, untended, into her lap.

"Hence it is," Warren went on, "that they are ever to be dreaded as the ready engines of tyranny and oppression . . ."

There were ready assents to that from the crowd. Faith's hands clasped tightly in her lap.

". . . And this will be more especially the case, when the troops are informed that the intention of their being in the city is to overawe the inhabitants. That this was the avowed design of stationing an armed force in this town is sufficiently known; and we, my fellow citizens, have seen, we have felt, the tragical effects! The fatal fifth of March, 1770, can never be forgotten!"

Faith's lips were slightly parted. Her mouth felt dry. Overhead, on the heavy roof of the meeting house, the rain fell and ran off with the beat of a slowly dying drum. Oh, Lord, she thought. Am I traitor to my people?

She looked at the perspiration standing out on Warren's brow, the tears on his lashes, as he went on, about judgment and repentance, about murder, and the innocent. Faith shuddered.

"May we ever be a people favored of God," said Warren, concluding his speech. "May our land be a land of liberty; the seat of virtue, the asylum of the oppressed, a name and a praise in the whole earth, until the last shock of time shall bury the empires of the world in one common undistinguished ruin!"

The cannonade of applause and the stamping of feet effortlessly obscured the snickers of the officers in their powdered wigs and scarlet coats. From his chair among several of the town's selectmen, Adams leaped up. Even at thirty feet, Faith could see the quivering of emotion that enveloped him. Raising both arms above his head, Adams turned to the assembly, entreating that they not allow themselves to forget the importance of the occasion and that they attend the next anniversary of the bloody Massacre. A murmur of astonishment coursed through the crowd. Faith sucked her breath in sharply. It had not passed her notice that Dr. Warren had refrained from use of the word *bloody* during his entire oration, as explicit as it was, for though it held nothing but the obvious definition for a Bostonian, to the British it was a singularly potent profanity. She knew this. In the heat of anger, Fletcher himself had used it.

Curious of the reaction of the officers in front of her, Faith tilted her head, peering at the place where the redcoats had been sitting. They were no longer there, but had risen to their feet. Somehow, she had not expected that the usage of the word, which had probably been entirely innocent, even for Adams, could result in such excitement.

Muttering exclamations, the British spun at last to gape back over the crowd to the gallery above. Faith turned also, following a thousand heads, to stare up at an unsettling sight of another officer leaning dangerously close to the low gallery wall. Tall and thin, he was frantically slapping his hands in what appeared a frantic search over his scarlet jacket. Faith thought that she heard him shout down a curt phrase concerning his handkerchief, but she was not sure, and in the next instant he had thrown up his hands, crying out, "Oh, fie! Fie!"

It was a bewildering ejaculation that was immediately taken up by others in the gallery, as "Fire!"

Fire.

Following the alarm was a hollow pause of fear; a fear that was forever and uniquely resident in the heart of every man and woman who recalled the pernicious speed with which flame spread through a town almost solely constructed of wood. It was a pause in which the blood pulsed in Faith's temples with the roaring force of the sea through a narrow rocky channel. In that space of paralyzing terror, she saw that the man in the gallery had become inordinately calm and was staring intently at something or someone below. Faith forced her gaze to follow his, to view that which he viewed, and found herself witness to another soldier, wearing the uniform of a private in the infantry, who was fighting against a humanity surging toward panic; his one hand was beneath his black-lapelled jacket, and in that hand was an instrument, wooden stock, black bore, gleaming brass fittings. His gaze was heated, yet burning with a strange satisfaction. Faith's own eyes sprinted along the path of the man's gaze before fully realizing that it was a pistol which he held secreted beneath his coat. His target, standing in urgent plea for the people to remain sensible and retreat in orderly fashion, was Joseph Warren.

Faith lunged forward, shouting.

But the strength of a panicked populace was overwhelming, and she was swept from the scene, adding her futile screams to those of a multitude, as she strained to hear that sound of irreversible violence: the explosion of gunfire beneath timbers quaking from chaos.

The green silk fan was torn from her hands. The hem of her dark brown skirt trod upon, causing her to stumble, catching herself on the arm of a man who pulled her along, then shook her off. A child, small and pale and terrified, stood wailing in the aisle. Faith could not imagine how she had not been trampled. She lifted the child in her arms, barely managing to pass the babe into the mother's grateful embrace before the two were borne from sight. The meeting house rumbled. Fighting for secure footing, Faith attempted to turn around. Grasping the back of a mahogany pew, she anchored herself by the fingernails to the smooth wood. But the force of panic to gain the street and safety ripped her away and bore her on.

"Dr. Warren!"

Her cry mingled with a thousand others, calling out names and instructions. Beneath the shadow of the gallery, the terrible volume of noise increased, as did the rush for the doors so near. No gunfire, Faith thought, in a whirl of relief and horror; she turned again, hearing above the clamor a strange and unearthly sound, a scream of pure fear that came so quickly upon the sight that followed as to almost precede it. A bundle of clothing in human form plummeted from the gallery above, falling with a sickening thud upon the shoulders of someone below, bearing both down onto the damp, muddied floor. This waking nightmare was followed by another, and still another, until Faith closed her eyes and at last allowed herself to be propelled into the tumult of the street.

The townspeople continued to scream and weep, shouting themselves hoarse with the repetition of the single word of alarm: "Fire!"

Making a final attempt to escape the hysteria that had nearly enveloped her and which still had a firm grasp on her quaking limbs, Faith struggled back toward the building. Her fear of fire was not forgotten, but her determination was strong enough to urge her on, breathlessly, lungs heaving. Her bonnet was torn from her head, painfully, leaving the ribbons still entangled in her hair. She pushed, and pushed again, extricating herself from hands that tried to drag her away from her goal.

"Dr. Warren!"

"Come away! Come away!" urged a shaken stranger. "Don't be foolish!"

"I must—I cannot—" shouted Faith, incoherent and winded, eluding fingers extended to clutch at her sleeve. "Let me pass!" she cried, forcing a passage through the shifting mass. "Let me through!" Again, a hand came down across her wrist, and again, she tried to free herself. But the person who had taken hold of her fought against release, tightening fingers to the point of pain. Viciously, Faith swung about. "I tell you, leave go of me, or I shall—" and then her mouth slackened at the familiar, angry countenance glaring down at her with gray eyes unyielding. "Fletcher!"

In her confusion, she left herself unguarded, and the lieutenant reached out his other hand to catch her by the elbow.

"Mrs. Ashley," he demanded hotly, his fingers still fastened, vicelike, about her narrow wrist, "exactly what do you suppose you are doing? Have you gone mad?"

"I have no time to argue my sanity, Lieutenant! Please, let me go! I must find him!"

"Find—him?" Fletcher repeated, so unbalanced by her declaration that he loosened his hold and the widow pulled away from him.

"I must find Dr. Warren, Lieutenant. I saw—" Faith hesitated, realizing for the first time that Fletcher was not in his uniform, but garbed as a civilian, as he had been on the day of their initial meeting. "Why are you here?" she demanded suspiciously, almost wildly.

"What does that matter at this time?" Fletcher retorted fiercely. "Do you not know your danger? A building afire, an hysterical population, and out on the street what appears to be the entire Forty-third Regiment, muskets leveled at the crowd, and the good townspeople screaming 'fire' at the fullest extent of their lungs. In another moment, you may very well have a repetition of past events."

"What?" In shock, Faith spun toward the street, unconsciously anchoring herself to Fletcher by clasping her hand to his arm. She could see nothing through the milling crowd. Once again, Fletcher took her by the wrist, catching her against his chest when she would have fallen. For a moment, she clung breathlessly to him, listening to the beat of his heart, the reassurance of it, steady, swift, and strong. Then she stepped back. He dropped his arms.

"Faith," he shouted, "Come away from this now. I will go into the street and put an end to this madness, if I can."

"Yes," agreed Faith. "Do as you must. As," she added, turning quickly away, "shall I!"

She dodged beyond the lieutenant's grasp and heard him swear, loudly. She did not wait to give him time to close the gap between them, but pressed on with a burst of relentless energy, finally stumbling clear of the throng in the unexpected freedom of vacant space.

Wonderingly, she stared at the empty area just outside the meeting-house doors. The threshold above the trampled grass and pathway was occupied only by several of the British officers who had been seated in the front pew.

"Where is Dr. Warren?" Faith demanded of them.

There was a brief hesitation. "Inside," one replied, grimly.

"Is he dead?"

"Dead?"

"Dead?" echoed another officer, exchanging a disconcerted glance with the first. "Why do you ask that? He is inside, helping those who have been injured."

"Should they not be brought out?" Faith insisted. "The fire—"

"Madam," declared another of the redcoated Britishers with a weary resignation, "there is no fire."

Faith's gaze snapped upward to view Old South standing undamaged beneath the gray, misting sky, belying the image she had held of the structure involved in a dreadful conflagration. There were no black vapors, boiling above ochreous tongues of flame. No crackling blaze, nor groaning timbers. The wind blew against her back, lifting her hair in swirls about her face. Lowering her head, Faith lifted her wet skirts and went forward, pausing before the group in the doorway. "Pray, permit me to pass through," she said wearily.

"Wait!"

Faith glanced up at the oldest of the officers, wary of his protest. He touched Faith lightly on her sleeve. "One moment," he said.

"Yes?" she responded with a quiet impatience.

"Madam," the officer replied, revealing a spasmodic twitch beside his mouth, "you did return here, believing the meeting house was in flames. Am I correct?"

"Yes," said Faith.

"Why? What is this Dr. Warren to you, that you should disregard your own safety and enter willingly into danger?"

"In the past," she answered, "he was a friend to my late husband."

"A friend?" responded the older officer, shocked. "Oh, God bless you, madam, and pity us!"

"Sir?" said Faith, drawing her brows together in surprise.

"It is exactly this sort of selfless loyalty," continued the officer, "that may be our undoing."

At this juncture, one of his companions interjected testily, "Let the woman through and be done with it. Do not encourage her. I, for one, have heard enough and do not care to hear anymore!"

Without waiting for further bickering, Faith angled past, into the shadows beyond the doorway. Behind her, the officers descended, arguing, into the street.

Someone was working to the left of the doorway, dousing a smoldering area of planking some three feet in diameter with a bucket of water. On the floor at the man's feet lay the quilted blanket, rings and all, once colorful and now crumpled and blackened with soot.

"I was told that there was no fire," Faith said.

The fellow with the bucket looked up sharply from his task, startled at the presence of a woman. He had hoped the entry to be that of another man, coming to lend him a hand. "Ain't none," he said, applying the quilt once more to the smoking floorboards. Faith watched the destruction of her handiwork, and of the others, impassively. "Lamp knocked down. Praise Lord, no more damage 'us done."

"Amen," concurred Faith. "Where is Dr. Warren?"

"Doc Warren?" With a jerk of his head, the fellow directed her further inside. "In there."

Faith strode into the main body of the building. In the center aisle, three men made unsteady progress toward her, two supporting the one in the middle as he held a hand to his bandaged head. Faith moved aside, standing between two pews in her stained and greasy dress, to provide room for their passage. There she waited, watching the figure of a man in a white robe checking a woman's wrist for breakage. Apparently, most of those hurt had been able to leave the church under their own volition, for there were few people left inside.

Completing his examination, Warren came upright, weariness evident in the effort. Turning, he seemed to recover, and strode briskly in Faith's direction, a stocky, sandy-haired youth at his side. Drawing abreast of the young widow he stopped, manner solicitous. "Are you hurt? You're bleeding."

"Am I?" replied Faith in dull surprise. "Where?"

"Here," said the doctor, reaching out to touch the curved bone of her cheek. "A small abrasion—" Slowly, he withdrew his hand, once again studying the woman's face. "You are William Ashley's widow, aren't you?"

"Yes," said Faith, and marvelled how his calm, assured manner made it seem as though there had been no cause for loneliness and tears. "I must speak to you, Dr. Warren, if I may."

"Immediately?"

Faith nodded. "I would suggest it, yes."

He hesitated only briefly before sending the boy away with orders to discover the reason for the continued commotion outside.

"Go on," Warren urged Faith.

She shivered, in an instinctive lingering fear. Looking directly into the physician's grave eyes, she said, "I saw a British soldier who had a pistol hidden beneath his jacket and was pushing toward the pulpit when the first alarm of fire was given. I believe his intent was assassination. Yours, Dr. Warren."

Joseph Warren, who had started to remove the theatrical outer garment from his working clothes as he listened, paused, the folds of white wrapped about his throat and shoulders. "You are blunt, Mrs. Ashley. Are you certain of this?"

"I am certain of what I witnessed. I may be wrong concerning the man's intent, but I do not think so. He was only prevented from carrying out his deed by the panic around him. Furthermore, I would assume that the officer who started the entire uproar by standing forward and shouting over the heads of the congregation was merely doing so as a diversion, for I saw him, later, watching the infantryman with the pistol without alarm."

Dr. Warren was silent. His expression raised the short hairs along Faith's forearms and the nape of her neck, for her words had caused the physician to foresee his own demise. Yet, he found that death did not sorrow him, nor did not knowing the outcome of the rebellion he had fought so hard to maintain. Rather, he was deeply upset that the compassion for humankind which had motivated him throughout his lifetime should, in the end, be abandoned for a musket on a bloody hillside.

"Mrs. Ashley," he said, when the moment had passed, "I shall have the matter investigated, if possible. You are a courageous woman to return to me with this information. I am grateful."

"I could not, in clear conscience, do otherwise."

Warren smiled. "Then we understand each other. I—" He stopped, turning his attention to the lanky young man rushing in from outside. "What is toward, Andrew?"

"There's a whole regiment of lobsterbacks in the street, hot for blood, and I reckon we could use your help, sir," the lad explained with a bewildered shake of his head.

Warren muttered a quick oath, whether curse or prayer no one but he and God did know. "They will not fire. Not again. They cannot." Snatching the toga from about his neck, he thrust it at Faith, striding away rapidly without another word. Faith grasped at the garment and missed, watching in dismay as it fluttered, whispering, to the floor. It opened over the dark planks, still snow-white, yet streaked with the vermilion stain of blood.

Lowering herself into the nearest pew, Faith awaited the outcome of the conflict outside, almost coldly anticipating the sound of gunfire, the screams. But in time, the crowd dispersed, peaceably, as did the soldiers, the rhythm of marching feet a simpler echo of her own heartbeat. The meeting house emptied, and its emptiness was tangible, oppressive, unnerving. Directly before her feet, on the dampened floor and half-hidden beneath the dropped back of the bench, Faith saw a small leg, porcelain and broken in two, held together by the flounce of a doll's petticoat. Faith kicked it, hiding the doll from her eyes, then lowered her head into her hands, wondering why it was so hard for her to be strong of late.

After a time, Faith heard footsteps, a soft, measured tread, and a hand brushed against her hair. Wordlessly, she rose. Lifting her eyes, she found Fletcher's own gazing down at her, darkly troubled. She felt no surprise that he was there beside her, no question. He removed his greatcoat from about his shoulders and settled it over her diminutive, shivering form. Gently, he pulled the front closed, turning the collar up beneath her chin.

"Come," he said, "I will take you home."

Chapter Twelve

Rain spattered fitfully against the window, creating small runnels that reflected the lamplight in the room behind. Fletcher jerked the curtains closed against the night. He had built a small fire on Faith's hearth, and now he crouched before it, warming his hands. Beside him, in a basket, he could see the folds and brilliant colors of her needlework. Upstairs, Faith was going about some strange and quiet business. If it had not been for the occasional squeak of a particular floorboard, Fletcher would have wondered if she had, in utter exhaustion, fallen asleep.

Warmed, Fletcher straightened, taking a thoughtful turn about the room, hands folded beneath the tail of his brown jacket. He admired the widow's taste in furnishing and decoration at a tangent. He fingered the edge of a lace doily, gently. He rubbed the back of his hand across an embroidered cushion, then along the flat, mitered edge of a frame, studying the painting it held: a stormy scene of a ship rolling in high seas. He lifted a small vase, salt-glazed in a tiny lilac pattern, and held it between his palms, then returned it to the exact spot he had found it. He picked up a miniature in a silver frame, palmed it, and brought it nearer to the lamplight. It was a portrait of a man, youngish, with brown hair and angular features, made quite handsome by the smile and the set of his friendly eyes. Fletcher thought it must be William, though he supposed it might have been anyone, a brother, perhaps. Carefully, he replaced the miniature, staring at it for some time longer before turning away. He did not touch anything else. He walked back to the fire.

"Lieutenant Irons, I thought that you had gone."

Slowly, Fletcher turned to the staircase. He had not even

heard her coming. How careless he was of late. How damnably careless. "I am still here," he said, his voice drained of emotion, unintentionally. She was on the stair, dressed in a heavy robe, her hair unbound and combed out, wet and dark about her shoulders, her eyes reflecting a faceted light as she stood looking down at him from a small height. He caught his breath, and crossed the floor without thinking to lift a decanter of brandy from a sideboard. He could not reason what he was doing, but it seemed his only recourse, his only distraction.

"May I?" he asked self-consciously. "You might benefit from one yourself."

Faith did not appear shocked. She merely nodded her head, watching as he poured the honey-colored liquid into a glass. When he pulled a second glass nearer, she voiced her objection. "It is the Sabbath," she reminded him, "and even were it not, I do not imbibe."

"Nor," Fletcher retorted, "do I. Normally. Today, I believe that I shall make an exception. As for the Sabbath, I noticed your laundry hanging as I went for the wood."

"Did you indeed?" said Faith, descending the stair. "My laundry is none of your business, Lieutenant."

"Fletcher," he said.

"No."

"As you wish."

Lowering her gaze, Faith strode quickly past him, drawing a footstool close to the fire to sit upon. She hugged her knees tightly, shivering, and dropped her chin to her folded hands, riveting her eyes to the flames. She felt that if she looked at him, even once, directly, she would disgrace herself. "There is no need for you to remain any longer, I am quite safe," she said, but was answered by silence. Rolling her head on her hands, and looking over her shoulder, she saw him lift his glass and take a long pull, grimacing at the unaccustomed taste.

"I thought that you would be in need of support, after the events of today," he said, addressing the painting on the wall. Faith turned her head back to the flames.

"Forgive me if I seem ungrateful." She thought of the brandy covetously. She did not drink, it was true, but the chill invading her seemed to go beyond bones and mortal flesh.

Suppressing a shiver, she glanced back again to watch the lieutenant finish off his glass and pour himself another. She almost spoke out, but instead turned away.

"One mouthful," Fletcher said, moving noiselessly to stand above her, "will do no harm."

After an instant's hesitation, she received the glass gratefully into her hands, taking in exactly one mouthful over her lips, swallowing quickly. It burned! Coughing, and spilling the liquor onto her fingers, she wiped the moisture from her eyes. But a nearly immediate warmth descended along her throat into her belly, radiating outward to her limbs. "Thank you," she said, holding the glass out to him. He crouched down beside her to take it.

"You are quite welcome to it. The brandy is yours, after all."

For some time after, he stayed beside her, balancing his weight over his heels, as he might in the field. He held the glass between his thighs, swinging it slightly, while with the other arm slung across his knees he took up the poker and worried the fire.

"Lieutenant Irons," Faith said, wondering why she persisted in fighting him when to have him beside her as he was, a silent companion, was an experience both gentle and sweet. "Did you, by chance, hear the speech Dr. Warren made today?"

"Yes," said Fletcher.

"And what," she said, remembering the guilt, the idea that she was, in essence, a traitor to her people, "do you have to say in your defense?" She lowered her head to her hands again. The fire was warm against her forehead and in the dampness of her hair.

"Defense?" Fletcher echoed. "Of all those things which I, and my fellows, have been accused, of which do I need defend myself? Surely, you do not believe I took part in the so-called Massacre? I was not even in Boston then. Perhaps you mean a soldier's training is only to settle all dispute by the use of arms alone? Can it be that you believe this of me? Where is the proof upon which you pride yourself? That you demand so often of me?"

"It is true," Faith retorted against the skin of her forearm, desperate. "I have witnessed it for myself."

"In me?" asked Fletcher, quietly. "You have witnessed such cruelty in me? Such lack of conscience and ability of judgment? Even in general, it is not true."

There was silence. Faith turned her head away, pressing her eyes hard into her forearm. "No," she said at last. "In you, I have not."

"I could not believe you would have," he said. "Faith, I would not hurt you."

"Still," retorted Faith in a whispering bitter laugh, "the thought has crossed your mind."

Fletcher threw back his head to laugh. "I did say that, did I not?" he said, dropping fully onto his knees beside the stool and the heavy, fanned folds of Faith's robe. He extended his hand to her hair, brushing it back from her temple. "Faith, look at me. Look at me." Slowly, he slid two of his fingers beneath her chin until she had lifted her head and turned to him. He had dread that she might be weeping, but she was not. Her eyes were dry, crystalline in the firelight. Her skin felt warm. "It's not true, I swear to you. I would not hurt you. I will not hurt you." A shudder ran through her. He kissed her very tenderly then, on the brow, and she accepted it with a small sigh. "It's not wrong to care," he whispered against her temple, and the little hairs there, disturbed by the passing of his breath, tickled his mouth. "There is no wrong in this." With his hand slipping into her hair he kissed her again, on the closed lid of her eye, and her mouth. She trembled, and he put his arms about her.

"Fletcher," she said, with her forehead against his chin.

"What is it, my little one?"

"Fletcher," she repeated, "I am afraid."

"Of what?"

"Of . . . of loving you."

"Ah." It was a sigh of relief, in its own fashion, and of sadness, and of longing for an assurance that would put her heart at ease. He lifted his chin to the crown of her head, and rested it there, drawing her nearer. He could feel her breathing, within his arms. She seemed so small, and fragile; so easily broken, like a child's porcelain doll. Yet, he knew she was strong; or was that merely a facade? He moved his hand beneath her hair, caressing the nape of her neck.

"Faith?"

"Yes?"

"May I extinguish the lamp?"

"Yes."

He released her then, reluctantly, and rose, crossing the floor to turn down the wick and snuff the lamp's bright flame. For a moment he stood there, watching the curl of smoke drift toward the ceiling; then he returned to her and knelt on the stone of the hearth. The firelight limned the soft curve of her cheek and the line of her jaw, and set in relief the tiny pulse beating at the side of her throat. Lifting his hand, he traced the contours of her cheek, her brow, and her mouth with his fingers. Faith closed her eyes, concealed them, probing the deep and physical ache that time had pressed upon her.

"Do not leave me," she said.

"I will stay, Faith. I promise you."

In the darkness, he came and crouched behind her, enveloping her, very gently, in his embrace. She released her held breath and leaned her head back against his chest. He could smell the rain in her hair, could feel the locks where they had dried, like curling flame, brushing up against his jaw. "Faith," he said, and she shook her head.

For a long while, they were silent. Occasionally, he stroked her hair back from her brow, or kissed her there, upon the temple; and she, in turn, ran her hand absently over the length of his sleeve, fingering the material, the stiff, weather-stained velvet. Each time, he caught his breath, in fear that she would question him on the reason for his attire, but she said nothing, and eventually he realized that the touch of her fingers in the folds of his coat was no more than a caress.

"Faith," he murmured quietly, taking her by the shoulders and turning her about, "I will do nothing which you do not wish me to do. But let me look at you, so near to my hand,

and to my heart.'' She glided her fingers over his cheekbones, his jaw, his brow, and the curve of his lips, lingering there. He scarcely moved. He could hear his own breathing.

"Faith . . .''

Without speaking, Faith slid from the footstool and rose up onto her knees. She touched him again, with both hands, loosening the ribbon at his nape, removing it, allowing his hair, black and silky, to fall over her fingers.

"Kiss me,'' she whispered.

This he did, a light touch upon her lips, and then he took her hand, pressing his mouth to the palm, then to the wrist, touching the pulse there with the tip of his tongue. He could feel the beat, rapid and warm.

"Again?'' she said.

And he did so, stronger this time, holding himself away from her body, keeping her hand still in his own. She responded breathlessly, then pulled away, her green eyes half-open, yet their expression marked both by desire, and fear.

"Three years,'' she said.

"My love, I will not hurt you.''

She smiled, then, almost laughed at her own trepidation. Her eyes were faceted with flame. Leaning with both her hands on his chest, she kissed him; he parted her lips, testing his tongue upon her own: a small caress, and then another, and then with leisure and grace. He slipped his arms behind her back, across her shoulders and her hips, drawing her nearer, onto his lap. For an instant, she struggled, but he had forgotten his promise to do nothing she didn't wish and held her close until her own arms came up around him, around his neck, and she settled against him.

She was small, within his embrace, and trembling, and strong. Though she was hesitant, she was no virginal child, but a woman who had known love in the past, and who hoped for it again.

"I will never hurt you,'' he repeated, against her ear, as he took her by the waist, in both hands, and lifted her from his lap, to her knees again. For a long moment, he merely watched her watching him, her eyes wide and patient. He had never seen her like this: calm and waiting. There had always been too much of turmoil in her gaze, of suspicion, of the fire of anger. It moved him, to witness the trust, like innocence, in her countenance. He brushed the loose tendrils of hair from about her face, then brushed the tangled, drying locks from her shoulders. In the fire's shimmering illumination, her lashes made thin, wavering lines over her skin, and he could see the freckles he found so endearing spanning the bridge of her nose. He touched them, with a fingertip, then traced a line along her cheekbone to her throat, and to the opening of her robe. As Faith knelt before him, his fingers slipped inside the soft garment, ruffling the lace edge of her chemise, following the contours of her collarbone and then of her breast, above the fine cloth. He flattened his palm and grazed her nipple, stiff against his flesh. He felt the warmth of her skin and bent forward as her chin tilted upward, kissing her throat as his hand pushed aside the robe, the chemise, off her shoulder, down her arm, and his mouth moved over her naked breast.

His touch was like fire, burning without pain. She had known it would be so, since she had first moved into his arms and met his eyes, and felt the grasp of his hands across her back; now she arched against him, gripped in his embrace as his lips circled the fullness of her breast, finding the nipple beneath his tongue.

"No, Fletcher," she gasped, "not here. Come . . . upstairs . . ."

Without reply, Fletcher came upright, lifting her bodily from the floor, and carried Faith up the steep staircase, all the while kissing her hair, her face, wherever there was bare skin to come beneath his touch. Faith wrapped her slender arms about his neck.

"Take care," she whispered, "of the runner. Do not stumble in the dark."

He answered with a laugh, as much as if to say that there was nothing, not even darkness so deep that it was too deep for shadow, that could bring him down from his desire. Inside of her bedchamber, he shut the door and turned the key, and despite her assurances that they were alone, only then did he set her on her feet. "Light a candle, Faith," he said.

With trembling fingers, Faith did so, listening to the small sounds he was making behind her as he divested himself of his jacket and waistcoat. She heard his shoes drop, quietly, onto the floor. Candle in hand, she turned to look at him. Clad only in his shirt and breeches, Fletcher took a step forward, then paused, an arm's length away. His jet black hair was highlighted by the candle flame, as were his eyes, gray as storm. He brushed her cheek with the backs of his fingers; a gesture fraught with such tenderness that she felt her throat contract against tears.

"Fletcher," she said, and placed the candle on the dressing table, so that mirrored flame shot about the room. He unfastened her robe, slid it from her shoulders, her arms, and hung it neatly on the hook behind the door. He was smiling, secretively, when he returned.

"Do you love me, Faith?" he said. "If you have any question, you need only speak, and I shall leave you. But not forever, Faith. I will not freely give you up."

Faith stood before him in her white gown, suddenly as shy as a blushing young girl. She ducked her head, raising her eyes to view him in his beauty. She smiled, also. "I do love you, Fletcher."

For an instant, he made no response, and then Fletcher swung her up into his arms, circling across the floor to drop onto the bed's high mattress with Faith pinned beneath him. He took her head in his hands, kissing her eyes, her mouth, her neck and shoulder. "My love," he said, rolling away from her to stand upright beside the bed, where he yanked his shirt over his head and tossed it heedlessly onto the bedpost. Faith scrambled onto her knees. She ran her fingers through the hair on his chest, up over his shoulders, then drew him forward, kissing him with an ache of longing on the mouth. His chest was firm, against her breasts, and his arms were filled with a strength restrained. She felt his hands, bunching the fine material of her gown, slowly lifting it along her thighs, over her buttocks, past her waist, lingering teasingly about her breasts, before he eased it clear of her arms and her head, and disentangled it from her hair. His hands came down upon her body, fingers splayed across her rib cage, holding her still beneath his gaze.

"You are more lovely than I had dreamed," he said. "No," as she would have moved to cover herself modestly, "do not conceal your beauty. Why should you? From me, of anyone? I love you. All that I know of you, I love, dearly. Your hair," he said, running the fingers of one hand through the locks about her crown, "your eyes, the intelligence behind them, that would put many of my peers to shame. Those freckles," he said, and made an attempt at kissing them all. "Your mouth," and he touched his to her own, lightly. "Your tongue, sharp though it may be," he said, his tongue entering her mouth with a sensual caress. Faith felt her heart pounding within her bosom. He took her hand, pressing it to his own heart.

"There," he said, "beats the blood of a man. Of the man who is more than the soldier, much less than the enemy. Do you feel it? I am a man, Faith; do not doubt me."

Faith shook her head at him. "I do not," she said.

"And here," he continued, "is the hand that I love," kissing it; "the wrists, the arms, the shoulders; the breasts that are driving me to madness." He took them, separately, into his mouth, suckling gently. "The hollow," as he went, kissing downward, "beneath your rib cage, the curve of your belly, the firm flesh of your thighs." Faith shuddered with delight of his touch. "And here," he went on, "is that which all men desire, but I, most of all, for you are my love, and I will give all to you, and take all that you have to offer me."

She drew in her breath, but let her legs remain open; her only movement was the curling of her fingers over his forearms. He kissed her gently at first, and then more harshly. He released his arms from her grasp, and rose, tearing at the fastenings to his breeches, pushing them down, free of his legs. In one fluid motion, he put his arms about her, lifting her from the bed, high, until she wrapped her arms and legs about him, and he entered her that way, turned to the wall, stifling the sounds she made with the pressure of his mouth against her throat. There was no control, only desperate need, as their mouths searched for the same gratification of the body and of the soul.

He cried out, in the candlelit darkness, like a weeping child, for love, and Faith trembled in ecstasy as her own desire consumed and soothed her.

In the small hours of the morning, Faith awoke, startled to find that she had dozed. Sitting up, she turned her head to view her lover by the diminished light of the guttering stub of the candle. Fletcher lay on his back, the rumpled sheet pulled up around his loins, one arm flung over his eyes, his black hair fanned and tangled on the pillow beneath his head. The shadowed illumination of the flame revealed his chest lifting in slow, deep respiration. Even before she called his name softly, Faith knew that he was sleeping.

Rising onto her knees, Faith searched quietly for her discarded gown. Unable to find it, she rose shivering from the mattress, and removed Fletcher's shirt from the footboard, slipping it over her head. She pulled her hair free from the collar. Glancing over her shoulder, she saw that Fletcher slept on, undisturbed.

With a look of affection, Faith crossed the cold floor on tiptoe to stand before the window. She parted the curtains, peering out into the moonless night. Below, the street was empty, save for the presence of a thin, scruffy dog snuffling about fence posts. Houses were dark and silent. Nearby, a cock crowed, followed by another at a short distance.

Faith lifted the material of Fletcher's shirt to her cheek, breathing in its musky odor. She shut her eyes, remembering the passing hours of the night. She had permitted him to touch, to caress, to kiss her where no man—not even William—had ever done. Why? In her loneliness had she become wanton? Or merely without pride? No. Oh, no. The path he had taken with her had only been wondrous, and beautiful.

Turning, she let the curtain fall, standing for a moment in shivering contentment watching Fletcher as he slept. Had she ever really hated him? It was difficult to imagine that she could have. Perhaps, she had loved him from the first. A day had not gone by since the beginning when she had not been giving something of herself to him. She had fought him mostly, or the thought of him. Yet, here he was, in her bed, in her life, irrevocably.

For a time, she indulged herself in the wistful dreaming of a woman who has found love with a man of her own choosing, who is neither enemy nor forbidden, but is only the man she needs. She thought of waking in the night to find him beside her, watching, or asleep. She thought of the arguments they had had, and undoubtedly would have, in the passing of time; she thought of the love they had made, and the balance between. In her dreaming by the window, she forgot momentarily that he was a British officer, and knew him only as a man— and that he loved her. It was hard to visualize what was between them in any other way, easy to forget that there were those parts of her life where he did not, and could not, enter. He loved her, she knew that; she remembered the sound of his declarations whispered harsh or soft against her ear. And the sound of her own voice, the last time they had made love. She had been weeping, and her hair had been damp across her brow. She loved him, and had never meant to make him suffer so.

She drew a ragged breath, in memory. For now she recalled against her will all that she had, in dreaming, forgotten: the advent of tomorrow outside of this room, the pain to be renewed, their disparate responsibilities to return them to their own designs, their own causes.

Slowly, Faith's eyes drew away from Fletcher to the large wardrobe no more than ten feet away from him. Inside, hung the doubled petticoat that she had designed specifically for the smuggling of the pewter-shot when it was made. Looking there, her chest tightened, closing the breath off in her throat. She thought of Fletcher, of his strong hands, his mouth and eyes, the way he loved her. What would become of him, and his mortal flesh, if, indeed, there would be war?

Yet, when the time came to perform as duty bade her, she could not think of that. She could not.

In silence, Faith moved to the dressing table and took up her silver-backed brush. Bending, she pursed her lips to extinguish the drowning flame, and then she returned to the bed, easing herself gently onto the mattress. She sat, brush in hand, running her fingers over the intricate design of the backing. Then she took it, engaging the bristles to untangle her hair, with long strokes from the crown of her head, to the wisping, curling ends, lying over her breast. The brush whispered over the silk of Fletcher's shirt.

Faith paused, brow creasing. Fletcher's shirt, she thought, lifting the hem away from her body into her hands to study its make. No officer's shirt, this, but she had known that, all along. A brocade waistcoat, jacket and breeches of velvet. Downstairs, before the fire, she had considered the implications of such attire, and had set them aside, but they had caused her, even then, to act with desperation; to initiate their love-making, in order that he might prove she had no cause to doubt him, in anything. In that, her reasoning had been childish. Only love had been proven; no more. And no less. She did not belittle love—she cherished it. And with a British lieutenant, of all the people she might have chosen. But he was not an enemy to her heart, he was but a man. I am a man, he had said. Worthy of love, and loving . . . but what if her suspicions should prove true?

Would her heart change at the calling of her conscience? She did not think so, ah, she did not think so. And it was here that confusion seized her, of disparate loyalties and emotions; it was here that she felt her courage falter.

I must know, she told herself, for good or bad. I must ask him to be honest with me.

From beneath the covering crook of his arm, Fletcher watched the expression of sadness on Faith's face. He had been watching her for some time, silhouetted at the window against the silver night, and then beside him, brushing her hair with long, thoughtful strokes. In the shadowed room, in his shirt, she was a bewitching sight. "Are you troubled?" he asked her. She stirred in surprise at the sound of his voice.

"How long have you been awake?"

"Long enough," he answered. "Have you any notion of the time?"

"Somewhere around three, I would guess," she said. Her

voice seemed distant, under the reins of control. Fletcher studied her face more carefully, saw the sudden hollow beneath her eyes, the haunting uncertainty of her look. She avoided his gaze, instead staring down at the fabric of his shirt.

"What is it, Faith? Tell me." And then, thinking that she doubted him, said, "I love you, my heart. Do you not believe me?"

"Do you attempt," said Faith, biting her lip, "to convince me, or yourself?"

There was silence. Fletcher frowned.

"Don't," said Fletcher at last. "Don't ever say that. There is no just cause."

Faith's eyelids closed. The salt of tears stung her. Blindly, she reached across the bed to Fletcher, searching for his hand on the mattress. Finding it, she closed her fingers around his own, squeezing tightly. "Fletcher?"

Wordlessly, he slid closer to her, propping himself up on one elbow. He touched a tear escaping along her cheekbone, then brushed her hair back, away from her face. The sheet slipped from his hips and he pulled it back up. There was nothing of nakedness that she wanted from him now. He sensed this with a small fear that chilled him.

"What is it, Faith?"

For a full minute, Faith said nothing. Once that I have asked, she thought, what hope will there be in the answering? Lies, or truth, there is no difference. Not in this.

"Faith?" he prompted.

"Fletcher, I . . . you are a British officer . . ."

"Yes," he said, warily.

"Yet, I have seen you dressed as no soldier would be, unless . . ." Her voice trailed off, despairingly.

For a long time, Fletcher did not answer. He, who had faced countless battles, with the threat of death so near, was afraid. Not of the woman, not of his precious love, but of the hurt he would deal her with the truth. Yet, he could not hope to keep it secret from her. It had only been a matter of time, after all. He must tell her now, or lose her. He sat up, taking the brush from her hand. He began stroking her hair, lifting it up and pulling gently from beneath, from the nape of her neck to the fine ends.

"Unless?" said Fletcher. "Unless," he said again, putting the brush down and placing both hands on her shoulders, "I do not care to be known for who I am."

"Why?" she said, guessing now that she had been right. "Won't you tell me that, at least?"

There was that, in her voice, which nearly broke his heart. He pulled her into his arms. She came, without protest, nestling against him.

"Faith, Faith," he said, hoarsely. "Betrayed on all counts, then, little one. I am sorry. But it is required of me, as an officer, to commit espionage for my country. Unfortunately, I do it well. And I am not one who could perform a job poorly for the sake of leaving it. It is my duty. Do you understand? It is my duty." Faith shook her head against his chest in bewilderment. He saw her hand come up, a small fist, and turned his head away, but she merely tapped him, once, on his breast. There was no pain, in the touch, but he felt as if he were choking.

"Tell me you are not using me, now. Please, please, tell me you are not using me—"

"Oh, God in heaven, Faith! No! No. I love you. If nothing else has proven it, then this, my confession, should have done so. I have given my life into your hands, Faith. Should there be war, my life will be forfeit to you for what I have revealed. My very life."

Her fist opened then, and he felt her fingers moving over his unshaven jawline, to his mouth. She touched him there, and then touched his brow, pushing back his hair. She turned in his arms, sitting back on her heels, taking his face in her hands. He saw unshed tears on her lashes. Her eyes were very bright, glistening in the darkness. She kissed him on the mouth, deeply.

"I do not want your life, Fletcher," she said. "All I desire is your love. Nothing more. I cannot expect more. Nor can you, from me. There is no betrayal in that. We know who we are, beyond this room. When we are together, thus, what is beyond will not exist."

"It does," Fletcher insisted softly.

"*It will not*," said Faith. She gathered him against her breast, with an ache in her, in her soul, that defied naming. Fletcher, also, was smitten by both pain, and pleasure. He had not expected both to grip him so overwhelmingly, to shake him as something in the mouth of an angry dog, threatening to tear him apart. He wanted to make love to her again, to dry her tears with the warmth of his breath, to banish the pain with the feel of her, beneath him, around him, pushing it away. And, in her embrace, he bore her down, onto the counterpane, with a mouth that was both generous and demanding, and a need that was more than desire, making love to her with a ferocity that only equaled her own.

Later, lying beside her, Fletcher held Faith in the curve of his body, the coverlet pulled around her chilled shoulders. Lovingly, he stroked the damp hair from her brow. Soon, it would be dawn. For Faith's sake, as well as his own, he would have to leave before first light. There would be eyes to witness his departure once the sun had risen.

He lifted a lock of her hair, wrapping it around his forefinger, toying with it absently. He felt Faith press closer to the warmth of his body, though she was sleeping. Her lids were rounded over her green eyes, moving in dream. Tenderly, he placed his lips on her bare shoulder. He caressed her throat, lightly, and kissed her there. Her skin shivered beneath the touch.

"Faith," he said. She moved, but did not waken.

"Faith," he said again, more quietly now. "You are my love, my only love. Be my wife, little one."

Knowing she would not reply, he pressed himself more closely about her, enveloping her in the coverlet and his strong limbs, holding her as she slept.

Chapter Thirteen

Faith held the fragile tea cup in her hands, cupped as if for warmth despite the cider within being quite cool, and stared intently at the violets glazed upon its surface. Gentle strokes they were, of lavender and pale green leaves, rimming the cup and appearing, in miniature, on the inside. She ran her thumb over them and could feel, in certain instances, that the paint was slightly thicker beneath the glaze, where the artist's hand had applied the tint too freely. But it was a beautiful piece, nonetheless.

Setting the cup down, Faith smiled across the dinner table at Ezra. She saw the flickering flame of the lantern overhead reflected in the dual lenses of his spectacles, but the eyes behind were hidden from her witness.

"It does my soul good to be with you again, my dear," he said, the edges of his mouth curling upward in a strangely compact smile that wrinkled the skin of his jowls like the crust of a pastry, when the filling beneath has cooled too quickly, and withdrawn. Faith nodded her head.

"So you have said, Ezra," she chided him good-naturedly. "Three or four times, since I have walked in."

"Have I?" he countered. She was instantly sorry for the bewilderment that seemed to overtake him. "I am forgetful, of late. You must forgive me."

"Oh, Ezra! You may say whatever you like, as often as you wish," she said. "I will be pleased to sit through it all." She reached across the table, touching her fingers to the back of his hand. She had been impressed, first thing, with the visible signs of his ageing; these other signs, more subtle, she found distressing. It was distressing to realize that the years which yet sat so lightly upon her shoulders were bending his into

133

decline. Sadder yet, was that her own neglect of this dearest, oldest friend had not only marked the process more clearly upon his face but had much been the cause of it as well. Sitting across from him, she gazed upon an ageing man who had once looked to her for happiness in his life; and she had denied it to him.

It no longer mattered what he had chosen to do with her denial of him, sending Fletcher to her side. That the lieutenant loved her, he had known, though what he had expected of her was less certain. Perhaps, he had anticipated her acceptance of his own proposal, when she had had the time to think better of it? Somehow, she did not think so, for he gave no indication that this was true. What, then, did he hope for?

Faith turned Ezra's hand over in her own, feeling how cool it was, and smooth, remembering that once she had thought to find safety in the touch, to flee from the fire which she had found so unexpectedly in Fletcher's. In her fear, she would have used him. In his loneliness, he would have accepted.

Am I not using him now? she wondered, straightening her back, releasing his hand. Fletcher had been gone for two weeks now and her loneliness was tenfold what it had been before. She had received no word as to his whereabouts, and had turned to Ezra when she could stand no more. She felt selfish. The independence that she had so prided herself upon seemed gone.

The last time she had seen Fletcher, he had been thoughtful, less talkative than usual, and he had asked her, several times, if she trusted him, though he would not confess to her the importance of her reply. He had said only that he relied on her level head, her intelligence, in the times to come. He had known, then, that he was leaving. Faith was certain of it. Duty, she thought. He was out there among her unsuspecting countrymen, performing a duty that was odious to her. But she could not speak against him, in warning to her fellow patriots, for it was his life in her hands, as he had said. And though she might abhor the duties which he performed in his service to his king, she loved him no less.

Closing her eyes, Faith uttered a silent prayer for strength and guidance. She knew that she had sinned, in her knowledge of a man without benefit of the sanctions of God and Church,

but she felt that He understood her confusion and the breadth
of her devotion to this particular man.

Ezra stirred, staring at Faith through cloudy eyes in bemuse-
ment. Faith was quiet and meditative, and he would console
her, but for the altered footing upon which their relationship
now stood.

With a sigh, he removed the flask from his pocket, the
one comfort he had left him, and caressed the etched pattern
with the ball of his thumb. Then he unstoppered it, and
drank.

In his chair, Ezra dozed, his chin against his chest, his wig
askew on his pate. He was snoring, deeply, and contentedly,
disturbing the lace bib of his shirt. Faith stood at the window,
watching the wing of night, rose and gray, curve across the
sky. Apple blossoms from the tree behind Ezra's house were
blowing across the brick pathway, a minute snowfall through
the growing shadows of the April evening. Not very long ago,
she had spent just such a lovely evening, though it had been
March, in a discreet walk along the river with Fletcher. It had
been a risky thing to do, but she so longed for the simple
pleasures which lovers came to expect unconditionally that she
had asked him to take her. He had spent the time amusing her
with tales of the grand exploits of his childhood, and in kissing
her under the cover of every tree. Before the window, Faith
smiled at the sweetness of memory.

Yet soon, her smile vanished, for the following day she had
found herself lying to him. Standing before him, as she prepared to leave town under pretense of attending a quilting with
a handful of her acquaintances, with the pewter-shot sewn
tightly into the hooped hemlines of their petticoats, she had
denied, when asked by him, any knowledge of wrongdoing
about to occur in Roxbury.

"Ride out there, if you do not believe me," she had suggested angrily.

"I trust you," he had said. Not his first mention of trust.
Later, on subsequent days, she had repeated the phrase, and
on that last, asking that she trust him also . . . Oh, Fletcher,
thought Faith, we are at odds, God help us. Yet, you knew
that we would be.

But she had lied, and he had accepted her words as truth. It was wrong.

She turned to look at Ezra, asleep and sputtering in his chair, on the verge of waking from his nap. Walking over to him, she touched his cheek, weathered and empty. "Ezra," she said, "it is getting late. I must go now."

"Will you come back," he asked, "on the morrow?"

His question was childlike in its sincerity and artlessness.

Standing above him, Faith set Ezra's wig to rights on his balding pate, then bent to touch her lips to it. "Of course," she said to him. "Of course, I will return tomorrow. How could I not?"

The sunlight across the water dappled the surface, and the fertile earth beneath the trees, rolling and sparking like so many newly minted coins. The tiny bell flowers had appeared along the roadside, and the pristine white stars had bloomed early, for April. All along the road leading down from Concord to Lexington, foliage hung close over the path, and the air was filled with midges, swarming about the nostrils and the eyes. Beneath his thighs, Fletcher felt the flesh of his mount shiver, in annoyance. He cocked the tricorne hat he wore closer over his face, shading his eyes in the morning sun. It was not the tricorne of an officer, with braid and decoration, but one that was simple, and black, and dusty.

A marsh fly landed on his arm, in the folds of his brown woolen coat. He shook it off.

"Damn," he swore, and dismounted, leading his horse from the road, to drink. He removed his hat, slapping at his dusty clothing with it, then tethered the horse and drank too, from a point slightly upstream. The sun was warm on the grassy bank; it eased the tired lines about his eyes, and he crouched down, eyes slitted, waving a hand every now and then to keep the insects at bay. He stared into the water, at the colors there, muddied brown, new copper and burnished gold, the vivid green of spring, the ivory of clouds still rouged by dawn's rosy hues; and he thought of Faith, and longed for her.

He wondered, not for the first time, if she had conceived a

child through the natural course of their lovemaking. If she had, he would not allow her to refuse his offer of marriage though he suspected that she might stubbornly do so. How could she expect him to accept his child being named bastard, no matter the circumstances? And how could he bear it in his heart if his beloved were named whore by those who wished her ill? Worst, worst of all his fears, was that one in which he saw her take a child of theirs away because of those things which might never be resolved between them.

He heard a sound, suddenly, out in the stream, where the water ran deepest. A plopping at the surface, as of a fish rising in pursuit of its morning meal. He opened his eyes fully, slowly, as it occurred to him that he had been careless in his musing, inattentive, and that the sound might be other than it seemed. Again, he heard it, this time preceded by a movement above his head as a stone sailed through the air to land with a musical note in the tumbling water.

Easing to his feet, he stretched his arms above his head, in plain sight of whomever was behind him, and turned without haste to face the scowling countenance of a young boy, about thirteen years of age. He was tall though, and stockily built, with a musket over his shoulder, and the bags of powder and shot swinging against his long, thick thigh.

"Mornin'," he said, gruffly. Fletcher inclined his head. "Stranger aroun' here?"

"Yes," said Fletcher.

"Reckoned so. Wher'ya heading?"

"To Concord," Fletcher answered. It was best to tell the truth, when possible. Lies could be detected in the eyes, especially by suspicious young men.

"That so?" said the youth, coming forward, propping his gun against a tree so that he could bend before the stream and drink. Enjoying his fill, he moved over, crouching on his heels. Fletcher did the same, beside him.

"Beautiful day, this one," said Fletcher.

"Aye, t'is that," responded the boy, nodding his head and gazing up through the trees at the sky overhead.

Fletcher observed him, surreptitiously, watching as the boy yanked at the green growth between his feet. His boots were muddy and grass-stained. Lowering his head, the boy reached up behind his neck, scratching a place where an insect had bitten, just below the hair on the nape of his neck. The ribbon holding his blond hair in place came loose and he pulled it out.

"My sweethea't," he remarked, "was for giving this to me."

Fletcher made no reply. None was called for. It seemed to him then that the boy was only a lonely youth, who had probably started the morning hunting with dismal results—a fact that would account for his surliness—and wanted nothing more than to talk, aimlessly, with a stranger chance met.

"Where ya from?" the boy asked, after a minute.

"Boston," Fletcher answered, without hesitation.

The boy rocked on his heels a bit. "Them Boston girls are fine, I hear. Full of spirit, spunk. They ain't about to let them British keep 'em scared."

"Is that what you hear?" replied Fletcher without commitment. His knee was getting stiff. Carefully, he shifted his weight. Across the narrow water, a bird trilled, high and sweet.

"Aye, t'is what I am told." He was silent for a moment, running the ribbon between his fingers, snaking it in and out. His brow lowered over his heavy, young features.

"I ain't never killed a man," he said, without preamble.

Beside him, Fletcher eyed the narrow ribbon in the boy's large hands, without much concern, and then the gun, just beyond the youth's shoulder. "Not many of us have," he said cautiously.

"I don' reckon that I would want to," continued the young stranger.

"Why should you be concerned about such a thing?" suggested Fletcher. "You are only a boy."

Suddenly, the youth's scowling expression became animate with open anger. "T'is the lobsterbacks I be talkin' about, sir!" And then he calmed, turning his face away, to stare at the sparkling water. "A man is a man, and the Lord says: Thou shalt not kill. But what if they take it into their heads to kill us? There be talk they may be coming. N'one knows when.

If'n we vote to stand up against 'em, what then? How many of 'em do there be in Boston, sir?''

"Thousands," Fletcher answered, quite honestly. "Many thousands."

"Thousands," echoed the boy, and it was clear that the amount was beyond his ability to cipher. It awed him. "An' only a few of us, scattered here and there," he whispered. He shook his head.

"If you don't bear arms against them," said Fletcher, "they will have no cause to fight you."

For a long moment, the boy was silent, narrowing his eyes as he plucked up a handful of grass and tossed it down, into the moving stream, watching as it was borne away, in swift, circling eddies. He cleared his throat, harshly.

"You don' strike me a coward," he said.

"No," said Fletcher. "I have never been known as such."

"Well. I ain't gonna be one, either," he retorted, quietly. "I ain't gonna be. I will stand up, as a man, if there be need."

Fletcher sighed. A man. He was only a boy, and his own militia would refuse him. He felt his throat tighten, and his breath choke short in his chest, and he turned away, pretending a study of his sleeve, of the stitches coming loose. "I am certain that you will," he replied.

"What's your lady like, in Boston?" the boy asked, in an abrupt change of topic. "Ya got one, ain't ya? Is she pretty?"

"As the sun," Fletcher found himself replying.

"Sweet?"

"No sweeter than yours, I would wager," he said, smiling at the pale blue ribbon.

"But she's brave, ain't she?" the boy went on, more as a factual statement than a question.

"Yes," said Fletcher. "Yes, she is."

"All them Boston patr'ot girls are. They smuggled them musket balls out, didn't they? Right past the guard, sewed into the hem of their petticoats. Said they was goin' to a quilting circle somewhere hereabouts, and fooled 'em blind. Made 'em look downright foolish."

Fletcher stared at the boy, at his earnest, proud expression.

He felt cold, suddenly, from the pit of his stomach to the tips of his fingers. He realized the boy spoke the truth, for a man would not have dared say that to a stranger. Youth spoke what it countenanced as truth.

Slowly, he stood up. In his ears, the surrounding sounds were strangely loud: the tumbling of the water; the birds, whistling from place to place through the rustling foliage; the tearing of grass beneath the horse's great teeth; his own respiration; and the beat of his blood. The boy stood, also, unfolding his thick, long limbs, and met his gaze with a confused squint.

"Boy," said Fletcher. The youth took a startled step backward at his tone. "Pick up your gun, and go home. There are certain things which you do not reveal, especially to a stranger. If I were your father, I would whip your hide for your loose tongue."

"S-sir," he stammered, "I didn't mean no harm."

"Where are you from?" Fletcher demanded, as if he had not spoken.

"Lexington," said the boy. "Not far."

"For your sake, son, and theirs, I hope that the inhabitants of that place show a little more sense than do you."

"Yes, sir," said the youth, head bowed in shame. He scuffed his feet in the mud he had left after ripping at the undergrowth. His cheeks were red, burning.

Fletcher backed away, cold with fury. He untethered his horse. With an uncharacteristic disregard for horseflesh, he mounted the beast and jerked its head around viciously, so that the bit cut deeply in the mouth, causing the horse to snort in hot protest, tossing against the rein. In alarm, the boy jumped clear. Wheeling about, Fletcher charged his mount recklessly through the trees to the road, leaping the rock wall, and even as hooves came down ringing on stone, he realized that, for the first time in his military career, he was about to disregard his professional duty for that of personal obligation; he hoped that it would be the last time. Yet, he rode on at breakneck speed, away from Concord and the further town of Worcester, to return to Boston. To Faith. For he knew, oh, he knew, as surely as his true instinct did guide him, that her hand was in that smuggling.

Chapter Fourteen

Standing at the base of the staircase, Faith leaned against the newel post and called Elizabeth's name once, loudly, then again, in soft constraint. The house echoed with her absence. Walking through to the kitchen behind the house, Faith paused, and called the girl's name once more, although it was plain that the room was unoccupied. The shadows of the waning day were long across the tidy floor. Faith turned about and returned to the parlor, where she sat down, removing her bonnet. She held the head covering in her hands, momentarily turning it over and over, and then she stood again, climbing the stairs to her bedchamber above.

Carelessly tucking the ribbons of the bonnet inside the head-piece, Faith placed the garment on the dressing table. She sat down on the edge of the bed, removing her walking shoes for the relief of soft-soled slippers. Then she lay back across the mattress, with complete neglect of the stiff fabric of the dress creasing beneath her, and closed her eyes.

She thought of the dream, the nightmare that had haunted her in the small hours of the morning, but in the light of another day, it had meant nothing. It had been of Ezra, poor man, but today she had dined with him again, and taken the air, strolling the length of several streets with her arm tucked into his elbow as he leaned heavily upon his walking stick. It pained her to see him so debilitated, but he had seemed to flourish in her care and company; even the pale flesh of his cheeks had taken on some of its old ruddiness. They had even argued, in their amiable way, and she had, for once, given him the last word.

She stretched her arms above her head, yawning, and the pull of her muscles across her body, a pleasant ache, reminded her of Fletcher . . . of the second half of her dream: his anger, and the aloneness, in a dwelling of fearful darkness. Biting her lip, Faith rolled onto her side, eyes wide and staring. For a full minute, she retained the position, as though her own thoughts had startled her to dumbness, and then an object on the pillow came gradually into focus, though it was sometime more before she sat up and took the letter into her hand.

At the window, she broke the seal of the parchment with her blunted nail, cracking the wax across the center. The flowing script was unfamiliar, hastily dried with sand so that some of the characters were smeared. Faith knew that it was not from Elizabeth, for the girl scarcely knew how to read and could not write at all, though it had to have been her who placed it on the pillow, for Faith to find. Quickly, scanning the end of the page, she found what she had hoped for: Fletcher's beloved name. For an instant, she squeezed her eyes shut, clasping the note against her bodice, for all the world like an innocent young girl with a sweetheart's note. And then she pulled it away, reading voraciously of the words. The message was brief.

"*Faith*," it read—just like an Englishman, she thought, with no grand salutations, no endearments—"*I trust this message to reach you safely. The boy who carries it is known to me, and he will be the same to return for you this night, to escort you to a place which we have cause to know. It has been long since last we were together—too long, I fear. There is much to be said, and all of it most urgent. I will await your arrival at eight o'clock. Do not forget . . .*" and here, he appeared to have hesitated, for the ink dragged a little along the page, "*that I love you. Fletcher.*"

Faith sat down, hard, in the chair beside the window. She held the message open upon her lap, head bowed in the warm sun arrowing through the casement. Tears of happy relief were shed from shining eyes, rolling along her cheeks to puddle the ink in those places where the quill had seemed to score the paper with particular vigor.

Immersing himself in the tepid water of a much-needed bath, Fletcher flinched at the sting of various scrapes and cuts occasioned by his hasty gallop through the woods. One that would not have been necessary, had he not lost his temper, and his reason, and become reckless. Sliding down with his knees against his chest, he completely submerged his head, allowing the water to soak his hair as tiny bubbles escaped through his nose and parted lips. Then he burst through the surface, reaching for the soap. The water dripped from his arms and head, splashing against the side of the tin hip-bath and back into the water, as musically pleasing as the sound of rain on a shed's tin roof. He dashed a hand across his eyes.

And spied Faith, standing in shocked immobility in the open doorway.

For a moment, he said nothing, but was as shocked as she. And then he said, with more calm than he could believe himself capable of mustering, "I did not expect you, so soon. I thought to be done with my bath."

Faith averted her eyes. "The boy you sent after me knew ways that were swift. And which," she added, "in daylight I might have been hesitant to travel."

"Harry, that is. Still, I thought that you would be longer."

"I should wait without, then," said Faith, "in the stair-well."

"Of course not! Faith, have you not seen more of me, when we have been together? Sit down," he said coolly, as if the anger, of which she was blissfully unaware, was quit of him. *Deception. It was not kind.* "Tell me how you have occupied yourself, since last I held you."

Faith blushed and ducked her head, pulling a chair from the wall, sitting on the edge of it, avoiding the sight of the bath in the center of the parlor floor. She felt ridiculously modest. "Oh, Fletcher," she said, and, covering her eyes with her fingers, laughed shortly. "I feel so silly, being shy before you."

The lieutenant laughed, also, but without much humor.

"It is kind," said Faith, from behind her hands, "for your friend to allow you the use of his rooms, so often."

Fletcher grunted. He splashed water over his body, and began to lather the soap on his hands.

"The boy," Faith continued, "knows you as Mr. Irons, not Lieutenant. I did not, of course, correct him."

"For which I am grateful," said Fletcher. She was a mystery, was his Faith. On the one hand, she would not betray him, but lied by lack of admission, for his sake; while on the other, she willfully pursued that which could easily bring about the maiming and death of many a man. Did she not realize?

Angrily, he took up the sponge from the water and applied it with vicious intent to his skin. He washed his neck, his shoulders, his chest, his groin, then the length of his long limbs. He was possessed of no false modesty; his years as a soldier had cured him of that. And before Faith, whom he knew more intimately than any woman of his life, there was no cause. But, even with that knowledge, his anger, which he felt was justified, did not abate. He had planned not to be in the tub, but fully clothed, when she arrived, so that he might address her on the issue. For that which he felt certain she had done—and he trusted to the certainty of his instinct more naturally than to any witnessed fact of the eye—was both dangerous, and treasonous; to her sovereign, not only his. They were one and the same, no matter to whom she felt she owed her allegiance.

"Fletcher, I have missed you."

Damn it, Faith, he thought, no. He saw that she was watching him now, quite openly, with her chin cupped on the heel of her palm, her elbow on her burgundy-clad knee. For the first time since she had arrived, he noticed that she was not dressed in her usual homespun colors, but in something more seductive. He turned his head from her half-lidded green gaze.

Biting the soft inside of his cheek, he splashed water over his body to rinse away the harsh lather.

"You have missed your back," she said. "Let me wash it for you."

He shook his head, almost desperately. He could not permit her to distract him. He must speak, now, and allow her her anger, or her contrition, before ever he thought to make love.

"Here," she persisted, "give me the sponge. Lean forward, darling." Removing her cloak, she folded back the gathered cuff of her sleeve a second time, tucking the lace flounce about her elbow into the turned material. From the corner of his eye, Fletcher viewed the shape of her arms, so well remembered, softly rounded, tapering to a narrow wrist and slender hands; all misleading in their appearance of fragility. He knew well their strength.

"Faith, I—"

"Hush," Faith warned him. "If you will complain, I shall be forced to push this soap in your ear." She was laughing, an earnest, gentle sound that warmed his blood, even as he tried to ignore it.

She took the soap, then, a very little of it, and lathered the sponge before applying it with both hands to his back. The strokes were long and relaxing, up, and down, the entire length of his spine.

"You will wet your gown in the water," said Fletcher, eyes closing as his head tipped back. Faith, he thought, as his tension eased, you are a witch, to bind me so, and make me forsake even my righteous anger.

"Fletcher?"

"Yes, Faith." His voice was barely a whisper.

But she said nothing. On her knees, she shifted her body-weight forward, kissing the side of his neck, the line of his jaw, following it around to his mouth where she lingered, tasting the blood where he had bitten himself. Her hands loosed the sponge into the water and, still soapy, came up over his shoulders, caressing his chest, running over the nipples, and down, over his stomach, as she released his mouth to sink her teeth, gently, into his shoulder.

"Oh, God, Faith!" he moaned, "Do not do this to me." His right arm came up, across the back of her neck, and he held her like that, for just a moment, without moving. She could feel him, in her hand, growing in the way of a man. He let go of her, and turned, slipping his fingers into her hair, to kiss her, with the pain of his desire, so long that she felt she would weep with it. He stood, then, straight out of the water with his mouth still on her own. His hands went to her bodice, to the velvet lacings there, slipping the length of each through eyelet after eyelet, until the whole of it parted beneath his touch. Her body beneath her clothing was warm, pressed against him.

In the bedchamber, he stood for a time, only watching her. He had forgotten, the affect she had on him. No. He had hoped to forget, just long enough. But she was beautiful, and daring, and wanting him to make love with her, to know love with her, and he could not forget. He had never forgotten, even in the heat of his most flagrant anger.

He gazed at her soaked gown, knowing that she had dressed for him, and then, with infinite care, he slipped the open bodice from her arms, and her skirt and petticoat from about her waist, so that they fell as one to the floor. The chemise she wore was exceptionally thin and delicate, and the light thrown through the open door revealed every angle and curve of her body. Very slowly, he pushed the chemise from her arms, rolling it down, little by little, over her breasts, to her waist, and then released it. It floated down about her ankles. The shadows caressed her body where his hands did not, marking curves and hollows and structure of bone. Her flesh was warm, as she turned against him, as naked, at last, as he.

Holding her, he trembled, overwhelmed by the sensation of the stroke of her hands, the touch of her mouth. Could he ever want more than this? To feel her again, like this, sinew and bone and rounded flesh; to anticipate the surprise of pleasure at her responses to his touch; to know that she elicited the same in him. And the words she kept, only for him, the gentleness, that she might deny another, the whispered dreams and confessions; the silences between. She was not just a vessel for his enjoyment; she was his love, as true and honest as ever a man could hope to find.

Bending, he swung her into his arms, kicking the door closed with his foot. She was as light as a child. "Oh, Faith, my heart," he said, and kissed her, deeply, only beginning to fill the emptiness of his longing. She could not know his love for her; in a lifetime, she could not know.

They made love in the darkness; not by choice, but by chance, for by the time they realized there was not a taper lit, they were too deeply embroiled to remove themselves for such mundane occupations. There was a strangeness to their lovemaking, and an urgency, that the days, the weeks of absence could not fully explain. Both were aware, deep in their minds, of the shaping of the times; perhaps, this was cause for desperation, before a chasm should open between them that they could not cross. Perhaps it was no more than what love, at that point, had driven them to. Whatever the cause, Fletcher took her, and found himself pushing her, with mouth and tongue and teeth, to a climax that left her weeping, and afterward he plunged deep, with no hope of coming back, as he was swept circling down and down, and her hands, her arms, held claim to him, and her mouth, so that he wondered if he could get enough of it all, or if he should die.

"I love you, Faith."

In the shadowed bed, Faith rolled onto her elbow, smiling, leaning with her breasts upon Fletcher's rib cage. Reaching up, she ran her slender fingers through his dark, damp hair, smoothing it back from his forehead. She felt him turn his head against her palm, pressing his lips to the inside of her wrist. She moved her hand, down, to caress his jaw, his throat, and on under the linen sheet, where she slipped her arms behind his back to embrace him.

"Fletcher, I love you," she said. He held her, kissing the top of her head, disturbing wisps of flame-colored hair with the vibrations of his breath. She was small, in his arms, and beautiful, and he wanted never to release her, but to keep her there, protected, and loved.

"Faith," he said, knowing that what he was to say was perhaps a waste of time, but he could not hold it back. He wanted it, more than anything else. "I must do the honorable thing by you—"

"Must?" Faith interrupted.

"No, not must. I desire it, very much."

"And what is the honorable thing to do?" she taunted him. For a moment, there was silence. She let her finger roam lazily over his stomach, describing lopsided circles.

"For you to take my name, Faith. For you to be my wife."

"You are asking me to marry you?"

"Yes."

Faith expelled a soft, weary breath that she hoped he had not heard. How many times in the days past had she allowed herself to dream of that state? To imagine what it would be like; to pretend that it was. But she was no fool, and no girl, and recognized dreams for what they were: fancied, twice-removed from life itself.

Abruptly, Faith sat up and turned from him, bringing her knees up beneath her chin with the sheet tucked around them. Dismayed, he sat up behind her. He brushed the hair from her shoulder and placed his hand there.

"Fletcher," she said, "I cannot."

Although she could not see them, his eyes betrayed his pain. "Why not, my little one? Faith, it seems to me that our love should overrule that which separates us beyond this room."

She shook her head, leaning back against his chest. "Please," she begged him for silence.

"If I beget a child upon you?" he insisted, determined, suddenly, to play that hand. "I will give you no choice, then, no rest."

"There is no cause to concern yourself with that, I am afraid," Faith replied, her small voice bitter.

"Is that so?" said Fletcher, with irony. "Do you propose to know the will of God?"

"No," she said. "No. His will is often a mystery to me. But Fletcher, my love, my deepest love . . . I am barren."

He felt, quite abruptly, as if someone had hit him, hard, in his abdomen. He felt sick. His ears rang.

As far as Faith was concerned, the confession, to him, her lover—her love—caused something to crack inside. She felt it, nearly heard it, the crumbling of defenses. Without restraint, she broke down and wept against her knees.

Fletcher felt the moisture, in his own eyes. He blinked, smoothing her hair. His arms went about her. "I do not care, Faith. It is not necessarily your children that I want. It is you, only you."

She shook her head, again, still crying. "No child, Fletcher. No child. It hurts me, grievously. Marriage cannot be," she said, "between us. There is no hope for that. What can I give

you? What happiness can I possibly provide you but—this?''
she said, indicating the bed in which they lay. "There is much
that keeps us apart, Fletcher, and it will do so, always."

He sighed, and pressed his cheek against her hair. "We are
not enemies, Faith, you and I. We are not." Releasing his
hold on her, Fletcher produced a handkerchief, and held it out
to her. She wiped her eyes, and blew her nose.

"Fletcher, listen to me. You know that if I were to wed
you, I would become a traitor to people whose beliefs I share,
and revere. I thought that you understood that."

For a long time, he did not answer. The only sounds were
those of Faith's sniffling, and his breathing, close beside her
ear. There was truth to her words, he knew. But to him, her
priorities seemed misplaced. Not in the matter of loyalty, naturally. He understood that concept clearly. But why did love
not take precedence? Or was he merely a romantic, a dreamer?

"Lay down, then," he said, "and let me hold you." He
embraced her, in the curve of his body, and stroked her hair.
Above her, in the blackness, he shook his dark head.

Faith lay very still, hoping, for a time, at least, he would
think her sleeping. The stroke of his fingers was soothing,
repetitive, erotic, but still she did not move. She loved Fletcher
more than she had cared for any other man in her life, including
William, God forgive her.

"Faith?"

His mouth was against her ear, softly.

"Yes?"

"Are you content to remain lovers, then? Meeting, as we
have, whenever the moment presents itself?"

Faith stirred, sat up, leaning her weight on one hand beside
him.

"It does not make me happy, Fletcher, having to steal our
time as thieves. But to be with you is worth the risks."

"And it seems to you that our lives can be managed in that
fashion?"

Faith strained in the darkness to see him, but he was reclined
into the pillow, in shadow. "That is how it must be."

"And you do love me?" he continued.

"Fletcher, you know that I do. You need not ask."

"Needn't I?" he said.

"That is not fair!" she cried, dismayed.

"No," he said, "I suppose it is not."

He moved away, then, to the edge of the bed, the mattress sagging as he leaned forward, in noisy search across the bureau. There was a brief, but blinding, flare, as he touched tinder to a candle.

"I need to look at you," he said.

He turned, to face her. She had expected to find that his expression matched the iciness of his tone, but instead, he looked unhappy; miserably so. His brow, beneath the black peak of his hair, was furrowed; his eyes, sad, yet cautious.

"I must ask you something. I meant to do so as soon as you arrived, but I—found myself distracted." Here, he made an attempt at laughter, and failed.

"Go on," said Faith, despairing, for she thought she had been the matter of importance that had sent the message flying to her, but all along it had been something else.

"I only want you to answer me yea or nay, and we will continue from there. Do you agree?"

Faith extended her fingers to him, to smooth away the line between his brows, but he caught her hand and held it for an instant before placing it back in her lap. Something about the manner in which he did that, almost as a correction, to her behavior, caused Faith to cringe inside. She pulled the sheet up, beneath her arms, holding it tightly across her nakedness.

"I agree," she said, however foolishly.

Fletcher nodded, rising from the bed to pull on his breeches. They were not those of an officer's uniform, but another pair, brown and worn. Lifting the candle, he came around the foot of the bed, and set the light down on the circular table. He sat down, in a chair. His shadow danced across the wall. He noted how wide Faith's eyes had become, and how frightened. He regretted that, but it did not deter him. Now, more than ever, he needed to know the truths in her life.

"I have heard," he said, "that ammunition was smuggled out of Boston in the hem of women's petticoats. These women who wore the petticoats came across the Neck on the pretense of attending a quilting circle in Roxbury, I do believe. No! Do not speak yet. I have not asked the question."

Faith subsided, staring at Fletcher. She knew what the question would be, of course, though how he had found out, she did not care to know, nor did she dare to inquire. She held her breath, feeling a cold dread creeping over her flesh.

"Recall: yea or nay. That is all the answer I expect from you. Did you, Faith, participate in this treasonous activity?"

Feeling a flush of anger, Faith bent her head. It would serve no purpose to lie. Not now. She nodded, and heard him sigh. He clapped his hands, flat, on his thighs, and stood.

"Another question, Faith," he said.

"You said one."

"Another," Fletcher repeated. "Was this smuggling of your instigation?"

Ah, but this question was different, more dangerous. Faith looked up to find Fletcher's gaze turned cold, unyielding. He expected an answer from her. Any lack would also be a conviction. She straightened her shoulders, defiantly.

"Yea," she said, in accordance with the agreement. He had pushed her to it, on the basis of their trust. It remained to be seen what he would do next.

He stood a moment, and the candle flame threw his shadow across the ceiling, dwarfing the bed, and the woman in it. He looked down at her, at the sudden defiance of her gaze, at her anger, and he felt himself betrayed.

"Faith! In God's good name," he demanded violently, controlling urges more wicked, "why did you lie to me? 'Ride out there,' you said to me, 'and see for yourself.' It was that day, was it not?"

Faith bowed her head, in guilt that crushed her anger. "Yes," she said, quietly.

"What was that? I did not quite hear you," he persisted. His fury was returning to him, coldly reasoning, hard as a wall thrown up between them.

At his continued tone of derision, Faith lifted her head again. "Yes! I said, yes." *And I have dwelt on the guilt of my lie, day and night; if only you knew*. But she could not bring herself to confess it, for she was a stubborn woman, and she bristled beneath his enraged glare, angered again by his coldness, his lack of understanding.

"Faith," he said, his voice only slightly raised, yet snaking through the shadowed room, "how could you be so stupid?"

She reeled back slightly, as if struck. "Stupid?" she said, breathing heavily. Her cheeks flamed like roses. "How so?" she said, smarting from the sarcasm that he turned upon her. "We succeeded, did we not?"

He had turned away, but in midstride, Fletcher swung back around. He could barely trust his ears to what he had heard. Rage rang in the blood pulsing in his temples. What insolence allowed such speech? Such disregard for the fact of law, order, and his own faith in her? "You bloody idiot How dare you? Do you not realize the implication of what you, and your— your damned patriot friends!—have done? It was simple, was it? And what of the harm that may come? And my knowledge of what you have done? Have you thought of that? What, my sweet little Faith, do you expect me to do about that?"

Faith leaped from the bed, tearing the sheet off behind her as she swung it about to cover her nakedness. Always quick-tempered, she reacted to his charges with a turbulent swiftness. "Why, whatever you please, I would suppose," she stressed. "Arrest me, if you choose, or have someone else perform the distasteful task for you. It is said that the officers of the British army would not know their own bodily functions, without first receiving the proper paperwork. As for arrest, it is the price to be paid. I have done what is right, for my own conscience, and for the Body of the People."

"Listen to yourself, Faith! The Body of the People. I don't want to hear that expression, again, do you understand me? It is nothing but utter nonsense. There is no unity in your rebellion; merely a lot of rabble, running about without true leadership." Faith huffed, but would not rise to the bait; she was not about to reveal the names of those she knew. Fletcher went on. "If I am worth my salt at all, a point on which you are doubtful, my dear, I will see that the orders for arrest are requested, signed, and issued, since that seems to be your heart's desire. That, Faith, is my responsibility now, and it will be done." His voice resounded with a loss of control that he had never experienced before. And she turned her back on him.

"Face me when I am speaking to you! I will not tolerate cowardice, from anyone."

Gathering her strewn clothing from the floor, Faith hissed fiercely, "I am not one of your men to be ordered about. Go to hell . . . Lieutenant!"

Fletcher caught his breath. "Blasphemy, is it? Was it only an hour ago that you claimed to love me? That you were moaning in my bloody arms?"

Faith gasped where she stood, holding her clothes against her breast. Quickly, she began to dress as the fury building lit her face, her eyes, with fire. "Bastard!" she cried, struggling with her skirt, appalled at her own choice of words, but continuing without check. "You bastard! You knew, when I walked in here, and yet, you let me demean myself, shame myself—how could you make love to me, when all along you planned these accusations?"

"Accusations are not accusations, when they are no more than the truth. You have admitted to all that I have said."

"And truth?" continued Faith, as if she had heard only that one word. "You lied to me! These rooms belong to a friend, do they? How often do you use them? Just how often? For other women? And—and, for this," she said, tossing his shirt at him. "You filthy spy! No, we are not enemies, you and I, Fletcher. We are two of a kind."

She stopped then, staring at him through eyes that shed tears, long and silent, over her skin. Her ears seemed to echo with those final phrases, screamed, against his utter shock. She could not believe what she had said; it horrified her. She stepped toward him, witnessing his withdrawal from her with a sickening wrench to her heart.

It was done, over. All existence of joy, all possibility, was now gone. She felt ashamed, visualizing her hasty state of dress, remembering the need that had driven her to him and caused him to take her, in spite of the doubt that plagued his mind.

"Oh, Fletcher," she said, and brought her hands to her face.

"Oh, Fletcher." What had she done? To him? To herself? Where were they to go, from this point? Nowhere. *Nowhere*.

Words, such as those which had passed between them, could not be retrieved.

"Faith . . ."

"No, Fletcher," she said, choking. "Let me be. Where is my cloak?" Blindly, she cast about for it, until she recalled how she had dropped it from her shoulders, in the parlor. Where she had tempted him. She remembered his words: *Oh, God, Faith, do not do this to me.* She drew in her breath, sharply, stifling the tears.

"I will see you home."

She shook her head, and would not look at him, would not look at the pain and anger on his face. She wiped the back of her hand across her eyes and walked away from him, leaving him alone.

Fletcher sat down, heavily, in the chair beside the bed. He watched Faith through the open door as she slipped into her cloak. She did not turn, but he saw her shoulders shake, beneath the drape of her garment. And when she left him, he made no move to stop her.

After a time, he extinguished the candle, lapsing into the shadows left behind. The smoke of the tallow, of the wick, lingered in the air, along with Faith's perfume.

There was nothing else.

Chapter Fifteen

Elizabeth held the leather pouch tightly against her abdomen. The pouch, worn and scarred, and wrapped round about with a bit of twine, contained the remnants of notes scrawled by British officers which had been afterward discarded, either by those who had received them, or by the authors themselves, and then gathered up discreetly by maidservants, to find their way, through one deceit or another, into the hands of the rebellion. This particular bundle had come to Mrs. Ashley, and though the woman was not certain if they were helpful, it was her duty to pass them on to an individual who waited, every week, for their delivery at an appointed place. This week, it was to be the ink-scented shop of the Boston Observer.

Elizabeth hurried along her own Salt Lane, toward the Observer, musing on Mrs. Ashley's new reluctance to perform those duties which once she had hastened to do. For Elizabeth had a long time known what her benefactor was about, though she had not revealed as much. Oh, Faith Ashley still did what was asked of her, but she had come to rely on Elizabeth in ways that once she had not. It seemed to Elizabeth that her heart had pulled away from her duty, leaving only a dull sense of obligation. It worried the girl to witness the sudden dissatisfaction; it worried her more to know that there was a sadness beneath it all, kept quiet and close within.

She was less talkative, less responsive, less inclined to speak with fire on the matter of her patriotism, although her views and her beliefs had not changed. Her once effervescent enthusiasms for her life and for her cause had been dampened, it seemed, and with what reason Elizabeth was unable to determine. She imagined all manner of causes, but could not attribute any of them to Mrs. Ashley, to what she knew of her, and felt ashamed, sometimes, of what she was thinking, and also of her inability to understand.

Since the onset of her strange moodiness, the woman had begun again to see much of Ezra Briggs, and even this day planned to bring him soup and a posset she had prepared, to ease him through a bout of illness. Elizabeth was aware that the man was a lifelong friend to Mrs. Ashley, but, nevertheless, she cared little for him, and in her own mind had christened him, with uncharacteristic cruelty, the Rumtart, for his predilection for those two: rum, and any tart or pastry that came within his grasp.

Elizabeth stepped out of the street and into the front room of the printing establishment. She blinked in the change from bright sunlight. The smell of ink was strong, and she heard the familiar clack of the printer's set and the sound of voices, which gradually ceased as the speakers became aware of the presence of a young lady.

"Might I be of help to you, miss?"

Elizabeth knew the voice. It was that of the printer's apprentice, a tall, dark-haired youth. He came around from behind the press, passing before the narrow, open window. His long legs were dressed in black breeches and white stockings, and he had a much-stained apron over his brown shirt. The other man present was a stranger, somewhat older, and standing back a little in the shadow beyond the thrown light of the window. Elizabeth saw only that his hat was in his hand and that his hair was nearly as yellow as her own.

"Oh, it's only you, Miss Elizabeth. Did your mama send you down for the morning edition?"

Hearing a small laugh from the stranger, Elizabeth's cheeks colored. Her eyes slid to the figure in the shadow, and away, as she ducked her head.

"Now, you know that I have been boardin' with Mrs. Ashley since before you came to be 'prenticed here," she said. "Indeed, t'is for Mrs. Ashley's benefit that I came, today. I—" and she faltered, remembering the stranger.

"Yes?" said the apprentice, "what is it that you want?"

"Mrs. Ashley . . . don't you know?"

"I don't know anything," he said, " 'ceptin' that you are the prettiest thing to walk in here so far this morning."

Blushing more deeply, Elizabeth stamped her foot on the planked floor. The fellow in the shadow laughed again, and agreed with his friend.

"I am supposed to be deliverin' this," Elizabeth insisted, lifting the pouch in her hands, "for Mrs. Ashley. H'ain't you any notion of what I'm saying?" Perhaps, she had gotten the place wrong, she thought, with a feeling of panic. But no, she had listened very carefully to what Mrs. Ashley had told her, and besides, she was not likely to forget the shop when it was on her own street.

"Oh, I do, I do, Miss Elizabeth. I was only playing with you, though the Lord knows that I shouldn' be; not over this. Do you forgive me?"

Elizabeth huffed, and turned her head away. "You are a rude boy," she said. "I don't know you that well, that you should reckon you could tease me, in any way."

The apprentice grunted. "Here," he said to her, "you should meet this fellow, then. He is the one you seek. I have known him for many a year. And if he torments me, I am not likely to take insult. Jack, kindly meet Elizabeth Watts. She used," he stressed, "to have her home on this street."

"Jacques," corrected the stranger, without rudeness, and came forward. "I will take that from you, Miss Watts."

Taking a tiny, sliding step backward, Elizabeth stared up at the fellow, clutching the satchel closer to her chest. There had to be some mistake. The young man was French.

Sensing her trepidation, he smiled. "My mother is English," he said, "and I am a patriot, proud as are you to be so. There is no reason to doubt me. Please, deliver your goods unto me."

The young apprentice chuckled at that, and walked out behind the shop. Elizabeth turned her eyes to Jacques, or Jack, as she was already calling him in her mind, knowing that she would be unable to get her tongue around the proper pronunciation. She looked at the face beneath the blonde shock of hair; it was wide and honest in expression, and the dark eyes stood out in contrast, coal black they seemed, regarding her in a rather open admiration. He held out his large hand.

She deposited the pouch into it.

"*Merçi*," he said, lapsing into French. Elizabeth cocked her head at him, frowning. "It means, my thanks, Miss Watts. I will deliver this to the proper place, now. There are others who await what is inside. You see? From there, to here, to there. No one must know any more than the man, or the woman, behind him." He took her hand, then, and kissed it, lightly. Elizabeth snatched it back, as if she had been burned.

"Jack!" she cried, and found him laughing at her for the abuse of his name.

"May I call on you? At your home that is *not* on Salt Lane?" And he laughed again, his smile one of brilliant teeth.

Elizabeth stared, feeling the pound of her heart within her breast. What would Mrs. Ashley say? Nothing, she thought, for she sees and says little these days.

She looked at him again, and saw that he was, in his own way, handsome. And not too old. He could not have been more than twenty, or twenty-one years. And she would soon be seventeen herself.

"Aye," she said. "Pray, do that."

Mingling clouds of smoke, of Virginia tobacco burning, of candlewick, and of the dark smoke of lamp oil, curled upward to the tavern ceiling where they remained, suspended in sheets of haze and shadow. Below, men diced, or played cards, or indulged themselves in debate, laughing overloud at their own recklessness as the yeasty house-ale settled in their veins. The harbor breeze blew in through the propped doors, drying sweat on brow and back, and guttering the candle flames. At a corner table, Lieutenant Fletcher Irons had his hand cupped as a shield about a shivering tongue of light, observing, with the amateur artist's eye, the tallow dripping into drying, twisting configurations that overflowed the dish. Then he withdrew his protection and sat back, rather clumsily, tilting his chair onto its back legs; a feat of marvelous agility, as he had consumed a half-dozen pints of ale in succession. Across the table, his nose and mouth ringed by yellow foam at which he was gingerly swiping with his tongue, sat Brian Upton, equally as intoxicated. Clutched tightly in his fist was an empty tankard, and he looked into it, smiling bewilderedly.

"Ah, Brian," said Fletcher, "you resemble nothing short of a mad cur."

Upton scratched his chin, then belched, loudly. "Thank you. I informed you that I intended to do this, if you recall."

"To do what? Make a ninny of yourself?" tormented Fletcher affectionately.

"Of course not," slurred Brian. "To get hopelessly drunk. I am not there, yet."

"No?" said Fletcher, brows arched. "Pray, inform me when you attain your goal. I should very much enjoy being witness to that momentous occasion in your life."

Ignoring him, the younger lieutenant turned away, calling for another tankard. Fletcher looked past him, to the crowded room, occupied almost entirely by British soldiers in their scarlet coats. Officers, for the most part, though he noted several non-commissioned men scattered about. An unruly lot, all of them, he reflected, and included himself in that opinion, vacillating between anger and indifference. He yawned, then, and stretched, and very nearly upended himself before regaining his balance.

He cursed, quietly, under his breath.

"Eh? What was that, Irons? I do believe you are drunk, not I."

"I would call it equal, you young pup!" laughed Fletcher.

"Young pup?" repeated Brian. "There are not that many years separating us, Fletcher," he said.

"A woman can age a man, so that he outstrips his peers," said Fletcher, and frowned, regretting that he had spoken. It was not something he would have said had he been sober, and he realized it. Yet, he was not deterred from drinking down the next pint without pause for breath.

"What a maudlin comment," remarked Brian, and consumed his own. He called for two more. Sitting back, he loosened his black cravat and opened his waistcoat, top to bottom, revealing a slight paunch. He patted his stomach self-consciously.

"Not enough action, by far, Irons," he said. He could not help noticing that the older lieutenant was still buttoned and in order and retaining his air of dignity, despite the fact that he was tipped back in his chair like a classless colonial, tossing comments at him that were nothing, if not out of character. "Could use a bit of action," he continued, "and not necessarily warfare, if you understand me."

Fletcher growled, dropping his chair down with a loud scuff across the floor. "Only too well, I am afraid. You are a lecherous soul."

"Ah, no, I am too young to be lecherous! Only fools and old men can be considered lecherous. We who are young have our youth to excuse us."

Fletcher laughed, then, and extended his hand to cover the flame as a fresh gust of wind blew through the door. Well, he mused, which was he? Briggs was the old man, therefore he must be the fool. And, Brian, he had yet to know that pain, Fletcher was certain.

"Here you are, sweet lass!" cried Brian, of a sudden, and Fletcher looked up to witness the crossing of the floor by the serving maid, dressed in her billowy dark skirt and her stained white bodice and apron, smiling a gap-toothed smile that was somehow seductive. Her eyes were blue, Fletcher noticed, for the first time, and her hair, flying in disarray from beneath her mob cap, was the same shade of flaming red as Faith's.

He cast his eyes down, away from her.

"One for me, and one for you," chanted Upton, as in a child's game, and the tankard thumped heavily on the table before Fletcher's gaze. Ale foaming over her fingers, the girl reached across in front of him to collect his empty vessel, deliberately rubbing across his scarlet sleeve. He glanced at her naked arm, plump beneath her own rolled sleeve, and then he gazed up to the sagging neckline of her bodice, which hung away from throat and collarbone to expose a view of the curve of her left breast and the rosy aureole of a stiffened nipple. The muscle in his jaw twitched, and his eyes, for a full moment, remained fixed. Yet, he did not see her, nor her dirty breast, ample and full, but another, infinitely more clean, more inviting, that he had come to know in every detail.

"I do believe that she's yours, Fletcher," mourned Upton from his side of the table. "I suppose I must find myself another." And he pinched the curve of the girl's buttock. She giggled, and straightened, pushing her abdomen against the table. In response, Fletcher laughed, somewhat cruelly, and shook his dark head.

"No," he said, "I don't want her."

The girl's mouth gaped, and then her eyes narrowed angrily. With a haughty toss of her red curls, she spun about and strode away. Fletcher glimpsed a flash of metal in the lamplight as the coin she had pilfered from the small pile at his elbow was deposited into the soiled folds of her apron.

Her hair, he decided, was not the same shade at all.

"Have you gone insane, man?" declared Brian, before the maid was barely out of earshot.

"Whatever do you mean?" responded Fletcher carelessly. "The girl was willing!"

"I am not interested."

"Why not?" the younger man demanded.

Why not, indeed. Fletcher lifted the tankard to his mouth, holding it in both hands. The pewter was cool within his palms, chilled by the cellar-stored ale. He thought of his conversation with Ezra three days before; a conversation that had been preying on his mind ever since. It seemed, from what Ezra had to say, that Faith and the lawyer had been much in each other's company. Apparently, she had turned to Ezra for comfort after their bitter argument. Was she reconsidering the man's proposal, now that their own relationship had met with such disaster?

He only knew one thing: he could not forsake his love for Faith. Nothing could tempt him save her own glorious smile. "For one thing," he said, not caring what reasons he gave, "the wench is not clean."

Brian choked on a mouthful of brew. "Instruct her in bathing then, but do not turn her away."

"It is too late," said Fletcher, "she is gone."

"I will call her back."

"No," said Fletcher. "No."

He tipped his chair back against the wall, where there was a place, worn into the panelling, from the continual scraping of chairs into that one position. He closed his eyes, folded his arms across his broad chest, in an attitude that suggested no more would be said on the subject. But Brian was not to be put off. He could be a persistent young man when he so chose, and he had, upon a considerable amount of convoluted reflection, drawn certain conclusions that he would not permit to rest.

"Who is she?" he asked, at last. Not from curiosity so much as friendship.

In his chair, Fletcher did not stir, not even to open his eyes, but his mouth moved, curving into a slow, wicked grin. He looked more dangerous than he had at any other time in Upton's knowledge of him.

"None," he said, "of your bloody business."

* * *

"Lieutenant Irons! T'is you, is it not?"

Alone at his corner table, Fletcher glanced up from the small puddle that had formed beneath his cup, spreading across the scarred wood. He had been toying with it, languidly, with the tips of his fingers. He was no longer drinking; he had ceased after the exit of Lieutenant Upton and the flame-haired serving girl. He could not have said why. Now, the sound of the voice calling his name struck him oddly, with a dissatisfying familiarity, and he looked about the tavern without turning his head. Ah, yes, he thought, spying the face to accompany the voice, pale in the lamplight no more than fifteen feet away, I should have known those odious tones immediately.

"Johnston," he said, coldly, without greeting.

The man moved closer, in the company of several acquaintances. All the men were gaudily dressed, but Johnston's jacket, Fletcher noted, was particularly well made, silk, dark, with gold frogs and turned cuffs. The color was burgundy. It put him in mind of the dress Faith had worn to tempt him. It put him in mind of the feel of it in his hands, and the way it had fallen, like water, to the floor.

"Well? Will you not invite us to be seated, Irons?"

There was a stiff moment in which Fletcher did not respond, and then he dropped his feet from the chair opposite to the floor, and said, still cold, "Of course. Sit down."

"Thank you," said Charles, and promptly did so. The men with him excused themselves, and drifted off; with the exception of one who draped himself in the chair to Fletcher's right, offering no introductions. Fletcher inclined his head, then turned away.

"An extraordinarily lovely night, Irons," said Charles conversationally. "Do you not think so, Lieutenant?"

"It is that," agreed Fletcher shortly. He could smell the wine on Johnston's breath from across the table. So he had smelled that night when he had been inclined to take liberties with Faith, grasping at her arm, her hands, her waist. Fletcher felt his spine stiffen and the hair on his nape rise, as might a dog's, beside its enemy.

"Dry weather," continued Johnston, oblivious to Fletcher's animosity. "Good weather for racing. Do you know anything about horseflesh, Lieutenant?" His companion released a brief guffaw, as at some trifling jest at Fletcher's expense. The latter inhaled, sharply.

"Enough," he said. "More than enough."

"I would suspect as much," said Charles, still with that same tendency toward friendliness that left Fletcher wary. "Have you a mount of your own?" The other fellow exploded again and Fletcher glared at him in annoyance.

"Yes," he said. His mouth felt dry. "But he is trained for the rigors of battle, Johnston, not to race for sport."

"That is too bad," remarked Johnston, glancing disinterestedly around the room. "We might have made an amusing match, you and I. Perhaps, we may yet. Winner take all." At this, his young companion nearly choked on his humor. Charles smiled at him affectionately. "Go away, Robert. I believe that you are annoying the lieutenant. He does not understand why you are laughing. I expect that he will, soon enough."

Still chortling, the fellow rose and departed. Fletcher watched him, through eyes gray and slitted.

"You must forgive my friend," said Charles. "He finds a double meaning in everything I say. It is his nature to search for innuendo in conversation. Sometimes, of course, he is right. But not always." He shifted in his chair and crossed his silk-clad knees, satisfied with the lieutenant's answering silence. "Irons," he went on, "I must confess that I am surprised to find you in this establishment. It seems a bit—out of the ordinary?—for a man such as yourself to frequent. Yet, since we are both here, may I purchase your next drink? And that of your guest, also, of course," he added, indicating Upton's half-empty tankard. His manner was smugly accommodating. He raised his eyes to Fletcher's, and the candlelight revealed them in a strange lack of color.

"No," said Fletcher, "thank you. My friend has gone, and will, in all probability, be detained for some time. As for myself, I am through. I recognize my limitations."

Charles winced. He flicked the lace on his sleeve irritably. "From our former association, Lieutenant, I take your meaning, clearly. And will ignore it, naturally. I am a gentle-man.''

"Indeed?" retorted Fletcher, dryly.

Johnston inhaled, swelling his chest against the sunny yellow fabric of his shirt. "I have news," he said. "Would you be interested in hearing it, Irons?"

"Only," Fletcher replied, "if it is not idle gossip."

"Oh, no, no," said Charles. "Hardly that. It concerns a mutual acquaintance of ours, Irons. A lovely lady the mere sight of whom makes my heart beat swifter. Oh, surely you know of whom I speak, Lieutenant? Ah. I see that you do."

"Where—" began Fletcher, and paused to swallow the con-striction in his throat, "where did you happen upon . . . Mrs. Ashley?"

"I did not say that I happened upon her, Lieutenant, but as it so happens, I did. At the home of another of our acquain-tances, Irons: Ezra Briggs. He is ill, did you know?"

"I did," he said.

"He is recovering quickly, under Mrs. Ashley's tender care. I am certain that I would do the same, given the opportunity. And you, Lieutenant? What about you?"

Fletcher was silent, controlling an urge to throttle the man. Charles chuckled, maliciously. His foppish demeanor had de-serted him, and he faced Fletcher as an adversary, his expres-sion both amused, and wicked.

"Ezra is still abed, poor man, and therefore Fai—Mrs. Ash-ley found that it behooved her to entertain me for the duration of my stay. She is an admirable hostess, Lieutenant. Most dedicated and efficient. Yet, before I took my leave, I discov-ered myself forced to remind her of that other night, when first we met." Extending his tongue to lick his index finger and thumb, he leaned forward, snuffing the wick of the guttering candle. "You remember that night, do you not, Lieutenant?"

"Yes," said Fletcher. He felt cold, suddenly, and entirely sober. Slowly, he sat up. No more than that. His respiration remained even, unaffected.

"The lady was not pleased, by my reminder—"

"Should she have been?" Fletcher interrupted. "You were

drunk. You behaved toward Mrs. Ashley in abominable fashion.''

"Ah," said Johnston, leaning back into his chair, "but you
have more cause to remember that night than do I, Irons. And
I was not drunk. I saw the two of you, in the street; I saw her
in your arms, Irons. Our little loyal patriot tossed me off, to
cling to you, Lieutenant, an officer in the British army. What
do we suppose she was about, Lieutenant? Was she playing
with you, trifling with you, in order to gain information? I will
wager that our pretty little patriot would be willing to do anything, to further her treasonous causes.''

Fletcher's chair slid back, wood on wood, slamming against
the wall. He stood up, catching the lantern above with the edge
of his shoulder so that it swung, casting his features in and
out of darkness.

"I believe that our conversation is concluded, Johnston,"
he said, flatly.

Coming to his feet, Johnston spread his hands in the air. He
regarded the stillness of the lieutenant's stance with a false
security. He did not perceive the danger of the man's immobility: the danger of a coiled spring in tenuous restraint. He
laughed.

"Did you return to her that night, Irons, once we had parted
company? Was it worth it, being allowed to her bed, to be
betrayed—''

He could not complete the sentence. His head jerked on his
neck, as a broken doll's and his blood spattered onto the lieutenant's white waistcoat. Johnston had not even seen Fletcher's
movement that split his lip. But the second time, he did see it
and reacted, far too slowly. Pulling away, raising his arm, he
took the brunt of the blow in his jaw, spinning his head on his
shoulders, tumbling him backwards, through space and sparking darkness onto a table. Irons strode past him, not bothering
to turn his head.

Chapter Sixteen

In the center of the kitchen, with a stew pot bubbling cheerily upon the hearth, a fresh-baked bread laid out upon the table that was wrapped in cloths of soft cambric, and the scent of dried herbs a perfume in the warm air, Elizabeth was crying as if someone had pulled the world she had known for sixteen years away and apart, and left her standing alone.

"Oh, Jack, Jack," she wailed.

He put his arm about her, and gave her shoulders a little shake. "Hush," he said, "or someone shall hear you. Why do you weep so? It is not the end, for us."

"B-but you are leaving, t-tonight," she stammered tearfully. Her blonde hair was wet, where it had fallen across her cheeks and into the path of her tears.

"I must," said the young man, bravely. "Should there be fighting, my Betsy, the British will soon detain all men who are of military age. I will not be able to fight, then. I will be as a caged animal, staring out at its captors."

"J-Jack, I am afraid! I do not want you to fight! Supposin' you are hurt? Or—or—" and she could not complete her sentence. Over the girl's nodding head, the young man named Jacques Sabot, who had been introduced, quaintly, by Elizabeth as Jack Shoe, caught the eye of the woman seated in the corner.

Faith rose.

She had been home no more than an hour when the young fellow had appeared, with stealth, at the kitchen door. As if prearranged, Elizabeth had been waiting for him. She had already been crying at some earlier time, for her eyes were red-rimmed and swollen.

"Elizabeth, please, you are only making it harder on poor

Jack. I assume that he desires to perform his duty," Faith said, "to sign on with the militia; to stand with the others, should the British come. Stop your crying, and gather provisions for him. Bread, and cheese, and some salted meat, if we have any. Fill his skin with fresh water. It is a long haul to Lexington." And then, "Jack, sit down. The stew is fine. Elizabeth made it. You may as well eat. You cannot leave before nightfall."

All the while that she had been talking, Faith had been leading Elizabeth from Jack's embrace, drying her tears, prodding her in the proper direction to perform those things which she had asked. "Be brave, be brave," she whispered. "That is what Jack needs most. Not tears."

Elizabeth marvelled that the woman never asked the nature of her relationship with Jack.

In due time, Faith sent the girl to fetch a small bootknife from her bedroom. It had been William's, and he had taken it with him, often, on his journeys, though he had left it behind on the fateful trip that had killed him. Quickly, Faith ladled the stew into a deep bowl, tore a hunk of bread from a fresh loaf, and set them down before the yellow-haired youth. She sat down opposite him, watching approvingly as he bowed his head in prayer before eating. He ripped into the bread with clean white teeth, spooning the stew in after as though he were starved. Faith waited a moment, listening to the sounds of Elizabeth's searching, above.

After a time, Faith rose again, with a little frown, and walked to the window. She gazed out at the lowering sky, rosy-fingered and shadowed with dark blue. Normally, she would have prepared to light the candles above the table, but she knew that it would be best to not do so, this night. "It will be twilight, soon," she said, "and then night. Tell me, Jacques, what you know. I have learned little, these past days, except that the tension grows. However, it is common knowledge that the British sergeants were seen through the town calling in the men which General Gage relieved from garrison duty on Saturday. For the purpose, it was said, of learning new evolutions." At this, she made a small, unfeminine, snort of derision.

"Yes," said Jack, chewing. His admiration grew at her

grasp of the situation, and her willingness to learn more. "The grenadiers are the strongest of the units, tall and well built; the light-infantry more mobile, to be sent out ahead. Their endurance is better than any other. But they fight, ah, with too much order. It is no good. Not this time."

Wrapping a heavy towel about the handle of the stew pot, Faith removed it from the flame. The infantry. Fletcher was light-infantry. Suddenly, she could scarcely breath.

"They are gathering on the Common at moonrise, it is said. Equipped for an expedition. I do not know how many. But they will move tonight. If I had anything worthwhile to wager, Mrs. Ashley, I would say that by tomorrow we will meet with them, in Lexington, or some other place, depending on their route and inclination. But meet them we shall. My legs will have to carry me far and swift this night, Mrs. Ashley." He paused, to spoon another helping of stew into his mouth, and chew. There was a noise, and a gasp. "Betsy! You are returned."

Elizabeth stood in the archway, her blue eyes wide and round. To her breast in pale brown homespun, she clutched a sheathed blade, its handle carved with the relief of a leaping deer embossed in silver. "Is this the one?" she asked, her voice no more than a whisper. "There was no other."

"Yes," said Faith. "Give it to him." Her shortness of breath made it difficult to speak in any other than the briefest of sentences. She turned, in time to see the Frenchman draw out the blade and hold it to the sunlight. It glimmered and glinted with the twist of his hand. The point of it was very sharp, as was the length of the blade. Faith began to wonder why she had given it to him. Protection, she had decided initially. But now she could think only of one thing.

"A beautiful gift, Mrs. Ashley," said Jack. "I do not think that I may accept it . . ."

"Please, do," begged Elizabeth, wringing her hands.

"Very well," said Jack, and smiled. Bending, he tucked it straightaway into the folded top of his boot, so that it was nearly hidden completely. Only the tip could be seen: just enough to take hold of. "My musket awaits me, outside of town, if I may reach it. And then—"

"Oh, Jack," cried Elizabeth again. "You are so anxious to go! To leave me!"

"Not to leave you, Betsy, my pet," he said. "But tomorrow, all able-bodied men will be needed to stand firm among the militia. I may not—I may not—" and here, he seemed to lose his words, and said, "unshoulder—my duties. Today, perhaps, you believe that I desert you. But tomorrow, or the next day, or some day soon after, you will have cause to be proud."

Abruptly, Elizabeth threw herself into his arms, nearly overturning the steaming bowl of stew. "Tomorrow! Will you pray with me, Jack?"

Faith felt a drying of her mouth, a sickness in the pit of her stomach. In caring for Ezra, she had been too much withdrawn from the news and from the drift of men toward violence. There had once been hope, that the demands of the Provincial Congress would be met. There was now none, Faith knew. The letters for which General Gage had been waiting had come.

Tomorrow, thought Faith, or the next day, or some day soon after, the British would march upon the countryside. There would be the grenadiers; the light-infantry; Fletcher. She closed her eyes. There would be other men; brave men, such as Jack. A possibility of violence. A danger of war, begun. Light-infantry, at moonrise. Tomorrow, or the next day, light-infantry, to the fore; and Fletcher. To Concord? The militia, armed, and waiting, to disperse, or stand. Men like Jack would stand, tomorrow; and Fletcher . . .

"Mrs. Ashley, I must be on my way. I thank you, for your hospitality. I shall not forget."

Recalling herself, Faith turned to Jack and took his hand, shaking it, as a man would do. Slightly surprised, Jack laughed, showing his large, white teeth, and brought the hand to his lips.

"Fare thee well, Jack Shoe," said Faith. "Godspeed."

"And Betsy," said Jack, spinning away, "I would have that kiss which you have denied me. To bear in my heart, as a memory, and a device against harm. Come, my Elizabeth, and kiss me."

For a moment, Faith gazed at the sight of their two blonde heads together, so suited and nearly matched, one large and the other oval and narrow beneath a white pinner. And then she sighed, long and shuddering, and turned away.

She did not turn back until she heard the door quietly close.

"Will he make it, tonight?" asked Elizabeth. "They are closing all the ways."

Faith stared at the girl's drawn expression, at the sad, shadowed eyes, the quivering lip. Her cheeks were blotched with the efforts of her sobbing. Even the fair skin above her bodice was patched with pink discoloration, like a rash. She could very easily cause herself to become ill, Faith realized, if any more worry fell upon her.

"He will," said Faith, attempting to sound convincing, when she was not certain of it herself. "Not all ways are closed."

The girl fell upon her, then, sobbing dryly, as if all her tears had been spent. With an arm about her shoulders, Faith led her out of the dark kitchen, and up the stairs, to bed. Urging her to lie down, she smoothed the hair from her brow, and wiped at the trailing moisture from her eyes.

"Sleep," she said. "You have exhausted yourself, Elizabeth. Sleep, and it will all seem better come the morning." She felt the girl shiver beneath her hand, and wondered, as did Elizabeth, if it would all seem better in the morning, or far, far worse. Taking the coverlet, she drew it up over the girl's shoulders, and rose from the mattress, turning away. At the door, she looked back. Elizabeth's eyes were closed. She was breathing, evenly, with just a small, shuddering sob breaking the peaceful sound every so often.

"I must go out, soon, but I will not be gone long," Faith whispered, half hoping that she would not be heard. But Elizabeth stirred, lifting her swollen lids sleepily.

"Where?"

Faith shook her head. "Nowhere," she said. "Do not ask."

"Mrs. Ashley?"

"Yes, Elizabeth?"

"I hate them redcoats. They might kill my poor Jack. I hate them, God forgive me. As much as you do."

For a full minute, Faith was silent. When she moved, nearer

into the room, she realized that Elizabeth had drifted off to sleep.

"No, Elizabeth," she whispered. "Not all of them."

Chapter Seventeen

Faith slipped quietly through the town, avoiding the groups of soldiers who were marching, with as little noise as possible, to the Common. The moon was on the rise, just peering above the treetops and the black shadows of the buildings, creating a nimbus in the night sky. Faith's heart pounded furiously in her breast. She clutched her shawl tightly, covering both her shoulders and her head, concealing the brightness of her hair and the cap she still wore. The night was sweet and warm.

Onward, she went; quickly; striving to reach the Common before the soldiers made whatever move had been planned, and she missed them altogether. She could not help but recall the boats, straining at their moors since Easter morning. Some had said it was merely a ruse, to confuse the rebels. Lifting her skirt above her knee, knowing that no one, in the dark, could see, Faith hurried along, stumbling over cracks and un- seen obstructions. She had not changed her shoes, though she should have, for ease of walking, and soon they began to pain her. In the torment of a twisted ankle, one heel broke loose. She paused, to break the other, to restore balance, and slipped both heels into the pocket at her waist. The soldiers were on every street, moving in both small and large groups, but always with stealth to their destination. And it was only a picked group of men, for Faith passed many an unshuttered window, viewing inside the officers and soldiers that had been billeted upon the private homes of Boston's citizens, as they were sitting down to cards, and drink, and other unhealthy activity.

Abruptly, she came upon a dozen soldiers, directly on the street before her. The pavement shimmered in the damp moonlight beneath their boots, where a light mist had fallen at twilight. Their breeches were like snow under a winter sky; their jackets subdued. Every button gleamed with polishing, as did every buckle. Thinking quickly, Faith stepped out of the street, in search of a place to keep clear of their passage. But all the homes on that street met with the gutter, providing no sidewalk or doorstone that was not in plain view. Quietly marching feet brought the soldiers nearer. Faith turned around to meet them. She set her face into lines of impassivity, to avoid suspicion. The clapboard of a darkened home was cold against her spine.

"Will you look at this now, eh?"

A British regular, younger than Faith, paused in the street. He reached an arm out to bring one of his companions to an abrupt halt, then turned his hand to more pleasurable pursuits, touching Faith's shawl, fingering the edges of it, then the sleeve beneath.

"Come to see us off, 'ave ye?" he said. "A pretty 'un, too, Billy, wouldn't you suppose?"

"Dunno," said the other. "Can't see 'er."

"Let's arrange it so's we can get a good look," said the first, readying to pull the shawl from about Faith's head.

Faith found the solid wall unwilling to give against pressure, and the turn of her head insufficient to warn the boy off. "Where is your superior?" she demanded.

"Up a'ead, somewhere," said the soldier. "'e don't know we stopped, ya see?" He turned to his companion. "'as to be an alley roundabouts, eh? We'll duck in, and—"

"If I scream loud enough," said Faith, "he will know exactly where you are, I am certain. And these homes are not unoccupied, if you have not noticed, boy. Some actually contain officers who might not look kindly upon the molestation of a lady."

"What'd she say, Billy? Don't think I cared for it, though." With a grunt, he shoved at her shoulder. "Don't matter, any'ow. 'aven't got the time to lift yer skirts—milady. The moon's up."

And with stifled laughter, they went on.

Faith let out her breath in a rush. Her hands were shaking. Pushing away from the house, she ran, following close behind the soldiers. Theirs would be the quickest route, if she could keep up with them yet avoid another confrontation.

Hearing another burst of low laughter, muffled by distance, she wondered in earnest how Fletcher could be one with these men. As they hurried through the night, late to their destination, there seemed nothing gentle about them, nor even strong, but merely a desire to meet with their enemy, to bear arms, to do harm. Fletcher was not like that. He was not such a man. Or was he? When the call came to arms, to the obligation of battle, was he?

In time, she was surrounded, left and right, by soldiers filing through the streets that led onto the Common. There were fewer houses, and only the shadows of trees kept Faith's presence hidden from probing eyes. Hundreds of men dressed in scarlet and black and white, converged on the expanse of field and tree and trampled ground where already thousands had been encamped. Hundreds of men, soldiers, fully equipped for war, were making their way down to the riverside. Faith felt her heart sink into her stomach.

There came a point where she could go no farther, and she halted, beneath the spreading boughs of an oak tree. She leaned against the rough bark with both hands, pressing her forehead to the backs of her fingers, feeling the ridge of knuckle as a comfort. She felt expended of energy, and the tramping of feet, the vast shuffling of heavy boots over the earth, rushed with the blood through her ears.

Hundreds of soldiers, gathered on the bank of the Charles, beneath the moonlight. Faith could see them, silent and distant, mannequins embarking into toy boats, and rowing across the river. The water rippled, silver and black, reflecting the cold beacon of the moon. An unnerving sight it was, taken together with the unearthly tension that had been mounting. Observing the scene, Faith attempted to count their number, to read the regimental marking that might signify Fletcher's presence among them. But that much refused to reveal itself in the moon's chilly radiance. As if purposely, the men were turned from her eyes, and none came near enough that she could step ahead to view the numbers of their buckles and headgear.

She saw, however, that other townsfolk were about, standing along the roads and beneath the night sky, not caring if they were seen. There was no longer any secret to the soldiers' movements, if ever there had been. The last hundred or so men were on shore, waiting, showing a sullen, ugliness of mood.

"The lights are burning in Cambridge. They are marching that way," she heard someone say.

"From there, to Concord, I'd speculate."

"And with good reason. The largest public stores of arms are held there; the nasty beggers are after 'em."

"How many, do you reckon?"

"In the boats? Seven, eight hundred? What do you think?"

The speculation continued. Faith lent half an ear to the conversation along the barricade, where men had gathered. Beneath the shadow of the hoary oak, she was alone. She gazed down to the shoreline until her eyes hurt, watching as the last men boarded, preparing to row to the other side. In a sudden stillness, she heard the splash and suck of the oars, even at that distance, and the hoarse orders, called from one boat to another. Eventually, there was nothing to be seen of the boats upon the river but faint movement, over the lapping, silvered water, and then they were gone. Even the voices faded, held close, in stealth. They were on their way to Lexington, to Concord, where the Minute Men awaited them bravely.

Faith bowed her head in prayer.

Very quickly, she raised it again, alerted by a sound nearby. She turned, and stopped, seeing that several men had gathered near, and that one was speaking in a dark, angered voice of the march of the redcoats.

"I have had enough," he said. "I declare myself tonight a patriot, though I find myself condemned by those other men with whom I am acquainted. I find myself, gentlemen, converted to your cause."

Faith folded the shawl from her face, moved by the man's declaration. It should be so, with all of us, she thought, and stepped forward, pausing just beyond the shadow of the oak. The moon's light touched her skin, making it fairer, even, than by day, and bleached the color from her eyes, so that they only hinted at the green of summer, and suggested more the spring beneath the ice. She opened her mouth, to speak out to those men, but no sound issued. She had seen something move, beneath the darkness of the oak's overhanging branches, a shadow within the shadows. Though she made no offer to scream, the tall figure detached itself from the blackness with startling swiftness, and took hold of her, covering her mouth to stifle both breath, and sound.

"Faith, Faith," whispered a voice against her struggling, "do not be frightened. Keep still," it said, and released the grip across her mouth.

"Fletcher!" gasped Faith, drawing away. She looked up at him, but his features were hidden from her view. "Fletcher, what are you doing here? I thought that you had—"

"Hush," he said. "Faith, I followed you, from your home. I saw you leave it. Prior to that, I had planned to come to you, to exchange a few words with you, nothing more. However, when I saw you slip away, I decided otherwise. I . . . I wanted to know where you were going. I lost you, once or twice," he went on, "but I suspected, in time, your direction. You were searching for me, were you not?"

"Yes," said Faith, quietly.

"You thought that I was leaving tonight, didn't you?"

"Yes," she said again, and her voice broke. She saw his hand come up, and drop.

"Allay your fears, dear heart," he said, "we have not been called. Still, that is no cause for rejoicing. Tomorrow . . . ah, tomorrow, there will be trouble enough, with those who have gone and your countrymen."

"Fletcher," Faith whispered, clinging to the endearment with which he had addressed her, "had you been called upon to leave this night, would you have gone without word?"

"No," he said, after a minute silence, "no. Oh, my love," and he stepped nearer, lifting a hand to stroke her hair, pale beneath the moon. "I am sorry that we fought. It was vicious, and unthinking, and we have lost two weeks of precious time in our anger. What is done, is done, and may not be altered now.''

Faith turned her cheek into his hand, and held it there. It was a warm and welcomed fit. She brought her own hand to cover his, then, and kissed his palm, and his wrist, above his scarlet sleeve.

Fletcher made a noise, in his chest.

''Come with me,'' he said.

The smell of the hay was sweet, but it gave off dust that floated in the air and irritated the nose. Faith sneezed, once. The crickets beneath her head ceased to chirp.

She turned her eyes to the stall nearby, where a placid-looking beast gazed down over the box at her, blinking with lashes like a woman's. The horse had small ears, Faith noticed; it was as small as a pony, and just as curious. Bits of straw hung from its mouth and clung to the long mane. She could not see the body beyond the sleek and beautiful head, but the roof above was planked, and dripping with moss. Faith sat up, brushing hay from her bodice and skirt. The crickets hushed again.

On a hook near the door, the lantern hung, a rusted one, with little oil, so that it burned with wavering light. He had hung it there, before he had slipped out, into the night. He was troubled, Faith knew. His lovemaking had been particularly volatile, and brief as if some subtle fury drove him more than anything else. But he was no longer angry with her; he had said so, and she believed him.

Shaking the straw from her unbound hair, Faith opened the barn door, pulling at it with no small show of strength. Slipping through a crack not wider than her own body, she stepped outside, forcing the door shut again, so that no light showed beyond the building. Once there, she stood a moment, poised and listening, as a deer does before flight.

In the soft breeze, the foliage rustled in whispers, driving the apple blossoms from the trees to flutter, small and white, over the long grass. The air carried a scent of woodsmoke that stung her eyes. Inside the barn, the horse was moving about, thumping its shod hooves over the stall floor. There were crickets in the grass and in the hay, and there were other insects, whose soft wings brushed across her cheek. She listened beyond them, for another sound, and heard it, the cadence of Fletcher's breathing, steady and deep.

Moving through the star emblazoned darkness, with the moon webbed in the branches of a twisted crab apple, Faith found him, leaning against the barn wall, his arms at his sides, and his head tilted back, staring upward at the night sky. She touched his hand, and he moved as if awakening, taking her into his embrace.

"Faith," he said.

He straightened, then, to walk with her a little distance beneath the trees. His arm was about her shoulders.

"Did I hurt you?" he asked, after a silence.

"No," Faith whispered.

"I am sorry if I did, my love. It was not my intent."

"I know."

He was silent again. Together, they came into a clear place, where the moon shone down in full, revealing her love in his hated uniform from the waist down, though above, he wore only his jacket to cover his nakedness. Turning her about, he put his hands in her hair, then suddenly laughed, shaking the length of it through his fingers.

"Your hair is full of straw! It will take hours to remove it all."

"More time than we have, I suppose," said Faith.

Fletcher glanced up at the sky. "Yes," he agreed. "More time than we have." He pulled her close against his chest. Faith felt the rise and fall of his respiration beneath her cheek. His flesh was warm, the hair upon it damp.

"Faith," he said, "look at the stars. How often have we had the opportunity to stand in the open under the stars, to gaze up, in wonder, in each other's arms?"

Tipping her chin, Faith gazed up into the sky. The stars were bright and softly focused, scattered across the black dome of the earth. "Never," she said.

"Once," said Fletcher.

"No," said Faith. "It was not night; not a night, such as this."

He kissed the top of her head, allowing his hand to roam down her bodice to her waist. Her stays were loosened, and he slipped his hand beneath, touching her ribs through the material of her chemise. "I came upon you, on the Common, as you went into hiding beneath the old oak tree. I stood there, in that shadow with you, and you never noticed that I was near. Not once did you turn, instead you kept your eyes steady on the embarkment, and I knew why you had come. Yet, I would have gone away, for it had come upon me that it would be better, until the trouble was passed, if contact between us remained broken. Better, if I never spoke to you again, never looked upon you again, never . . . touched . . ." Here, he drew a haggard breath, and withdrew his hand. "I don't know what happened to me, my love. Suffice it to say that when you turned your head about, looking over your shoulder with the moon on your face, in your hair, in your eyes, I felt my heart would break from the sight of you. Am I being, as you once expressed it, melodramatic? I thought you would scream when you saw me move."

"I had no intention of doing so, no," said Faith.

Above her head, Fletcher smiled.

"Do not blame me for what followed, Faith," he said. "Or, perhaps, you should. I am a man, and responsible for my actions. And this barn," he said, gesturing, "this barn was the nearest, available place. I wanted to make love to you again so badly that I did not care. But I have compromised you, and I am sorry."

Faith pulled back from him. She rose up onto her tiptoes, smoothing the black hair from his brow and around his face, then slid her hands beneath his scarlet coat. "Do not be," she said, grasping the front of his breeches between her thumb and forefinger. She tugged on the stiff cloth. "I would have you, any place. And weep with joy."

His smoky eyes darkened, in grief, it seemed, and his brows lowered. There was a scar of old pain in the expression. Tenderly, he kissed her eyes, her lips, and then felt the tip of her tongue inside his mouth. He pulled her close, and close again, searching with his fingers for the gauzy rent that he knew he had made in the chemise, and slipped his hand inside, opening it over her naked skin.

"Come inside," said Faith, in throaty suggestion.

Fletcher stood back, holding her at arm's length.

"You are a passionate creature," he said.

"Always."

She ran, then, lightly, on bare feet. For a moment, he stared after her, suppressing the laughter that rolled to his lips. Following in pursuit, he caught her up outside of the barn and lifted her in his arms, shouldering the door aside. Faith blew softly on the lamp as they passed.

Fletcher's low chuckle rumbled through the darkness.

"Faith, you are a darling tease," he said huskily. "Come, kiss me again."

But she merely laughed, and skipped behind him, catching the edge of his jacket as she went.

"Take it off."

Wordlessly, he slipped out of it, and felt her snatch it away from his hands, into the shadows. Beside him, the horse thumped in its stall, and snorted sweet breath into the air.

"Faith," Fletcher called, without moving, "where are you now?"

"Your shoes," he heard her say, quietly, "and your stockings."

Still chuckling, he did as was bade him, allowing the removal of both from his grasp. Her fingers touched the skin of his forearm, lightly, as she backed away, then trailed across his naked back. His laughter faded. "My love," he whispered; and her empty hands came across his abdomen from behind, tugging gently on his breeches. Slowly, with tormenting leisure, she rolled them down, and down, until she was kneeling beside him, unfastening the buttons at the knees, and they were off, cast away into the darkness. Her mouth was warm on his flesh.

"Faith," he said, and stopped, as the peak of sensation ran hot into his blood. He made a noise, a word, without form, deep in his chest. His eyes closed. "Faith, no," he said, and reached for her. She stood, her skirt rustling across the straw as she rose. "I have not the strength to resist," he said. "You bewitch me."

"Unfasten me," said Faith, and took his hands, guiding them to the closures on her bodice, and on her skirt. He would have removed her clothing, but she would not permit it, and stepped away, out of arm's reach, to perform the task herself. In the blackness, he was guided only by sound, and he listened, with closed eyes, to the fall of her garments. In time, he knew that she stood naked before him, beyond his touch, yet near enough that he could smell the sweetness of her hair, and the perfume of her skin.

"I love you, Fletcher," she said.

Faith felt the brush of his fingers, across her collarbone, and then onto her shoulder, and up beneath her chin. Bending, he put his mouth over her own, kissing her with an odd restraint.

"What," he said, against the side of her throat, "will you have me do, now, my heart?"

"Take me in your arms," Faith answered.

"Thusly?"

"Yes," said Faith, "yes," as he embraced her, and the warmth of his flesh touched her own. She pressed closer, and for a long moment they stood only like that, swaying slightly in the colorless night. She felt his lips moving across her hair, her brow, seeking her mouth, where he lingered. His hands opened across her hips, and she was aware of the strength of them, as she had been the first time that he had touched her, that he had taken her hand, and would not release it . . . as he would not release her now, his mouth on her own, holding her, in his hands, as he sank down slowly to the floor, causing her to follow.

They knelt, facing each other. His breath was warm against her throat, his teeth gentle on her shoulder. He circled her breast with tiny kisses, teasingly, until her head dropped back on her shoulders in delicious anticipation. Her hair brushed the floor and cascaded across the soles of her feet. She pulled away from him, to lie down.

"No," he said, still kneeling. "No, my love. Come, and I will support you. In my arms, you are without weight, and I want only to have you before me, beneath my touch." And he lifted her, across his legs, pushing deep, and deep again, many times, as his arms held her close and he felt hers about his neck; he adored the height of her responses, the wondrous sensation of trembling warmth, the small sounds she made; he marvelled at the power and strength of the calling of his name, when uttered from her lips. Robbing him of breath, of restraint, until his voice intermingled with her own, rich and dark, and was stilled, in the end, by a kiss long and sweet.

"You are my one love," said Faith, toying with the brass buttons on Fletcher's jacket. In the darkness, it did not appear so red, nor so hateful. "You are not my enemy, Fletcher, and it was cruel of me ever to speak so to you. When I hold you in my arms, you are my life, my soul's desire. Could I ever have known you as any other?"

Fletcher grunted, eyes closed, reveling in the touch of Faith's fingers across his chest, curling in the dark hair.

"Ah, Fletcher," said Faith, "shall we make a pact never to be so heartless again?"

"Pacts," murmured Fletcher, running his hand along Faith's spine and over the roundness of her hips, "are for children. Adults argue, and go on. But cruelty; cruelty is another thing, entirely. I shall never be cruel to you again."

"Nor I you, Fletcher."

"Do you think we will manage to keep that promise?"

"Possibly not," said Faith, and collapsed across Fletcher's abdomen. But shortly, she was clinging to him, breathless with the force of her emotion. He gathered her into his arms, and held her there; neither of them spoke, yet all that was unsaid was made clear in the silence. Through the slight crack in the door, the last of the night was gleaming, making a fine, pale line across the hay-strewn floor. In the stall, the horse was sleeping, legs locked, its head hanging over the stout gate.

"I must see you home, Faith. Let me help you dress."

"No," said Faith. "Do not help me. We would be here for three days, and what would the rider of that horse have to say, if he were to come in upon us?"

"Would you care to find out?"

"Oh, no!" cried Faith, rolling away from him. "Only help me to find my clothing, and I shall put it on, thank you!"

It was joy, to find herself with him again, anger forgotten, all sorrows in temporary abeyance. And this night was possibly the most perfect of all, like an island of peace, inspiring forgetfulness and forgiveness.

Yet, as they parted, in an hour's time, Fletcher looked unmistakably grim. He touched Faith's hair with his palm.

"I cannot know when I will see you," he said.

"Soon," Faith answered.

Fletcher shook his head. "Not soon," he said. "Though I will try." He spoke the statement like a dire prediction, solemn and matter-of-fact. Faith felt a chill course along her spine. She took his hand, and squeezed it.

"Soon," she said again.

Catching the drift of her nervousness, he kissed her, soundly, almost desperately, taking her up in his arms so that she was nearly off her feet.

"Yes, soon," he agreed, "God willing."

Faith stood in the open doorway, the scent of the bread and stew still lingering after so many hours, and watched as Fletcher glided away into the dark hour that preceded the dawn. Tonight had been a reprieve, she knew, from the fear that had so overwhelmed her before when she witnessed Elizabeth and Jack parting. Once again, the insinuative phrase of the evening made itself heard, within her ear, echoing in many voices, recalling the fear tenfold. She had seen the truth of it, in the town, and in Fletcher's eyes and in the words that he had not spoken. War. It would come soon. If not tomorrow, then the next day, or one day soon after.

Chapter Eighteen

That Wednesday dawned bright and clear and windless. Not a breeze drifted from the mainland, to carry the sound of bells to Boston's straining ears, ringing out in warning from town to town, bearing testimony to the British march to Concord. Major Pitcairn's cry of "Disperse, ye rebels . . . Lay down your arms!" was no more than an echo shattering the misted peace about Lexington's Village Green as the militia stood, bravely facing the columns of British regulars across the expanse of dew-laden grass. Boys and men faced the glint, in the rising sun, of fixed bayones, of the eyes behind them which looked black, and polished: the bore of British muskets. Scarcely trained men were pitted against those who had drilled, day after day, in preparation for just such a moment.

Defending the splintered tranquility of the lives they had known, the Minute Men stood firm upon Lexington's Green, and would not lay down their arms.

The first shot was fired. War was begun.

"Elizabeth, are you certain?"

Quickly, Faith tipped the pitcher of scented water over her hair, and stood up, wrapping her head in the damp towel. The last of the straw had been difficult to remove, even with a brush, and wisps of it were floating amidst the bubbles in the basin.

"I seen it for myself, Mrs. Ashley, when I went out hopin' for news of my Jack. To be sure he ain't been caught, you understand. And I come upon 'em, plain as you are before me, a whip-tail end, marching around the corner. I followed for a bit, wondering what they were all about, with such purpose—more than usual, I mean—"

"Elizabeth," interrupted Faith. "Please. Tell me one thing: whose men were they?"

"I ain't sure," the girl confessed, disappointed. "Marines, is all I know. And late, too, from what I could tell, for there was a great deal of grumblin' about that. Lobsterbacks are all the same to my eye. But they were meeting on the Common. I didn't go that far, but came back here to tell the news to you. You said I was to keep my eyes open, whenever I went out." The last was uttered defensively.

"Oh, yes, Elizabeth. Especially this morning! You did well, very well," she hastened to commend her, patting soaked red locks with the edges of the towel. She shrugged her bodice over her damp undergarment. "I will comb my hair, and then together we shall see what, if anything, this is about."

In the streets, however, Faith saw immediately that the girl had been correct in her assumption that something was amiss. Groups of Boston's citizens were knotting in debate, neglecting their day's work as if Sunday had come upon them unawares. There was much speculation wherever men gathered, wondering at the latest signs of activity. Faith hurried Elizabeth along, following the curious who moved silently to the Common.

"What do you think it is?" asked Elizabeth, in a breathless whisper. "Is it war, come upon us at last?"

"Oh, do hush, Elizabeth," begged Faith, and increased their pace.

There had been no official word of war, but it was possible that no one, as yet, bore that knowledge, thought Faith. Why, then, was there the mustering of soldiers? Shaking her damp head, she banished Elizabeth's questing. The sudden activity could mean anything; and that was the point: it could mean anything at all.

Faith walked swiftly, despite the ache in her legs from the previous night when her heels had been broken. Elizabeth paused behind her several times to ask after the men who had attempted to leave Boston before the soldiers, before moonrise.

"You must be careful," warned Faith, more than once. "Not everyone to whom you speak is a Whig. There are Loyalists here; more than there were. Many have fled to our town, to seek the protection of the British."

Chastised, Elizabeth nodded her head.

Schools and shops were closing. Children capered in the streets, while their mothers chastened them to keep still and come indoors. Faith felt the hair along her arms rise as she heard that five hundred of the marines billeted around North Square had, indeed, marched in quick pace toward the Common. They were joining the soldiers waiting on them since shortly after sunrise.

Faith took Elizabeth's hand. "Do not leave go," she said.

They found themselves too quickly at the tail end of the long rank of soldiers that twisted to the contour of the street, and ended, they were told, upon the Common itself.

"How many men?" asked Faith.

"Twelve hundred, at a guess," was the reply.

Clutching Elizabeth's hand, Faith looked out over the scarlet tide of soldiers. She saw artillery equipment, and the stocky horses that would draw the wagons harnessed to their burden. Every man shouldered a musket, affixed with a bayonet that mirrored the sun. Every cartridge box appeared full. These were not men engaging in an exercise. It has come, she thought. It has come.

All about her, camp-women were crying, bidding their loved ones farewell. Beside her, Elizabeth condemned them with unthinking disgust. Faith moved on, dragging the girl with her. And then she came to a halt. There was no need to go further. Lord Percy was there, slim and haughty astride his snow white mount, but it was not really he that Faith had been seeking. Only the affirmation that these were his men, standing beneath the still, open sky, with their perfect weapons, their military stance, and their readiness to fight, to endure, to follow their battle training, to kill all enemies of their rightful sovereign. Faith remembered the day when she had delivered the shot to Roxbury, and she shuddered. They had been farmers, and members of the militia, without military training, with ancient, inefficient weapons, fowling pieces, a blunderbuss or two. God help them, she thought. God help us all. We thought to stand firm, but perhaps we are fools.

Faith turned and saw the fluid, flashing arc of Lord Percy's sword in the air. The drums began a brittle rolling as the shouted, distorted orders flew from mouth to mouth. The horses of the cannon leapt against the solid harness, dragging the heavy burden forward, straining, until the wheels of the wagons began to roll. The soldiers lifted their feet, a conditioned response to the drummer's call, first with uneven tramp, and then in synchronous rhythm. The earth trembled to their fall.

On the breath of a breeze, the flag of England fluttered out.

Faith turned desperate eyes to the moving formation, searching, among the uniformity of the British army, for one man. She saw the mark of his regiment, without denial; she knew that he had been called. She looked at the uniforms, and thought how handsome Fletcher was in the cut of his own, and how she hated the sight of it.

Faith stood, silently bidding her love Godspeed, while guilt at such a betrayal, of her fellow, untrained patriots consumed her.

Long after the dust of the soldiers passing had settled, Faith stood alone on the cobbled street. She had not distinguished Fletcher in the crowd. Among the handful of mounted officers riding flank to Lord Percy, there had been several lieutenants. Faith would have expected Fletcher's place to be there, but the officers had ridden to the fore, at a slow and stately pace, and she had not seen him.

Dazed, she turned her head, looking for Elizabeth. The girl had wandered down the street, doubtless to make further inquiries after the Frenchmen. Faith had heard that the French were fierce fighters. It was said that fighting was in their blood.

Closing her eyes, Faith tilted her chin to the sun. She wiped the dust from her face; the air and sun warm on her eyelids. A weak and intermittent breeze wafted the scent of woodsmoke; of green, living things; of the river, fresh and sharp; of horse dung, on the street; and human sweat, still lingering where the soldiers had been. The crows cawed in the trees. Once, she had been wary of them, for her mother had told tales of crows as the harbingers of death. But they were always there, as was death, and she had ceased to fear them.

"Elizabeth! I am for home, now. Are you coming?"

"One moment, Mrs. Ashley."

Sighing, Faith shook the dust from the hem of her skirt and petticoat, then brushed it from her bosom. It clung to her damp hair tenaciously, like a fine spray. Everyone else looked as disheveled and as wary as she. Across the broad expanse of the Common, the encamped soldiers remaining of Percy's First Brigade watched them with sullen eyes.

"Elizabeth . . ."

"Coming, Mrs. Ashley!"

Returning much as they had come, Faith noticed that shops were still closed, the children still cavorting in the streets, chanting in singsong voices of the day's events. The soldiers they met here were not as churlish as those who had been left on the Common, instead they were inclined to good humor or to a swaggering conceit that suggested they held expectations of the upper hand against the rebels in the countryside. At the sight of their confidence, Faith felt a growing sickness in the pit of her stomach.

"I had news of Jack," said Elizabeth at last, in a loud whisper. Faith paused, turning to look at her, wondering how she had managed to contain herself for so long during her own silence.

"And?" she prompted. "Is he safe, Elizabeth?"

Elizabeth nodded her head vigorously. "I reckon so. He got out, anyways. If he made it to his friends, then he is ready, right now, to stand with 'em and fight."

"If they are fighting," said Faith.

"What do you mean?" cried Elizabeth, forgetting herself. "'Course they are. You don't mean to say they would run away, do you?"

"No, Elizabeth, no. That is not what I am saying, at all. But you must remember: They are up against the British army, which is fully prepared to meet them. This morning, on the Green at Lexington, there could not have been more than one hundred men. Last night, Elizabeth, six or seven hundred of the army's fiercest fighters slipped across the river to march toward them. I am not saying that Jack was among those at Lexington, Elizabeth. He could not have made it there so soon. Indeed, I pray that he did not.''

Elizabeth was frowning. A spark of fire was in her eye, darker now than even the sky on that morning. ''Are you sayin' they should run?'' she insisted.

Faith shook her head. ''No. I do not know what I am saying, exactly. But I am worried.''

She turned away, then, in wonder at the change in Elizabeth. Only hours before she had been weeping in fear and sorrow over Jack's departure; now, she wanted nothing more than for him to fight, and there was pride in that desire, a pride that once had been hers. It still was, but she had seen something more today in the march of those soldiers. She had known the departure of one whom she loved more than life itself, and her heart was torn both ways.

In the street of her home, standing beside the well, she saw Rachel Revere, in her arms was her babe, grown fat and pleasant. As soon as the silversmith's wife caught sight of Faith, she came forward. There was no gentleness in her eyes.

''He got away,'' she said, ''last night. Rowed across beneath the very bow of the Somerset, God bless him!'' She laughed with a touch of hysteria, then took control of herself once again. ''He alerted the countryside. The militia were waiting at Lexington when dawn came.'' Then the reason for the bitter sadness in her eyes was revealed. ''But the British fired right through them, and went on. On, to Concord.''

''Oh, Rachel,'' breathed Faith, eyes closing. She heard Elizabeth stir, and lifted her lids, glancing sidelong at the girl, whose face had paled and was ashen.

''H-how many,'' she stammered, ''h-how many were—''

''I don't know, Elizabeth,'' said Rachel. ''But there were men killed. Here in Boston, the soldiers and the officers are trying to convince the people that nothing has happened, that not a shot has been fired, but it just is not true. Believe me, it is not true.'' Faith put her arm about the woman's neck, and for a moment they clung together, the baby balanced on Rachel's hip. Elizabeth stood, transfixed.

"How it goes now, I do not know," Rachel added as they parted, "though as the day passes, I am certain we shall discover."

Faith nodded. She thought of Fletcher, of the troops, equipped and trained beneath him; she thought of the men of Lexington, and the others, waiting.

"The Lord help us, now," she said. Shivering, she turned her gaze toward the west, toward the mainland, unseen beyond roof peaks and church spires. Birds dipped in the cloudless blue sky, as did the ever-present gulls, which cried like babes. Woodsmoke, dark and curling, drifted up and up, thinning far above Boston's brick chimneys as its women began preparing for the hearty midday meal.

For an instant, Faith visualized an officer, handsome, virile, passionate, and warm, giving whatever orders were necessary to impel the men beneath him into battle; wielding his own saber; observing the routing of his enemies, the wounding of her countrymen, the death of liberty's hope.

She turned her head again, lifting it to the sky. There was an ache in her that seemed to rend her soul. Beside her, both Rachel and Elizabeth were uttering prayerful whispers. She did not pray; she no longer knew what to pray for.

Fletcher removed his headgear, holding it in his hand as he swept his sleeve across his sweating brow. With the other hand, he reined his horse about, sharply, so that the beast canted onto its rear legs for a step or two, and then down, with an angry stamp. He looked along the road that they had come in retreat, lined with soldiers, haggard and on edge, moving without military formation or restraint, back toward Charlestown. His men walked with their eyes scanning everywhere as they attempted to discern from what point the next attack would appear. Puffs of smoke from the trees, beyond the rock wall that edged the road, were accompanied by the explosion of gunfire. Some men were being ordered to leap the wall, in pursuit of the rebels, but Fletcher would not permit his men to do so. It was dangerous: the militia, the farmers, even the boys who hunted rabbit in the fields, were more familiar with the characteristics of the surrounding landscape. Countless British soldiers had been wounded already. Many were dying, or dead. The rebels fought without order, without the restriction of regulated warfare; they attacked from any vantage point, under cover of tree or rock or barn. At Concord, they had turned back the British army, freeing the town from Colonel Smith's foothold—a town lacking in ammunition, for the depot had been emptied long before the British arrived—and forced the colonel's troops into retreat to Lexington. Here, Percy had met Smith outside of Munroe Tavern with the reserve troops, but to no avail. Neither they, nor the cannon, blasting houses to ruin and barns to rubble, could deter the rebel numbers. In their fervor for the course of liberty they held so dear, they were beating the best-trained soldiers in the world.

We are, as the locals would have it, being licked, quite soundly, thought Fletcher with a wry and bitter twist to his lips. He shook his head, urging his men to stay in formation and remain calm. The last thing he wanted was a headlong flight, uncontrolled, along a road where ambush lay at every point that offered concealment. His first responsibility was to his men, to their safety.

Surrender, as the thirty-three year old Lord Earl Percy had stated, was simply out of the question. But, considering the growing danger of their position, a hasty retreat was not. They would go to Charlestown, where they would be under the protection of the *Somerset*'s guns in the mouth of the Charles. Fletcher had concurred.

There was no longer any room, or time, for the application of cannon. But they could not be left to fall into the hands of the rebels, and so the lathered, heaving horses lumbered onward, dragging the huge weight of the iron weapons. The baggage wagons were utilized for the transport of wounded soldiers, who were bandaged and bleeding, and suppressing any cry of pain at being jolted along on the rutted, mucked roads. The dead were left where they fell, their souls committed to God, silent, free from pain and fear.

The rebels seemed to be staying ahead of them along the entire length of the tortuous road. They urged the British on with musket fire from behind. It was an unearthly sound, preying on the men's nerves. Many of them, developed for rigors of war, were becoming weary, and they panicked. Fletcher spoke to them, his head low over his horse in the flash of powder, urging them onward. Above the road, the smoke was heavy, like a pall, gray, dimming the sun. Fletcher remained astride his mount, feeling the quiver of its flesh beneath the saddle, yet he knew the animal would not falter, or bolt; such had been its training.

"Irons!"

Fletcher's head whipped around. Running along the lines, dodging between the regulars of the infantry, was Lieutenant Upton. His young face was flushed, his brown eyes feverish. He stopped, up against Fletcher's bootstrap.

"Why aren't you with your men, Brian?" shouted Fletcher, above the din. "Where is your horse?"

"Shot out from under me," explained Upton, breathless. "Not the men—my horse. They're trying to pick off the officers, out there."

"That's the first thing they've done that makes military sense," said Fletcher.

"You're a sitting duck up there, Fletcher. Get down, for God's sake."

The older lieutenant shook his head, slowly. An explosion rent the air nearby. He could smell the sulfurous reek of powder. "I will be where my men can see me, Brian. I owe them that much. I must get them out of this."

"For God's sake, Fletcher, you are no more than target practice."

"Where is old Percy?" asked Fletcher, bending low. "Old" was as a joke between them. The earl was not much older than he, himself.

"On that white charger of his, of course. But—damn it, you've made your point!" Brian pulled away from the horse's flank. "Don't get yourself killed."

"I am trying not to allow any of us to be killed."

"How much longer, do you think?"

"Of this? Until their powder holds, I suppose."

"No, the road man, the road. I cannot judge the distance any longer. How much farther?"

Shielding his eyes, Fletcher gazed along the road, but could see no familiar landmarks through the smoky haze. All was in near chaos, as the harried red-coated soldiers retreated. It was not the sort of retreat that took place on an organized field, but one of madness. Fletcher shook his head, his blue-gray eyes dark. "I do not know."

"Sweet Lord, save us," whispered Brian, but Fletcher heard him, and patted his shoulder. Such had been the subtle changes in their relationship that he felt able to offer him that comfort, that touch among friends. He shook the younger man's shoulder affectionately. Suddenly, there was a commotion in the road ahead, directly among the ranks.

"What the devil is that?"

With something that resembled a salute to his friend, Fletcher spurred forward. The horse leapt over a fallen soldier.

"See to that man!" Fletcher shouted.

It was difficult now to tell where one regiment ended and the next began. Fletcher reined in behind a quarreling, shoving knot of soldiers, ordering them to part. Two, one of his own regiment, the other a footsoldier, had, under impossible reasoning, come to blows and were rolling, cursing, in the rutted, muddy road.

"Enough!" he shouted. "I don't want to know what this is about, I only want the two of you on your feet, immediately. You are endangering the lives of every man here. You, and you, pick up their weapons. Keep moving. The rebels are on your heels, men. You know that, by now. Keep moving."

As he uttered this last, something came plummeting down from the sky; he lifted his head, in time to witness a black male duck, blue-and-buff wings like the planes of a board, sailing across the space before him, to land, with a rolling thump of feet, on the grass beside the road. All eyes turned as did his, to see the duck rise, and waddle off, as though nothing more natural were expected of it in the midst of battle. It was a comical sight, telling of saner times, and Fletcher twisted in his creaking saddle, wondering if Upton had seen it too.

He saw Brian's look of dismayed horror, too late, it seemed, for already the reek of powder was in Fletcher's nose, burning; and pain exploded in his brain with a flash of light so bright it blinded. Fairfax, his faithful, well-taught mount, reared up onto his hind legs.

He knew no more.

Chapter Nineteen

As night fell, the ferry slip of North Boston was aglow with the tossing flare of torches and swinging lanterns as the boats were rowed across from Charlestown, bringing in the wounded British soldiers. In Charlestown itself, every house was well lit, for the people there were in fear of what might become of them when the remains of a beaten army, surly and exhausted, came into their midst. A goodly number of townspeople gathered in Boston near the wharf to witness the debarking of men, pale and in pain, some barely conscious. No civilian was permitted access to a closer point, save the physicians who had offered their services.

Faith stood at the mouth of a narrow dirt alley, shivering in her shawl as the renewed breeze blew off the water, assaulting her tired body, tugging the hair on her head, swirling it into her eyes so that she had to continually brush it away in order to keep a constant vigil over the soldiers being brought across. She could scarcely stand to look at them, with their flesh ashen with pain, their once-perfect uniforms slashed, sometimes to shreds, and bloodied. These were the proud and eager men who had stolen from Boston in the night. They were Colonel Smith's men, harried and besieged by the elusive militia for nearly twenty-four hours without ease. Lord Percy's men were also being rowed over, interspersed with the others, depending on the gravity of their wounds. Clasping her hands together, Faith leaned against the stone base of a warehouse, the cold of the rounded river-rock dampening her clothing.

We have beaten them, she thought, watching the sad parade of the soldiers who were capable of walking away from the boats moving toward the hospital. There was pride in that realization, and relief, but there was no rejoicing, for the suffering appeared too great.

Each time a boat came in without a full load, Faith would stiffen, for she had recognized the better treatment given officers, and she searched for Fletcher among them, praying, as she could not before when she had stood on the street with Elizabeth and Rachel Revere, that she would not see him there, knowing his absence would not necessarily mean that he was alive.

I would know, she kept telling herself; I would know, had he been killed.

We are beating them, Faith thought again, staring into the hollow eyes of a young private as he stumbled in her direction beneath the flaring torches, mistaking his way in his pain. She backed against the wall, hands flat, for there were two more soldiers, coming to fetch the first, and if she were seen she would surely be removed from such proximity. She had dared to come closer than most of the others; too close, if it came to that. If she were a man, she would likely receive the butt of a musket across her back, or even the side of her skull, for her daring.

"Aye, here comes another one! Only three on board! Officers! Step lively!"

Faith collected herself, stepping away from the wall. The breeze tugged the small hairs above the curve of her ears and flattened her dark skirt against her hips. As if in a lull, she heard the lapping of water against the undersides of the rowboat, then the groaning turn of the oars, the scrape of wood against wood as the boat was eased into the slip. Three officers were on board, their uniforms disheveled, even ravaged. With pity that surprised her, Faith observed the first man remove himself from the boat, half supported beneath one arm by a foot soldier on the shore. There came another behind him, dark-haired and dark-eyed, with a bandage around his head that was soaked with blood. The third, whose back was to her, was also dark-haired, leaning forward with his arms upon his knees. He, too, was bandaged about the head with a horizontal strip of gauze rather than vertical. Faith grimaced.

The sight of so much blood and agony was making her physically ill. Unable to stand any more, she turned her face away, leaning her forehead against the cool stone of the warehouse. Bile rose in her throat.

Suddenly, she swung back. They were helping the third man from the boat.

"Take care with the lieutenant," warned the second. "He's been shot through the leg, also."

She should have known him straightaway; but the breadth of his shoulder, the carriage of his head, and the height and strength of his masculine form that she had expected to recognize beneath the color of his uniform, had been transformed in the unrelenting grip of his suffering. Her hand flew to her mouth to stifle a cry as she watched Fletcher lifted from the boat, aided from behind by one of the oarmen. His face was turned full into the light, the countenance that she so loved was gray and contorted, his lips were compressed to keep any sound of his agony from escaping. The bandage slung across his head and over his eye was caked with crusted blood, black in the illumination of the torch's flame. Faith swayed dizzily.

He walked, then, supported by the young officer who had spoken, and Faith saw the torn breeches, ripped purposely to the hip, with a wide swath of bloody cloth wrapped around his thigh. Faith's breath came fast, and she stepped forward, still in shadow, her lover's name on her lips. Without thinking, she began to speak it, but abruptly he turned, and slipped down onto one knee. The other fellow went down with him, an arm about his waist. Others reached out to assist them.

"Bloody hell," Fletcher swore softly. "I can do it myself. I—I am—" And then his words failed him, for he scented something familiar in the night, near his shoulder, on his blind left-side, and there was a tender touch upon his jaw. And then a voice that he could not fail to know said softly in his ear, "Fletcher, oh, Fletcher, I have been so—Oh! Leave go of me! Release me at once, you abusive dog! How dare you handle me in that way?"

He could hear the struggle, at his flank, as someone tried to remove her from his side. A grunt, from the man, in all probability receiving a swift kick to the shin. For a moment Fletcher could not prevent a low chuckle, even as he crouched low over his knee, his torn leg at an angle behind him, the pain shooting through his spine. Then he ordered, quietly at first, and then louder:

"Let her go, man. I said, let her go. Do you not recognize an order? Assist me to my feet, and leave us. Not you, Brian," he said, quiet again. "Please, stay."

Standing, Fletcher locked his knees, and his jaw, in time to witness Faith casting off the hand of a heavy, sour-faced sergeant with her usual finesse. Her green eyes sparked with indignation. He cocked his head, staring out at her through his good eye. She was as beautiful as was the image of her he had kept in his heart throughout the entire course of the nightmarish day—full of fire and sensuality, even in anger. But something had changed, too. He could see it, when she turned to him, and it was more than the weariness which suddenly revealed itself in her expression as she regarded him.

"Oh, Fletcher," she said, and there was the sound of unshed tears in her voice. Beside him, Brian shifted, and sighed. "This is the one," he whispered.

"Yes," said Fletcher.

Coming no closer than what his grasp, in better times, might have attained, Faith stared at the bandages, bloody and hastily applied, across his forehead.

"Your eye," she said.

She had still come no closer, but merely stared, breathing hard, as if she had been running. Fletcher reached up, fingering the dressing across his brow.

"It is still mine, I am told," said Fletcher. "I have not lost it. Yet. Would you love me any the less if I had?" He attempted levity, in the hope of erasing the chiseled mark between her auburn brows. She did not take it as such, but blinked back tears, frowning. If there had not been so many witnesses to her actions, she would have thrown herself into his arms, and wept there. But he needed strength, not feminine weakness. He needed care to make him whole again.

"Of course not," she said, with cool efficiency that did not fool him. "And your leg? Is the ball lodged within, or has it been removed?"

"Straight through," he answered, flatly. "And out the other side. Caught my horse in the shoulder. He threw me."

His voice was growing breathless, weaker than was his wont. Of course, thought Faith, he has lost a goodly amount of blood. She tried to visualize the violence that had brought him to this pass; the disgust that must accompany the knowledge of such violence; the fear. What is it, she wondered, that allows a man to perform such deeds, as killing? Is it duty? And what is it in a woman that enables her to pick up the pieces which are left, into her hands, to make them whole, or cast them down? Shaking her head, Faith moved to Fletcher's side, peering around him at the younger lieutenant who stood opposite. She felt Fletcher lower his weight to her shoulder, unconsciously seeking support.

"He is coming with me," she informed the other man.

"He cannot," said Lieutenant Upton.

"Do you doubt that I can tend to him?"

"Not at all," said Brian. "I am certain your abilities are more than satisfactory," and he grinned, followed by a painful wince under Fletcher's weight. Fletcher did not notice. He was gazing at a particularly bright shell, crushed into the paving material at his feet.

"Then, leave him to me, sir."

"You will not be capable of supporting him for any distance," insisted the lieutenant.

"Would you care to watch me?" said Faith.

"Are you always so bad-tempered to men who are fighting for your Crown?"

At this, Fletcher bestirred himself from the echoing, spinning focus of the shell, and said, in a hushed tone, "Faith is a Patriot. She cares not for the Crown, nor for England, but only for her founded country. And me, Brian." He could not believe he was speaking so glibly, but it was as if, in his pain, he was left without barriers.

Brian was silent. He felt a shortness of breath, in his chest. He remembered that night in the tavern, when he had witnessed that look of pain on his friend's face; when Fletcher had passed the comment pertaining to a woman ageing a man beyond his years, or something of the sort; when he had told Upton, in no uncertain terms, that the female in question was none of his bloody business. He had not known what to expect, but certainly not this vision of loveliness, with her acid tongue.

"We must report," Brian told Faith quietly. "The surgeon must be seen. For Fletcher's sake, more than mine. His eye's injury is more serious than he lets on . . . No, Fletcher. If you love her, then the truth must be spoken. Leave us go," he said, avoiding the bitterness he should have felt at the knowledge of her beliefs, "and I will return to you with news. I promise you. If the surgeon will permit him to be committed to your care, then I will support him to your home, unaided . . . If you desire it, Irons. I have not considered you, have I?"

"I do want it," said Fletcher, so low now that he found himself having to repeat the statement. The air before him shimmered in unnatural brightness, and the pain of his eye was increasing tenfold, a stabbing, as of a knife, through his skull. He brought a hand to his face, and felt the fresh oozing of blood, warm and sticky. He heard Faith gasp, and wanted to comfort her, to assure her that everything was as it should be, but it was not, and he had not the strength to convince her otherwise.

The British military surgeon had been relieved to find someone capable and willing to take the burden from his overworked hands and those of the civilian doctors. He had instructed Faith in certain procedures, and bade her turn her head as he removed the torn flesh from the leg wound, where the shot had made its exit. Fletcher had made no sound, and Faith, in order not to weaken his resolve, had bitten down on her lip so hard that it had bled. The injury to Fletcher's eye had taken considerably more time in its tending, and for this, the doctor had asked Faith to step outside of the makeshift screen, and wait. He knew that he could get her to go no further than that, and he was touched, by her strength, and her stubbornness.

Faith listened to the sounds emanating from behind the screen with her slender hands balled tightly against her thighs. She knew that Fletcher wanted nothing more than to scream out his agony, and that it was perhaps only her presence that prevented him doing so. Or, perhaps, it was his years of training. She could not be sure. She only knew that she felt it, welling up inside of her, ready to burst from her own lips in wordless cry.

Standing with her back to the screen, Faith attempted to avoid the gaze of the other wounded men, lying prone on the floor, on someone's lovely woven rugs, or sitting propped in the set of Chippendale chairs that lined the wall, staining the seat covers with the mud from their uniforms, their boots, and the blood from their wounds. Fletcher, himself, had been assigned a place on the table; indeed, it was here that all surgery was taking place. The stench of sweat and caking wounds was very nearly unbearable. Just for a moment, Faith moved to the open window and stood before it, breathing in the fresh air.

She felt the presence of the wounded soldiers behind her, even though she knew that their eyes were not upon her, for in their misery, they were not curious. I have hated them for so long, she thought, and at this moment I can feel nothing but pity.

"Mrs. Ashley?"

Faith turned her head. The breeze touched her cheek, drying traces of saline moisture from her skin. The surgeon was beside her, sandy hair frazzled, his red coat cast aside and his shirt-sleeves rolled up.

"I did all I could," he said. "The rest is up to his own healing powers, and God, of course. Unfortunately, I can spare no men to bear him on a litter. Do you have someone with you?"

Faith turned on the doctor, shaking her head, dumbly. Where was the other fellow, the lieutenant who had also been in the boat? "There was an officer, who offered . . . a lieutenant, not greatly injured. I do not know his name. Dark-haired, dark-eyed, with a bandage about his head, so." And she indicated how it had been, with her hands. The surgeon shook his head.

"There are too many this night to remember just one," he said.

"I was to wait outside, but I did not. I thank you for permitting me entry. I know that no civilian was—" and she stopped. "Can he walk? I might support him, if we go slowly."

"He is weak, Mrs. Ashley. And you are small. He should not walk, anywhere. I had hoped you had a means of transportation for him. I will ask about for you, but . . . I am busy, Mrs Ashley, and there looks to be no let-up for some time. I must get the men in, and out, as quickly as is humanly possible. You understand."

Faith nodded gratefully, marvelling that she should feel such gratitude to an enemy. "May he rest," she asked, "for a time, until I can find some means of taking him away?"

"Naturally," said the surgeon. "I did not mean to imply otherwise. There are other tables, and some of these men here can be treated where they sit."

Smiling wanly, Faith crossed the room and stepped behind the screening. Fletcher lay still, upon the table, with nothing beneath him but the hard surface of wood. Faith saw that his eye was freshly bandaged, and a small amount of blood, bright and red, was leaking through the dressing. The other eye was closed, immobile, as he slept the sleep of exhaustion. Tenderly, Faith smoothed the black peak of his hair, tugging the locks with gentle care, to free them from the gauzy band that encircled his head. She touched his cheek, felt how oddly cool it was, and damp, and stubbled with the dark growth of his sprouting beard. He looked gray and haggard, and oh, so close to slipping away from her.

With a small sound, Faith gazed at the scarlet jacket, torn and stained with blood, a deserving end to such hated garb. But not to the man who wore it, even proudly, as Fletcher had done. Throat contracting, she recalled how it had hung, in such attractive negligence, over his naked chest only the night before. Swallowing her tears, she took his limp hand in hers, lifting it to her lips, and kissed it.

"Faith."

His eye was open, his mouth twisting into a grimace of a smile, a ghost of the boyish smile she knew so well. Faith stood very still. Beyond the curtain, she could hear the slight moaning of the men who waited, and beyond that, through other rooms, an earsplitting scream was cut short. Faith shuddered.

"I love you, Faith."

Teeth clenched, she choked on a sob. "Oh, Fletcher, I want you with me. I'm taking you home with me."

"My love," he said, and his eye closed again.

Faith continued to stare down at him, listening closely to his breathing. She wanted him whole again, well, but it occurred to her that she stood a greater chance of losing him then. For the fighting would continue, she knew it, for there would be no ending it now, without victory, entire and complete. He was an officer. She understood the pride he took in his commission. He would return to his men, again, and again, until it was done.

Lifting her head, Faith turned to gaze through a chink in the curtain, back to the window by which she had been standing. It was nearing midnight, but still the wounded were being rowed over from Charlestown, seeking the medical attention to heal their tormented flesh. Faith wondered bitterly how many more of her own countrymen, since the battle at Lexington, had been victim to British musket-fire, cannon, bayonet, and saber. The misery and destruction made her breathless with horror.

We are all a part of it, she thought, each in our own way. And she squeezed her eyes shut, compressing her lips. All of us, she thought, remembering the pewter-shot, the organizing of the collection, and the smuggling of the completed ammunition into the countryside. She had been so damnably self-righteous, even to Fletcher, nearly causing the demise of their relationship because of it. And what had been impossible to visualize when she had been working so hard in the singleness of her pursuit she saw now, in the hollow, shadowed eyes of the men about her: the outrage of human suffering. Fletcher had known what would happen; he had tried to tell her. And now he lay beneath her hand, a victim, also.

She felt the sting of tears beneath her dark lashes, and she dashed them away, with the heel of her palm. Her shoulders trembled. From the open window, she heard the sound of carriages and carts and wheels rumbling over the pavement, the clatter of shod hooves, the bellow of orders, as the wounded who had been treated and dismissed were taken away. Fletcher, as an officer, would have been among them, borne with respectful handling to the inn where he was quartered. Yet, she could not command a carriage to transport him to her home. What was she to do?

"Fletcher," she whispered, smoothing the hair from his brow. "Fletcher, my darling, wake up, if only for a moment." But he did not.

In the instant in which her heart paused, then beat again, Faith stared down at his ashen face. Then she saw the rise and fall of his chest, heard the rasp of the air through his lungs. He licked his dry lips, in his sleep, and made a soft moaning. Faith bent, pressing her lips to his creased brow. Did it feel warm, now? Perhaps, yes. But anything was better than the lifeless cold that had gripped it before, that spoke of death.

Hearing a step just on the other side of the divider, Faith lifted her head and turned in that direction. Two men spoke quietly. She recognized the voice of the absent lieutenant.

"It is nothing to me who this Mrs. Ashley is to your friend, Lieutenant, of course, and I do not ask. I believe she is well able to tend to his wounds. But she needs help, as I have stated, bearing him to her home. It is a dilemma for which I have no time. I am sorry."

"Understood," said the other. "I have already commandeered a wagon for that purpose. I was expecting this trouble."

"Good for you, Lieutenant! That is some relief to me."

"Well, yes," murmured the younger lieutenant, somewhat embarrassed. "All you need with these people is a little show of force—No," he said. "No. I suppose that is not quite true any longer, is it?"

"No," said the surgeon. Faith heard him stride away, followed by the sound of the young man's sigh. He came around the divider. His jaw had been stitched and dressed, and, with the exception of the deplorable state of his uniform, he looked none the worse for his experience. He nodded in silent greeting to Faith, then gazed down at the unconscious form of his fellow officer. He ran a hand through his short-cropped, dark brown hair, so that it stood up about his crown.

"Do you know," he said, almost as if to himself, "how I would have missed you, old fellow? You are a good officer, Fletcher, and a good man."

Faith brought her hand to her mouth, watching the lieutenant with a frown between her brows. She shook her head in tiny movements, left and right.

"It was not so close," she whispered.

"No? Did the surgeon not tell you? His eye was missed by such a small degree, that the shards of metal lodged into the bone of his brow and had to be removed. Had they gone into his eye, the force would have driven them through, to the brain behind. He would have been dead, Mrs. Ashley. Dead. Your fellow 'patriots' would have killed him."

"It is war," she said.

"High treason, and murder," snapped the lieutenant.

"And on Lexington Green? What name, sir, do you give to that?"

"The same. Not only Lexington men have died this day."

"I am aware of that, Lieutenant—"

"Upton."

"Upton," she repeated. "I have been here long enough to witness more than I had ever cared to. And it is not only your heart that is bleeding—"

"Stop."

Both turned at once to find Fletcher watching them through his single eye. "Stop," he said again, thickly, his tongue swollen and scarcely manageable. "The two I love . . . bickering . . . as . . . children . . . as if the outcome of your . . . arguing . . . will make any difference . . . in the end."

Brian stepped forward, into his vision. "A wagon awaits

you outside, if you can manage to walk that far. If not, I can call for assistance.''

''No,'' said Fletcher, struggling to sit up. ''Help me . . . to rise.'' Upton grasped his left arm in both hands while Faith moved in to the right, slipping her arm behind his back. His muscles quivered with the strain. Once he had positioned himself upright, he swung his leg over the edge of the table, then took the other in hand, easing it likewise. Faith would have bent to help him, but something in the expression on Lieutenant Upton's face as he watched the efforts of his friend made her hesitate, and decide against it. She stood with hands clasped, to prevent their flying to Fletcher's aid, and waited.

''Faith,'' he said, head bowed, breathing sharply through his nose. After a moment, he lifted his head on his shoulders, and raised his hand to touch her face, so near to him. She turned her cheek into the curve of his fingers, nearing tears.

''Do not cry, my love,'' he said. ''I will survive. Only . . . take me home, Faith, before it is beyond me to make it. Take me home.''

Chapter Twenty

Faith dipped a folded towel into the basin of water that Elizabeth had brought to her, wringing the excess liquid with a twist of her hands. In the ferocity of that motion, the sinews in her wrist stood momentarily in relief beneath her blue-veined skin, then she relaxed, and they receded. Laying the cloth across Fletcher's feverish forehead, she pressed it down gently. He made a small sound. Faith sat back on her heels, regarding his still, pale face. The color in his cheeks was unnaturally ruddy; and his eye, when he chose to open it, was overbright. He had vomited, once, while Lieutenant Upton was still there with them in the attic, before that younger officer had been forced by his own fatigue to leave them. Faith's own countenance was drawn, her eyes darkly circled with sleeplessness. Outside of the attic window, the dawn of another day was breaking.

Faith heard the noise of Elizabeth's restless movement, and glanced up to where the girl stood, clad in a nightdress and shawl, as she had been since Faith had awakened her for her aid in making up the bed in the attic, whose linens were pulled over an old, but useable, mattress placed atop a line of sturdy crates. It was almost ludicrous, secreting the man who was her lover in a bed in the attic, considering there would be stair after stair to climb by the hour in order to care for him, but for the sake of Elizabeth's young sensibilities, and even that of decorum, she supposed, Fletcher had been made comfortable at the top of the house. It was clean up there, after all, and airy when the windows were ajar, and the extra steps were not something that she minded. But in her glance at Elizabeth, who clutched the shawl and the front of her nightdress as one, she witnessed an expression directed first at Fletcher that was as unyielding as stone, and then at herself, that was without forgiveness.

"Elizabeth," she said, choosing to ignore it in her exhaustion, "I must make one more request of you, and then you may return to your bed. After that, I will not require your help again, as I know it is distasteful to you. Please, will you boil a pan of water, and bring it to me here? There is infection somewhere, causing this fever. I must try to draw it out."

Elizabeth made no move to do as she was bade. She stared down at the man in the bed, naked beneath the linen sheets and the cover of several blankets. Mrs. Ashley had removed his clothing herself—the tattered, bloody uniform of a redcoat—while the girl had averted her eyes and had folded them, finally dropping them into a corner. The man's shoes and gaiters were mud-spattered and lying at the top of the attic stairs. Elizabeth felt the gall rising in her blood.

She drew a deep, angry breath. "Who is he, Mrs. Ashley?" she asked. "Why is he here?"

Without looking at the girl, Faith eased the blankets up over

Fletcher's shoulders, though he very nearly shook them off. In her fatigue, her inclination was to snap at Elizabeth, but she controlled the rise of her temper.

Her voice was roughened by lack of proper sleep, yet soft. "Elizabeth," she said, "his name is Fletcher Irons. He is a lieutenant in the British army. One of Lord Percy's command this very day. That fact is not something of which I am proud, nor do I expect your pardon. But I do love the man, and he has been seriously wounded, and that is why he is here." There, she thought, it is said. She pivoted away, turning the cloth on his forehead. At the moment, his well-being mattered far more than Elizabeth's feelings and lack of compassion for a man who was her enemy. It seemed that Faith had become cruel and uncaring, where all else was concerned. Or perhaps it was merely exhaustion that had so narrowed her vision and her loyalties.

Elizabeth blinked, watching Faith's tender ministrations. The girl wondered how long Mrs. Ashley had loved him, and how she could still deal with the activities of a patriot with a true heart. When the British officer had appeared at the door, greatly distressing Mrs. Ashley, and taking her away, she had suspected her employer was attaining information for the patriots' cause, as Mrs. Revere had suggested.

"I will fetch the water," she said. "An' some clean dressing."

"Thank you, Elizabeth."

From over her shoulder, Faith observed the girl's descent. Then she turned to Fletcher, pulling back the blankets from his bandaged thigh. He shivered in protest, grasping the hand that touched his skin. His eye was open.

"What are you doing?" he asked. The words rolled from his mouth in thickened articulation. He needed to drink, and asked for something. Lifting his head in her hand, Faith brought a cup to his lips.

"What is this?" he asked, smelling mint.

"Herbs in water and brandy."

"Brandy?" said Fletcher.

"For the pain. Open. Drink."

He grimaced at the curt, one-word commands, but opened his mouth gratefully. The cartilage at the front of his throat bobbed up and down with the pain of swallowing. "Thank you," he said.

"Lay back, then, dear, and let me unwind your bandages. I must clean and examine your wounds." As he made no further protest, Faith turned back the sheet, untying the knot that bound the bandage-ends together, and carefully rolled it round and round his naked thigh. His flesh quivered beneath her touch; his muscles tightened.

"Am I hurting you?" she asked.

"No."

It was a lie, made quite obvious by the whistling of his breath through his teeth.

The gauze lay in a stained heap on the floor. Only the dressing remained, that which had been packed about the wound. Faith removed this also, carefully easing the material from the site. For a full minute she stared at the hole which the ball had left in his leg, roughly circular where it had entered, and on the opposite side, where it had found its exit, somewhat larger, jagged about the edges, but clean: the result of the surgeon's knife. Already it appeared to be scabbing over healthfully. Holding his thigh in her hands, Faith recalled the size of the pewter-shot, the feel of it in her fingers, as she had dropped it, ball by ball, into the tiny pockets sewn into her petticoat . . .

"Well?" said Fletcher, voice grating. "What judgment? Live or die?"

"Do not tease like that!" cried Faith angrily. She felt her heart clench, like a fist, and closed her eyes. Oh, it could not have happened that way, with ammunition that she had supplied. It would just be too cruel, too weighty a payment for her sins.

"Faith, what is wrong?"

"Nothing." As Elizabeth had not returned, Faith could not redress the wound, and she merely covered it once again with the sheet, so that it would not chill. On her knees, she went to his head, and crouched beside the bed for a moment, gazing into the eye that looked back out at her. Then, wordlessly, she took up the cloth, to soak away the encrusted blood that edged the patch, and began to remove it, little by little. The dressing was weighty in her hand, with freshening blood; it had the smell about it of a new iron kettle. She threw it down, in a heap beside the rest.

"Turn this way, to the light," she said.

Her stomach heaved, rather painfully, and she swallowed the bile that rose into her throat. Yet, she could not remove her gaze from the blood-crusted lid behind which his eye, smoky blue and incomparable in beauty, had so often looked upon her, providing a window to his thoughts, to his soul. Biting her lip, she picked up the cloth, to clean about his face, touching the edges of the curving ridge of bone, avoiding the wound in his brow, where two parallel lines, running upward, showed once again the surgeon's knife had done its work, cutting down through flesh to the bone beneath, to take out the metal. It was stitched now, and closed, with no smell of putridity about it. Below, as she cleared away the black crust of dried blood, his eyelid creased and opened.

"Thank God," she said on an expulsion of held breath, as though she had not believed his eye still whole until that moment. "Oh, thank God."

She thought of the pain he had endured, in receiving the wound, and in its tending, silently bearing the agony of the knife in his brow, and she wanted to weep at his bravery and suffering.

"Fletcher," she said quietly, "I am sorry, for my part . . . in the maiming of men . . . in the killing. You were correct, of course. I had no right. It was stupid. And one day, you said, I would know the truth . . . One day I would come to know the damage I had begun. I witnessed it tonight, Fletcher, and it is not something I will forget. And out there, in the countryside, my own countrymen are wounded, dead, or dying, Fletcher—"

Silencing her with the touch of his burning fingers upon her lips, he said, "Do not lay too much blame at your own door, my love. It is war, Faith. It is fighting because each man believes in himself, and will stand up for what he feels is right. I witnessed that, Faith, for myself today. Come, lay your head down here, upon my chest. Let me look at you, and you may cry if you wish. I do not mind getting wet."

Gently, she obeyed him, placing her head against the curve of his naked chest. He touched her hair, smoothing it away from her eyes, and then traced the tears, falling singly and simply, without noise or outburst, across the bridge of her nose to drip into the dark, curling hair of his chest.

"You have been long without sleep," he said, so lucidly that she could scarce believe he was so fevered. But the flesh beneath her cheek, beneath her hand, was raging with it.

"Whore!"

Faith squeezed her eyes shut, trembling with the force of that accusation, even though she knew that he was not speaking to her, but to someone else, another woman that he had known, or imagined that he had known, in the depths of his fevered brain. This, and other, spectres had been hovering about him for hours, so that he spoke out to them, at times so loudly that she had been forced to shut the windows at either end of the attic, closing off the circulation of fresh air.

"Your favors are as nothing to me . . ."

Faith wanted to cover her ears with her hands, to stop the sound of his incoherence. It was as if all his thoughts, memories, and past lay open to her, revealed without connection, and she was made to bear witness to it. She felt like a trespasser in Fletcher's most private life. Sitting cross-legged on the floor, Faith drew her knees up, wrapped her hands about her ankles, and buried her head into the voluminous folds of her gingham skirt. The material was damp, from the constant wringing of water from the towel, and from her own perspiration.

"Charles," he said suddenly, and she wondered to whom he spoke now, "you risk more than you know . . . bastard . . . so close . . . I will not . . ."

Faith lifted her head, and dipped the towel into the basin of cool water once again. She wrung it fiercely, listening with a vague and weary fascination to the sound the water made in falling. "Fletcher," she crooned, placing the towel across his forehead, "my love, my darling, hush."

Reaching up with a barely guided hand, he shoved the cloth away. Picking it up from the floor at her knees, Faith replaced it, wiping the water from her fingers along his jaw. His hand came up again, clamping about her wrist with unrelenting, no longer surprising, strength. Faith was still, making no attempt to free herself. In time, she knew, he would release her, as he had before.

He turned his head, seeming to look directly at her. This was something new, that he had not previously done. For a moment, it unnerved her. And then she met the challenge in his eye, the fevered glint, the sudden, violent impulse. She wondered, fleetingly, if he would, in his illness, attempt to do her bodily harm. This was not something she had expected. His suffering, his loss of blood, the virulence of an infection she could not locate, had weakened him, yet something of his mind continually gave him his issue of strength. An incubus of nightmare, perhaps. What prevented him from seeing in her person the face of someone else?

She spoke his name, softly, trying to recall him from that place where he had gone.

He shook his head slightly, frowning. "He calls her Janie," he said, barely above a whisper, "as if she were a street urchin, but it is only because he loves her so."

Faith leaned forward, feeling the urgency of the grasp on her wrist, knowing that here was something of great import to him. She stared into his eyes, which were the color of thunderheads in summer sky and glazed, and she understood that his mind still wandered. She tried to recall what she knew of his past, and she smiled suddenly in relief.

"Your father calls your mother Janie," she said. "It is his pet name for her."

She felt as if she were talking to a child, making simple conversation, to assure the child that she understood the idea he wished to convey.

"What else, Fletcher?" she said.

"Don't you know?"

He sounded oddly bitter, and he turned away, releasing her hand, like a child who had been hurt. Faith closed her eyes, holding in her tears. Illness was wasting away the man so quickly into something less than what he was.

No! That sounded as if she were giving up hope. She would not.

Turning, she soaked the cloth again, and laid it across his brow.

For nearly six days, Fletcher lay flat and still on the dampened mattress. Perspiration soaked his flesh; fresh blood continually beaded along the sutures above his eye; his breath was shallow and sawing. He grew thin, by obvious degrees. The fever raged, in spite of all that Faith could do, in spite of all her prayers, in spite of the ministrations of the herb woman and the physician. Yet, he lived on, breaking Faith's heart in his weakness.

It seemed, at times, that there could be no hope.

Daily, Faith removed the soiled linens from beneath him, which were saturated with his body's precious moisture, then she wiped down his fevered flesh as he groaned. She washed his face, and brushed the length of his jet hair. She caressed often the dark peak on his forehead, curling it back and away from his wound with her fingers. Using her voice to anchor him to the world, she refused, tearfully, to let him slip away, speaking on any subject that came to her mind, or reading to him, quietly, from a Bible on her lap. Elizabeth watched the woman's loyalty, her efforts, her neglect for her own health, in distress, but it was as if, for Faith, the world beyond the attic did not exist.

"The fig tree," read Faith, one night shortly after midnight, from the Song of Solomon, "putteth forth her green figs, and the vines with the tender grapes give a good smell. Arise, my love, my fair one, and come away . . ." Her voice drifted off, for it had come to her earlier that she was merely waiting, now, and nothing more. It had come to her that this man, who meant more to her than her own life, would soon be gone. She tried to continue, but before long she realized she could not.

Faith closed the pages, and bent her head, blinking tears from her auburn lashes. She could not go on. Beside her, from Fletcher's prone form, a sound issued, one of many that he made often, without sense, or reason, and she turned, to inhale sharply. Fletcher's head was angled on the pillow, and his smoky eyes were wide, unglazed at last. They met her own.

"Go on," he said, hoarsely. "Finish . . ."

Faith faltered, gazing for a long time upon his countenance without speaking, her elbow on her knee.

"My beloved is mine," she said, at last, "and I am his . . ."

With the little of strength that he had, he pushed forward, physically nearer to the startled joy in her eyes, and felt himself falling, down, first head, then chest, then hips. But somehow she caught him, in the curve of her arms. She embraced him in arms that were stronger than his.

Chapter Twenty-one

Faith crossed the creaking attic floor, sinking to her knees beside the cot where Fletcher lay, still weak and pale. He smiled at her, lifting his fingers to graze the bone of her cheek, then the curve of her jaw. He flicked his fingers through her hair, curling a lock about his thumb, then he allowed his hand to slide to her lap, without energy, across the pink and gray folds of her skirt.

"Fletcher," said Faith, "the militia has surrounded Boston."

He said nothing; he just looked patient, and quiet. He did not look surprised.

"Boston is surrounded," she repeated, stiffening her spine, "by our ragtag army of farmers, as your associate, Lieutenant Upton, is wont to describe the militia. He is a very contemptuous fellow, that one. Despite the fact that my countrymen are spread from Roxbury as far north as Cambridge, and aligned east to Chelsea on the north shore of the Mystic, and show no signs of departing, he thinks them of no concern to himself and his fellow officers. What do you think?''

Fletcher sighed wearily. "Is it honesty you want from me, Faith? I will admit to you that I think he is wrong. From a military standpoint, we are quite vulnerable here, if we cannot displace your 'ragtag' patriots. But I know the pride of the British, and we will not allow the insult of siege, which appears to be their intent. We will fight, and they will fight, and no one will soon see the harsh end, I can assure you.''

"Is there no chance of surrender on your part? General Gage seems—''

"There will be no surrender. It is too late. On that long nightmarish road back from Concord, there were officers who wanted to surrender then, because fear had overtaken them. But no more. The fear is gone, and anger alone has replaced it. I heard it, on the wharf, in the hospital. Anger, which will resurface as wounded pride, and there will be no surrender.'' Suddenly, he struggled to sit up. With Faith's aid, he managed the feat, holding himself upright with quivering forearms. His chest heaved. The sheet fell away from it, revealing the multiple ridges of his ribcage along his side. She fitted her fingers into the skeletal suggestion of shadow and light, touching him ever so gently.

"Fletcher,'' she said, staring at the evidence of his loss of flesh, "Gage has given permission for all Whigs and sympathizers of the revolt to leave Boston. Some were against it, I hear, declaring we were of value as . . . hostages. But we are of more trouble behind his lines, I suppose, than we are worth as hostages, even if it means that there will be no qualms among my own countrymen, once we are gone, over attacking the town . . . or burning it . . .''

"When?'' was all that Fletcher had to say.

"Tomorrow,'' replied Faith. "All firearms must be turned in. We have none here, so it matters not.''

"Tomorrow,'' echoed Fletcher, and his hand came up, into the hair at the back of her head. He was unsteady, on his one arm, and Faith caught him across the back. Here, more than elsewhere, his ribs were evident in relief beneath her fingers. She lifted her head, and he turned it in his hand, full to the lamp's illumination.

"I had thought to protect you, to keep you safe under my hand, for as long as I was able. I did not expect the time to come so quickly when I could not."

Faith looked at him. "You misunderstand me, my heart. Do you think that I could leave you now?" she said. "That I would, even were you well? I will not go, and Elizabeth has decided to stay with me, though her family has tried to convince her otherwise. We will stay here, where we belong. No one will cast us out, and we shall not go willingly. If it is known that even one Patriot remains behind, then perhaps I may be doing a service to this town that is my home."

"And perhaps," said Fletcher quietly, "a disservice to your countrymen, for if you could conceivably cause them to stay their hand, when it might otherwise be militarily prudent to move, you may cost them more than what it would suffer them in the rebuilding of homes."

"How can you speak to me of the cost to men whom you claim as your enemies?" she demanded. "How can you be so fair and just?"

"They are men, Faith."

"Well, Fletcher Irons," declared Faith, suddenly finding herself in full support of his sagging form, "you will not dissuade me from the course I have chosen. You should know better than to try," as she helped him back on to the raised pillow, "for I am stubborn, and selfish—"

"—and you would not let me die, isn't that so, Faith? And you seek to protect me, now, by remaining here in Boston, as a deterrent against violence. It has nothing to do with your house, or that of anyone else. I know you too well, indeed. I have witnessed your behavior in the past firsthand, and you would not stand in this way for your cause, when there are others, more efficient than this. You are doing this for me, Faith. And I can scarce believe that you love me so."

Fletcher's attempts thereafter to convince Faith to leave were earnest, but futile, for she refused him, adamantly. The following day, Faith and Elizabeth stood by the gate to observe the procession of Boston's patriot citizens as they moved out across the Neck. Far off, beyond the range of British guns, stood the militia, ranged across the horizon. Their number was hard to realize, for they dressed without uniformity, without bright color, melting into the earthy hues of the landscape. Faith watched the departure with her heart beating in her throat.

It seemed that all of them were going, and none would be left within Boston who shared her sympathies. Had it not been for Fletcher, and Elizabeth's faithfulness, foolhardy as it might be, she would have quailed at the idea of being alone among a town swelling with Loyalists and a population of angered British troops.

Sighing against the tight confines of her bodice, Faith turned to watch Elizabeth, standing a foot or two in front of her, her blue eyes intently scanning the militiamen. The tearing of her heart was plain in her expression as she observed the exodus; her thoughts were of Jack, Faith knew. The girl could hardly be blamed for that. Here was possibly her opportunity to locate him, among the militia, though it was said that thousands of men were out there, and she might search for days and not find him, if he was there to be found at all. He might have been wounded, lying up in some home along the road, or . . . Faith, at this point, was quick to divert her thoughts, for Elizabeth's sake. Jack was not dead. After all, was it not true that the British suffered more losses than Americans, by double, and triple?

But in the end, the girl was staying with Faith, for it had been Jack's wish that she do so. He wanted her to remain where he could find her when all of the trouble had passed over; remain where she was safe, in a patriot household. Yet, Boston was no longer safe, for anyone, and as for the patriot household, what would Jack have to say of the fact that a British lieutenant was residing beneath its roof?

For Faith, there was Fletcher, whom she could not, and would not, forsake, though the quality of her life depended upon it. She could have gone, with the rest, finding transportation to her family home in Longmeadow, but Boston had become her home, for she had established it as such. And Ezra, too, was a factor, she realized. He was still in Boston, and, being a Loyalist, he was far safer than she, but she knew he would find himself in need of the comforts which she alone seemed able to offer him.

And she did not care that she was not going, she told herself, and stepped forward, her chin angled high, placing her hand on Elizabeth's shoulder. Yet, her heart continued to pulse in her throat as she watched until the last patriot had walked out through the fort's gate and started out across the Neck.

After that, the rebels settled down for a long and uncomfortable siege of Boston, once the heart of dissidence and activity, and now a town housing more Tories and troops than treason. Faith continued in her care of Fletcher, nursing him back to health, feeding him, bathing him, eventually dressing him in the clothing which Lieutenant Upton brought to him, until, in time, he was capable of performing these things for himself. The younger lieutenant scoffed at the presence of the militia skirting Boston's borders, especially when their numbers began to dwindle, as farmers returned to their fields and other men returned to their craft, which had been left too long idle. It seemed, from his talk, that the heart was seeping from the revolution. Faith refused to believe so, and often said as much. She realized that the young man despised her. If Elizabeth chanced to be about during one of these discussions, she merely listened in brooding silence.

And so the days passed, into a week, and then two, until April became May, and flowers that had been riotous in one month became utter madness in the next; wildflowers and cultured flora grew untended in the gardens of the town, and Faith plucked them by the handful, to brighten the attic, setting them about in vases and small bowls. Fletcher sat in his chair by the window, watching her deft arranging of blooms for his pleasure. He smiled, holding out linen-clad arms. Wordlessly, she slid into them, standing between his knees.

"Look at you, Faith!" he said. "What a treat for the eyes in your guise of domesticity. But you are a soldier at heart; more than I, my love."

And Faith laughed, a trifle oddly.

"If we were husband and wife, by law, would you still honor me with flowers?"

"Until it was of too much trouble, I suppose that I might," she teased in reply.

He took her face in his hands, and though it felt somehow rounder than it had in the past, he knew that this must be but an illusion, brought on by his own thinness. Her cheeks blossomed with color beneath his gaze, and her eyes were bright, reflecting the panes of the window behind his head. "Then you would marry me?" he said.

"You would need permission for that, wouldn't you? In time of war, such a thing is not granted."

"You are right, of course. Yet, you have avoided answering me. Would you consent to be my wife if we were not at war? if it were ended, done?"

Faith looked past him to the yard, overgrown with waving grass, and to the heavy branches of a pair of wide and ancient chestnut trees. There was a puddle of standing water, in the dirt before the shed, reflecting the sky above. Faith could see the clouds moving in it, like grazing sheep.

"I don't know," she said, at last.

Fletcher dropped his hands from her face with a sigh. "So be it," he said.

Faith returned to her flowers.

The time came when Fletcher did more than sit in a chair beside the window, or walk slowly about the attic, ducking his head beneath the rafters of the roof's sharp angles, as he leaned heavily upon a stout stick in support. He began to exercise himself, moving without the cane, carrying weight upon his shoulders and back, strengthening himself toward the fitness of a soldier. Faith fed him well, watching the flesh return to his form, his ribs disappear from view, the muscles of arms and chest and thighs regain their sleek power and beauty. And though overjoyed, she was touched by the sadness of inevitability, of the knowledge that soon he would be wearing his officer's uniform again, with breeches of white and the hated coat of scarlet and black.

Meanwhile, he wore only the buff breeches and white shirt that Lieutenant Upton had brought to him, looking more like the man she had known with each passing day. The healthy glow had returned to his hair, and he wore it pulled back in a ponytail rather than braided, tying it with one of Faith's ribbons. He spoke with energy, and at length, on all manner of topics, now that Faith was so often near him. It was evident in all his movements, in his speech, in the turn of his head when he sought her out, there in the peaked confines of the attic, that he was cherishing moments, storing them, to keep him sane and buoyant in the rough seas of an uncertain future.

"Faith," he said, one day, when he had been standing for some time, wordlessly gazing at her bent head as she sat mending in his chair beside the window, "would you return to England with me?"

Faith lifted her head. The sunlight fell across her brow. "This is my home," she said. "I do not know England."

"England is my home," he countered. "Though I have resided in other lands, they have never been home to me. Not even," he added, "the colonies of America."

Nodding, she bent to her mending again, jabbing the needle through the thick fabric in her hands. "I understand," she said to him, biting off the knotted thread with her even, white teeth. She set the garment aside and folded her hands in her lap. Her spine was very straight. "What would I do there?" she asked. "I would know no one but you, Fletcher, and though I am aware that there are sympathizers even in your country, they could not come close to comprehending what I feel about my own. What of the pride I take in this fight for liberty, firsthand? They do not know this land, with its newness and beauty and opportunities for those of us who want to be something more than what we have been. I know," she forestalled him, "that a wife forsakes much for her husband. I know that."

"Have I asked," he reminded her, quietly, "that you forsake anything, Faith? I miss my home," he said. "That is all. And I would like—I would like my father to meet you. We have drifted apart, over the years."

"I am sorry."

"Do not be. It happens, and there may yet be time, to make that up. Now, my mother," he went on, leaning with his forearm against the window frame, "she would delight in you."

"No doubt," said Faith, lifting her green eyes to his gray ones, to the healing wound above the one, and away, "she would think me quaint."

"My mother is quite quaint, herself, my dear."

"You say that with affection," commented Faith. "But frankly, I believe she would be horrified to find her son taken up with a woman of the Colonies. The son of a noble, and the daughter of a non-titled colonial; widow, besides, of a smuggler? Quaint, indeed."

"Do not forget rebel, and he, a soldier of good King George."

"Exactly," said Faith.

"No," he said. "No. Not exactly. Just a man and a woman, with a love between them that seems, at times, rather hopeless. Yet, indulge me, Faith. Imagine yourself crossing the sea with me, to my fair isle, to the ancestral home of my forebears. My mother would kiss you, twice on each cheek, and a third time for good measure, exclaiming over your loveliness, and the beauty of your flame-colored hair." At this, Faith stood up, walking away from him in a huff of embarrassment. He followed, close behind.

"My father, of course, would come at a more dignified pace down those grand stone-stairs, measuring you slowly with his eye, taking his time, and then he would turn to me with that nod of his, as if I had just bought myself a good horse. I would, quite naturally, be annoyed by his pompousness, until he smiled, and took my hand, and I would see in him, then, the youth who had swept my mother off her feet."

Faith halted in the center of the floor. She turned to Fletcher, staring at him in disconcert. Fully aware with startling clarity of the loneliness he must feel, far from home, and those whom he loved. It was more than a matter of distance: it was a matter of his life, his chosen life, and the years dedicated to it, forcing a wedge between a man, and the past, the family, he cherished. It might be unintentional, perhaps, but undeniable.

"What . . . what then?" she said to him. "What then would we do?"

Fletcher smiled down at her. He lifted her hand so that her fingers lay loosely across his open palm.

"Doubtless," he continued, "you will be introduced to my elder brother, who will fawn over you, kissing your hand, thusly," and he proceeded to enact the scenario, a smile of mischief in his eyes. "He fancies himself a Frenchman at heart, though you would die at dawn, should ever you say so to his face. And there would be his wife, naturally, and their children—I have no idea how many they have now: three, at least. They would call you Auntie Faith, and probably poke their tongues out at you behind your back."

"Indeed?" said Faith, and pretended to look over her shoulder severely.

"Yes. And that night, or perhaps the next, there would be a ball, in your honor. All the neighbors would come, dying for a glimpse of the little colonial woman—" (here, he laughed, still holding her hand), "—who had so enamored Jonathan Winfield Irons' second son. My other brothers would be there, also, trying to claim you for a dance, but they would all be reserved for me . . . wouldn't they?"

"Is that not considered rude?"

"So?" said Fletcher, with a flip of his incised eyebrow that made him wince. "You would wear a gown of white satin and tulle, cut to reveal your shoulders, so." With both hands, he partially unfastened the front of her bodice, pushing it down over the curve of her narrow shoulders. "There," he said.

"Will it be hooped and draped with ruchings and bows?" Faith asked him inquisitively.

"If you desire it, my love."

"And the finest pair of stockings ever to be worn by a lady?"

"They would be as insubstantial as the air beneath my hand," he said, running his fingers suggestively along the front of her skirt, over her thigh. Faith held her breath in delight, both real and imagined.

"Would you care to dance, Mrs. Ashley?" Taking up her hand again, Fletcher held the palm against his lips.

"I rarely have," Faith confessed honestly. "I have gone to Lexington, on occasion, but in Boston we do not dance. Nor at home."

"There is nothing to it," he assured her, slipping his arm behind her waist. "Follow my lead, dear heart."

Taking Faith completely into his arms, Fletcher began to dance her around the creaking floor, first this way, and then that, with remarkable grace despite the slight limp of his healing leg, humming a refrain in the air above her head. It was not a familiar tune to Faith, but, as it was repetitious, she soon found her voice joining his, and then her laughter, as he whirled her faster and faster until she was dizzied, and the dust motes in the sunshine rose beneath their steps, clouding in a golden mist before her eyes.

"Oh, stop! Stop!" she cried, but joy was in her voice and in her heart.

He brought her to a stop, and she leaned against his chest, catching her breath. She could hear the beat of his heart, a deep drumbeat, beneath her ear.

"Yes," he said, "we would dance the whole night through—"

"Not so wildly!" Faith protested.

"You would become used to it. And enjoy it, little one. Then after, a bedchamber would be prepared in that rambling old stone monstrosity, just for you and I, far from family, and guests, and there . . ."

"Yes?" said Faith, pulling back from him, so that she could raise her head and view the expression marking his handsome countenance. His eyes were dark as smoke, blue-gray, shadowed by the length of black lashes.

"There," he repeated, "as my wife, as Mrs. Irons, at last, my love, I would give you the one thing which would make you happiest, which would make you forsake all that had passed, without regret, and it would be so, because we would make it so . . ."

"And what is that?" asked Faith, in a hush, as he slid the sleeves of her gown further down her arms.

"A child, Faith . . . a child."

"No," she said. "I cannot—" But the rising of old sorrows forced her tongue to silence.

"I want to give you that, Faith. I wish that I could—oh, God, I wish that I could! It breaks my heart, Faith, to be unable to give you that which you want most."

Blindly, Faith reached up a hand to silence him, but he caught it, and held it, close against his throat.

"In that chamber, Fletcher," she whispered, "where the miracle takes place, is it quietly that we make love; gently, for you are a man healing from illness and injury?"

"Quietly, yes," he said, "And gently."

"And do you hold me after, and promise never to stop loving me?"

"And promise never to stop loving you," he said. "On my honor, and on my life."

For a moment, Faith envisioned it all as they had spoken it, and then rose up onto her toes, to kiss him lightly on the mouth. She took the ribbon from his nape, felt the silk caress of black hair across her cheek and the lowered lids of her eyes. She stepped away from him, standing in the afternoon light angling through the window. She felt the sun's warmth, against her back, her head. Outside the day was sleepy; below, the house was quiet, for Elizabeth had gone out. Faith closed her eyes.

The dawn approaches, she thought, and we have danced the whole night through. I remove my gown with care, for I have never possessed any other so fine and rich; my underthings; the stockings of smoothest silk. And he comes to me across the floor, with desire in his eyes, handsome, even more so for the scar that mars his brow; and there is nothing I will not give him, nothing I will not take.

She felt his arms go around her, there in the sun, unclothed and warm against her naked skin. She opened her eyes, to cast away the trappings of her dreaming, to see him only, lifting her effortlessly from the colorful circle of discarded garments about their feet to carry her to his bed.

"And the lowering circle of the moon shines through the window," he said, in continuation of his tale, "as the cock crows. We will smell the sweet scent of scythed grass, and of garden roses, and," as he lowered his face against her hair, "of honeysuckle, twining through the stones . . ."

Chapter Twenty-two

June 1775

Quietly, Elizabeth stood on the attic stairs. Her skirt was in her hand, twisted up away from the wooden treads so that not even the whisper of sound had escaped as she had ascended. She had avoided those places where she knew the treads were warped, and tended to squeak, intent on her purpose as she went. For she knew that the other lieutenant was up there, and she was determined to learn what it was that brought the tone of urgency to his voice.

"You understand that you must come back to us, soon; we need your level head. There is much to be done in the coming days. Besides," Upton was saying, "your men do not much care for my command."

"Do they not?" she heard the other man counter, softly.

"I have been sent, unofficially, to request your return."

"By whom?" came Lieutenant Irons's voice, casually, it seemed. "My men?"

"No," said the younger lieutenant, annoyed, "by Lord Percy himself. He could, of course, command your return, and should actually, which he has not failed to point out to me. He knows that you are recovered, and is glad for it, as he also knows your value. Your record speaks highly for you."

"Indeed."

"Damn it, Fletch! Don't behave so much as if you do not care. That is not the officer I have known, believe me."

Elizabeth flattened herself silently against the wall at the sound of movement above.

"Is it that you do not want to leave here? Declare this house for quartering, then."

"No," said Fletcher, "no. I would not do that. Although I

am accepted, what I do is not, and it would be wrong of me to attempt to force the issue. We stand on opposite sides of a fence, Faith and I, which, for her, needs nothing more than tearing down, while my view is that it requires restructuring. Our lives are divergent, Brian, meeting only where love does; and this war delineates the differences between us with hopeless clarity."

"Love," said Brian. "What a tragedy."

On the darkened staircase, Elizabeth lowered her eyes in disturbance, feeling her cheeks heat in an awkward blush. This was not the sort of conversation that she had anticipated. Nothing so intimate, nor so revealing of the character of both men. She felt ashamed, suddenly, and confused, and released the hem of her skirt to brush along the stair treads as an announcement of her presence. But, at least one of the men took no notice of the sound, for Lieutenant Upton was saying, as if in continuation of an earlier topic:

"I understand, Fletcher. But you do have your duty, to your uniform, and to our king, and the plan to seize Charlestown on the eighteenth will go through. You must be prepared to— what is it?"

Elizabeth was alerted by the creaking of the floorboards, and was able to adopt a posture of innocence just as the elder lieutenant appeared, crouching over the opening to the narrow staircase. Elizabeth lifted her pointed chin to stare up at him, her expression defiant. But Lieutenant Irons appeared amused, smoky eyes wide, his brow lifted in a jagged, piratical arch.

"Good evening, Elizabeth," he said.

Blushing deeply, Elizabeth nodded her head.

"Mrs. Ashley has sent me to call you for supper," she said.

"Did she, now?" drawled Fletcher. "Did she send you to eavesdrop on me, also?"

"She did not," the girl stated. "And besides, I ain't been listenin' to a word said! Why should I be interested in the conversation of the likes of you two?"

"Ah, young Elizabeth," scolded Fletcher, "you take too closely after your benefactress, I do believe. But, I suppose I can attain your promise that you will not utter a word to anyone of what you have not heard?"

Behind him, Brian chuckled appreciatively.

"T'is suppertime," she said again, tonelessly.

"I suspect you are hinting that I must be on my way," said Brian, stepping forward to gaze over his friend's shoulder at Elizabeth's blonde head.

Frowning, Elizabeth made her confession reluctantly. "Mrs. Ashley has meant for both of you to come."

"Has she now?" said Brian. "Fletcher, I believe we should commandeer this place for our own use. I am beginning to take a liking to it." And he winked, broadly, in Elizabeth's direction.

Elizabeth drew herself up, bristling. "Supper," she stated once more, and spun on her heel, her skirts dusting the walls, to descend the stairs, leaving the two men to follow, or not, as they chose.

Faith waited below, and was displeased by the expression on Elizabeth's face as the girl swept past her, into the kitchen.

"Are they coming?" she asked.

Elizabeth nodded, sinking a ladle into the contents of the pot on the fire. She stamped her foot, once, and gave her apron a little flip of annoyance. Faith observed the display with a small frown chiseled between her brows.

"Is there something wrong?"

Elizabeth stirred the pot without speaking. After a moment, she turned her head to gaze at the woman over her shoulder. Picking up a towel, Faith wiped her hands on it, and came forward.

"What has happened?" she whispered.

Hooking the ladle to the side of the fire-blackened pot, Elizabeth listened for a moment. Faith took the discarded implement and began to ladle the steaming dumplings from the water into a salt-glazed tureen.

"Well?" she urged, wondering at the girl's reticence.

"They . . . them British, I mean," whispered Elizabeth, in a rush, "are planning an attack on Charlestown, less than a week from today."

Faith paused in her task. "How do you know this?" she demanded. "Did you hear them say as much upstairs? Were you listening, Elizabeth?"

Head bowed, the girl admitted to her eavesdropping. Yet, the glint of her blue eye was anything but contrite as she gazed at the planking beyond the petticoat hem of her green gown.

Faith glanced toward the open door, listening for the sounds of descent. "When, exactly?" she whispered hurriedly.

"The eighteenth. When is that? The Sabbath?"

"Yes," Faith answered, shuddering with a sense of outrage. "How do they dare? We must get word out to the lines, if they have not already received it. Most likely, it is known among our men, and yet—" Abruptly, she stilled. Fletcher's voice, his laughter, came to her from the lower stair; the sound of his footfalls now a familiar rhythm within the routine of her household. She stood smitten by the recollection of the night when she had waited long beside the North Wharf, seeking his face in that of every man rowed across the Charles. And then came the guilt, in the knowledge that her hand had been deep in the suffering of men, on both sides.

But, if her countrymen were not forewarned of this coming event, then misery would be assured, as they would be caught, without defense. It was cowardice to hope that others would learn of it without her aid, and channel it through to the outside. Her eyes were wide as she turned to Elizabeth.

"There is a man," she said, "on Tremont Street—"

"And what is that delicious aroma?" It was Lieutenant Upton, more jovial than usual. Faith continued, rapidly.

"I must go there, tonight, and—"

Elizabeth was not looking at her, but gazed past her shoulder. Faith clutched the towel-wrapped tureen against her breast. The steam rose, heating her bosom and face. Following the girl's gaze, she turned, also, to the two men in the doorway. Fletcher stood behind the younger lieutenant, taller than he, by a head. His eyes locked with hers. He knows, Faith thought, what passes here. But there was nothing she could do, or say, to prevent the accusation that flared in the attitude of his countenance and then was gone. Calmly, she pivoted away, taking the cover of the deep dish and depositing it firmly on top.

"Elizabeth—" she began, and was interrupted.

"I understand," the girl said, "and I will do it."

* * *

Fog floated at knee level above the streets as the heat of the day escaped the cobbled pavement to meet with the chill of the night air. Dampness penetrated the fabric of Elizabeth's skirt, clinging to her petticoat and the sleeveless shift she wore beneath her garments. Within the confines of her bodice, her heart was hammering incessantly, until she thought that she might faint. She swallowed dryly, several times, as she waited for the summons upon the door on Tremont Street to be answered. She had only knocked lightly, but in the silence of the night, she had not dared to announce herself with more resonance.

"Yes? Who is there?"

The voice was dull, subdued, so that Elizabeth could not be certain if it were male or female.

"Elizabeth Watts," the girl said, pressing her mouth close to the shut door. "Mrs. Ashley has sent me, with a message for Mr. Housemann—" Abruptly, the door was yanked inward.

"Hush, child. Come in, quickly."

For an instant, Elizabeth only stared, dumbfounded, at the tiny woman who had answered the door: she was wizened and dressed in black, with an overlarge mobcap flattened around her head. And then, as the woman's thin fingers clutched about her wrist, she stepped inside. The door closed behind.

"He ain't in, I am afraid, my dear," said the woman.

"Ain't he?"

The woman shook her head, so vigorously that the cap mushroomed about her face. "No, but you can wait, if'n you wish. He shan't be long."

"I—I wish," Elizabeth stammered, feeling uneasy in the dark enclosure behind the door. She could hear voices elsewhere in the house. A thin bar of light provided illumination, slanting across the floor from beneath a heavy curtain.

Suddenly, the curtain was whipped aside.

"Who is that, old woman?"

Elizabeth started. The man standing outlined in the brilliant doorway was a British soldier. Behind him, several more were seated about a table, playing cards on the surface, their glasses of brandy and water forming rings upon the cloth. The smell from the room was of liquor and sweat.

"T'is my niece," stated the woman, without the blink of an eye.

"Is that so?" said the officer. "Your relatives pick strange hours for social calls, do they not?"

"T'is my home," said the woman, "and as I do not mind, why should ye?"

"Bah, the woman's right!" called another man, from inside. "It is your play. Are you stalling? Ha, I suppose that I can count on winning this one!"

But the officer in the doorway was not to be deterred. "Come here," he directed Elizabeth. "Let me look at you."

Elizabeth would have refused had it not been for the shove she received from behind. Angry, but silent, she stood before the man as he studied her face in the light, then allowed his gaze to slide downward, disdainfully.

"She does not look much like the other," he commented.

"Need she?" retorted the woman. "We ain't all born of the same mother. This is my sister's granddaughter. And that's all I will trouble myself to say."

"Oh, leave off!" hounded the man from inside. "Look at the hair; there's hardly a bit of difference there. Satisfied? Leave the woman and her niece alone and return to the game. The stakes are high, man, and I do not care to wait all night."

With a breathless exclamation that Elizabeth pretended not to understand, the officer stepped back, flipping the curtain shut.

"Upstairs," said the old woman.

Feeling for the banister, Elizabeth obeyed, moving carefully up the steps as the woman followed close behind. "Are you Whig or Tory?" she asked, over her shoulder.

"Ah," the woman cackled, "Whig, through and through. Them redcoats were billeted on me months ago, and it don't look as if I'll be rid of them any time soon. We fight, constantly, but no harm done. It's the old man they try to fire up, but he won't have none of it. Makes them furious, it does!" And she laughed again.

"Where are you takin' me, now?" Elizabeth ventured further.

"To cool your heels a bit," she said. "Until me husband returns. Mrs. Ashley sent ye, ye said?" Elizabeth nodded, but the woman did not see her. "Eh?"

"Aye," said Elizabeth. "With a message."

"Ah, then there is something afoot, we can be sure. Go through that door, there, lassie—oh, goodness! wait!"

But it was too late. Elizabeth had already thrown open the door to the dimly lit chamber and walked inside. Yet, she paused at the woman's outcry, and at the sight of a man's back as he crouched over a satchel against his knee, working furiously to close it. Beside him, a small pile of paper had scattered over the floor; they were much inscribed and ink-stained, with more than a few pages crumpled and smoothed over, as if they had been meant to be thrown away. With a furtive movement, the man whisked the paper into one of his large hands. In the other, across his thigh, a gun appeared, dark metal and shining wood.

"F-forgive me, I—I didn' mean to—"

At the sound of her voice, the man lifted his golden blond head, and turned it, revealing his profile and the shade of his dark brown eyes.

"Jack!"

"Betsy?" And he laughed, a low, triumphant crow, that did not carry beyond the room. "Is that truly you, my Betsy?" he said, swinging himself about, and unfolding to a height that Elizabeth did not remember. The gun disappeared, as did the pages. "What brings you here? Need I ask? God has brought you here, to me. How else would you know to come the very hour that I have arrived?" He spoke rapidly, and his accent was heavy. His face seemed different to Elizabeth, not so young as when last she had seen it aglow with the excitement of anticipation. He was thinner, too. With an exclamation, Elizabeth rushed into his arms.

"Oh, Jack!" she cried again. He touched his fingers to her lips.

"Hush," he said. "We must be quiet."

"Ah, well, isn't this a good one?" declared Mrs. Housemann in amusement. "The two of you are acquainted, and
very well, it seems to me. I should stay right here, to keep an
eye on you both, but I won't. Nay, I won't. T'is privacy you
need, for you may not have it long. But," she said, backing
out of the door, "pray be good children, so that I ain't ashamed
of myself later." And she vanished, leaving the door nearly
shut.

"Jack, Jack . . ." moaned Elizabeth tearfully.

"I have missed you, Betsy."

"Oh, Jack, I've been so worried! I thought—I wondered—
if you'd been killed, I would've just died, too. I heard that
Lexington was horrible, and I—" Suddenly, she faltered.
"What are you doing here, Jack?" she asked, lifting her head.

"Does it matter, Betsy?" he countered, after a moment. "I
am here, safe and sound." Grasping her head in his large
hands, he kissed her, soundly. Elizabeth pulled back with a
gasp.

"Jack," she said.

Laughing again, he kissed her a second time, and a third,
and on and on, in a different manner than any she had been
used to, until she felt dizzy.

"Jack, don't," she protested, weakly enough.

"And why not?" he asked her, still smiling.

"I, well, I don't know. It's not right . . . is it?"

He was silent a moment, brows lowered over his dark eyes.
"Who has told you so? Why do you believe it wrong to express
oneself with a touch of the lips?"

Elizabeth hesitated, shyly, cheek mantling. "It . . . it leads
to . . . other things . . ." she demurred.

"Other things?" Jack echoed alluringly, taking her hand
and leading her to a chair, where he sat down, pulling her onto
his lap. She squirmed, trying to remove herself from his embrace halfheartedly. "What 'other things' do you mean, my
Betsy?"

"I . . . ain't sure," she said, turning her head from the
expression in his eyes. It almost frightened her, the way he
stared so intently, and yet so softly. Expecting something of

her that was vague knowledge, suspicion, guesswork, yet that was enough to make her tremble. He touched her, carefully, on the cheek, the arm, along her shoulders, finally taking her by the chin to turn her face to his.

"Do I make you afraid?"

Elizabeth nodded.

"Do not be afraid. I ask nothing of you. Lay your head against me, and be silent, so," he said, as she nestled against his chest. "I have missed you, truly." For some time, they sat together, without speaking, his head bent over her own, the golden against the yellow of corn, and then his hands began to rove, in a seemingly aimless pattern, across her back, over the roundness of her upper arms, around her waist, dropping along the dull green skirt covering her hip and the length of her leg. With her head angled against his collarbone, Elizabeth watched his movements in fascination. She knew that she should demand that he stop, but she was breathless with trepidation, and the pleasure of sensation. Beneath her ear, she listened to his heart beating in conjunction with hers. There was, in that moment, no more perfect sound.

"Elizabeth," he said, "you are young, innocent, and we have not known each other long, except in absence. Still, I love you, and I will not hurt you. You must not be afraid. I only want to touch you, in this way, to remember. I do not want more."

Trustingly, Elizabeth permitted his touch, and returned his kisses with a growing, startling passion. She turned in his arms and clung to him.

"What brought you here, this night? You did not tell me."

Elizabeth stood before the mirror, squinting in the low light as she ran her fingers through her tumbled yellow locks. Jack was reflected behind her, a hulking shadow against the wall. She turned to look at him. She would almost have rathered that he had not asked. The spell of ardor, the impassioned descent into captivity, was broken by the question. She gave him a little frown.

"Mrs. Ashley sent me. I found something out tonight," she

said. "The redcoats are going to attack Charlestown, this very Sunday."

Jack's expression did not alter. "Betsy," he asked, "how did you discover this?"

"I—I overhead two officers, talkin'. It wasn't just light talk, Jack. They were serious."

"I have heard this, also," he told her.

"Have you? Then, t'is true! I knew, if'n I listened long enough, I'd hear somethin' worthwhile."

"Listened to whom?" asked Jack, with a wariness that caused the girl's tongue to slip out between her lips in worry. "Where did this conversation take place?"

Elizabeth noted the severity of his expression. What had happened to the man who had held her with such passion only minutes before?

"On the street today," she lied without so much as a second thought, for her allegiance to Faith could not easily be cast aside. "They—they did not know I was near," she said, which, at least, was a partial truth. Unconsciously, she wrung her hands together. "Jack," she said, "it ain't nothing to be suspicious about. I just heard them, that's all."

After a moment, Jack nodded.

"I required affirmation of some sort. You have provided it, Betsy. This means that I must leave, tonight. I may not rest here, as I had planned."

Elizabeth turned, looking where Jack had been furtively working, on the floor, when she had entered. She saw a large leather bag, packed haphazardly with rags, perhaps, or unfolded clothing, crammed hurriedly into place.

"You ain't just come," Elizabeth whispered, "have you? You were going, weren't you? Without ever tellin' me you were here in Boston."

"No, Betsy, no," he said.

"Yes, you were. You were packing when I came in. How long, Jack? Tell me."

He sighed, reaching for her, but she pulled away.

"Very well, my heart. I have been in Boston for four days, but here, only one. I did not think it wise, to let you know, for I am only to gather what information I may, and then go,

at a moment's notice. You have given me that notice. This is
information that General Warren must know straightaway.''

Elizabeth's shoulders dropped as she stared at him heavily.
She wanted nothing more than to cry, but she refused to allow
that before him; instead, she merely stood there, lip quivering.
''I—I thought that you were with the militia. I've worried,
an' worried, and you, you were here, in Boston—''

''Betsy . . .''

''How did you get in?'' she demanded, cuttingly.

''To Boston? With this,'' he said, reaching inside of his
jacket. He withdrew a much-folded square of paper that bore
the signatures of the Provincial Congress: a Loyalist pass.
Elizabeth shook her blonde head in horrified disbelief. ''No,''
he said, ''it is not what you think. The pass provides the safe
passage. And here,'' he went on, bending to reach into the top
of his stocking, ''is the means for departure. Do you see?''
With a flourish, he produced yet another pass, this one stamped
with General Gage's seal. ''Whigs are still permitted to depart
the town, provided they turn in their worldly goods. I have
nothing,'' he said slyly, ''so I give nothing. And, as a man
who limps and whose vision is poor,'' he added, enacting both,
''I shall not be detained for the fact that I am of military age.
But alas, there is nothing written here that provides for my
identity to bring a wife, so I cannot, in safety, smuggle you
out disguised as such.''

Elizabeth's mouth dropped a little, and she felt her heart
flutter against her ribs. ''What're you sayin', Jack?'' she asked
him cautiously.

''I am overjoyed that you are here, Betsy. It is in answer
to my prayers, believe me. You are the light of my life. I have
thought of you, nearly every waking minute, since we have
parted, and dreamed of you at night. Do not be angry with
me. I love you. If you could, I would ask you to leave with
me, tonight. But it is not safe for you. Wait for me, as I have
asked you before. Wait for me, and when next I return, perhaps
this war will be done, and we will—''

''No.''

''Betsy—''

''No.''

"Please—"

This was not what she had imagined, standing all those weeks ago before the gate at the fort, watching the exodus of thousands of patriots across the Neck and longing to go with them, only to now find Jack, to hear him ask her to wait for him. Shaking her head, she backed away from the offer of his arms, taking in the expression of his dark eyes, the color of his hair, the funny tilt of his nose, and the new fullness to his jaw, the man's strength of it, and of his body. She loved him, but her love had changed, from that of a girl's romantic dreaming to that of a woman's reality. She wanted to go with him, not to wait idly in Boston. The hurt that disappointed the one and resigned the other ran too deeply for clear thought. She wondered if she could bear it. Turning on her heel, she slammed open the door and fled down the stairs, startling Mrs. Housemann at the base of the staircase.

"I must go," Elizabeth said to her, unaware of her own tears. "I have delivered my message. I must go."

As the door closed behind the girl, the old woman lifted her eyes to the stairhead, to the young man standing there, to the son of her beloved niece and the Frenchman. "Jacques," she said, for she had always called him so, "what has happened?" But her voice dwindled in bewilderment as she witnessed, even in the darkness, the spasm of pain around his mouth and in his eyes. Her ageing heart grieved.

Chapter Twenty-three

Faith turned restlessly on the bed, seeking an absent warmth, and reached in sleep for the body that had been lying next to her own. She moved her head, into the valley of a vacated pillow; the tousle of her flame red hair fell across her cheek, over her shoulder. The sheet of unbleached linen had tangled about her legs and she kicked, once, exposing the curve of her back as it gentled into the roundness of her hips. Her skin was luminous in the starlight.

At the opposite end of the attic, Fletcher observed her. Quiescent, he sat with feet propped on a stool as he leaned back in his chair, arms folded over his naked chest. The unshaven line of his jaw was rigid, his eyes dark as the night sky beyond the window. His unbound hair hung, coal black, along his neck.

"God in Heaven, Faith," he said, allowing his whisper to fade into silence. She slept on, undisturbed by the soft flow of his voice. He had known, that night when he had discovered Elizabeth on the stairs, listening, what would come of it: the rebels had learned of the British plans. It did not matter to him any longer if they had been enlightened through Faith's instigation. Perhaps, there was some truth to the saying that love could blind a man; perhaps, it was merely understanding. At any rate, he found that he could not condemn her, but merely wonder at her conscience.

Noiselessly, he rose, padding across the floor barefoot, clad only in his breeches, to pause beside the bed. With an expression of tender affection, he gazed down upon Faith's sleeping form and touched her hair, brushing the unruly locks from her shoulder and face. How soft they were, beneath his hand. And how trustingly she slept, lying in innocence rather than immodesty, naked before his eyes, his caress. He curved his fingers over the contour of her hip, and held them there, against the warmth of beloved flesh. He bent and kissed her, in the small of her back. Then he walked away.

Tomorrow, the frigates in the river mouth would bombard the fort which the rebels had built, seemingly overnight, on Breed's Hill in response to the information they had received. And in the morning, he would return to uniform, and duty, to lead his men in the afternoon frontal assault. As ordered. It was not, as far as he was concerned, a sound military strategy, but it was not his place to do more than suggest, especially now, when he had been away from the core of tactical discussions. The idyllic existence that he and Faith had created for themselves was having its payments. He had lost a degree of the authority that had been important to him: in maintaining the control over his men that could guarantee their safety. Worse, in personal terms, was the misgiving with which he now greeted duty that once was so clear to him. And all because of Faith. Ah, how hard it would be to leave her now, altering the course of their lives once again, canting their relationship with such misery that it might, like a listing ship, sink beyond hope of retrieval.

He stood before the window, leaning, his arms folded above the casement and his forehead pressed against the cool glass, staring down into the shadows of the yard below. The chestnuts, mushrooming clouds of blackness, whispered into the night, obscuring the ground beneath. Fletcher could hear the movement of a large animal, a dog, he suspected, or perhaps a fox. Crickets chirped, close to the house. An owl hooted from the shed's roof. There was the flutter of insects; the call of men, in the distance; too far to concern himself over their words. He closed his eyes, and turned his head, feeling the glide of glass over the scarring wounds that intersected his brow.

Faith, he thought, pressing close to the chill of the windowpane, tomorrow I leave you.

It was only a day sooner than he had anticipated, yet it seemed astoundingly precipitant, and it filled him with a passionate aching. She was not aware, he knew, of the situation at hand; she did not realize that he could not give her the extra day she had hoped to have with him, a hope she had expressed this very night, as she lay in his arms. He had not been able to tell her because he could give her no assurances, despite all of her love and all that she had done in caring for him, that he would return alive this time from that wide-open hill that belied military common sense. He did not hope to die; he did not plan to die; but hopes and plans meant naught in the ferocity of bloodshed. Men behaved viciously, at such times, and British soldiers obeyed their superiors, without question.

Swinging from the window, he returned to the bedside, ducking his head beneath the rafter as he lowered himself onto the bed beside her. Sensing the sagging of his weight into the mattress, Faith rolled, onto her back, flinging her arm above her head. Briefly, Fletcher gazed down at the beauty of her naked form, and then, with solicitous care, he disentangled the sheet from her legs and pulled it up, tucking it beneath her arms. He lay down, with his right arm crooked beneath his head, his left traversing her waist.

It seemed that she had an ability, he reflected, in taking the world and turning it about in such a manner that he saw all those things which he had witnessed before in a new light. Her grace and beauty, her willingness to give, and to take, raised up the quality of their love to a height previously unattainable. She was open with him, full of life, and the image of life. In the past months, she embraced what they had together without question, ignoring, he knew, the condemnation of her neighbors, or enduring it, without complaint. He loved her, for all these things, and more; he would sorrow over their loss.

"Faith," he said, disturbing the tendrils of hair about her ear, "I love you."

Without waking, she turned onto her side, backing into the warm, familiar curve of his body. He kissed the top of her head, her temple, the side of her neck, and considered how effortless a thing it would be for him to weep.

Brian witnessed the coming of day in the golden fire shimmering along the silhouette of treetops; a fire that promised warmth for that June day. For a tremulous moment, it shivered through the spreading black branches in a sky of pale yellow and amethyst, and then it lifted on hazy wings, chasing shadow before its flame. Brian rose, and dressed, pulling open a dresser drawer to gaze, with regret, at a still unopened bottle of cognac. He had meant to share it with Fletcher, long ago, but something had always precluded his doing so. Frowning, he pulled it out, and walked to the window.

He looked into the yard below where grooms were already at work, mucking the stalls, walking the horses outside of the stable. He knew, personally, that one of those boys was a patriot, and only continued his work for the British in order to gain what information he could for the rebels. But it would have been difficult to prove.

This bloody rebellion! he thought angrily. The impudence of these rebels, to think they could keep the British army contained within Boston for very long! He felt confident that today would be the deciding battle. Breed's Hill had become an important focal point since yesterday, and the British were proving themselves efficient in that matter, as long their record had proven them to be. They would gain the hill, oust the rebels, fortify that vantage point for themselves, and break the siege once and for all.

He would feel a certain satisfaction in the surprise element, in the reaction it would have among Boston's remaining patriots. Mrs. Ashley was one in particular, with her impertinent manner, her quick tongue, her intelligence that was not in keeping with the loveliness of her face and form. Had she been his, surely she would have pushed him to madness long ago. Perhaps, she had already driven Fletcher to that insanity; he certainly behaved as though he were bewitched beyond redemption. He imagined it a pleasant insanity, at times; and at others, he supposed, quite painful.

Prying the seal from the cognac, Brian twisted out the cork. Glancing about for a glass, and not finding one, he lifted the bottle into the air.

"To you, my friend," he said aloud, "I drink your health now, and tomorrow, God willing, you will drink mine."

He brought the neck to his lips, inhaling briefly of the bouquet, and then he tipped the bottle upward. The liquor burned in the dryness of his throat, and he welcomed it.

Not long after, with the bottle recorked and returned to the drawer with his other dear possessions, Lieutenant Upton left, marching along the hall to the room of a man who had once been his fellow officer; who still was, even if he needed forceful reminding. In war, friendship might save a man's life, but the enticements of a woman could destroy reason, and the ability for preservation. Fletcher could not abandon his commission. He could not be allowed to do so, when the orders had already been issued demanding him to lead his men up Breed's Hill. To refuse would be tantamount to treason. He would be hung.

* * *

Rolling unbaked loaves into dampened towels, Faith carried them, one by one, to the warm bricks beside the fire for rising. She brushed flour from her hands and forearms. The scent of fresh, yeasty dough was a pleasant permeation. Humming a quaint, disjointed tune beneath her breath, she returned to the table and began to clean her work area, sweeping bits of drying dough into the pocket of her apron that she had created with her arm. She strode to the back door and opened it, flinging the dough into the yard with a sharp strike of the cloth. In the rising sun it would dry completely, and the birds would feast upon it merrily.

Faith stepped over the doorstone, into the dirt path that the years of treading had worn deep, and then on, into the grass beneath the trees. It needed scything, for it had grown long, above her knees. Her skirt caught in it as she walked. Pausing to lean against the trunk of the largest of the two chestnuts, Faith dashed a hand across her perspiring brow. She leaned her head back against the fissured plates of the bark, shutting her eyes against the shaft of the sun through the tree's long, lanceolate leaves. There was a peace to the morning that was out of keeping with the tide of events, of revolution, of Fletcher's imminent departure. There was not even the sound of the drilling that had become so much a part of daily life.

Faith opened her eyes, sensing a gaze upon her where she stood beneath the rustling shade of the spreading branches. She looked to the attic window, smiling. But Fletcher was not there. She looked then to the open rectangle of the doorway in the whitewashed expanse of the kitchen wall. That was empty also, as were all the rear-facing windows. The sensation grew stronger, as did another, at the edge of her mind, coming to her in a small vibration through the air. She pushed off from the tree, propelled by urgency. At that precise instant, an explosion of cannonade in the near distance rent the peace of the morning. The earth rocked beneath her feet. She spread her hands before her in an instinctive reflex and cried out wordlessly.

"Mrs. Ashley!"

An arm, on her elbow, supported her. Faith spun to blink at the young countenance of Lieutenant Upton. His expression was one of concern, yet he seemed to be trying to quell that sentiment. Breathing deeply, she said, "Pray tell, Lieutenant, what was the cause of that uproar?" With only a slightly shaking hand, she pushed the hair from her eyes and tucked it up beneath the edge of her starched pinner. At his hesitation, she glanced at him sharply. "It cannot have begun so soon?"

Lieutenant Upton regarded her display of fortitude with some disconcert. He was singularly touched by her lack of hysteria, and her attempt to remain calm. He stared at her in confusion, for he felt a foolish need, for a sudden, to protect her, to guard this flame of her courage. It occurred to him that what was passing in his mind and through his heart, in that instant, was knowledge of some part of the love that Fletcher held for her. He could understand Fletcher's love and respect for her, though he despised himself for knowing it.

"The frigates in the river are bombarding the fort," he said, with a harshness that was meant to cow, but only came out sounding kindly, more emotional than he had originally intended. He had thought to gloat over the fact, to hold it over her patriotic ideals, to make her understand that the British army was not one to be trifled with, or to be taken by surprise a second time. But he found, gazing into the roundness of her startled green gaze, that, after all, he could not.

She sighed. "And Fletcher knew this," she said, not as a question, but as a statement without question. Brian was silent, uncertain of his reply. He withdrew his hand from her arm. Wordlessly, he watched as her eyes moved from his face to that which he held, folded double, over his forearm. He wished now that he had hidden it beneath a cover of sheeting, or, as a last resort, behind his back. But it was there, in plain view, crying out for her attention: the scarlet coat against his own, trimmed in black and lined in utter contrast with white. He had polished the brass buttons himself, so that they winked in the morning like sunshine itself. Folded beneath were the other garments of the uniform. He held Fletcher's shoes under his arm.

Faith stared with her lips slightly parted, so that her upper teeth showed, white and even.

"Today is not the day," she said, and her voice was barely audible.

"It is," he answered, flatly.

"No—"

"I must go in, now," he said, and made to move past her.

"He is not awake." Faith pleaded.

"It matters not," said Brian, softly, turning to look back at her. "I will wake him. He must come with me. He must, Mrs. Ashley. Such are his orders. I am sorry." As he spoke, there was another bombardment of cannon fire directed toward the hill. The birds fled the tree above them, winging into the sky. He saw her shudder, her shoulders trembling. "Will you come upstairs?" he asked. He did not want to leave her outside, alone.

Faith shook her head. "When he is ready," she said bravely, "I will come to him."

Brian nodded, reluctantly. He looked at her small face, at the halo of fiery hair floating above it, at the green eyes that spoke the truth of her emotions, telling him what her voice did not; that she was afraid. Not of the cannon fire, which continued as quickly as the cannon could be reloaded on the ships, but for the sake of the man whose love she claimed. Ah, Fletcher, he thought, I both pity and envy you, for this love of yours is wondrous to behold, and must surely break your heart.

Faith watched as he pivoted smartly on his heel, striding across the yard and through the open doorway, clutching the uniform close to his body. "Good morning, Miss Watts," he said, as he passed into the kitchen and out of sight. Elizabeth appeared on the threshold without a reply, her face pale, her eyes showing white all around.

"Mrs. Ashley," she said. "What's goin' on?"

"The British warships are firing upon our fort on Breed's Hill, Elizabeth," Faith informed her. Another roaring blast followed, with the thunder of impact upon the hill itself.

Elizabeth raised her hands to cover her ears. "Our men!" she cried.

Faith bowed her head. "Dear God, I know," she said. She felt that she should pray, but in the turmoil of what she should pray for, she felt her abdomen tighten, and sicken. For a moment, she covered her face in her hands, breathing deeply to stop the heaving of her stomach. It was not the first time in the past days that she had felt so ill when she thought of Fletcher returning to battle.

Drawing another breath, Faith dropped her hands. Elizabeth had not moved. Faith went forward, taking the girl's hand. "I am frightened, too. I do not know what the outcome of this day will be, Elizabeth."

"You are worried, for him," Elizabeth said, bitterly.

Faith's eyes narrowed. She felt a tightening, in her chest. The girl's tone of criticism was biting, injuring her greatly. "Yes," she said, "I am." Releasing her hand, Faith turned away, yet as she did so, she saw tears fill the girl's blue eyes. "If the noise continues to make you afraid," she said coldly, "go to the root cellar until it is done."

Lifting her skirts high, Faith swept through the kitchen to the staircase and took the steps in swift succession. Even before she neared the narrow attic-stair, she heard the voices of the two men, raised in apparent argument. She went quickly on, climbing the ladder-like steps at a near run, bursting into the attic breathlessly. "Fletcher," she said.

He was stationed in the position that she had grown to recognize as his own, one arm hooked above the window casement and his tall form leaning forward as he stared, without purpose. He moved sluggishly in response to her voice, dropping his arm, and came forward, slowly.

"Fletcher," she said, quietly, "do not leave me."

He responded with smoky gray eyes inundated with pain. She took a step nearer, and stopped.

"I love you, Fletcher," she said, careless of the younger officer's presence. He stirred behind her.

"Mrs. Ashley—" Upton began.

Fletcher made a cutting gesture with his hand, his entire body. "Brian," he stated sharply, "speak not. It is not your place. Keep still."

Faith glanced at the lieutenant over her shoulder, startling a look of grief. She turned back. "Fletcher," she implored, "my love, I beg of you with all of my heart, do not go. I . . . I meant to be strong, for you," and her hand came up, across her cheek and her eye as she forced back the tears, "I truly did, I swear to you." Her voice broke, and she waited to regain it before going on, in the midst of silence. "But I find I cannot. You may be killed," she whispered hoarsely. "God forgive me, you may, Fletcher. I am not unwilling to face that, but . . . what will I do, without you, my heart? What will I do?"

"Faith, Faith, come to me." Fletcher opened his arms, and Faith stumbled into them, burying her face against his chest. "You are brave, Faith, and strong, and if I die today, you shall go on, as you have before . . . No, hush, my darling. I must go. I know," he said, gazing long at Brian over Faith's head, "what my duties are, without threats or inducements. And you must understand, not only for my sake, but for your own, Faith." He bent his head, then, pressing his cheek against her hair. "My little one," he murmured, "nothing means more to me than do you. But what kind of man would I be, if I should abandon the service to which I am sworn, and in which I believe? Could you truly love me then, as you do now? I do not believe so, ah, I do not believe so."

Yet, even as he spoke those words, his arms convulsed around her, holding her tight against his breast. He compressed his lips, shut his eyes, preventing the spillage of his tears.

"Fletcher . . ." It was Brian, reminding him of the time.

"Very well," he said.

Faith pulled away first, standing at a short distance, her hands on his arms. She looked in his eyes; determined to convey her willingness to be strong.

"Godspeed, Fletcher," she said. Defiantly, she threw her arms about his neck. "Godspeed, my love," she said again. "Come back to me, I beg of you. Only come back to me."

"Faith," said he, and buried his face into the side of her neck.

"Fletcher," said Brian again, with his eyes averted, and a catch in his throat that he could not rid himself of, "we must be going."

Releasing Faith, Fletcher stood away, gazing down at her

with something of a smile crossing his features. He touched her cheek with the back of his fingers.

"Farewell," he said, and was gone, moving quickly down the stairs. She watched his stride, erect and proud; the handsome carriage of his head; the perfection of his profile when he refused, at the stairhead, to look back at her again: she was staring about the attic, knowing that it was over, that it could not be the same, evermore.

The smile that Faith had forced in return, faded at his disappearance, and she swayed on her feet, near to fainting. Lieutenant Upton grabbed her with both hands by the upper arms, assisting her to a chair. He cupped her chin in his palm and bent, kissing her lightly on the forehead. He had not meant to do it, and was not certain why he had, or had dared. He remembered then the promise that Fletcher had wrung from him, in the name of friendship. If the worst should happen, Brian, he had said, you must take the news of my death to her yourself. Swear to that, he had asked.

"I will watch over Fletcher for you," he said, suddenly. "I vow, I will keep him from harm."

She nodded, blankly.

"Good-bye," he said, "Mrs. Ashley."

"Good-bye."

Once he had gone, she crumpled like a child's rag doll, over the pale skirt of her gown, and wept across her knees.

Chapter Twenty-four

The sun on the slope was strong, casting shadows long behind the marching troops. Flesh beneath scarlet coats shivered in the discomfort of the heat; it prickled with sweat and the chafing of field-packs against back and shoulder. Guns were held in hands slick with moisture; bayonets, honed to killing sharpness, gleamed as water in the afternoon light. Fletcher's sabre flashed at his side. From behind, came the rumbling of heavy wheels as the cannon was drawn up the hillside.

Four hundred feet from the top, Fletcher ordered his men to stop and regroup around the bodies of men, dead, or dying. He looked to the fort, shading his eyes with his hand. As before, the rebels were holding back their fire, waiting, motionless, behind the earthen walls. He saw a man, striding swiftly through the lines, hatless, sandy-haired, young and slim. Fletcher recognized Dr. Joseph Warren, a kind man, one to be admired, even in his rebel dissidence. Fletcher narrowed his eyes, lifting his hand from his scarred brow in a salute of respect.

"Advance!"

Slowly, inexorably, the line moved forward, British muskets raised, column upon column. Fletcher waited, counting down the seconds beneath his breath.

"Fire!"

The volley of the first line exploded. The soldiers dropped, to their knees, to reload. The second line moved into place.

"Fire!" And again, "Fire!" Across the slope, the soldiers responded to their officers' command with simultaneous gunfire, explosive and reverberating. From the fort there was no return. Fletcher's nostrils pinched. He would have to order his men closer, yet. It was a dangerous game that the Americans were engaging in, but it was damn effective.

Abruptly, he scented an odor of smoke that had nothing to do with the flash of powder, and he turned his head to witness a billowing black cloud pouring up the hillside behind from the direction of Charlestown. He saw a wisp of flame, and then another, somewhere in the streets. Within a minute's time, the smoke had obliterated the rear line and the slow progress of the cannon on creaking, metal-rimmed wheels; yet the pinnacle of Breed's Hill remained clear, and the sky above pale and limitless with the heat.

"Advance!" he commanded again. "Fire!"

The earth was slick with blood, here, where so many had fallen. Obstructed by bodies in scarlet and white, dotting the hillside with color.

"Advance! Fire!"

Why the hell didn't they return the volley? Did their commanders have that much control over the men that they could prevent them from doing so, even as their own men were being killed? Or was it as he had suspected? That ammunition was in short supply, and not to be wasted on any but the most definite of marks?

"Advance! Fi—"

In a puff of sulfurous yellow, the first shot rang forth from the rebel fortification, followed by another and yet another, in rapid succession. This was not the explosive volley that had greeted the British before, but something infinitely more deadly, for the Americans were taking careful aim of their targets, and did not miss. Teeth clenched, Fletcher watched as his men were cut down in the horrendous accuracy of the rebel assault. They had come within sixty feet of the fort. One could see a man's eyes, the perspiration on his brow, and the blood that ran, untended.

Unbuckling his sabre, Fletcher ordered his men to drop their field packs.

A bullet rang on stone, spitting dirt at his feet. He stepped back, holding his sabre aloft.

"Prepare," he yelled, "for bayonet charge!"

Muskets dropped forward with a clatter against the palm's curved flesh. The affixed bayonets glittered like glass, without order. And men fell.

And fell.

"Steady . . . !"

God help us, now, he prayed.

"And . . ." swinging his blade in a loose arc . . .

"CHARGE!"

They surged toward the wall, toward the muskets, lowered and deadly, toward the men who remained, standing strong. One could see them, as clearly as one might upon passing in the street, with the hatred of expression no longer concealed, the bitterness, the anger, the fear. Fletcher felt his foot slip on the first incline, and he righted himself, plunging onward, side-by-side with the men beneath his command. He shouted words of encouragement and of praise, for their bravery, their swiftness. He was no longer aware of the sweat running into his eyes. The gunshot rang with strange echoes within his ears. He thought of Faith, but only for an instant.

"Irons!"

Fletcher paused, turned, and saw Upton standing behind with his sabre at his side. For all of the younger lieutenant's attitude, he might have been waiting for the onset of breakfast, rather than preparing to charge over the wall.

"God, Brian, what the hell are you doing?" Fletcher demanded, as if, for a moment, he had forgotten that the man existed within the realm of danger and had been safe, all along, in some other place.

"Fletch, I'm here, old boy!" Brian shouted back, waving his weapon in greeting. "We'll do it! I said as much, did I not? We will take it!"

Fletcher found himself grinning. His slate eyes lit with a vicious fire. "We may!" he shouted to Brian, as the young lieutenant turned to swing his sabre against the gaping bore of a fowling gun. "We just may!"

The cannon cartridges had been opened, the powder distributed, and even with that most of the men had only three shots left; some, only one. Jack reloaded his musket, ramming the charge into place angrily. This is all of it, he thought; I must choose well.

He stood to fire, leaning over the dead body of his neighbor, and sighted down the barrel. An officer, he determined, but there were so damn few left. At any rate, a retreat was not likely this time. The ranks were decimated, and still they came on. The British were not about to give up, not until the last man was dead. And with no more powder, it was not likely that his rebel friends could arrange that.

Squinting only slightly, he gazed along the barrel, preparing to fire. But a bullet from a British musket struck the stone beside his head, chipping off a hefty sliver that caught him in the forehead. He backed down, wiping the blood away with his stained and tattered sleeve. "*Infernal batard*," he muttered in French. He was up again, aiming, with a little more haste, at a black-haired lieutenant. The shot went astray, striking the ground at the officer's feet. Spitting over his shoulder, Jack dropped, searching the dead man for powder.

"There is no more."

Jack glanced up. "General Warren," he said, "I only hoped—"

"There is no more. There are only a few minutes left, Jack. If the British wait that long. No," said the physician, wryly, "listen. Already the order is being given for bayonet charge. Use your gun now as best you are able. It may yet save your life."

Slowly, Jack rose. He extended his hand to the doctor, who took it, in a warm shake. "What will be, will be," said Jack.

Warren nodded. "You must be brave, Jack."

"Yes, sir."

"And if today is your last, Jack, you must go to God who has made you, humbled by the task which you have undertaken. He will forgive you then. As I pray He shall forgive me."

"Sir—" began Jack, but the doctor continued as if he had not heard.

"Once," he said, "I envisioned this very place . . . I saw myself, standing as I am . . . with a gun, in my hands . . ."

Jack shivered. He turned at the sounds at the other side of the wall. He reached, for the doctor's arm. The British were over the parapet, their bayonets gleaming, jabbing, spitting men like meat, pulling away stained with the crimson rust of blood. So many more than he had thought remained to the army, overwhelming their own numbers.

"Jack," said Warren, "there is one shot left. In my gun. Take it, and give me yours. Do as I say. Withdraw enough to use it, or run, my boy, if such is your desire for life."

"I am no coward!" Jack cried.

"I know that, Jack. Who better than I?"

And Joseph Warren turned, with the young Frenchman beside him. It was too late for the exchange of guns; too late for anything more. A shot rang out from the wall, and pierced the physician's skull, through the forehead. He died where he stood.

"No!"

Enraged, Jack charged the soldiers wielding the bayonets, swinging the empty musket left and right with a madman's strength, intent on maiming, on death. He grappled a man's gun from him, then turned it upon him, slicing with the blade without care or hesitancy. Then he went for another, and yet another, frenzied with fear and despair. Somewhere to his right there was an explosion as the fort was rent by the force of British cannon. The American right-wing was crippled. And the troops that had been expected from Charlestown did not come. It was over, it was over, there was no point in surrender, no point in yielding, without death. With loss of hope, there came a certain peace to Jacques's mind, and he fought on, gaily almost, as the fort was breached, and the scarlet deluge swept over the walls, and beyond.

With his elbows on his knees, Fletcher cradled his dark head in his hands, staring down at a small beetle that was making its way across the russet-colored, woven rug. It moved between his spread feet, in and out of the mountains and valleys of the rug's weave. Fletcher observed it, until it had gone on, under his shoe, and even then he merely stared at the place where it had vanished.

The skin of his face, which had paled in illness, was sunburned, tight, tender beneath the pressure of his fingers. Yet, he noticed the pain only as a secondary discomfort, minor, and of no consequence. There was other pain, more serious, and which had nothing to do with physical distress.

After a moment, he lifted his head to gaze through the open window. There were gulls, above the wash-house, as there always had been. And he knew that if he stood, and looked down, he would see the black laundress, sheets in her arms, her mouth full of pegs; he would see the stable boys, for the horses had not gone, and the soldiers who were alive. Possibly, he would smell the lye soap, and the grass, and the strangely sweet scent of manure. He would hear the boys laughing, if he listened closely, and the flapping of the laundry across the lines. But he did not stand. He had no desire to witness the normal things, the everyday, the mundane.

But for the gulls, the sky was empty, heat-hazed, and bland. He stared into it, until his eyes hurt, and then he looked away. The haze made his eyes water. He wiped at them with his fingers.

Slowly, he rose, walking stiffly around the tiny inn-chamber. He stared at the walls, whitewashed and barren. He glanced at the neatly made bed, at the dresser, and the half-empty bottle of cognac upon it. The sunlight shone through the amber liquid, making patterns of brilliance in the whorls of wood. We waited overlong, to drink that, he thought; and looked elsewhere.

Coming about to the left side of the bed, he paused. He touched the pillow, clean now. All traces of bloodstains were gone.

Why did you do it? Why did you leap in front of me that way? he asked the question once more.

"Because," Brian had said, a transparency undermining his browned countenance and his dark eyes circled in lavender, of which Fletcher had grown so fond, "because I made a promise."

"That was not your promise, Brian," Fletcher had said, holding tight to his hand. "That was not your promise, at all."

"Not to you," Brian had answered, quietly. "To her."

Fletcher closed his eyes, held the moisture in, against his lashes. He took down the bottle of cognac, blindly, turning it in his hands. The glass was cool.

I loved you, Brian.

Had he said that, at the last? Perhaps not. He wished that he had.

Chapter Twenty-five

Faith was seated at table, staring listlessly into a cup of black, cold coffee when the news came to her that the British had won; that they had, in the end, overrun the fort, and were now in the process of constructing a stronger one, on nearby Bunker Hill.

She raised her eyes to view Elizabeth's expression as the girl relayed the information with a cant of her blue eyes and a twist of her mouth that seemed to say: Are you satisfied?

"How many . . . died?" Faith asked, slowly.

"I don't know the British number," said Elizabeth sullenly.

"Oh, Elizabeth!" cried Faith, smacking her open palm down on the table top. "You know that is not what I mean. In God's holy name, you know that is not what I mean."

"Ain't it?" retorted the girl. "I would have thought that you'd be worryin' about him."

Faith frowned. The nausea that had been plaguing her for days rolled in her stomach. "I am," she said, quietly, gazing down into the oily contents of her cup. Elizabeth was silent, watching her carefully. Beside the widow, there was a plate of uneaten toast and congealed eggs. Elizabeth had finished her own, before even she had gone out into the town, seeking news.

"A hundred," the girl said. "A hundred dead, and more."

Faith closed her green eyes. Over one hundred Americans killed, in a battle to retain a bit of earthwork, a stronghold, a dubious military advantage over the redcoats.

Elizabeth took a step closer. Her petticoat rustled. Faith did not turn her head, or open her eyes.

"Doc Warren . . . is dead."

Faith's mouth moved, lips closed, a muscle twitching in her jaw. "Dead," she said.

"He died," continued Elizabeth, waxing eloquent, "a general, with his musket in his hands."

Silently, Faith began to weep. She brought her elbow up onto the table, lowering her forehead into the heel of her palm. Were they to lose them all? she wondered sorrowfully. All of the men that they admired and revered, before this thing was done?

Behind her, Elizabeth's eyes widened, and grew tearful. She stepped closer still, reaching out her hand to touch the woman's shoulder, and then stopped, allowing her arm to drop to her side.

"Those eggs are cold," she said. "Let me fry you up some more. An' a new slice of toast. I'll eat that one. It don' look too bad."

In her posture of grief, Faith slowly smiled. She looked up, sniffling, and dashed a hand over her eyes. "Are you still hungry?" she said.

"Oh, no, Mrs. Ashley! I ain't hungry at all. I just—I—"

"Sit down."

Elizabeth sat. She pulled her chair close.

Pushing her coffee away, Faith leaned her head on her hand, tangling her fingers into her hair, and stared across at Elizabeth. "Do you hate me so very much," she asked, "for loving a man who is the king's own?"

Elizabeth swallowed, tears starting afresh. "No," she whispered. "I don' hate you any, Mrs. Ashley."

"There is no need," Faith went on, in a quiet, husky voice, "for punishing me for what you view as my wrongdoing. I have suffered conscience enough. I am torn enough. There is no greater punishment, I would suppose, than knowing that the man you love, whom you would die for, is at odds with all else that you believe in, and stand for, in your life. Do you understand what I am saying?"

Lips parted, Elizabeth nodded. Her blue eyes were wide as a baby's.

"Twenty years ago," Faith said, "your Jack might have been a prisoner of war in this very town. He is a Frenchman, after all. Would you not love him because of that, though your heart bade you otherwise? I tried to deny what I felt, for a little while. But I did no more than hurt myself, and him." She paused, thoughtfully, and her green eyes were dark, and sad. "In different circumstances, I would be his wife, Elizabeth. I hold on to that, very dearly.

"But circumstances are not different," she added, "and he continues to serve his uniform, and the king."

Elizabeth was silent. She looked at Mrs. Ashley, at her green eyes, red-rimmed from tears, and her open, lovely face.

"We have kept good company, you and I, Elizabeth. You are as a sister to me, and more."

Slowly, Faith's left hand crept across the table and settled over the girl's own. She squeezed it, gently.

"And if he is dead, Elizabeth—if he is—"

Without another word, the girl came up from her chair, and threw her arms about the widow's shoulders. She buried her face into the curling mass of the woman's red hair and felt the squared edge of Faith's chin, against her collarbone.

"I have not done anything wrong," Faith grieved. "I have done nothing of which I am ashamed. I want him back, Elizabeth, that is all. If he is dead, I shall not be able to endure . . ."

"Hush, Mrs. Ashley," said Elizabeth, stroking her hair. "Hush."

It was almost habit that brought him to Faith's back door, for Fletcher had been wandering without aim beneath the heat of the sun, measuring grief in the length of his stride. In a sad self-deceit, he found himself outside of her back door, although he had possessed no inclination, upon leaving the inn, to come there.

The door was open. Through the shallow depth of the lean-to, he stared inside. He stared, and did not notice that Faith sat alone in the kitchen, at the table, with her head bowed into her hands. The creases and folds of her dull green gown blended into the misted shade beyond the mote-filled sunshine pouring through the window. He lifted his heavy-soled shoes over the threshold, setting them down quietly on the brick floor before the inner doorstone.

Faith.

The sight of her brought him up short. He frowned at her profile, as lovely as always, and at the linen handkerchief balled into her fist. In all that had occurred, he had not paused to think of her suffering over the losses of her own countrymen, of Joseph Warren, a man whom she had known for some years, nor of her worry concerning his own well-being. He had not sent word. Too much had occurred, too quickly.

Faith raised her head. She wiped her eyes with closed fingers. "Elizabeth?" she called. "Are you back, so soon?" she turned, slowly, toward the back door. She saw him there, saw the scarlet of his uniform, the coal black of his hair, the face, worn and tired and beautiful. His eyes regarded her silently. With a gasp, she stood up so quickly that she upended the chair. It fell with a clatter of wood.

"Fletcher? Oh, dear God!"

She was in his arms in a twinkling, clutching to his black lapels desperately, and sobbing against his chest. "You're alive, you're alive," she said, over and over. Above her, he was very still, jaw set, his eyes fixed straight ahead. After a moment, he bent, kissing her hair, and lay his cheek upon it.

"Faith," he said, in a desperation that she misunderstood, "I love you."

Squeezing shut his gray eyes, he embraced her close, and drew several deep, ragged breaths.

"Might I sit down?" he said.

Taking his hands, Faith led him to the table and her vacated chair; he lifted it, easing down onto it, wearily. Faith knelt on the floor before him. She turned his hands over in her own, and kissed them both.

"We took the fort. I suppose that you have heard."

Faith nodded. Barely able to countenance the fact that she had not lost Fletcher, Faith gazed up at him with single-minded devotion and intent. Absently, Fletcher rubbed his hand across her wet cheeks.

"Joseph Warren is dead."

"Elizabeth told me, my love."

"Despite what you might hear from the troops, he did not turn and run, but died, standing firm, as a man."

"I would not have believed otherwise," said Faith.

"I suppose not," Fletcher sighed. He lifted his eyes to the window, to the ripple of the curtain in a vagrant breeze that did no more than waft the heat and dust into the kitchen. "The siege has not been raised," he said. "We have accomplished nothing. Men have died for naught."

Faith was silent. She lifted his hand again, interlacing her fingers with his own. With her other, she traced the bridge that their fingers made, studying it, swallowing painfully.

"Two-hundred and twenty-six soldiers died, Faith. Over eight hundred—eight hundred, Faith, have been wounded. Of the entire Eighteenth Regiment, only twenty-five men survive. Every officer in General Howe's staff was shot down in the first volley. And why?" he said. "For the sake of thirty American prisoners, and a fort which we abandoned in the end to construct another? The siege is not raised. And this war goes on."

Faith looked up, and made a small sound. From Fletcher's wide-open eyes the tears were rolling, unchecked, over the high planes of his cheekbones. His shoulders shook. He would not take his gaze from the window, the wind, the glimpse of pale sky beyond the trunk of hornbeam beside the house.

"Fletcher," began Faith, "please," and would have risen, but he held her fast.

"Brian's dead," he said. His teeth were bared, in a grimace of pain and sorrow. "God in heaven," he said, "save me, or damn me to hell. Brian is dead, Faith; he is dead."

He caught her, then, to pull her up against his breast, and wept like a child in the embrace of her arms. In shock, Faith held his convulsing form, listening to the heartrending depth of his sobbing.

Holding his head in her hands, she kissed his black hair, and cried into it, without noise.

Ezra sat, knees aching, back stiff, deep in the cushions of his favorite chair. The hearth before his feet was, in summer, swept clean, empty, yet he gazed down into it out of habit. Beyond the open window, night was lowering, and the birds were in the trees, singing contentedly. They had no stake in war, no care for it, and so were unaffected. Ezra pulled his spectacles from his nose, polishing them halfheartedly with his handkerchief, his thoughts deep in melancholy.

Somehow, all of his wandering musing of war and loss and sad anger had dwindled down to the image of one person, and that was his Faith. Ah, when last he had seen her, her content and inner happiness in the midst of all this turmoil had seemed so evident that it had nearly broken his heart, when, in truth, he should have been overjoyed for her. It was the cause of her happiness that had hurt him so, that had made him realize, once and for all, that there was no hope that he would ever be the recipient of the love he had desired for himself.

And that cause was Fletcher Irons. Wounded in battle, the man was in Faith's tender care, in her home, and Faith had been fairly blooming with the joy of having the man whom she loved so near.

Sighing, Ezra shifted painfully in his seat. For his own sake, Faith had tried not to exhibit her happiness too plainly, but he knew her too well, in the passage of the years. It had been obvious, quite obvious.

He had considered himself resigned to the fact that she did not love him, long ago. It had taken this to remind him of what he had already known. And had he not brought them together? he thought, with regret.

Sighing again, he made to rise from his chair, but the sound of movement in his office stayed him. Frowning, he stared with clouded eyes toward the open doorway.

"Who is there?" he called; quietly, calmly.

After a moment, a shadow appeared in the darkened rectangle, and hovered there, peering in.

"Ezra?"

In shock, Ezra stirred, replacing his spectacles with shaking, blue-veined hands. "Faith, is that you?" he said, wondering at the catch in her voice which indicated to him that she had been weeping.

"Yes," she said.

"Come in, then!" he cried, with more harshness than he had intended. "Don't stand about in the doorway like a frightened child. Come in, and sit down."

Obediently, she did so, moving to the chair opposite him, and sat, smoothing the folds of her green skirt. Her eyes were red-rimmed. She smiled at Ezra, wanly.

"It is good to see you," she said. "I am sorry to come, unannounced."

"Unannounced?" he retorted. "It has never mattered before; why should it now?"

"Yes," said Faith, lowering her head to stare at her hands in her lap, "Yes, of course."

A silence entered between them, awkward, and full of questions, unspoken. Finally, Ezra asked her, bluntly:

"What is it, Faith? Why have you come?"

Faith hesitated, a small frown between her brows.

"Trouble?" Ezra prompted, rubbing his ridged knuckles with swollen fingers.

"No," said Faith. "It is not trouble."

Ezra inhaled. "Does this war frighten you at last, my dear? Do you realize now what it is that is being done in the name of this elusive, ill-defined, liberty of yours?"

"I have known," Faith answered, listlessly, "all along."

Closing his eyes, Ezra formulated the question that he had meant to ask the moment he realized her distress. He licked his dry lips. "The lieutenant?" he said. "Did he return to duty? Has he—has he—"

"He is gone, Ezra."

"Oh, no."

"Ezra, you misunderstand," Faith hastened. "He was not killed, thank God. But he . . . he is gone. Returned to his duty, Ezra, to the service to which he is sworn."

"He is a man of honor, Faith," Ezra answered, after a moment. "I have long known that, as have you. He would not forsake his commission, his allegiance to Britain. Did you expect otherwise, my dear? Do you have some . . . cause . . . to expect this?" The young lieutenant had assured Ezra that he would treat her with respect. The elderly man would not think otherwise.

"No," said Faith, quietly, "I had no cause to expect it." Ezra let loose an unconscious sigh of relief, not realizing that her response had little to do with the path of his reflection. Faith rose, then, and went to the window, to gaze out at the darkening sky. The chimney swifts darted through the air above the rooftops on arrowed wings. "I let him go, Ezra. I could not stop him. I knew," she added, almost as to herself, "when he donned his uniform again, what the end result would be."

Ezra frowned. A sharp pain gripped him, low in his chest, and was gone. "I am sorry, my dear," he said. "You love him very much."

"Of course, I do, Ezra," she answered. "And you knew that I would, didn't you? You forfeited a great deal, on a gamble for my happiness." She turned from her observation of the night, moving slowly to stand before Ezra in his chair. "Thank you," she said, and burst into tears behind the cover of her hand.

"Hush, hush," said Ezra, and took her hand. "Kneel here, and lay your head on my knee, Faith, as once you used to do, before your sorrows had grown beyond my ability to erase. Put your head there, Faith, and do not worry," he said, and his old voice quavered. "He will be back, my dear." Tenderly, with shaking fingers, he stroked her flame red hair.

Faith's tears fell onto the satin fabric of Ezra's breeches, staining the cloth that strained about his swollen knee.

Chapter Twenty-six

Boston
January, 1776

Summer had passed, and autumn, and the new year had begun; and there was no reprieve from the siege, or from the coldest winter in years. Great chunks of ice floated down the Charles River toward the sea, and the British garrison was doubled there, lest the ice pack together and freeze, and thus provide a bridge over which the rebels could attack. In November, Old North Church had been pulled down for firewood; the townspeople found the steeple of West Church torn down by January, and, by the month's end, sixty additional buildings had been dismantled. Trenches scarred the slope of the Common, dug out of the frozen earth. The pews of Old South, where once Joseph Warren had enthralled thousands of listeners with his appeal to their sense of righteousness and yearning for liberty, were ripped out to be burned, and the floor was covered with dirt and gravel so that the royal officers could exercise their horses out of the weather.

The opulent mansions of Beacon Hill lost their paint, their look of wealth, having been left abandoned by so many. Throughout the town, the gardens which were the pride of Boston, were, in winter, no more than beds of ice-slicked weeds, sparkling in brittle sunshine with their own sad beauty. Stray animals roamed the streets, thin, and shivering, and nearly too undernourished to provide a meal for a starving man. Nearly.

Behind Faith's own house, her beloved chestnuts had been removed in October by the British, and were now broad stumps upon an earth where the snow had frozen into sheeted layers, and the stumps themselves glistened like glass. In December, the shed was gone, also, plied apart with Elizabeth's help, and piled within the confines of the lean-to along with the pickets of the fence; by January, nearly all of it had been burned.

The two women took to residing in close proximity to the kitchen hearth, for there was no possibility of warming the entire house. Shutters were closed, and what blankets could be spared were thrown over doors as a barrier to the cold. Neither of them ventured out of doors except at such time as they were to collect their ration of meat and flour. The larder had been well stocked, but had dwindled, and the food within it was consumed sparingly, carefully. They did not starve.

And, as the months progressed, so did the obvious state of Faith's condition, for she had found herself, against all hope and expectation, with Fletcher's child.

"Elizabeth," said Faith, standing before the fire, holding her hands to the heat. She wore heavy brown knit-gloves upon them; they were fingerless from the second joint, for freedom of movement. The girl looked up from her seat upon the brick hearth. She noted that the woman's flying brows were lowered over the bridge of her nose, and her head was tilted, as if listening.

"Do you hear someone knocking?" Faith went on to ask her.

Elizabeth listened, also, and it seemed that there was the sound of a summons coming from the front of the house. "Shall I go see?" she asked.

"I will," answered Faith. "Stay here, where it is, at least, warm." Pulling her shawl over her well-rounded belly, she lifted the quilt from the inner door of the kitchen, and opened it, stepping quickly through to shut it behind. Her breath smoked in the near darkness beyond.

"Coming!" she cried. "I am coming!"

With all the shutters secured against the elements, the house was very dim, and she fumbled a moment with the door latch before opening it. The blast of wind whipping around the door blew it back with such force that it slammed against her elbow, and knocked her backwards, off balance. Snow swirled in a great cloud of hazy light, coating the floor.

"Oh!"

"My dear!" cried a strangely familiar voice, "Are you hurt?" And she felt a hand on her arm, lifting her, as the door was pushed closed with a theatrical grunt. For a moment, she stood shivering, clutching the swell of her abdomen from beneath, and breathing heavily.

"Who is that?" Faith asked, blinking in the abrupt absence of frigid, filtering sunshine.

"It is rather dark in here," commented the voice, in irksome smoothness, without answering her question. "Is there no lamp, Mrs. Ashley?"

"Not here," said Faith, in growing irritation. "Who—?"

He interrupted her with a laugh that struck a chord of memory. Yet, before she could speak again, he said, "Are you truly unable to fathom my identity? Oh, Mrs. Ashley, what a joy you are! It is Charles Johnston, my dear, come to pay you a call."

Faith said nothing. Unthinkingly, she jerked her arm free of his grasp and took a step away from him, thankful, now, for the dim circumstance. The last thing she needed was for that odious man to spy her in her flagrantly pregnant condition.

"Is there someplace else where you, ah, entertain your

guests?" he went on. "It is a trifle uncomfortable standing here, unable to see you."

"Why did you come?" Faith asked him, pointblank.

"My," he retorted, "as waspish as ever, I see. I thought that you had accepted my apologies, long ago. Have you forgotten our walk together? Naturally, it would have been far more pleasant, had we not been accompanied by that oaf, Irons."

"Would it?" responded Faith. "How so?"

He laughed, with a decadent wickedness. "I don't suppose that I should say," he answered her. "However, I was merely passing through the area today, and I thought it quite the neighborly thing to do, to drop in, and assure myself that you are well. The situation that prevails being what it is, I mean."

"Passing through?" repeated Faith. "In this weather? You should have taken more care to stay at home, sir."

Johnston grunted. "You are, perhaps, correct. It seems a good bit cooler in here than I have found it outside. Yet, you would not turn me away without first offering me a little something to sustain me on my journey homeward, would you?"

Faith narrowed her eyes in the darkness. "We have no wine, here," she said.

He seemed genuinely hurt, as he said, "I was not asking, Mrs. Ashley. Just a little something to eat."

Faith frowned, thinking how absurd it was to be bandying words with the man in a shadowed house, and how uncharitable a thing it was to bear a grudge, for so long. She had only met the man twice, and though both meetings had been unpleasant, they were, perhaps, no cause by which to wholly judge the man.

"We have not much to spare, Mr. Johnston. But I am certain that something may be mustered for your pleasure. If you will follow me, carefully, sir, I will lead you to the kitchen. That is the only part of the house open for use."

She listened to the sound of his clipped footfalls, assuring herself that they were not coming too near, and at the kitchen door, she ducked in ahead of him, to seat herself at one of the two chairs which remained at the table. The others had been burned, as had the long-retired butter churn, the block board, which she'd had to take an ax to, in order to break it, and anything else of wood that could be spared. One shutter was open, to allow some degree of light to illuminate the room. Elizabeth turned sharply from the fireside, eyes wide, and wider still at the entry of a stranger, behind.

Faith nodded to her, in a peculiar, stressful manner. "Elizabeth," she said, "this is Mr. Charles Johnston, an—an acquaintance of mine. Mr. Johnston, Miss Watts."

Charles strolled slowly into the kitchen, speculatively. He greeted Elizabeth with a sensual glance that made the girl frown angrily. She looked at Faith. The woman shook her head, very slightly, and pushed in closer to the table, bringing the folds of her shawl up to drape over her arms like a curtain. Elizabeth understood.

"Sit down, Mr. Johnston," the girl said, not caring for the way he was hovering about. He was a well-dressed man, she noticed, upon removal of his coat, though his clothes hung on him rather loosely. Tall, also, and dandified in his mannerisms. As he made his way, casually, across the floor, holding his ostentatiously ornamented hat in his hand, he looked at Mrs. Ashley with an open expression that startled the girl.

From beneath lowered lids, Faith observed every movement the man made. He looked different than she remembered him; not quite disheveled, but not the impeccable dresser that he had prided himself in being. He's lost a noticeable amount of weight, also. But hadn't they all? His face was drawn, shadowed. And the eyes that had always been pale, were now colorless above the darker flesh beneath.

My goodness, Faith thought; he looks to be starving.

"Elizabeth," she said, carefully, "do we have any eggs left that you might fry up for Mr. Johnston? And a cup of hot water, to warm him. I am afraid that we have no tea here, even if we were of a mind to drink it, Mr. Johnston, and the cider is gone."

"Ale?" suggested the man. Faith shook her head.

"Not at all."

He sighed, gazing about the kitchen with his blanched eyes. He raised his hand, to smooth back the graying hair at his temple; it was his natural hair, not the wig he usually sported.

The hand shook, a tiny tremor, and was stilled with an angry clench. No, he was not the same man that Faith recalled, drunken, and forward, taking liberties. Until he spoke. There was no altering the haughty tone of his voice.

"You have come down a bit in the world, Mrs. Ashley."

Faith shook her head in a motion of surprise.

"I would not say so, Mr. Johnston. I have never possessed much more than that which I possess now."

"Indeed?" said he. "Considering the way that you dressed at dinner when we met, and your contemptuous attitude, I thought that you had some wealth to back you up."

"Is that why you are here?" she asked.

"I beg your pardon?" he said, severely.

"I thought that you were, perhaps, in need of a handout."

"I resent that, Mrs. Ashley!" the man cried in indignation, but remained seated, his eyes gliding from Faith's to the eggs spattering in the pan over the fire. With expertise, Elizabeth flipped them, then she set a piece of bread into the toasting rack, sliding it nearer to the flames. He watched, gritting his teeth, as she tipped them into a plate, tucking the toast beside, and poured the water from the kettle, carrying all to the table before him. Wordlessly, the girl deposited a fork beside the plate, and a napkin, only slightly soiled. He hardly waited for the amenity before pulling the plate close. He ate, ravenously. Observing him, Faith was moved to pity him.

"I wish," she said at last, "that I had something more to offer you, but there is nothing."

Elizabeth cocked her head at the woman in confusion. Charles frowned. "There is no need for your pity," he said.

Faith nodded in acceptance. Charles wrinkled his nose in displeasure. He pushed the plate away, dabbing at his mouth delicately with the napkin. He discarded the cloth with a fillip of his fingers. His glance was hard, weighing potential gains in his mind. There was something cruel in the look, in the gaze he directed at Faith, in the flickering of his pale eyes, up and down. Elizabeth took a step closer to her, standing behind her shoulder. Faith did not move. She kept the shawl curtained across her distended abdomen, with the table between herself and the man.

264   *Robin Maderich*

"Do you have any coin, Mrs. Ashley?"

Elizabeth started.

Faith made a face of impatience.

"So then, it is a handout which you are looking for, after all, Mr. Johnston?"

"Indeed not," he said, and in his injured pride there was something real to him, something which made him attractive, gaunt as he was. "A loan, Mrs. Ashley; nothing more. I have a property in New York, and I want nothing more than to be there. But first, it seems, I must bribe my way out of this godforsaken town, for there is no ship that will depart in this weather."

Faith leaned forward, as far as she could manage. Her belly rubbed against the table. The baby kicked.

"What on earth made you think to come to me?"

"You are a woman, and women have always been a soft touch," he said, attempting to look seductive, but somehow, only appearing the more to be pitied.

"Mrs. Ashley ain't!" cried Elizabeth, suddenly.

"My," said Charles, his eyes raking the girl searingly, "what a lovely pet you keep on your shoulder. How many tricks can she perform? Any that I might find of interest?"

Faith ignored the remark, patting Elizabeth's hand to bid her to silence. She let her own breath out slowly, through her nose. "How much?" she said.

"Mrs. Ashley—!"

"Hush, Elizabeth," said Faith, quietly, looking directly at Johnston. He reached up, nervously brushing the hair at his temples.

Licking his lips with a frown, he said, "A sovereign will do, Mrs. Ashley."

"A sovereign!" cried Elizabeth, unable to contain herself. Faith admonished her with a squeeze of her hand.

"You forget, sir," said she, "that we are at war. I have a box of worthless scrip, but a sovereign I have not."

Johnston's frown deepened. "A few shillings, then. That will be enough."

Faith was silent, and then she laughed, at her own gullibility. "You are willing to settle for a few shillings, and yet you expect me to believe you may bribe your way through both the British army and the rebel forces? You are, you must remember, a Loyalist, and it is not likely that any patriot will allow you to pass from Boston—with, or without, a bribe. I see now that you want nothing more than to take whatever I might offer you, and slip it into your pocket. And to think that I nearly felt sorry for you. You are no better than a harlot, sir, now that your fancy ways have left you, and your clothes, like Boston, have come to ruin. Your friends, in all probability, have deserted. Elizabeth, I have a ha'penny, there on the mantelpiece. Give that to Mr. Johnston, and then, I am afraid, he shall have to leave.''

As she was bade, Elizabeth crossed to the hearth, and stretched up, running her hand over the mantelpiece until she found the coin. She turned, extending it to Mr. Johnston. He rose from his chair, sputtering.

"No," he said, "I am not so desperate as that! Keep your damned coin, Mrs. Ashley. You have not changed. There is a bitch in you," he said, shoving away from the table and stalking slowly around it, "unlike any I have ever known. Perhaps, there might have been some enjoyment in taming it. Perhaps not. Do you know, Mrs. Ashley, what I would have done to you, had I been the one whom you chose to walk you home, that night—how long ago? Unlike that blowhard, Irons, I would not have permitted any company to distract, or prevent me.'' He stood beside her chair, glaring down, and wondered why she did not move, did not rise, or turn away. "I suppose you bite," he said, "don't you?"

"To draw blood," said Faith.

With the howl of a desperate man, Johnston reached down, and swung Faith's chair about, shoving it back across the floor, so that the legs scored the planking. Faith stood up. Her shawl fell from her shoulders.

Charles brought himself up short, in shock. Casually, Faith held out her hand for the iron poker which Elizabeth had lifted from the firewell.

"Are you leaving, Mr. Johnston?"

Her red hair had loosened, and was falling about her shoulders. She breathed deeply, and with each intake of her breath,

her abdomen rose beneath her gown. Charles stared at it, at
the place where the child, whom Faith had so long desired,
curled in tender waiting.

"I am as a harlot?" he said, slowly. "Whom," he said,
"is the lucky father? Does he know? Do you know, my dear?"
And then he laughed, with bitterness. "I might hazard a guess,
myself, but it is not really necessary, is it? His name has already
come up, at least twice in our conversation."

"Mr. Johnston. Get out." Faith swung the poker up, and
let it fall. The sooty tip cracked down into the floor. Charles
leapt back.

"So you bedded him, did you? And where is he now? At
least I would have paid the price for pleasure, and married
you, even if faithfulness was not in my vow."

"How do you know that we are not wed?" Faith snapped.

"I have asked."

"What?"

"Oh, not him, naturally. But, I have a friend, with whom
your lover is acquainted, and he has been keeping a close watch
on the bastard. Irons lived here with you in sin, for a time. I
know this. I know, also, that he no longer sends you so much
as a single package to subsidize your meagre rations. He has
tossed you aside. And when the dog abandons the bitch, the
wolves are free to move in."

"Get out!" Faith cried. She could not stand to be reminded
that Fletcher had not contacted her in months.

Elizabeth rushed past Faith's speechless, immobile figure
with the pan from the fire raised above her head. Charles
gasped, and extended his arms to grapple with the girl. The
hot pan touched his hand, and he yelped, pulling away.

"Elizabeth! Elizabeth, come here, my dear. Put the pan
away." But the girl merely stood, with her arm hanging at her
side, keeping the pan, the handle of which was wrapped in a
towel, still raised parallel to the floor.

"I suggest," said Faith, moving to stand beside the girl,
"that you leave now, Mr. Johnston. What you have said is
unforgivable. I am not certain, yet, why you have come here,
but I do not believe that I care to know. Just get out."

"Do not play the innocent," said Johnston, picking up his

battered tricorne with its ridiculous cockade from the table
where he had deposited it, and sweeping it up onto his head.
He slipped into his heavy greatcoat. "But I would not ravish
a woman with child. Especially one who bears the child of a
man I abhor. Either way," he said, "you do not appeal to me
in that bloated state."

He started out the way that he had come in, but Faith stopped
him, pointing angrily toward the back door. "That way," she
said. "I will not tolerate your presence in my house any longer
than is necessary."

Poker in hand, she followed close behind. In the confines
of the lean-to, he turned on her, but thought better of his actions
at the sight of the raised length of iron, and threw the door
open. It banged loudly against the house. Snow as fine as dust
swirled in. He stepped out into it. The wind howled.

"Never dare," she shouted above the din, "to come onto
my property again! Or I swear to you, I will— use this, without
hesitation!"

Waving the poker threateningly, Faith went out into the snow
behind him, watching until he was out of sight. The wind
whipped at her hair and gown, and tore her shawl from her
shoulders so that it stretched out beside her, like a banner. She
dashed the ice from her eyes.

"Mrs. Ashley, you'll freeze like that! Come inside, now!
Please!"

With Elizabeth's hand on her arm, Faith returned to the
house. She bolted the door forcefully, her expletives angry.
Then she went to the fire and knelt before it. She was shaking;
and not entirely from the cold.

"Here," said Elizabeth, coming up behind her, "wrap yourself in this. T'wouldn' do to catch a chill." Solicitously, she
lowered a blanket over Faith's quivering form. Faith pulled it
close and bowed her head, spending a moment in catching her
breath and trying to calm her trembling. She moved her hands
over her abdomen, which had settled, in her kneeling position,
over her legs. She felt heavy, physically bound to the earth.
Beneath her hands, the child moved slowly, as though rolling.
Faith gasped, at the sensation. She had all she could do to keep
from urinating as the weight disposed itself above her bladder.

"Somethin' wrong, Mrs. Ashley?"

Faith shook her head.

"Who was that man?"

"Someone," said Faith, "of whom I have never been fond."

"I can understand the reasoning," muttered Elizabeth. "He seemed the dangerous sort."

"I believe that he can be," Faith agreed. "Thank you, Elizabeth, for coming to my defense."

"T'wasn't much," scoffed Elizabeth, waving it aside.

"It was," said Faith. "To me, it was. Unfortunately," she added, rising, her one hand supporting her belly, the other against the hearth. Elizabeth caught the falling blanket, and wrapped it about her shoulders. "I can imagine the consequences of this day's work. Oh, Elizabeth! I cannot have Fletcher finding out from that hateful man that I am with child! I should have told him myself, sooner than this. So much sooner. For even if he cares no longer for me, the child is his. He has the right to know, from me.

"Once, Elizabeth, when I had refused him again in marriage, he told me that he would not accept that answer if ever we made a child between us. I assured him there was no possibility of that. 'Do you propose to know the will of God?' he asked me. Lord forgive me, perhaps I thought that I did. A miracle, a miracle at last, and I am making such a mess of it."

She swayed on her feet. Elizabeth grabbed her, leading her to the chair that had been shoved across the floor. "Sit down, Mrs. Ashley. That man has upset you. Sit down."

For several minutes, Elizabeth observed Faith's bowed head, the movement of her hands over the gown that covered her swollen belly, as if speaking in tender words of silence to the infant within her womb.

"Why did he stop sending the packages?" Elizabeth asked.

Faith looked up. Her expression was dazed, distant. She thought of the time when she had danced with Fletcher in the attic. He had spoken then of a child. Oh, how hurt he would be to discover that she had kept this from him! Or would he not care? Had he gone beyond caring? She could not believe so. She wronged him in believing so . . .

"I asked that he cease," she said. "I was afraid that he was giving me what was otherwise reserved for himself, and I worried there would be trouble with his superiors. And I . . . Elizabeth, the last I saw of him he spoke as a man does who is finding himself faced with a choice in his life, a clear delineation, and who must follow one road, or the other." She remembered their last, strained conversation after Fletcher had wept for his friend, and she had known then that the war had taken on new meaning for him. She guessed he would be unable to compromise himself any longer. "I will not be a burden to him, when I am not what he wants; when I am not the road that he chooses to travel. I have not been entirely honest with you, these past months, Elizabeth. I explained Fletcher's absence as a result of his duty; that is half-truth only. And he does not know, Elizabeth, about the baby."

Elizabeth was silent, clasping her hands together against her apron. Her ability to speak was impaired by the news. Behind her, the fire reduced in warmth. She glanced at it, to see that the planks, the single, turned leg of a chair, were all burning steadily. She took a step backward, and collapsed onto the hearth, her hands between her knees. "Mrs. Ashley . . ."

"Hush, Elizabeth," Faith soothed in a whisper, "I know."

Elizabeth shook her head, over her lap. "How could you not tell him?" she asked. "He loves you."

"He did," said Faith, "once. How am I now to be sure? What is there between us now that tells me he would welcome the news I have?"

"But you still love him, don' you?" .

"Yes, Elizabeth."

The girl was silent again, staring at the planked flooring beyond the hem of her gown and the many petticoats that she wore beneath, for warmth. She lifted her eyes to where Faith sat, very straight, in her chair. The sun filtered through the ice that rimed the window panes, touching her with its pearly light, so that her skin, the cream of her shawl, the pale background of her gown, reflected in a diffuse glimmering. She moved her hand to caress the child as it fluttered within her belly, and her head lifted, thoughtfully. Elizabeth lowered her own head into her hands.

"What will you do?" she moaned. "If he willn't marry you, your child will be named bastard."

With her head up, Faith closed her eyes. Her posture spoke of dignity, and resignation, and marked her, strangely, with beauty.

"I know," she said.

Chapter Twenty-seven

Mrs. Hart bent double, picking up the remains of the sturdy sign that had once hung above Ezra's door. Above her head, the chains clanged in the wind, empty and without use. Shouldering the broken wood and dragging the axe carefully in one hand, she returned through the office, shoving the door shut with her hip. By the time she reached the parlor with her burden, she was breathing heavily. The snow that had clung to her was melted, dripping wetly from her gray hair and the thick shawl about her shoulders.

"Here," she said to the lawyer, sitting in his chair, blanketed in quilts. "This should burn right well." And she tossed the wood onto the meagre flames of the hearth, prodding the pyramid with the poker until tongues of orange broke out along the planed edges. The paint curled, and blackened, giving off a noxious odor. The housekeeper fanned the smoke with her apron.

"Thank you, Mrs. Hart."

The woman nodded, turning to peer intently at the lawyer's expression. "What be you thinking of now, sir?" she asked, as if she did not know any better.

He merely sighed.

"She is fine, Mr. Briggs. You musn't worry."

"I have not seen her since Christmas," retorted Ezra, miserably. Mrs. Hart shook her head.

"Aye, but what a fine time we all had then, don't you recall? Even young Elizabeth was here, and Mrs. Ashley had us all laughing, and she led us in carols, and hymns . . ." She paused, knowing that she had, in her attempt to cheer him, only made him more miserable.

"This weather is frightful; there is no wood, no food."

"If Mrs. Ashley needed anything, she would let you know. And you have sent her what you could, you know that."

"Yes," he said. And he turned his face away from her, to stare, blindly, at the leaping flames. "That feels better, Mrs. Hart. It is much warmer, now."

"Very good, sir," answered the housekeeper, wondering, as she did so, if she would be able to supply more wood for the fire when the time came. It was getting more and more difficult to keep even just this one room warm, and Ezra was not much help, now that he had grown so weak in his legs, and in his heart. Nodding again, she turned to go.

"Mrs. Hart?"

"Aye?"

"Read Faith's last letter to me again. Please." In his hand, he held a crumpled piece of paper, which he was never without, and carried with him, inside of his coat, since its arrival some weeks before.

"Must I, sir?" asked the housekeeper, reaching for it reluctantly. "It only upsets you, Mr. Briggs."

"I know."

"Mayhaps, if you wrote to her again, apologizing for your anger. She would know that you meant nothing. You have given her everything that you could, despite your words. She would know—"

"It matters not," said Ezra, and returned the letter to his pocket. Mrs. Hart observed him with a frown on her wizened brow, and then she left him.

Faith, pregnant, he thought. The child of Fletcher Irons burgeoning in her womb. And the lieutenant, an officer of high calibre, leaving her, in shame. How could he? Faith had insisted, in her letter, that the man did not know, but how could he not? If he had not so totally abandoned her, he would have witnessed it, for himself. Instead, they stood apart, his Faith and her lover, with nothing but desperation between. What fools. He had half a mind to tell Fletcher himself, but Faith had begged him not to; had pleaded with him, in writing, to keep her secret, and to forgive her. Forgive her. At Christmas, she had known, and yet she had kept it from him. Why? he thought angrily. Why did she not tell him to his face?

He grimaced, there beneath his mountain of quilts, as the pain in his chest tightened, a single fist, travelling into his stomach, his shoulder, his arm. His eyes glazed over with pain.

No, he thought, no, not now. Mrs. Hart was right. He should call her to him, offer more than what he had. Perhaps then, she would accept his hand, allow him to provide a name for the child, give him a few months of happiness before the end . . .

His breath grew short, and he could not swallow. All thought appeared to be spiralling down to one pinpoint of light, of blinding pain and light. He brought his right hand up, to clutch at his breast, to tear at the cloth there as the agony overran his senses. From his nerveless left hand, his spectacles slipped, splintering on the hearthstone. It seemed that he could hear Mrs. Hart, crying out, from some grave distance.

Faith, he thought, my Faith, and then:

It is too late.

Leaning over the bed, Faith gazed down at Ezra's beloved face. Now that his spectacles were gone, her eye was drawn to the depth of his sockets, to the shadows beneath. His skin was without color, but for a bluish tint around his pinched nostrils and along the edges of his stretched mouth. His pale eyes were closed, barely flickering. Faith caught her breath, in pain. Opening her hand, she smoothed the dry, frizzled corona of his hair with her flat palm, then touched his fingers. "They are so cold," she said, more to herself than to anyone else within the room behind her. She heard Mrs. Hart begin to cry.

"What are his chances, Doctor?" Faith heard herself ask, with more calm than she had ever expected to feel. Retaining her grip on Ezra's hand, she turned to face the physician. Her abdomen extended conspicuously before her from beneath the crossed sections of her shawl.

The doctor's expression was not one to instill hope. "Were you aware, Mrs—"

"Ashley," said Faith, without hesitation.

"Mrs. Ashley. Were you aware that Mr. Briggs has had a heart condition, an abnormality in its beating from which he has suffered for some time?"

Quietly, she answered, "No," and looked again to Ezra. A frown twisted her brows together. *Why did you not tell me?* she thought.

"It is my opinion that he has suffered an acute attack of apoplexy," continued the man. He uttered the words matter of factly, and his manner, in his dark frock, was inoffensive, yet Faith felt nothing more than an urge to scream at the fellow. "I am not certain that he will recover, Mrs. Ashley."

"What would have caused that?" Faith asked.

"Perhaps something upset him overmuch. I do not know."

She looked at Ezra again, at the skin beneath which the flesh had withered, like wintered fruit. His eyes opened suddenly, staring outward, at nothing, and then they closed again. His breathing clouded the air. Three braziers were scarcely enough to warm the room. Beneath the pile of quilted blankets, his body looked oddly small. And his hand in her own continued to feel so cold, as if the warmth of life had left it.

"He has not been well," the physician reminded her.

"Might I have a chair? I should like to sit down, beside the bed."

"Of course," said the doctor. "I will fetch one for you myself. It was not wise of you to venture forth at all, in your condition, but I understand that Mr. Briggs is a very dear friend of yours."

Faith colored slightly. It was the first time that anyone had made mention of her pregnancy. Mrs. Hart met her eyes around the broad, round shoulders of the physician.

"Mrs. Hart," she said, "Would you accompany the doctor, please? Show him where he might find a chair."

"Of course," said the housekeeper. "There is one in my room. One of the few," she said, "that are left to us here."

Faith waited until they had gone, Mrs. Hart's petticoats rustling like stiff linen and the doctor's shoes crunching with deplorable damage to the floors, before she responded to the tightening of Ezra's grasp around her fingers. Cumbersome as she was, she knelt on the floor beside his bed, caressing his face with the back of her hand.

"Ezra," she whispered. "Dear Ezra."

Behind the creased folds of his eyelids, Ezra's eyes rolled weakly in response to her voice. His lips moved, stretching thinly. They were dry, and they cracked, leaking blood. Faith drew out her handkerchief, dabbing at the crimson droplets.

"Ezra," she said. "Ezra, I am here. If there is any comfort in that, I beg of you to take it."

"Faith . . ."

Faith rocked back, over her heels. Lifting his hand, she kissed it. Ah, but this could only mean that the doctor was wrong, and that he was fighting to survive. That he would survive, because he had the will to do so.

"Ezra, rest," she said. "Do not waste your strength in speaking to me. I will be here, when you awaken again, and then we will work to make you well."

"No," said Ezra. "No . . . time."

"Don't," said Faith, in dismay. "Do not say that."

"Not . . . this time."

"Don't. Don't . . ."

"Tell me," he said.

"Tell you, what, Ezra? I will tell you anything, if only you will not give up," said Faith, holding his hand tight between both of her own pleadingly.

"Not giving up," said Ezra. "The Lord claims . . . me . . ."

"Does He? How do you propose to know?" demanded Faith. "Who are we to know His will? Once, I thought—I thought that I knew, but I was wrong, Ezra."

Ezra looked at her, and his pale eyes seemed knowledgeable, and understanding. "The Lord claims me," he repeated.

She bowed her head. The red-gold of her hair was as a flame in the fire-shot dimness of the bedchamber.

"Tell me . . . of the child," he said.

"Of the child?" Faith echoed faintly.

"A miracle—"

"Yes," said Faith.

"You are not ashamed . . ."

"No."

"If I . . . if I were not dying . . . would you . . . marry me? A name . . . for the child . . ."

Faith pressed her forehead against the back of his hand, against his gnarled knuckles, against the coldness of his flesh. What harm would there be in lying to him now? He would be happy. He would be happy, in the end.

"Yes," she said.

"Not true."

"Oh, Ezra," said Faith, and clung to his hand with both of her own. It was no use. No use, at all. He knew that she never would have wed him.

"Ahhh," he said, thrashing his head suddenly, "it hurts . . ."

"No, Ezra, no! Doctor!" she shouted over her shoulder, "Come at once! Oh, Ezra, hold on, please," she begged, knowing, as she did so, that only time stood between him, and the Death that waited to take him. "What," she said softly, "will I do without you?"

A foam appeared at the corners of Ezra's mouth, and he jerked on the bed in an effort to free himself of the agony tearing through his body.

"Doctor!"

"Ahhh," moaned Ezra, and subsided. Faith bent over his mouth, to feel his breath, and touched his brow, the pulse beating at the side of his neck. Outside of the room, there was a clatter of wood as the doctor dropped the chair and came rushing in. He eased Faith aside, without gentleness. Faith backed to the wall, glancing, with green eyes, to the figure of Mrs. Hart, waiting on the threshold with her craggy fist pressed to her mouth. Behind her, Elizabeth stood with her young countenance marked only by sympathy.

"Elizabeth," said Faith, shakily, "bring me the chair."

The physician spoke. "Whatever prayers you have to utter now, Mrs. Ashley, you may. It will not be long. All of you," he said, glancing toward the door, "trust in God. It will not be long."

Faith nodded, and lowered her head, to stare at her knees. Elizabeth and the housekeeper entered the room to kneel at the foot of the bed. In silence, the doctor moved to stand beyond the flickering illumination of the brazier.

"Dear Lord," Faith whispered, "Thy will be done."

Ezra died, in his sleep, toward midnight. Peacefully, at the last. There had been none in the room with him at the time, save Faith, nodding over her swollen abdomen. She had felt his hand move, beneath her own, and had started, lifting her eyes to see him turn his head away on the pillow, toward the wall. Nothing more than that. His final breath was drawn, shuddering, in unconsciousness. Faith sat by a long time, still, and quiet, knowing that he had gone.

Tears streamed in silence along her cheeks.

Chapter Twenty-eight

In the darkness of the firewell, an occasional flaring of the flames lit the soot-blackened walls. Embers glowed along the floor, brilliant and burning into themselves as they turned to grey ash. Faith stared, in mental numbness, and then she rolled again onto her back. The floor was hard. She wished for her bed.

The pains which had begun earlier in the evening had not ceased; rather, they had increased in intensity and regularity, until they were not more than minutes apart. With each contraction, she squeezed shut her eyes, gritting her teeth against the sensation, and prayed that it would be the last. Not because the pain was great, but because the child was coming too soon.

Lifting the quilt, Faith pushed her hand down between her thighs, and then pulled it out, moist. She held her fingers to the meagre illumination of the fire.

Blood.

Turning her head, she viewed Elizabeth's tousled blonde hair, the relaxed slope of her shoulders, the curl of her fingers through her yellow locks, as the girl lay, sleeping, on her side, her back to Faith.

"Elizabeth," Faith whispered. Outside, the cock crowed from his nested shelter. The snow blew between the vanes of the shutters, brushing, crystalline and soft, against the windowpanes.

"Elizabeth."

She closed her eyes, as the next wave took her. The pain was not bad, oh, the pain was not bad; but the baby was coming, too soon.

Reaching out her hand, she shook Elizabeth's shoulder, unintentionally leaving a smear of crimson on the girl's white gown. "Elizabeth!"

The girl started, shook herself, and twisted around to face Faith. She blinked in the low firelight. "You called me, Mrs. Ashley?" she asked sleepily, and then sat up onto her elbow, frowning at the woman's expression. "Mrs. Ashley?"

"The baby, Elizabeth," said Faith. "The baby is coming."

"Now?"

"Soon," said Faith. "I think. You must help me."

"O'course," said Elizabeth, slipping out from beneath her covers and into her robe. She belted it tightly around her waist.

"What shall I do?" she asked.

"Assist me up the stairs," Faith told her, quietly.

Elizabeth was horrified. "Up the stairs?" she said. "No, Mrs. Ashley. I don't reckon that you should do that. I will bring all that you need to you, here."

Faith shook her head determinedly. She lifted herself onto both elbows. "If you will but help me, I will manage it. I want to give birth to my child in my own bed, not here, on the kitchen floor. Give me your hand."

Though protesting, Elizabeth obeyed, crouching behind Faith with her arms beneath the woman's. Faith leaned into the girl, and stood. Another contraction seized her upon rising. Faith gave a slight gasp at the dramatic, and unexpected, increase in the pressure that standing upright brought.

"Oh, Mrs. Ashley," said Elizabeth, "this notion of yours is a foolish one."

"It is not," Faith insisted calmly, and started across the kitchen floor. There was no foolishness, she thought, in wanting her child to be born upon the bed where once she had fancied all children of her womb would start their life.

She paused at the kitchen door, fumbling with the blanket that covered it. Behind her, Elizabeth found the tinder box, and struck light to a candle. The girl gave a cry of alarm.

"There is blood," she said, "on your gown!"

Without answering, Faith opened the door, shivering in the chill air that wafted in. With one hand, she clutched her abdomen, and with the other, she found support against the wall, walking blindly into the blackness. "Bring the candle," she said to Elizabeth breathlessly. "Hurry." Faith went on to the stair where she paused, one hand to the newel post, and waited.

A moment later, Elizabeth appeared with the stub of a candle and three or four blankets rolled beneath her arm. She dropped the blankets on the floor at Faith's feet.

"I'll come back for them," she said. "Give me your arm."

Extending her arm to the girl, Faith leaned heavily upon her as they ascended. Elizabeth held the candle balanced in its holder. The wick hissed, and the flame flickered in the well of molten wax. Shadows danced near in the small light that it cast. Above them, Faith saw the cloud of their breath mingle, and rise.

Every step or so, Elizabeth muttered, "One more," and Faith nodded, as if she did not realize how far they were from the top. But with every lift of her foot, she glanced upward, praying to reach the landing above. How many times had she run up and down those stairs in the course of a day, without thought or notice of their steepness nor of the number of treads. She had forgotten, but now she had just cause to recall.

In the hallway above, Faith paused for breath, leaning against the railing. Wearing nothing but her nightdress, she shivered as the perspiration broke across her body.

"I'll go for the blankets, now," Elizabeth said, and set the candle down on the floor. Faith watched as she lifted her robe above her knees, racing down the stairs to retrieve the fallen quilts. Faith drew a deep breath. Quite suddenly, she found herself soaked with a warm fluid that flowed down her legs. She gave a strangled cry. She stood looking down, and felt tears of shame start to her eyes.

"What have I done?" she said.

"T'is nothing to worry about, Mrs. Ashley," called Elizabeth, hurrying back. "Your water has broken, that's all. I seen it happen for myself, twice, with Mama. I'll mop it up. First, you must get into bed."

Taking the candle from Elizabeth's hand, Faith held it high as she threw open the door to her bedchamber. The room was not as cold as she had anticipated it to be, for it had been shut up tight. She went to the dresser, and placed the candle before the mirror so that the light reflected outward, twofold.

"Help me out of my soiled gown, Elizabeth," she said, removing a fresh, dry gown that was icy to the touch from one of the drawers. The girl helped to pull the wet nightdress over her head, wiping the fluids and the blood from her legs with it as Faith settled the dry one about her body.

"We must heat this room, Mrs. Ashley. I will build up the fire, and bring up some coals in the braziers. You will freeze otherwise. Get into bed, and I will cover you."

Faith slipped between the frigid linens, and found herself shivering without control. With the quilts about her chin, she lay staring into a candlelit darkness, where the shadows reigned over the light and brought with them a host of memories. Strangely, her recollections of William were portraits of life, one dimensional, and painted with colors that had faded. But she could not help thinking of him as she lay in the bed that he had fashioned with his own hands, about to bear the child they had both longed for, to another man.

She thought of Ezra, and though she had been beside him when he had died, scarce hours before, she could not believe that he was gone. She would not dwell on it. She turned her mind to recalling him in animation, which only made her sadder still.

Her contemplation turned to Fletcher, of whom she fought against the most. She felt warmed by the thought of him, even in abandonment. She wished she could have been certain of him so that he would have known, long before this moment, about their child.

Another contraction, which stole her breath, was followed soon by the next, and then the next. With an effort, Faith controlled her shallow breathing, drew it out, made it deep, trying to ease the tightness of her pain. She turned her eyes to the sealed letter upon the dressing table, which she had written weeks before. To be delivered to Fletcher in the event of her death in childbirth. She must remember to tell Elizabeth of it.

In time, the girl returned with the braziers, and made another journey to the kitchen for a bundle of rags, and towels, and a basin of heated water, from snow which she had melted in the kettle over the fire. She had two lengths of cord, which she tied to the bedpost above Faith's head, within her grasp. Faith observed the confidence of her actions in amazed affection.

"The bleeding's stopped, ain't it?" the girl said.

Faith nodded. "Yes."

"I don' reckon that it will be long, now, a few hours, but I ain't one to say. Shall I go and fetch the midwife?"

Faith hesitated. It seemed ridiculous to send poor Elizabeth out in the dark hours of the morning when she might not reach the point where the midwife's services were needed for some time yet.

"No," said Faith. "Wait, until daylight."

Faith felt the coolness of a dampened towel as Elizabeth applied it to her perspiring brow. She could scarcely bring herself up out of half-consciousness to acknowledge the care which the girl was taking. She mouthed the words, but no sound came out. Forcing her eyelids open, she was greeted by a harshness of light that prevented her focus. Someone had opened the shutters? Who?

She closed her eyes again, and it was as if she were sleeping, as if the blackness between dreams had claimed her, and she drifted away . . . Her hands hung limply from the loops on the bedpost, slipped free, dropped to the pillow beneath her head with a dull sound of lifelessness; her wrists were chafed and bleeding . . . then the next contraction began, a minute and a half from the last, and dragged her up from her state of insensibility to the reality of pain which she had known for the past eighteen hours.

Twenty-seven hours, now, she had heard someone say, though she was not certain whom. All voices sounded the same, rather drifting and hazy, and without a point of origin. She turned her head, felt it roll without a will of her own, in response to the pain; a pain that she thought to grow used to, and each time it passed she told herself that she had, and that next time she would not suffer, but next time it only grew worse.

It was fear that made it so, she decided. Fear that she would die with the child unborn within her womb, or that the child alone would perish, without ever knowing life, without ever to be held living in the grasp of her arms, so that she might look upon the tiny face of the love that she had carried, manifested in her body.

She moaned, tightening her grip inside of the circle of the cords, but her grasp was feeble. Her head dropped to one side; her green eyes were wide, and staring. Thus far, the product of her labor had been but this: crimson-stained linens heaped upon the floor, as she poured her life's blood onto the sheets beneath her hips. Something was wrong. Something had gone wrong with the baby so that it would not come out . . . or was it herself, her own physical failure that prevented the birth? Whatever it was, not even the doctor, skilled in such matters, and bearing her blood upon his rolled sleeves and the front of his coat, could correct it.

As the contraction subsided, Faith's eyelids closed slowly. In a minute reprieve, she breathed slowly, without the swift bursts of panting which the contractions forced upon her. The voices drifted through her consciousness, as the sound of birds' wings had, among the rafters of Old South, many months ago.

She began to realize that the voices were not those of the people within the room, but of others, that she remembered well. Father, she thought, and she heard the deep cadences of his scolding tone. Father, I love you . . .

She was pulled up, back from darkness to the frosted sunlight, and she saw a face, above her own, swimming in the smoke-haze of pain.

"Mrs. Ashley," said the doctor. "Mrs. Ashley, listen to me."

Faith frowned. She felt a hand on her shoulder. Somehow, she knew that it did not belong to the physician. It felt small, and comforting. "Elizabeth," Faith whispered.

"What did she say?" the man asked.

"She called my name."

"Did she? Mrs. Ashley, I must speak to you, on the matter of the child."

Faith stared wordlessly.

"If we do not rid you of it, you are going to die. I have done everything else that is humanly possible. You are not built to bear a child with ease, and this one is twisted about beyond my reach, and will not pass the structure of your bone. The forceps will not avail."

In a rush, Elizabeth began to pray softly, and Faith felt the pressure of her hand increase.

"I know," continued the doctor, "that you are a month shy of your delivery time, but the baby is large. Perhaps, you miscalculated? Where is Mr. Ashley? I would like to speak with him on this matter. You are his wife, after all, and it is his child."

Faith swallowed. Her mouth was dry, tongue swollen. "Gone," she said.

"Where? We do not have much time to go fetching after him."

"He passed away," she heard Elizabeth answer for her, and tried to move her head, to seek out the girl's sweet face. The surface of the pillow was slick with perspiration, and her hair was matted beneath her. She could not lift her head enough to find the girl. She had not the strength.

"I see," said the doctor, after a moment's hesitation. "Then there is no choice. I must take the responsibility of the decision.''

''No,'' said Faith.

The expulsion of sound was so faint that Elizabeth, who was standing behind Faith's shoulder, barely perceived it. The doctor took no note of it at all.

Along the currents of her lapsing awareness, Faith watched as the physician lifted a mahogany box from the floor, and placed it on the dressing table. He lifted the lid, against the mirror. Beside him, the midwife, giving in to his interference, spread a towel across the dusty top of the table. The doctor drew out the instruments, one by one. Faith felt a shudder course through the wearied, punished length of her body. She had seen an obstetrician's kit but once in her life, and that, when only the forceps were being used; but she had never forgotten the others, and the intent of their design: To remove a stillborn child, or to destroy the child that endangered its mother's life. The names of those instruments were as horror in her mind, for in their names was the description of their nightmare: the perforator; the blunt hook and crochet; the bone crusher.

Slow tears rolled from the corners of Faith's staring eyes. My child, she thought, dear God, my child.

Curling her fingers in the cords above her head, Faith pulled on them with the last vestige of her strength, lifting her upper body from the soaked mattress. Her mouth opened. Her own voice echoed over and over in her head, until it escaped at last from her lips in an anguished, wordless scream for mercy.

Chapter Twenty-nine

The sky was pale grey, a pearly dome threatening another fall of snow. Sounds echoed in an unfamiliar manner, like vibrations in a jar. There was no wind, only an icy stillness that had caused temperatures to plummet. Fletcher stood on the frozen cobbles, staring with peculiar intentness at the brick face of Boston's gaol. His breath plumed before him, freezing in his nostrils. All about him, on either side of the street, beside the building, snow had been heaped taller than a man's head.

This same time last year, he thought, I was standing about in nothing but my uniform, quite comfortably. The nights were warm enough that Faith could appear at Ezra's in little more than her silk gown. He remembered the cut of it, and the colors, and the way she had worn her hair. His heart ached with the memory of it, for that had been the last moment of simplicity. Once he had kissed her—that they had kissed, in desperation, it seemed, even then—the course of their lives became one of tragedy and joy, intertwined and inseparable.

Fletcher frowned, and frowned again, and then he went forward, into the gate.

"Who goes there?" demanded the soldier, standing within the bricked entranceway, his musket shouldered.

"Lieutenant Fletcher Irons. Lord Percy's First Brigade, Light Infantry."

"State your business, sir."

Fletcher hid his annoyance as he answered. "I have come to see a prisoner before he is hanged—Sergeant," he stressed. "Do you mind?"

"Then, this is not official business, sir?"

"It is not," said Fletcher. He waited a moment longer as the soldier hesitated in indecision, and then he said, "It is cold, Sergeant."

"Of course, sir."

The soldier lifted a ring of keys hanging from a chain attached to his red coat. He inserted the largest into the lock of the gate. Iron grated against the tumblers. The barrier swung inward on well-greased hinges. Fletcher strode inside.

"I will lead the way for you, Lieutenant. There is a lantern, just inside the doorway, there. What is the name of the prisoner, sir?"

"Jacques," said Fletcher. "Jacques Sabot."

* * *

One hour. She had already been one hour in searching, and the doctor had not promised as much. Ah, what a horrible sound that had been, Mrs. Ashley screaming like that, drawing strength out of her weakness to protest the destruction of her child. She could not have stayed to witness the screams that followed, even if she had not determined to find the lieutenant, to bring him back. She had heard earlier in the day that British troops had once again returned to the inn, and she had expected that he would be there or close by, and to discover that he was not, and that no one else knew where he had gone, had reduced her to useless tears.

Out in the street, in the frigid temperature, the saline moisture froze to Elizabeth's lashes. She brought her mittened hands to her eyes. *I cannot go back, she thought, I cannot go back. The child may be dead; Mrs. Ashley may be dead. What will I do?*

She had to find Lieutenant Irons. He had a right to know the fate of his child, and to see the woman whom he loved, if only for the last time on this earth.

Dear God, she prayed, no. Let it not be so, let it not be so . . .

Exhaling a deep, smoking breath, Elizabeth dropped her hands to her sides. She pulled her cloak together, and the shawl beneath it. She would have to go back, without him. There was no good use in searching for a man who could not be found, when Mrs. Ashley was in need of her. It had been childish and weak and cowardly of her to run out, to leave Mrs. Ashley alone, just to retrieve her love to her side. Though it had been an honorable desire, an earnest one, to do right, she saw now that it was senseless. And if the deed was done, then Mrs. Ashley would need her caring, and comforting. And if childbirth had taken the woman's life, then Elizabeth needed to manage that, also.

The girl dashed another tear away; she saw it glisten, frozen, in the woolen knit of her mitten. She looked up; the sky was like a pewter dome. It is too cold to snow, she decided, and

I must go home. Mrs. Ashley, do not think that I have abandoned you; I have not.

"Pardon me."

Elizabeth turned with a start to stare at the man beside her:
a young, redcoated officer, breathless and apple-cheeked. The
air about his head fogged as he bent with his hands on his
knees, attempting to regain his composure.

"Are you—" he gasped, "the same young lady who was
inquiring after Lieutenant Irons?"

"Aye," said Elizabeth, slowly, "I am."

He straightened, his hands on his hips, and smiled: a smile
that had probably won the hearts of many, in the past, but
which left Elizabeth unaffected. "Glad I caught you up," he
said. "The lads said it seemed important to you. Where he's
gone, I mean," he added, with a remarkable blush. "The
lieutenant's gone to the gaol."

"He's been arrested?" Elizabeth asked incredulously.

"Ah, no, I don't mean that, miss," said the youthful officer.
"He's gone to look in on a prisoner."

"Why?" said Elizabeth.

"Dunno."

Elizabeth was silent for a full tenth of a second. It was fifteen
minutes there, if she ran as fast as she safely could on the ice-
slicked streets, and then twenty minutes home . . . Oh, more
time than she could hope for Mrs. Ashley's sake! But she must
do it.

Abruptly, she took the soldier's hand, and shook it in both
of her own. "Thank you," she said, "thank you," and turned
on her heel, to hurry away, leaving the officer to stare after
her in an amusement of misunderstanding.

The frozen ways were treacherous, but there was no going
aside from the streets, for the snow was too deep; though here
and there Elizabeth did manage to cross it, lifting her skirts
high, and walking carefully over the thick crust that had formed
on top. She fell once, twice, a third time, but with no more
damage done than a rent in her petticoat and a bruised elbow.
Picking herself up, she went on, without pause. She could not
delay.

The brick-and-timber structure of the prison was soon within sight. Elizabeth hurried to the iron gate, wrapping her mittened hands about the bars. The guards whom she had thought to find there were nowhere in sight. She called out. The sound of her voice echoed beneath the bricked arch.

Frustrated, she shook the gate.

"Allow me entry!"

There was no response.

"Please, someone! Let me in!"

Still, nothing, until she spied the swinging of a lantern beyond the wooden expanse of a partially shut door, and the rusty red of a coat sleeve, lifting the lantern onto its hook.

"Pray, you, let me in!" cried Elizabeth.

The body behind the door paused in its motions, and then went on, completing the task at hand. The door swung open. A burly sergeant stood framed by it, frowning out at Elizabeth.

"Eh, girl, what's that you want?"

"Has a Lieutenant Irons come?" she asked, pressing her face to the gate. The sergeant looked confused. "A Lieutenant Irons," she repeated.

It seemed that a wisping smile passed over the soldier's face, but it may just have been the cold.

"Ah, a Lieutenant Irons," he said. "Let me think. Are you certain of the name?"

"Yes!" Elizabeth practically shouted.

"No need to get huffy," the redcoat reacted defensively. "I believe you are correct, and an officer named Irons has just come in. Why," he said, "are you asking?"

"I got a message for him."

"Give it to me," said the sergeant.

"No," said Elizabeth, stepping back and giving another yank on the gate, "I must tell him myself. Will you call him here?"

The guard was pensive for a moment, and then he said, "But that would leave you out in the cold. Come in, and I will lead you down to him. Stand back, while I open the gate."

Grateful, Elizabeth did so; she waited while the man opened the gate, and then entered in under the arch as he shut it, turning the key in the lock. "This way," he said, stepping past her to lift the lantern from its hook. "Walk a little ahead of me, and I will hold the lantern high."

Elizabeth placed her feet carefully, for the paving of the floor was slick with dampness and frozen wherever water had been standing, and the swinging of the lantern chased her shadow up and down the walls in a manner that confounded the eye.

"Turn here," said the guard, and, "Turn here," again. "Take the steps, slow."

By this time, it seemed to Elizabeth that they had descended into a place of nightmares, for there was no light but that of the lantern, and from behind stout doors she heard the sounds of moaning, or of unearthly muttering. Some of the doors were merely barred, and these were worst of all, because she could see creatures that once had been men huddled upon cots, or in the corners of the floors. They were American prisoners of war, most of them. She could not bear to look closely.

"This way, through that door."

Receiving no assistance from the sergeant, Elizabeth shouldered the door open, and stepped inside, stumbling over a ridge of dirt just the opposite side of the threshold. The ridge moved, squealing roughly in protest. Elizabeth gave a small cry. The door closed. The lantern swung close to her face. She turned her head away.

"All right, miss?"

"Yes."

Elizabeth glanced around in the swinging arc of the lamp, and it appeared to her that the place that they had just entered was not another corridor, but a single cell, without occupancy; and the only way out, that which had just been closed off, was behind the guard, who had coincidentally planted himself there.

"See him anywhere, miss?"

Elizabeth peered again in confusion. "No," she said. "'course not. There's no one here."

"I did not think so."

Slowly, Elizabeth turned about. The sergeant was lowering the lantern to the dirt floor, revealing all manner of filth in elongated shadow. "Pray, let me pass, sir. You have made a mistake."

"Nay," said the soldier, "the mistake is yours. Never trust a man who stands about in the cold too long, with nothing to think about but the warmth of a woman in his bed. I am not one of the commissioned officers, free to steep myself in whatever pleasure of vice takes my fancy. But providence has seen fit to put you in my path today. The lieutenant does not need you; I do. I can make you as happy as he. Come here."

"No," said Elizabeth, backing away from the light that illuminated the man's features from beneath, "you do not understand. I've got a very important message for Lieutenant Irons."

"Oh. That. I told you to give it to me, and you would not. How important can it be?"

Elizabeth retreated still further, until she felt the ridged stone of the wall against her back. The chill permeated her heavy clothing instantly. Her heart hammered against her ribs, constricting her breathing. She swallowed, to speak again, and found that she could not.

"And you are a pretty one. I don't think I have ever seen eyes quite so blue."

Elizabeth shook her head. The man advanced, nearer. He was big, but not too big, though he seemed to possess a brute strength that would preclude a battle on her part. With wide eyes, she measured her chances of reaching the door around him, and wondered what she would have to do in order to escape. He came closer still, until he was standing no more than three feet away. He reached out and touched her hair. She turned her head. He touched her hair again, then tightened his fingers in it, pulling her head about painfully as he tried to kiss her, on the mouth. She spat on him. It was the only thing she could think of to do.

The sergeant raised his hand high above her, and came down with it, edged, across her jaw. She fell back against the wall, and to the floor, dazed, and the room spun in near darkness.

Oh, Mrs. Ashley, she thought, I will never reach him in time now; I hoped that he might save you; I hoped that he might save the child . . . I don't know why . . .

And then, as she felt her skirt lifted, above her knees, above her thighs, she thought of Jack. Somewhere out in the lines, he waited. "I will come back, and you will be my wife," he had said; *but not now, oh, not now, because this man above me will have taken away the innocence of my offering. You will not want me. And Mrs. Ashley will die. And all because of a redcoat's filthy perversity.* "Damn you!" she screamed, and he slapped her again, into silence.

Fletcher stood with his fingers hooked about the iron cross-bar of the door, staring wordlessly at the remnant of youth within the cell. This was not the bayonet-wielding giant of his haunted remembering; not the golden-haired madman; not the young soul that had entered the cell struggling more than half a year ago. He was an old man, gaunt and shivering beneath his stinking blanket, the sheen of health gone from his hair, gone from his dark eyes that reflected a listless soul; the vitality of his life was lost.

"Jacques," said Fletcher, "did you hear me?"

The man on the metal cot sat very still, as if deaf, leaning forward over the stool that stood before him. A single candle burned there, small, and guttering, and he held his rag-wrapped hands close above the flame, to warm them. Too close. The frayed ends of the rags caught, and he pulled back, watching the threads smolder for an instant before he brushed them out with fingers chilblained and bloody from the cold. Without looking at Fletcher, he said:

"I have heard you. What do you expect from me? You do not look like a confessor, and I am not in need of one."

"But you are to be hanged. You do understand this."

"Yes."

"Is there anyone you wish notified?" he asked, coldly. He did not wish this man to mistake his question for kindness.

Jack hesitated, long, and long. He lowered his head, shaking, over his hands. "No," he said.

"Who are you, Lieutenant?" he asked, in time. "I do not remember you."

"I would not expect you to. There is no cause, save that which is personal, to me. I am one of many, whom you, and your fellow patriots, fought that day on Breed's Hill."

Jack said nothing, but his eyes changed, lost some of the flatness, the lack of emotion and animation. Fletcher duly noted this, in the candlelight. His fingers tightened still more, until bits of rust broke off in his hand.

"I am one who has hated you, Jacques, for a long time."

At this, Jack turned his head. A look of genuine amusement appeared on his countenance, to lift the aged demeanor which prison had pressed upon him.

"For which of many reasons, Lieutenant?" he asked. "Because I am French? Because I am a patriot? Because I fought, without surrender? Ah, I had hoped to die rather than to surrender," he sighed, and his features reverted to pain and age. "I do not care much for prison, Lieutenant."

Against all expectations, Fletcher was moved by the man's brief confession. But he had no desire to feel compassion for the Frenchman's pain. Yet, it occurred to him that the Frenchman had not been seeking pity, or judgment, but had merely commented to him, as one man to another, as one soldier to another.

Fletcher bit the inside of his cheek. He removed his hand from the bar, rubbing the flat of it on his scarlet coat until it stung. Somewhere, in the distant, echoing corridors, he heard a door slam shut. The draft of it followed a moment later, guttering the candle flame. The young man called Jacques stooped over the precious fire, shielding the point of light with his hands.

"You killed a man," said Fletcher.

"Only one?" answered Jack, with a bitter irony, as if regretting his earlier admission. He coughed, and turned to expectorate, but thought better of the action, and subsided, shivering.

"The man was a friend," he said. "I loved him, very much. More in death, I sometimes think, than in life. Because in life, we are often fools."

Jack was silent. He looked about the tiny cell, at the accumulated filth of six months and more; at the weeping walls;
at the basin, where he was given water, once a day, if he was
remembered: lately, there was a thin layer of ice upon it at all
times. He looked to the place where a window might have
been, but was not. The sky was a memory; as was fresh air.
He knew that he stank, that everything in that prison stank, of
urine, and feces, of bodies unwashed, and of the places where
the rats held sway. He looked down at his hands, and thought
of the feel of a gun within them. He thought of Joseph Warren.
He thought of his family. He thought of Elizabeth.

Lowering his head into his hands, his dirty golden hair fell
about them, and over his forehead.

"I am sorry, Lieutenant," he said, "that war must put an
end to friendships with such finality. We lose all chances. There
is too much sadness."

"I have been haunted," said Fletcher, "as no soldier should,
by the memory of his death. He stepped in front of your bayonet, and took it in the chest. To save me. For the sake of a
promise that he had made to the lady that I love."

Jack shook his head. "A brave and noble man," he said.
"We met in battle, in war; he offered his life for you, and he
died. I did not know him. I do not recall him, but he is honored
by your grief, your memory of him."

Standing back, Fletcher placed both hands about the vertical
bars, and leaned into them, dropping his head forward.

"You do not recall killing him."

"No," said Jack. He sat up. The blanket slipped from his
shoulders and he clutched at it, bringing it about his body
again. Beneath, his clothing was worn, tattered, soiled. "How
is it that you would expect me to do so? Do you recall the face
of every man shot down, or run through with your sabre? It
is war, *mon ami*."

"Do not call me friend," said Fletcher.

Gazing through the bars at the single flame which was all
that was left to this man, at the candle which would count out
the hours until his death, Fletcher tried to dredge up the hatred
which had seemed so often overwhelming, but it was gone.
He had borne it for such a multitude of lonely, bitter hours

that he felt as if his skin was peeled away, and he was exposed, tender, and raw. He wanted to weep; not for Brian, who was gone, who had died as a result of a service in which he prided himself, of a promise in which he found himself sworn, though it was only in his own heart; no, he wanted to weep after Faith, for he had abandoned her, without truly realizing it. He had allowed time to slip between them, because of an empty hatred and a blame for his foible that he had laid at her feet. And he had called it duty. God, but he knew she had seen through his claim.

Straightening, Fletcher slammed his hand, palm open, against the iron barrier.

"What a fool!" he shouted. "What a bloody fool!"

The Frenchman frowned. He moved, and the candle flame reflected in his dark eyes.

"Why are you here?" he said. "Did you come seeking to free yourself from guilt? From your endless, useless hatred?"

Tipping his dark head back on his shoulders, Fletcher ran his fingers through the hair at his crown. "Yes," he said, his rich voice barely audible.

Jack watched him, seeing in him a man in search of stable ground. He narrowed his eyes, rubbing the back of his rag-covered hand beneath his nose. "Perhaps," he said, "I may do something else for you. It is said that a condemned man can afford to be generous."

Fletcher hesitated, breathing heavily. In the darkness of the corridor, his smoky eyes were as black as that of the prisoner.

"Is it possible," Jack said, "that you would permit a reason for killing your friend? Other than war. I did not single him out, Lieutenant, but I was enraged. I wanted all men who wore that scarlet coat to die. I was standing beside a man whom I, also, loved, when he was struck down, with a ball through the forehead. He was a good man, and kind, and when he died, I saw nothing else but his death."

"What was his name?" asked Fletcher, quietly.

"You knew him, or of him, I am certain. He was our general, and before that—"

"Dr. Warren," said Fletcher. "Yes, I knew him. A great loss, that. As you have said, he was both good, and kind, and struggled greatly for the welfare of the people of this town. I admired him.''

"Did you, Lieutenant? I will tell him so," remarked Jack, irreverently, "when I see him—if the kingdom of heaven is granted me, though I die the death of a dog on the gallows.''

Speechlessly, Fletcher met the valiant expression on Jack's haggard countenance with regret. For an instant, he pictured the wasted young body swinging from the scaffold, neck broken by the hangman's expert knot. Surrendering, in the end, to the king's justice.

"You have committed high treason, Jacques," he said.

"I would rather be blasted into pieces by the ball of a cannon, then to die this way, without honor. But, alas, the deed is done, and I pay the price. It is war, Lieutenant, and these are the stakes. When the rebels have won, you may swing, also."

Fletcher shook his head, with a laugh. "Do not be so certain of yourself, Frenchman."

Suddenly, Fletcher swung about, staring back along the corridor tensely. Jack, whose ability for abrupt movement had long ago been diminished by his captivity, rose protractedly, clinging to his ragged, stinking blanket.

A bubble of illumination appeared, careening wildly over the slick walls, reflecting light and shadow in the dampness. A moment later, a disheveled young woman appeared around the corner; she stumbled, then righted herself. She looked up, with round eyes, and opened a mouth that was purpled with bruising.

"Elizabeth!" cried Fletcher, and ran forward, to steady her in his arms. "What has happened to you? Who did this?"

"Lieutenant Irons," Elizabeth gasped, "I have been searching for you . . . but it is too late . . . too late . . . he . . . he tried to make me . . .'' and she broke into tears, hanging her head, with her arms at her side. Her yellow hair was streaked with oily filth, her gown beneath the cloak muddied, and torn. "Who?" said Fletcher. "Who do you mean?"

"The soldier," answered Elizabeth, "with the keys . . .''

Fletcher sucked in his breath. "Bastard," he snarled. "I will see him flogged for this. Where is he now?"

"In the cell," said Elizabeth, regaining her breath, "where

I left him, after I . . . I kicked him. He is puking, on the ground.''

"Show me where you have left him, Elizabeth. I will deal with him myself.''

"No," whispered Elizabeth, "there ain't time, Lieutenant. I . . .''

Her voice tapered off in bewilderment. In shivering trepidation, she gazed at the man in the cell behind Fletcher's shoulder. He had been moving, slowly, toward the barred door, but he had stopped, and was staring, without ease, directly at her. What a poor, unhealthy soul he was! Trembling beneath a dirty blanket, his body gaunt, and unclean; his hair untrimmed, unwashed; a beard upon his face half-shaven. The fingers clutching the blanket were chilblained, the rags wrapped about his hand filthy and putrid with the suppuration of his sores. How could anyone permit a man to suffer so? What had been his crime?

The man came a bit closer, stretching out his arms, and clasped the bars before him. Behind him, a single candle flame flickered. He looked at her with dark eyes from which the fire of hope had died.

"No," she said, quivering with the residue of fear, that any man should look upon her for his release, whether it be from the vagaries of lust, or merely from the ghosts of despair. "No," she said again, and turned her head away.

"Betsy . . .''

Elizabeth swayed. She turned back.

"Jack?" she said, her voice a crack of desperate unbelief.

"Have I so changed?" he said, and laughed. The tears ran down his face, coursing a path through the grime of his skin.

Elizabeth dropped the lantern. The glass cracked, but the light remained, as did the oil within. The lamp rolled, throwing a tumbling illumination over the walls and Elizabeth's bruised and grieving countenance.

"Oh, Jack!" she cried, and ran to him, throwing herself against the cell door, reaching in with both arms to embrace him. He slipped his own hands around her, pressing his face so close against the bars that the pitted iron ground into his flesh. He kissed her forehead. She clung to him, weeping.

"My Betsy, what has happened to you? Who has hurt you?"

"No one, no one," she wept, and kissed him, on the mouth, on the eyes, whatever she could reach of his face through the barrier. Behind her, Fletcher observed the piteous reunion with a sinking heart. It would have been better if she had not discovered her sweetheart within the bowels of the prison, for she would turn to Fletcher in the hopes that he could have the man removed. And he could not. *Tomorrow, Jacques Sabot was to die, hanged by the neck.*

Beneath his breath, Fletcher uttered a swift prayer.

Jack heard him, above Elizabeth's crying, and looked up. He met Fletcher's smoky gaze with his dark one. *Do not tell her; I beg of you, do not tell her*, it said.

"Elizabeth," said Fletcher, and repeated her name. "Elizabeth. You were searching for me. Why? Is something wrong at home?"

Elizabeth turned from the cell, still clutching Jack's hand. The rags were wet. She blinked dazedly. "Oh," she said at last, in a sigh of breath. "Oh, Lieutenant Irons, forgive me!" She brought her arm up, dashing it across her eyes. Her shoulders shook. "Mrs. Ashley . . . Mrs. Ashley bears your child."

Fletcher checked, in cold shock. "What? Elizabeth, what are you saying?"

"The baby," she said, still crying, "is come early, Lieutenant. She had a hard time of it . . . a real hard time. I don't—Oh, Lieutenant, there is something wrong, with the baby! It won't come, it won't come, and the doctor, he wants to . . . to destroy it. Mrs. Ashley's lost a lot of blood. Oh, I fear she may die!"

Fletcher closed his eyes. He felt the floor shift beneath his feet. Then he turned, smashing his fist into the rough-hewn wall, splitting the thin flesh above the knuckles wide so that crimson droplets exploded over the white fabric of his breeches.

"God!" he cried out. "Oh, dear God."

"I am sorry," said Jack, heartfelt, for he had been fond of the woman. He wondered at the association between herself and this British lieutenant, for the widow was a patriot. His curiosity was fleeting. Such things did not seem to matter very much, with his hours only limited to a very few.

"Elizabeth, she is home?" asked Fletcher.

"Aye," answered the girl. "She had me help her to her own bed. Lieutenant Irons?"

"Yes?"

"It may be too late. I pray that t'is not, but it may be." She burst into tears again. Jack rubbed her shoulder.

"Hush, my heart," he said.

Fletcher came forward. The blood from his hand dripped between his fingers and onto the floor. There was nothing in his face to reveal the impassioned anguish of his soul. *Why had she not told him? A child, his child, and might both be lost to him, before ever he reached her side.* "We must hurry," he said to Elizabeth. "Come."

The girl hesitated, torn. "Jack," she said, and not to the man whose name she spoke, but to Fletcher.

Fletcher shook his head. "You must not stay here, and he may not leave. Isn't that correct, Sabot?"

Within his cell, Jack closed his eyes. Behind him, the rats rustled through the straw, and the single candle burned, counting down his time.

"Yes," said he. "Kiss me once more, my dear heart, and then you must go. We . . . we will meet again."

Elizabeth spun about, and clung to him tenaciously while he stroked her hair with his cracked and bleeding fingers, the unyielding metal of the bars preventing the contact he longed for in a final embrace.

Fletcher turned from them. He crossed the floor, and bent, righting the lantern. He lifted it in his hand. Silently, he strode away, around the corner, to await Elizabeth's following. The corridor behind was now dark, but for the light of that single flame.

It was all, he thought, that he could give them.

Chapter Thirty

Sluggishly, the officer took in the pile of bloody sheets that had accumulated on the floor. A serpentine muscle traveled, along his jaw. He swallowed over a constriction in his throat, turning his head, to gaze at the woman on the bed.

How perfect she appeared: the glory of her red-gold hair brushed in a mass away from her crown and over the pillow; her hands, her arms, lying flat at her sides over the white counterpane; her face, in profile, the stuff of which his dreams had so long been made; even her paleness, like ivory, only added to the beauty of her repose.

Fletcher took a step forward. "Doctor," he said, "who did this—for her?" The grief caught at his tongue, causing it to stumble.

"The midwife," answered the physician. "She is a good and kindly matron, but her experience was lacking for the seriousness of the situation."

Fletcher closed his eyes.

"Go closer," urged the doctor. "Mrs. Ashley is very weak, it is true, but she would like to know that you are here."

Fletcher faltered, midstride, and turned to stare at the man. "Weak?" he echoed. "She is not—?"

The doctor's eyes widened in astonishment. "Take a good look at her, man! She breathes, she is alive. Did you come straight up here? You poor soul; to have entered here, believing that this woman had died! Who are you, sir? Lieutenant, I believe?"

"Lieutenant Irons, yes," said Fletcher, and felt tears of relief and gratitude start to his eyes. He wanted to drop to his knees, beside the bed, but he held himself in check. "I am—I am a friend," he said.

"Hmm," said the doctor. "A friend. Did you know her husband?"

"No," said Fletcher. "Not personally."

"What was his name?"

"William Ashley."

"Is yours, by chance, Fletcher, Lieutenant?" asked the doctor, dryly.

"Yes," he answered.

"She called out for you, in the end." Firmly, he shut the mahogany box of his kit, and secured the lid. There was no need for the officer to be subjected to a view of the instruments inside. Slipping the case under his arm, the doctor headed for the door. Fletcher moved closer to the bed, then paused again, turning about.

"Wait one moment, doctor," he said.

"Yes?"

Fletcher inhaled, with painful deepness. He felt ill in asking, but he uttered the next question, nonetheless, eyes flickering over the physician's crimson-stained clothing. He could smell the blood. He had smelled it, even before he had opened the door.

"What was the child?" he said. "Male, or female?"

The doctor nodded his head. He shifted the case in his arms. "Lieutenant," he said, "the child is a boy. You are the father of a perfect son, thank the Lord above. When you are done here, he awaits your inspection in the warmth of the kitchen below."

So speaking, the doctor turned about, and noiselessly shut the door.

Fletcher did then what he had thought to do, and lowered himself to his knees beside the bed. His clothes became dampened with melting snow as he knelt there, with his fingers clasped tightly together on the white counterpane. He stared at Faith.

The light that fell upon her was soft, filtered through the hissing fall of snow, and silvered, but for the faint blush of the braziers nearby. He saw now that the same blush tinted her cheeks, and the mouth that had seemed so pale but a moment before.

"Faith," he whispered. And again, "Faith, I am here, my love. Forgive me for having stayed away so long."

Her head rolled a little on the pillow, seeking his presence in his voice, but exhaustion prevented the opening of her eyes. Her movements declined, and, once again, she lay still.

Extending his arm, Fletcher touched his long fingers to her cheek. Her skin was smooth, and cool. He touched the bone of her brow, above her eye, following the contour of it, the beauty of its shape. He caressed the hair at her forehead, the hair over her ears; he grazed his fingertips across her chin. The blood from his own broken flesh had dried in the ridges of his split knuckles, and along his skin.

"You have borne me a son," he whispered, and felt worshipful, awed by the miracle, and the knowledge of the ordeal that Faith had endured. He thought that perhaps he understood the reasoning behind her secrecy, and why she had not told him of the child, for he had not treated with her as if he would have welcomed it. He was sorry for that.

And he might live to regret it more, he thought, for there were no assurances that when she awakened, Faith would accept his return. Nor that she would accept, at last, his offer of marriage.

Rising from his knees, Fletcher strode from the bed to the window, and stood before it with his hands clasped behind his back, staring out at a snow-swirled scene. Nearly every house was shuttered; from every chimney a thin and pallid column of smoke rose into the showering snow, attesting to the one fire that was kept burning against the elements. A man on horseback rode in the street below: a figure well-coated in ice. His tricorne was as a receptacle for the falling flakes as they accumulated around the brim. Several children, bundled to their noses, capered as though on holiday. They threw snowballs at a soldier, patently visible in his red coat. Fletcher leaned his head against the glass, clouding the panes with the warmth of his breath.

Then he heard a small, shuddering sigh from the bed behind him, and turned his head, to find that Faith had moved again, very slightly. He returned to her side.

"Faith," he called.

Her eyes opened, closed, opened again. As green as he recalled. Her mouth turned, in a vague, weak smile. But that she had smiled at him at all, was relief.

"Fletcher," said Faith, licking her dry lips. "How did you come—"

"To be here, my love?" Fletcher finished for her, smiling down at her moistly. "Elizabeth came after me, and brought me back. Do you mind that?"

"No," said Faith.

"I feared, then, to be too late. I feared to find that I had lost you both." He swiped at his eyes with his wounded hand, yet the tears appeared more quickly than he could banish them. He crouched down beside the mattress. Weakly, Faith lifted her hand, pushing her fingers into the dark length of his locks as he lay his head upon her breast.

"We have a son, Faith," he said.

"Have you seen him?"

"Not yet, my darling."

"I have," said Faith, and even in breathlessness her voice changed. Fletcher marvelled at the maternal blossoming of her countenance. "Mrs. Perry took him away from me very soon, though, because I had not the strength to hold him, and this room is not very warm. I lost consciousness, after. But I did see him, whole and sound, Fletcher. I counted his fingers, and his toes. Fletcher—" She paused, sleepily, drawing on the strength that remained to her. "I—I could not bear him. So many hours, that it seemed hopeless. The doctor and the mid-wife agreed. They were going to—destroy him, Fletcher. Kill our child, so that I might live. I could not let them. I did not want to live, knowing—" And she was weeping, soundlessly, her head turned against the pillow.

"Faith, it is all well now. Do not trouble yourself with the memory. It is over."

"I screamed," she gasped, "and screamed, and screamed. I called out for you. I called to God, to take us both, then and there, rather than to allow this unbearable thing to happen. And then . . . and then, I felt this great, ripping pain, and the doctor was swearing—worse than you, Fletcher—and he reached into his instrument box. But it was only for the forceps,

Fletcher. Our son . . . came into this world . . . just be—just before eleven . . .''

Fletcher was up and above her, kissing her brow and smoothing her hair. His chest ached with the agony of her pain. "I love you," he said, "I have never ceased to love you, Faith.

"Once," he continued, "you asked to make a pact that we would not argue again, and I told you then that arguments were nothing but what may happen, ever and anon. I made a promise, though, against cruelty. And in leaving you alone for so long, uncertain and wondering, I have dealt the cruelest blow of all. I did not know you were with child—you did not tell me. But I do not offer that as an excuse from blame. Faith, I was wrong, in many things. Will you forgive me, my heart?''

Faith took hold of his hand as it moved in frenzied distress about her face and hair, and stilled it. She kissed his palm, and held it to her wet cheek.

"There is no need," she said, "for forgiveness, for you have done nothing which defies my understanding. You are my love.''

On the kitchen hearth, the fire was leaping to heights unseen in past months; Mrs. Ashley's own wash-stand, and a chair from Elizabeth's room, had been sacrificed both to the flames. Curled, cross-legged, on the floor, Elizabeth sat scrubbed and in clean garments, tending the sleeping infant in the woolen folds of her lap. The midwife and the doctor had both departed, leaving the baby to her care, and leaving Faith to the lieutenant's. The fire was comforting, after the cold of a long and bitter day, and Elizabeth dozed lightly over the child, leaning her blonde head against the stonework.

Fletcher crept in quietly, crouching over his heels beside the fire. He gazed with affection at Elizabeth's sleeping countenance, and frowned at the mottled bruising of her lip, and along her tender jaw. That guard will be flogged, he thought. I will see to it, ah, I will see to it before the day is through.

"Elizabeth," he said.

The girl started, but only slightly, for she had only been half-dreaming.

"Where is my son?"

She blinked. "Here," she said, "in my lap." She moved the roll of her skirt and petticoat, so that he could see.

Fletcher leaned his weight forward, on one hand. He peered into the voluminous dark folds of Elizabeth's garment.

"There he sits," Fletcher breathed, "like a jewel in velvet. Like a king."

Elizabeth leaned forward, looking down, also. She frowned in puzzlement at Fletcher's loquacity.

"My son," said he, and lifted the infant from Elizabeth's lap into his own as he settled himself to the floor. He turned back the bunting of sheepskin and heavy cambric to better view the tiny body beneath. Wiping his hand self-consciously on his breeches, he stretched out a finger to the pale fuzz of the infant's hair, feeling the softness of it against his calloused skin. He touched his son's cheek, which felt nearly as fleshless and gentle as a cloud. The baby screwed up his face at the contact, then opened its eyes; a mere slit, that scarcely revealed them, one and then the other, in the expression of a drunken soldier. Fletcher lowered his hand, to the chest, then he turned the infant over, lifting him carefully from his bunting, so that he was naked before the firelight.

"Oh, Lieutenant!" cried Elizabeth. "What are you doing?"

"Checking," he said.

Elizabeth blushed, and withdrew, to lean her head against the stone again.

For a full minute, Fletcher struggled with the baby's swaddling clothes, and then he beseeched the girl for help. Elizabeth leaned over him, wrapping the infant with efficient assurance. Fletcher thanked her.

"You are welcome, Lieutenant," she said.

Fletcher arched his brow at her tone of amusement.

In awe of the mystery of life, Fletcher remained a long time with his son in his lap, studying the child's every feature, from the bulb of the closed eyelids, to the rosebud shape of the tiny, searching mouth. From the tiny, flat nose to the curving, shell-like shape of the ears. He admired, verbally, the color of the child's skin, and the healthy grip it took upon his finger. But when the infant attempted to pull that finger to its mouth, Fletcher's eyes widened in discomfort.

"Is he hungry?" he asked Elizabeth.

"Not really," answered the girl. "They usually ain't, for a while. He's merely sucking. When he starts to fret, I'll fetch him some sugar and water, until Mrs. Ashley's milk comes in."

Nodding, Fletcher folded his hand over his son's head. "Elizabeth," he said, "I am sorry for what happened to you, today. No man has the right to—to—Well, anyway, as soldiers, we are not all as he. And I will see him punished, I promise you."

Elizabeth said nothing for a moment, and then she commented, at a deliberate tangent, "He's big, that baby of yours, ain't he? For an early comer, I mean."

Fletcher glanced aside at the girl, and then down again, at his son. "Was he before his time? Why was that? Did something happen?"

"Aye," said Elizabeth, "it did at that! Two things, actually. First, that horrible man, Mr.—er, now, let me think—what was his name?"

Slowly, Fletcher turned his head. He waited. Beneath his hand, the baby's hair curled softly. The scalp was warm.

"Johnston," said Elizabeth, at last. "That Mr. Johnston came here—"

"What?" exclaimed Fletcher, so loudly that the baby started, but did not cry. "Johnston was here?"

"Yes," continued Elizabeth. "An' he gave Mrs. Ashley a dreadful time, after she tried to be so nice to him, an' all; she even had me fry him up some eggs because he seemed so hungry. With the little that we have! Was he grateful? Nay, he was not. He carried on, an' upset her, until I finally had to take after him with the frying pan." She did not bother to mention that Fletcher's own name had come up during that harrowing converse.

"Did you now?" said Fletcher, with a crooked, boyish grin. "Good for you, Elizabeth. Good for you. I regret that he came here, though. He had no business, nor right, to come to this house. He knows that well enough. Ah," he said suddenly, "then he saw that Faith was with child?"

"That he did," replied Elizabeth.

"It is a wonder," said Fletcher, "that he did not think to come to me to torment me with the knowledge. However, he was doubtlessly leary of that confrontation. I am afraid that I had previously taken him down a peg or two for his insinuations." He looked grim at the recollection.

"What was the second thing to upset Faith?" Fletcher asked.

Elizabeth bit her lip, and shook her head. She leaned forward and took the baby, cradling the child against her small breast.

"Mr. Briggs . . . Mr. Briggs died, sir, that same night. Mrs. Ashley was with him."

"Oh, no," Fletcher sighed, and looked away, to the fire, propping his chin atop his knee. The firelight danced through his Welsh mother's black hair like fairylight. A sadness settled over him.

"Lieutenant," said Elizabeth, softly, "please. Do not leave her again."

"I do not plan to," he said, and rose, tall before the fire. His shadow stretched up the wall behind. Beyond the shuttered window, the snowy twilight was falling. "I will go now," he said, "to collect my possessions. I will give word to my commanding officer that this is where I will be quartered. I will go forth each day from here, to my duty, and return to this place at night. You will have to accept that I cannot change the color of my uniform, Elizabeth."

"I already have," she said. He moved away, but she called him back. "Lieutenant."

"Yes?"

"I would ask that you do somethin' for me, sir."

He faltered, and felt something akin to fear strike him, for he knew what her request would be. "Yes, Elizabeth?" he said. His back was to her. His eyes were closed.

"Might you see to my Jack? I don' fool myself into believin' that you might get him out of that horrible prison, but could you see that he's cared for? An' that I could visit him, regular? I—I beg it of you, Lieutenant. I beg."

She clung to Fletcher's son, blue eyes wide and childlike, brimming with tears. But there was nothing puerile about her desire. In her longing to save the man she loved, she was as any woman.

"I shall see what I can do," Fletcher heard himself saying.

"Thank you," said Elizabeth, simply.

Fletcher nodded, and started for the door. Yet, he paused again. "If Mrs. Ashley awakens soon," he said, "tell her where I have gone, and that I will be back as quickly as possible. Take care of her well, Elizabeth, and of my son."

"'Course," said the girl. "You know that."

It was some time near to dawn before Fletcher returned. Elizabeth was sleeping before the hearth, curled about the nest of quilts she had formed for the newborn boy. Stealthily, Fletcher lowered the cradle he had carried through snow and rising wind to the floor. He took the few logs of seasoned oak from inside of it, and placed one on the dwindling fire. Bending beside Elizabeth's blonde head, he thought of the soldier who had attacked her, whom he had, as promised, seen flogged for his deed. "Elizabeth," he whispered, "you are avenged."

He turned, then, to depart, but she stirred, and spoke to him.

"Lieutenant," she whispered sleepily, her words ill-formed, "did you see my Jack?"

Fletcher faltered, frowning. He felt weary beyond relief. In the dark hour before the sun, his look was black, and cold.

"He is gone," he said, quietly. "He has escaped, from his cell."

Elizabeth rolled over, eyes wide. "Safely?" she asked.

Fletcher nodded, reluctantly.

"Where's he gone?"

"Do you expect me to know that, Elizabeth? If he is wise at all, he has left the town behind." His tone was deliberately stiff and unyielding.

"An' me," said the girl.

Fletcher sighed. "And you," he said. "Would you not rather that he is safe?"

"Yes," she said.

So definite, unhesitating, that Fletcher's heart dipped miserably. "Well then," he said, and gave the empty cradle an absent rocking with his foot before he stalked wretchedly from the kitchen.

There was no helping it, he thought. I have done the only thing that I could.

Chapter Thirty-one

Faith gazed down at the baby suckling at her breast. The sensation of his mouth was odd, slightly uncomfortable, yet immensely pleasant. She stroked the pale fuzz that wreathed his head so fine, like a spider's web. It was dark, she noticed, at the back of his neck. Perhaps, he would have his father's black hair when he was older. The coloration of his Welsh ancestry.

"Jonathan," she cooed, disturbing the down of his hair with her breath. Fletcher and she had named him during the first days of his life. A name for Fletcher's father, and for her own. It seemed to suit him well.

Faith raised her eyes to gaze at the ice that was frosting the glazing of the window and filtering the sunlight through its crystalline haze. The corners of her mouth turned down, and she quickly looked away, to the babe once more. For Fletcher had gone, into the frigid cold of the morning, to attend Ezra's funeral in her name. A vision of the open grave appeared before her mind's eye; yet, it did not trouble her so much as did the image that followed: of the coffin lowered, the dirt mounded over, raw and without life, as the winter denied it grass, or flower. The wind would be high, salty and bitter, blowing the snow across the barren earth. At least, she thought, he rests at Kathleen's side; and she pictured that, also, with the stone glazed in ice, and the sky overhead clouded, pearly gray.

Sighing, she lowered her cheek to the sated child's crown, and held it there.

Hearing a noise, Faith glanced up to find Fletcher standing on the threshold, his arm crooked against the doorframe, watching the two of them with a careworn countenance. He came forward, lowering himself to the edge of the bed.

"I am sorry," he said, not for the first time, "about Ezra."

Faith nodded.

"The estate," said Fletcher, "is unsettled, of course. All of his possessions have been locked up, and the key is for your safekeeping." He held it out to her, and she opened her palm to receive it. She held it a long moment before setting it aside, on the table beside the bed.

"I expected that you would be away all day, my love," she said.

"Well," Fletcher answered, running his fingers through his black hair and loosening the ribbon. "So did I."

"What has happened?"

"I put in a request for permission to marry, now that you have accepted me, Faith. It was refused. I am afraid that I made a bit of a scene about it, and was relieved from duties, until tomorrow. I may not wed a known traitor in the midst of insurrection, my dear. Your reputation, somehow, has reached the ears of Lord Percy."

"And we must wait for permission, Fletcher?" said Faith, after a minute of silence.

"It would be wise," answered Fletcher, "unless I am to allow myself to be cashiered, or plan to hide you away."

Faith said nothing, but lowered her eyes to the infant in her lap. She wiped the milky drool that dripped from his rosy lips. "As you say," she whispered.

In that, the coldest winter in years, the harbor froze over, though never quite firm enough to support the weight of troops or artillery, and so the siege continued. Fletcher came and went from the house in the pursuit of his sworn service; Faith held her tongue concerning that matter, and Elizabeth followed suit as best as she was able. The furniture within the house dwindled, burned upon the hearth, supplemented with the officer's supply which Fletcher continued to demand, and to which he was entitled.

Jonathan thrived at Faith's breast; grew plump, content. His hair darkened, beneath the fuzz of blond that stood out like down about his head. Fletcher marvelled at the miracle of life, the reality of a child, his child. It seemed that he could not get enough of holding him, of watching him suckling at Faith's nipple or sleeping in his cradle. It was as if, in the circle of his tiny family, he had found joy, at last.

Elizabeth, when the opportunity arose, took to caring for the child with selfless devotion, loving him as much as if he were her own. Having grown up the eldest of six siblings, she proved herself invaluable as a source of information, time and time again. She seemed to blossom, in her newfound importance, and one day, Faith realized that what there had been left of the girl was gone, and in her place was a serious young woman.

"Ain't he ever goin' to marry you, Mrs. Ashley?" she asked, one morning.

Faith turned to Elizabeth in wordless appraisal. Yet, when she spoke, it was with honesty. "When permission is granted by his superiors for Fletcher to do so, he will. That," she added, with unconscious bitterness, "is the way of war. Everything other than that one violent purpose must wait."

"Supposin' that he didn't? Wait, I mean to say."

"Then, he would be cashiered, or sent to some post that was equally as dishonorable."

"Does that matter so much to him?"

"Yes," said Faith, "it does."

Her admissions seemed so unreasonable, when viewed through Elizabeth's eyes, but a man's pride was his own, and could not be judged against another's conception of those same ideals. Fletcher was still torn by his loyalties and by his love, Faith knew, and she was trying, calmly, to give him the time he needed. But, she prayed nightly, in the long minutes before sleep, that he would not take much longer. She was afraid of the uncertainty of the future, for so much could occur, in wartime, that might sweep the two of them apart again. And this time, perhaps, forever.

Chapter Thirty-two

The sound that rent the air above Boston on the morning of March 2, 1776, was one which struck the true fear of conflict into the hearts of the town's remaining population; for the war had come to them. From the north shore of the Mystic, the Continental army was bombarding Boston with mortar fire.

With the first distant shock of impact, Faith's dishes rattled in the hutch, and a single cup fell from where it had been sitting upon the mantelpiece, shattering into a multitude of porcelain fragments over the floor. Elizabeth, who had been in the process of folding her bedding, dropped the blankets to the floor with an involuntary shriek of fright. In the cradle beside her, Jonathan opened his mouth to wail in response to her shrill distress and the thin crash of the shattering cup.

With her teeth in her lip, Faith removed the child from his bed, and sat down on an old sea-trunk, soothing and silencing the infant at her breast.

"There, there," she said. "Take hold of that, my sweet. Shhhh. Shhhhh." Rocking him, back and forth, she watched as Elizabeth wrung her hands, gazing, speechlessly, at the shards of porcelain.

"Sit down, Elizabeth," she said, "and be still. Leave the cup, for now."

Through the open shutter, Faith could see blue smoke rising. In the hutch, the dishes rattled like gunfire. And at the opposite side of the kitchen, Fletcher was shrugging into his coat and muttering such profanities that Faith would not have been surprised to witness a streak of blue fire trailing behind him.

"Elizabeth is a brave girl," Fletcher paused to comment. Neither he, nor the girl, had ever made mention to Faith of the incident in the gaol, but Fletcher had not forgotten. It had

310

been a cruel and wicked thing to have occurred, the robbing
of innocence in that manner. But he had personally seen that
the soldier had paid the price for his savagery. Jacques Sabot
had wanted to kill the man, he remembered, with his bare
hands.

"Will the house come down?" Elizabeth whispered to him
breathlessly.

"Not," said Fletcher, "without a direct hit."

"Hush, Elizabeth," said Faith. "All will be well."

Fletcher stomped toward the door, recalled that he had not
kissed Faith good-bye, and came back. He bent, pressing his
lips to her forehead in aggravation, then bent to kiss his son,
heedless to the fact that the babe was suckling at its mother's
breast. He nodded at Elizabeth.

"When will you return, Fletcher?" Faith asked, calmly. I
will not show him that I am afraid, she determined. A fresh
mortar burst, rumbling through the air like thunder. The ladle
fell from its hook beside the hearth with a bell-tone clatter.

Fletcher reached out, smoothed her hair, caressed her cheek.
"When the firing ceases," he said. "I can promise no more
than that."

Faith nodded, and did not let him see the despair in her
eyes. She moved her lips in silent prayer.

For three days, Faith awaited his return. The mortars burst,
sometimes falling short of their mark, sometimes not. The
damage was not what it could have been, as chimneys fell,
and dishes tumbled, and fires broke out to be quickly contained.
A few buildings were blasted into rubble, some lost a wall,
exposing the rooms inside to the elements without. The smell
of smoke was constant in the air, as were the cries of the
British, who attempted to halt the firing through retaliatory
attack. On the third day—by coincidence, or not, the anniversary of the Boston Massacre—the mortar ceased.

Faith stood in the center of the kitchen in her old gingham
skirt, with her hands on her hips, frowning thoughtfully as she
assessed the damage in her own home. She had lost many of
her dishes. Several windowpanes throughout the house had
cracked; the floor before the hearth was blackened by the soot
of a burning log. Only a few hours earlier, the copestone at

the chimney-top had broken loose, plummeting into the fire below, showering sparks and hissing, flaming wood over the planking. Faith had smothered the fire with a blanket, after which she had promptly moved Jonathan's cradle to a more discreet distance. One of her arms was blistered, slightly. Her hands were still shaking.

Outside, in the absence of explosion, the bitter, fierce wind that had arisen was more noticeable than ever. Faith listened to it keening over the broken chimney-top.

About midday, Fletcher arrived home. He stood a moment inside of the doorway, stamping his feet and blowing out his breath like a winded horse, as he gazed about at the wreck of the kitchen, and muttered, beneath his breath:

"Damn it all."

He dropped a kiss upon Faith's lips inattentively, so that he very nearly missed them. His eyes moved to the blackened section of the floor.

"Was anyone injured?" he asked.

"No," said Faith.

"Yes," said Elizabeth. Faith shot her a withering glance. "Well," said the girl, "t'is true. Lieutenant, Mrs. Ashley has burnt her arm."

"Let me look at it."

"It is nothing," said Faith, and would not let him see.

"As you wish," he said, rather curtly, and crossed the kitchen floor to lower himself beside the cradle. He folded his long legs before him, his back propped against the wall. Not a chair, not a table, remained to the room. Distractedly, he placed his hand on the cradle's rocker and began to tilt the bed, side to side. His expression was pained, lost, as he stared vacantly into the fire.

"This place is full of smoke," he said.

"There is a reason for that," Faith answered, nodding toward the floor, and its blackened, bubbled surface.

He grunted, and removed his hat, slapping it on his knee. He lifted Jonathan from the cradle, onto his lap. "You were awake in there, weren't you, my boy? Papa is home. Where's a smile for me, eh?" At the gurgling efforts of the child, he grinned, weakly.

Glancing at Elizabeth, curled in a blanket in the corner, Faith went to Fletcher and dropped down beside him. Her gingham skirt folded over his thigh.

"Fletcher," she said, "what has happened? We have seen no one; heard less. Will you not tell me, so that I may understand why you are so cross?"

Frowning, Fletcher said, "I have every right to be cross. It was a ruse, all of it. Your own countrymen endangered the lives of every man, woman, or child left to this town, patriot or not, for a ruse. To draw our attention from their true purpose, as we attempted to deter their fire. A general by the name of Thomas, and some two thousand men, have constructed a breastwork of ice on Dorchester Heights."

"Why are you so angry? It is war, as you have said, and each commander does as he sees fit. It was," Faith added, "a prudent move."

Fletcher's gaze was spiteful. "Your old fire, coming to the fore, Faith?" he said. His fury was barely contained.

"Fletcher," she said, softly, "I am sincere concerning the Patriot Cause. Nothing has happened to change that. If I am pleased by a minor victory, I am not necessarily pleased by your loss."

"Minor victory?" said Fletcher. "The entire British camp is now covered by rebel cannon, as is every ship in the harbor, Faith."

Faith had cause to welcome the news, with joy, but she held her tongue. The Faith that would have allowed her tongue to fly was gone.

"Is the siege ended, then?" Stirring in her corner, Elizabeth asked the question that was in Faith's mind.

"As of now," he answered, bouncing Jonathan on his knee, "we have no plans to surrender. I have only come home for a few hours." He turned then, and his gray-blue eyes met Faith's green ones without barrier. There was no longer any anger there; merely frustration.

"Tomorrow," he sighed, "we attack. That does not go beyond this room. Do you hear me, Elizabeth?" he said, purposefully. "I have no doubt that this will be the decisive battle of the siege, if not the war. The crisis is at a head. Time is short. Faith, as you know, I had hoped to be wed to you by now. I don't—I do not know what to say to you on that matter. The outcome of this battle may determine all, for you." He hooked his hand behind her neck, pushing his mouth against her hair. Jonathan reached up, his eye attracted by the gleaming locks, and entangled his round fist into them. Tenderly, Fletcher disengaged the infant's grasp.

"War is war, and once again, tomorrow I may face the loss of life. There is no truer enemy upon the battlefield," he said, "than the spectre of Death hovering near. I hope to come back to you. I pray to come back to you. We will decide, then, what to do."

Silently, Faith nodded.

"Ah, Faith," he said, "I do love you so."

Twilight descended, on wind-driven wings, and he was gone again. Faith had not wept over fear of his death. It was pointless, for all the tears shed could not prevent a single bullet from piercing flesh and bone. She took comfort in Elizabeth's voluble company, and the fact that the child at her breast was his.

The morning of the sixth dawned in misery, in a torrential rain that could drive a horse astray, and which poured down the chimney to soak the wood so that it smoked more pungently than before. Elizabeth stood before the hearth, fanning the flames with her apron in an attempt to keep the smoke out. Curling on the wind, the water battered the glass, its beat over the roof sounded in thudding drum rolls. Apparently, Jonathan found the noise soothing, for he was content to sleep the day away. Faith sat beside the cradle, preparing his first pair of stockings.

Every so often, she lifted her head, and listened.

"Do you hear something, Elizabeth?" she would say.

"No," Elizabeth would answer. "Nothing."

And it was true. Beyond the sounds of the rain, there was nothing of battle. No cannon, or gunfire; no cries of men. The wind rattled the shutters, moaning across the chimney and beneath the eaves. The rain fell.

After a time, Faith rose, and donned an old oilskin which had once been the property of the captain of her husband's ship. He was a huge man, Captain Eller, and the waterproof skin fell below her ankles.

"Mrs. Ashley, where are you going?" Elizabeth asked, in alarm.

"I will be back shortly. Take care of Jonathan," said Faith. "I want to know what is occurring in the town."

Faith had not gone far, however, when she was stopped by soldiers. She stood, glaring at them, narrow-eyed, as the rain beat against her face and soaked her hair.

"What are you doing out, m'am?" one of them asked her.

"Are citizens remanded to their houses?" she asked. "I was not aware of that edict. I have come to see what is occurring. Is the siege over?"

"You will know when, and if, that should occur," stated the other, firmly. "Go back to your home. You will catch your death."

Angrily, Faith turned away. She gathered the oilskin close over her gown, but it did no good: her skirt was soaked. She continued through the streets, searching out news, but there was none to be had, until she happened upon a knot of gentlemen, who were equally as wet as she, standing beneath the naked branches of a hornbeam; one of the few trees left standing, for its wood was too hard to burn without the proper amount of kindling, which was in short supply.

"Is there fighting?" she asked them. They turned to her in surprise.

"Nay. There is no fighting this day. Those damned rebels —my pardon—are going to take this town into their own hands! I guarantee it! We will all be fleeing like rabbits before long. It angers me, and puts us all to shame. Especially our British protectors, who have failed us miserably. Would you not agree, my friends?"

The men around the speaker nodded in agreement, or made verbal statements attesting to the same, while the rain poured from their hats, and over their shoulders. Faith left them.

Was it possible that the woeful conditions of the past months were coming to an end? If the British surrendered the town, then all Loyalist citizens, and all troops, would have to depart on the British ships. And that meant Fletcher, for she could not convince him otherwise. She did not dare to. To desert his commission at such a time would be no less than a sentence of death for both his life, and his honor. She understood him, and his need to do what was right. To him, it was often a very simple thing. Follow the course of his own devising, as long as it ran parallel to the path to which he was sworn. The only time during which he diverged from that path, was when it met with her own.

And what of her own convictions? When the man had spoken in such fierce negative of the patriot army, she had, conversely, felt a burning pride. A fire of respect for that which she and her countrymen strove for; for the liberty of vision, and ideal. A fire that had once waned, during the seclusion of her pregnancy, during the confusion of torn loyalties, though she may have known it not.

Until now.

I am a patriot, she thought, as she hurried homeward, and her heart was filled with the spitfire imagery that had driven her so thoroughly in earlier days. I will raise my son a Patriot, and my children henceforth, if any be granted to me. And Fletcher, dear Fletcher, what will you think of that? We must come to an agreement, and our time is so short . . .

As she passed before her neighboring houses, the wind blew her hood back, exposing her rain-drenched countenance. She struggled to pull it up, over her hair. Her eye was caught by a movement in a doorway. She turned; slowed. There was a woman in the open frame, frowning at the rain. Faith recognized her as someone whom she thought had left town during summer's exodus. Apparently, the woman recognized her, also.

"Turncoat!" the woman shouted, and stepped back, slamming shut the door. An instant later, the door opened again, and an unknown object was projected through the air to land, with a thud, upon the cobbles. Faith only glanced at it, and walked away. The woman had wrapped a lampoon around something heavy, and tossed it out at her. Faith had no need to study the picture, for there was another, not far away, nailed to a house frame. And another, placed elsewhere. There were more, and on her own house, several. She rushed over, and tore them all down. No name, not even of the woman depicted, but the face was familiar: it was her own. Waving a colonial flag, while being subjugated by a British soldier. It was a lewd depictment. The rain-washed ink ran onto her hands. She threw the lampoons down, and stormed to the back of the house, and inside.

Angrily, she whipped off the oilskin.

"Mrs. Ashley, you're soaked! Get out of them wet things! What's happened? Here, let me help you. Johnny's still asleep."

"Jonathan," said Faith, absently. "I swear, Elizabeth—"

"Oh, hush, don't swear, Mrs. Ashley," Elizabeth warned, wide-eyed.

Faith shrugged out of her bodice and skirt, standing before the fire in her petticoat and her chemise. "Do you doubt me, Elizabeth?" she said. "Do you doubt that I am a patriot still?"

"'course not," said Elizabeth, recalling uneasily those times when she had.

"Do you know what is being said about me?"

"No," Elizabeth lied.

"You do not want to know," said Faith. "I have given my best, for years," she said. "I still am; I still would. Am I not allowed to love whom I choose? Why should that make a difference? Lucy Gage does not earn the disrespect that I do, and she is married to the Governor-General, royally appointed. Yet her patriotism is not doubted. Why is mine?"

"I don't know," said Elizabeth. "Mayhaps, it ain't that it's doubted, but your ability to choose is."

"To choose?" said Faith, slowly. She held out her hands to the fire, and would not turn around.

"In the end," said Elizabeth, "you are goin' to have to choose, somehow. Lieutenant Fletcher is a proud man, Mrs. Ashley. An' an honorable one. He ain't goin' to forsake his red coat, just as you ain't goin' to forsake that colonial flag of yours." Realizing what she had said, the girl drew in her breath sharply.

Faith spun around, and then back again, to the fire, following Elizabeth's gaze. There, in the ashes, half-burned, lay the remains of another lampoon. She sighed, and then, quite uncharacteristically, she swore. Elizabeth gasped behind her.

* * *

The silence before the hearth had been long, and unbroken. Fletcher sat with his knees drawn up, staring into the flames, dry now, and fed. His scarlet coat hung on the edge of the mantel. Steam rose from the damp fabric into the air, making thin shadows on the wall. Behind him, Elizabeth was asleep in her corner, and Jonathan lay in his cradle, untroubled. Faith peeked in at him, pulling the blanket closer about his shoulders, and then came back to Fletcher's side, easing down onto the floor beside him.

"So," he said. "It is done. Dorchester Heights will not be taken. The boats could not even be manned in the rain, and Howe cancelled the orders for attack. It might have worked. It might just have worked."

Faith rubbed his shoulder, then dropped her hand to his thigh. It felt strong, sinewy, warm.

"Tomorrow, the order will be given for all royal provisions to be turned in. It will take several days to arrange a total surrender of the town. The horse transports will, no doubt, be moved into the harbor to remove the troops and citizens before your—countrymen—march in." He stared into the fire, his jaw set. Beside him, Faith drew her knees up, also, and lowered her chin onto them.

"You will," he said, "be coming with me, Faith."

Faith was silent.

"There is no longer any place for you here in Boston, Faith," he said, tossing the crumbled, ink-smeared paper that he had been holding in his fist to the flames. It opened, like a flower, as it caught, then burned, in petals of fire.

"Perhaps not," she said.

"I cannot stay," said Fletcher. "Even if I reveled in the idea of prison. I will not desert my commission, nor my country. Faith, I am a man of honor. I must see this war through, to its completion."

"And have me follow you about, like a camp-woman."

"No, Faith. Live with me, as my wife. We can marry, on shipboard. If Percy chooses to discharge me, then, he may."

"Then why do you not walk away, now? We will leave Boston, together. Settle elsewhere with Jonathan."

He shook his head, gazing silently into the dark well of the fireplace. Faith pushed her fingers through his damp, black hair. She touched the widow's peak at his forehead. How endearing that one feature was, standing out above the rest. His hair never seemed quite under control because of it, and when he grinned, in his boyish manner, he may as well have been the youth that had marched, years ago, on his first campaign. How she wished that she had known him then.

"I love you, Faith," said Fletcher, and compressed his lips. It was hard to say that now, without pain.

"I know that you do," Faith answered.

He closed his eyes, and the tears seeped out, glistening in the firelight. "You are my wife. In my heart, that is what you have always been. And Jonathan. I would not have him called bastard. That is not a thing to make a child's life easier."

"There is no need for that. From what you say, there is time, before the ship sails, Fletcher. No one else need know, save you and I. But we will make it right, Fletcher. Let it not be said that we made this one mistake."

"Faith, please," said Fletcher.

Her throat constricted. "It has to be this way; it must. I have never cared much for what people have said of me, but I have always cared what I have thought of myself. It is one thing, to love you, Fletcher; and love you I do, more than my heart seems able to contain. But I cannot live among my enemy, betrayer of my countrymen and of the liberty for which we have fought and must continue to fight—of my own honor, Fletcher. I have my own sense of honor. It is not only men who live and die by it."

"No," said Fletcher. "It is only men who make fools of themselves for its sake."

"For glory," said Faith.

"No. There is no glory in war. Only maiming and death, and the loss of loved ones . . . What will I do without you? You are my life, Faith."

"Don't," she said, and touched her fingers to his lips. He

pulled her closer, burying his mouth into her hair. Ah, but he would not forget the scent of her hair, like the honeysuckle that clung to the walls along the roadways, and to the fence-posts, in June . . .

"Will you remember me, when all of this misery is said and done?"

"Yes," said Faith. "I will not forget. I will never forget." And, suddenly, she was weeping. "Oh, Fletcher," she said, as he pulled her close, against his breast, and his heart beat loudly beneath her ear.

Faith stood very straight and still beside the barrier, observing the departing troops. Her shoulders were back, her fists curled so tightly that her nails dug half-moons into the soft flesh of her palms. Her cloak drifted on the breeze, as did her hair, unbound. Overhead, the gulls cried, like babes. The cobbled pavement vibrated to the marching of feet, toward the last of the waiting ships. Soldiers and Loyalist citizens alike were moving to board. The violence was over; the looting of shops and unprotected houses had ended, and the barricade had been erected to prevent anything further: committed against the soldiers, rather than by them. The orderly ranks of scarlet-coated regiments moved steadily onward. Faith breathed in their dust, and the crispness of the air.

All down the line, women were breaking free of the barricade to bid their loved ones farewell, for unless they were married to their men, they could not go. Faith waited, expression impassive, her head held high, not so much in pride, as in an unwillingness to move, lest she break the concentration that was preventing her tears.

"Faith."

Closing her eyes, she felt the touch of his hand upon her own, and bit, hard, into her lip.

"Faith," he said again.

She opened her eyes, green and moist. It was a cruel taunt, this, to find, upon her last sight of him, that he was more beautiful than ever she had known; tall, and well built, and handsome even in his hated uniform; and his mouth with its

boyish smile, and his eyes like smoke, or summer's quickening
thunderheads, and his thick, black hair; his mother's dark
Welsh hair . . .

He took her into his arms, and kissed her, for the last time.
There was such strength, in his embrace, such gentleness. It
had always been that way, from the moment when his hand
had touched her own, in the carriage, oh, so many years ago,
it seemed.

"Keep my memory for Jonathan. Do not let him think ill
of his father, Faith."

"I won't," she said.

"And you will take care of yourself."

"And you, Fletcher. Do not let any—any rebel shoot you,
do you understand me? Don't—"

"Hush, my love," he said softly. "You were not going to
weep, do you remember?" He lifted her hand, and held it, so
that the slim-banded ruby on her finger sparkled in the sunlight.
It is yours, he had said to her, through life, and unto death.
And she had wept, as she was weeping, now. He frowned,
and his eyes beneath their dark, mismatched brows were sor-
rowed. "I love you," he said.

"I love you, Fletcher."

He laughed, crookedly. "With all our love between us, what
are we doing, Faith?"

"Following our divergent paths," said she, and attempted
to laugh, too.

"I have never told you that I am proud of you, Faith, for
the strength of your conviction. Don't give up."

"Fletcher—"

"This, then," he said, "is the ending. After so many starts
and finishes, it has come, at last. It breaks my heart."

"Fletcher—"

"I must say farewell, now, Faith, or I shall not say it at all.
I cannot bear this parting."

And he kissed her again, on the crown of her head, as he
was wont to do in moments of great affection and tenderness,
and he strode away.

Faith watched, as she had that other time, when she had not
seen him, astride his horse. But now her eyes were riveted to

his diminishing form, as he marched among the men that were left to his command. Once, he seemed to falter, and turn, and then went on, until he had vanished from her sight.

Fletcher, dear God, Fletcher, don't go.

But he was gone. The last of the troops had emptied the streets, leaving them dusty, and echoing. At the wharf, the sails of the ships unfurled, billowing with a heartrending noise upon the breeze, preparing to leave Boston, forever.

Chapter Thirty-three

Longmeadow
October, 1781

The boy was tall, for his age, and slender, giving him the appearance of being older than he was. His hair was dark: coal black, thick and soft, and bound into a short tail behind his head with a length of dyed rawhide. He had a narrow, handsome face, with a squared chin and a slender nose. Beneath his brown lashes, his eyes were gentle ovals, green as the foliage of summer.

He wore his dark, Sunday meeting-clothes in a casual manner, careless of their cut or of their quality, and he needed constant reminders to take caution in his treatment of them as he ran on ahead of his mother along the river path. It was a wondrously lovely day for so late in October, crisp and blue and fleecy, with the colorful leaves falling about the path, or rustling in the trees. The river looked like a shining strip of silver beyond them. In the still, murky backwaters, the ducks paused to circle lazily on their way south, and the last of the midges swirled up in the final pattern of their dance. How could he be expected to contain himself, when there was so much to be seen? And so he ran on, and on, until he was out of sight of his mother's quick vision, and beyond her gently chiding voice. He slipped from the main path to another, quiet and private, to which he, alone, was privy. He went down beneath the branches under which he barely needed to stoop, skidding on the mud once, then righting himself, after soiling the knee of his breeches; on to where he knew the little-used path opened, just beside the riverbank, in a place where the water took a turn in upon itself, and had created a small peninsula. The undergrowth was a wealth of berries at that time of year, and was governed by a huge, old elm that leaned out, bent and twisted by the shadows of the trees on the bank above it, right over the tranquil pool beneath. He enjoyed scrambling up atop this elm, to pretend that he was on horseback, riding at full gallop rather than the sedate pace that his mother allowed; through heathered fields and green pastures, up into the face of his enemy. He would strike the enemy down proudly with his sword, swiping left, right, left, right. In his dreams he always seemed to fight only one man, and this man was his father. He could not understand why he fought his father, except that it made him angry to think that his father could have left him, and his mother, so alone. He did not believe that the man had died, as his mother was willing to allow all the others within the village to believe, for she never spoke of the man to him in terms of death; she never really told him that his father had died. She only told him good things about the man, and she never spoke as if he were gone.

Frowning, the boy scurried down through the underbrush, toward the old elm, wanting now, more than ever, to mount the tree and ride, to brandish his sword, and yell, and maybe even cry, as he sometimes did. But as he burst free of the berry-laden bushes, tearing his sleeve, and the back of his hand, he saw that someone had come to occupy the tree before him. It was a grown man.

It only took a moment for Faith to realize that she no longer heard Jonathan's running footsteps ahead, and she came to a halt on the path, listening. It was not that she was afraid for him, for it was safe here in the village where she had grown up, but it irked her that her son would shake her off in that playful manner, as if she were an annoyance.

She stood, pushing the flying tendrils of her red-gold hair from her forehead as the brisk autumn wind tugged at them, and at the black ribbons of her bonnet. The air put a fresh blush in her cheeks and a rose to her lips, and caused her eyes to sparkle in a manner that spoke of times past, when there had been hope within hopelessness, and she had thought that Fletcher would return. Now, she knew better, and her life in Longmeadow had settled into a quiet acquiescence, a stolid acceptance, that made her seem a different woman than the one who had left her father's house to return to Boston against his wishes more than a half-dozen years before.

She turned on her heel, tucking her hands beneath her cloak, to stare up over the gentle, wooded slope at the long lots of her neighbors, and the roofs of their homes, and the short spire of the town's meeting house. Beyond that, on the opposite side of the main street, were more homes, including her father's, and thence the fields where the men who remained worked hard, and beyond these, the forested hills. The sky above was as blue as she remembered Elizabeth's eyes to be, filled with clouds. Blackbirds roosted in the colorful trees, and a gaggle of long-necked geese, bodies gray-brown, heads black above necks banded in white, flew across the path of her vision, low, and heading toward the marshy land beside the river for a respite from their long journey just begun.

But the people of the village were not the same as once they had been, though the land itself might remain unchanged. With each passing year of the revolution, each month, each day, there had been small changes among them. Not all of them were readily noticeable, as pride was humbled, or the meek spirit made bold, by news of victory after defeat, of the changing tide of the battle over the past three years, away from the triumph of the British, to that of the Continental army. There were those men who returned from the war, wounded, and unable to fight any longer. They found their fields sown by their children, and their wives, and they suffered further wounding at the knowledge of this. Then, there were others, who were merely bitter, for they had been in the worst of it and had seen friends die. Such a man was William Bliss, once pleasant, and easy-natured, now gripped by sullen brooding. Faith preferred to think of him as the boy she had known in her youth, and she treated him in that manner. Because of her attitude he often responded with some of his old ease. For this reason, he sought out her company often in a stroll after Sunday worship, or he invited himself to dinner,—a fact which tended to amuse her father, since he remembered how persistent the man had been as a boy—or he otherwise insinuated himself into her society since his return a year earlier. This Sunday was no exception. Promptly at service's end, he appeared at her side, with arm extended, and took herself and her son out along Ely Highway to the meadow beyond, and thence, the riverside.

But now, Jonathan had run ahead and beyond sight.

"Jonathan!" she called. She startled the birds from the trees nearest.

"Oh, let him go, Faith," said Bliss. "Johnny's a good boy. You worry him too much. What harm can come to him so near to home?"

"None," she said, "I suppose. None at all."

William smiled, and nodded. "It is good," he said, "to have you as my friend again."

Faith eyed him askance and said nothing.

"Have I said that before?"

"No," said Faith.

"You know, of course, what the folk here are saying about us."

"No," Faith lied.

"No?" echoed Bliss. He laughed. "They say that the twice-widowed daughter of John Colton will make poor, crippled William a kindly wife."

Faith had, indeed, heard that said, though the wording had been somewhat different. "And what do you think?" she asked him, quietly.

"That they are all a bunch of cackling biddies, male and female alike. You have no more desire to wed me, than I you."

It was Faith's turn to be amused, and her laughter rang softly beneath the arch of trees above their heads. "How pleasant to hear you say so," she remarked. "But it is true: I have no desire to marry again, even . . ."

"Yes?"

"Even," she said, "if I was certain that my husband, that Jonathan's father, is gone. I cannot believe that he truly is. I —I would know, somehow."

"You have never spoken of this before," whispered William.

"No," said Faith. She tried not to think on it herself. When Fletcher had urged her to return to the safety of Longmeadow until the war was over, she did not think it would last so many years before he came for her. She prayed he had not abandoned her.

"You have led the townspeople to believe that his death was a fact."

"I know."

"And Johnny? What have you said to him?"

"The same that I have just said to you. It seemed wrong, to allow him hope, but it was worse to deny it to him."

William sighed, and was silent for a time. Faith walked a little ahead, her gloved hands folded before her. "Did he— did he—desert you, Faith?"

"Of course not!"

"No, no, of course not," Bliss repeated, and was quiet. After a moment, he spoke again. "If you discovered that Johnny's father was, indeed, dead, would you reconsider your statement? For I would marry you, if you thought it best. The boy needs a father, Faith, and though there is no great love between you and I, at least there is friendship."

"There is that," said Faith.

William nodded, and allowed the subject to drop. He did not love Faith, and he hoped for a woman, one day, who would make him happy. Yet, he was particularly fond of Johnny, and it was a shame to see such a boy growing up without a father's love and guidance.

"Jonathan!" Faith called suddenly. "Jonathan, where are you hiding?"

Faith walked on, ahead of William, to a place where the

path turned sharply toward the river, and collided with her son, coming up out of the underbrush. He fell, clutching to her skirt with his fists as he went down onto his knees. Grabbing him beneath the arm, Faith righted Jonathan on the path. She frowned at the state of his clothing, soiled and torn.

"Oh, Jonathan, look at you! What a sight you are! What am I going to do about this?" She fingered the frayed ends of the rent in his sleeve, brushed the mud from his torn knee. The boy accepted her ministrations with noble restraint, though his expression revealed that he was bursting with excitement. His mother recognized the look: he had had an adventure.

"So, Jonathan," she said, "just what have you been doing?"

His face opened to her, like a bursting seed-pod. "Oh, Mama, I have met a man, down there by the river! A stranger, Mama, who said that I look like you! How does he know that?"

Unthinkingly, Faith took Jonathan by the shoulders. Her countenance blanched. "Did he—did he say his name?"

"No, Mama, but he seems a nice man. Why do you look that way? He didn't try to hurt me, or nothing. The only time he was strange, was when he said that I look like you."

"What else did he say, Jonathan?"

"Uh, well, he asked me a lot of things, 'bout what I do, and if I like it here, and such . . ." His green eyes squinted as his forehead wrinkled in thought. "He asked about you, too, Mama."

Faith drew a steadying breath. "What did he ask?" she said, quietly.

"If I reckoned that you were happy," answered the boy in a sort of wonderment.

Faith felt a tremble in her knees. Behind her, she heard William Bliss approaching, shuffling along the path with his pronounced limp. "Is he . . . is he still there, this man?"

"I suppose so," said Jonathan.

"He did not want to come into the village?"

The boy shrugged his thin shoulders beneath her hands.

"Take me to see him, Jonathan," said Faith, releasing her grip on his arms to take his hand. At that instant, William called the boy's name, though he was as yet out of sight beyond the bend.

"Mr. Bliss is calling," said Jonathan.

"I have him!" Faith shouted back, then whispered to her son, hurriedly, "And how did this man look?"

"Like . . . like the trapper who came through here last year."

"Trapper? What trapper?"

"Don't you remember? Oh, no, I reckon you didn't see him. I didn't remember him, much, 'til now. I didn't really look close. But he has a big beard, and brown clothes, and dark hair, and a funny mark on his eyebrow, like the one on Mr. Bliss' leg, but smaller, that runs this way," he said, indicating with his finger two parallel lines. Before him, Faith felt a shudder course through her body, and she took a step backward. Her heart began to beat rapidly. William was closer, now, though still out of sight.

"Take me to him," said Faith.

Silently, in a conspiratorial manner, Jonathan took his mother's hand, and led her down the narrow path beneath the trees, holding the low branches aside for her passage. He saw her lift her skirts above her ankles, to avoid the mud. "This way," he whispered. "By the water."

Beneath the trees, the midges swarmed up from the back-water, and together mother and son descended below the level of the main path above.

"He was on my tree," whispered the boy, frowning. "He must've gone away."

"No," said Faith, in a blurred hush, "he could not have, knowing that I was near . . ."

"What, Mama?"

"He—" And she grew silent. Her skirt slipped from her hand in a rustling whisper. Under the shadow of the tree, beside the green, still water, another shadow crouched, and was slowly rising, tall as a man, on the opposite side of the twisted trunk, silhouetted against the gleaming river beyond. Faith released her son's hand, and went forward, hesitating a dozen feet away. She stared at the beard that made the man appear so strange, and at the battered hat pressed low over his forehead; she gazed at the eyes, gray-blue as slate, steady, earnest, and felt her throat contract.

"Fletcher," she said, huskily. The man did not answer, but his hand came up, and pushed back the hat, high onto his head, revealing the peak of dark hair, and the scar tissue upon his brow. Slowly, Faith moved nearer, one step at a time, until there was only the trunk of the tree between them. She placed her hands firmly on the fissured bark, and felt them shaking. "Fletcher—" she began.

He spoke, at last. "Am I welcome, after the passage of years, Faith?"

Without a word, she nodded, and leaned forward, and his arms closed around her, over the rounded expanse of the elm. Slipping her hands up along his coat, she embraced his shoulders, pulling him close. She felt him tremble in the circle of her limbs.

"Ah, Fletcher, Fletcher, I cannot believe that it is you. Let me look at you," she said, pulling back a little, and tipping her head to gaze up at him. He made to release her, to come around the tree, but she grasped his hand, and held it tight. "Do not completely let go," she said. "I do not trust my eyes."

"Mine," he said, opening his free hand over her cheek and along her jaw, "do not deceive me, my love." He kissed her, and his mouth was sweet; there was nothing of shyness, nor hesitancy in the kiss, nor discomfort; it was all that she remembered, and more for the secret longing that she had, until this moment, held in abeyance.

It was then that she recalled the presence of their son, standing wonderingly behind them, and she turned, hand outstretched to call his name. Small branches cracked, and there was a scuffling, sliding sound as William Bliss came down the narrow path, and halted beside Jonathan. The boy stood staring at Faith and the stranger with whom she had just made such a spectacle of herself, and it seemed to him that he knew. This was the one. He was not dead. He frowned, feeling betrayed. Bliss stumbled up behind him, glancing from the face of one to another intently, and lastly summing up the likenesses between Jonathan and the fellow with the beard. He looked sharply at the scar on Fletcher's brow. A grim expression settled over his countenance. He placed his hand firmly on Jonathan's young shoulder.

Faith felt Fletcher stiffen against her.

"Who is that?" he asked, flatly.

William Bliss stood on the path, with his hand on Jonathan's shoulder. His look was black.

Chapter Thirty-four

Fletcher sat with his hands between his knees, perched on the edge of a chair that seemed somehow too small for his tall frame. He had washed, and shaved, and now was in the presence of Faith's father, John Colton, in the man's high-ceilinged great-room. To Fletcher's right, a fire was blazing, and was a good deal too hot for his comfort, but it apparently suited the elder Colton perfectly. The mantel was of marble and wood, surprising in its elegance in an otherwise colonial setting; for John Colton was a man of simple tastes, and earthy desires, and his home reflected both of those facts. The only other concession to what had probably been his deceased wife's fancies were the Queen Anne chairs, with their curving legs and delicate patterns, and the chair in which Fletcher, himself, was seated. Colton sat opposite him, a man of medium frame, with a sandy peruke, brown eyes, a stern brow, and a jawline that was remarkably similar to that of his daughter. At the moment, his jaw was set, much like Faith often set hers, and his eyes were steady and sober as he regarded Fletcher. Behind him, Jonathan had stationed himself, and Fletcher could see the top of his head, from the nose upward, as he peered over the chair. But for all of the lieutenant's coaxing, he would not come out.

"So," said John Colton, and his voice was considerably

softer than one might have come to expect from his countenance, "you are my son-in-law, Mr. Irons. What a strange
meeting is this. I knew, of course, that you had not died, or
at least that my daughter kept that hope in her heart, and I kept
her secret. But, if I may be honest, I did not anticipate meeting
you, man. I felt that it was not likely, under what appeared to
be the circumstances."

"You thought that I had abandoned her, sir."

"Yes," said Colton.

"I am sorry that you should think so," answered Fletcher.
"Though you cannot be blamed for your assumptions. It must
have seemed most likely to you, as there had been no word
from me." Silently, the other man nodded in his chair. Behind
him, Jonathan's green eyes widened. Fletcher wished now that
his son was not in the room at all. He looked to him, smiling
at him in an attempt at reassurance, but the boy withdrew,
perceptibly. Frowning, Fletcher straightened his spine. "But
I did not abandon your daughter, sir, and I am here now to
make amends for the time that has been lost. We agreed—
rather foolishly, I believe now—Faith and I, that we could not
be together while the war lasted. Has she told you of this?"

"My daughter," said Colton, "is not one for explanations,
if it does not suit her to give them. I learned early that no
amount of anger can stand against her stubbornness."

"I learned that lesson, also, I am afraid," admitted Fletcher.
"The reasons which parted us were sound enough, but they
should not have been allowed to do so."

"It seems rather weak of you, to keep so far from my
daughter for so many years, when last you knew of her, she
carried your child in her arms."

"I admit that, freely," answered Fletcher, and a muscle
snaked along his jaw. "I do admit that. But I made a vow, to
myself, that I would return at the proper time, to settle the
differences between us for good and all. To see if she will take
me, or turn me away. Faith will understand this. The war is
done, and so did we prom—"

"The war?" echoed Colton. "What do you mean?"

"You have not heard?" Fletcher said. "Cornwallis surrendered at Yorktown, eleven days ago."

The man, in his shirtsleeves and waistcoat, nodded sagely. "Then," said he, "for all practical purposes, the war is ended. Britain's most successful general has been defeated."

"Yes," said Fletcher, schooling his voice to show no emotion.

"Doubtless," continued Colton, "it will be some time before the king admits as much."

Fletcher was silent.

"War wound?" said Colton, indicating the scar on Fletcher's brow.

"Yes, sir," he answered, slowly. Faith walked into the room, and her eyes widened, looking from one man to the other. Fletcher's countenance lit at the sight of her. She is as beautiful as ever, he thought, scarcely realizing that she was now thirty-two years old. She stirred his heart still, sweeping into the room in a panniered skirt of rose and gray, and sitting down, stiffly, on the edge of a chair. Her teeth came out to pull gently at her lip. Even that, Fletcher thought, has not changed.

"Have you been fighting all of these years?" John Colton asked, suddenly.

"Yes," said Fletcher.

"And you were not permitted furlough?"

"I was," he said. "I took it but twice. Once, to—"

"Come here," said Faith, in a quiet rush. "You were here, last year, and you did not let me know."

"Yes," answered Fletcher, and gave her no further explanation of his reasons, for there would be time later, he hoped, to tell her of the desire only to see her well, and contented, before he returned again to his duty. He had seen Jonathan, then, from afar, and the boy had run from him, in fear. It had nearly broken his heart. Happening upon the child by the river, this time, had been less than chance. "And once," he continued, "to return to England, when my father died."

"Oh, Fletcher!" This, from Faith, as she rose from her chair, but with a look from the lieutenant, she sat down again. "We never met, he and I," she said, sadly.

"No, you did not."

Faith's father observed the man who had married his daughter, unbeknownst to him, in Boston in the early stages of the war, and his brows lowered over his brown eyes. He did not think that the man realized the pain that he displayed, but it was there, nonetheless.

"Jonathan," said Faith, quietly, "why do you not go out into the yard, until I call you?"

"If the boy would wish to stay," said her father, "then I believe that you should let him."

"There may be things said that—"

"You must be careful, then," Colton replied quickly, "not to say them. But it is best that the boy is not kept in the dark, and learns what he can of his father through his actions with those whom he knows well, and loves."

Knows well, and loves, thought Faith. How could her son love a father whom he had hardly known, no matter all her words? He did not remember him. Jonathan's knowledge of his father had to start with this.

"Very well," she agreed.

For a long time, then, she sat in silent observation of the three men in her life who mattered most, and her heart went out to all of them, in their confusion, and their distress. She wanted to extend her hand to Jonathan, draw him out from behind her own father's chair, but somehow she felt that she should not, but allow him to be strong in his own way, in the way of a child, open, and aware.

So intent did she become on the discussion, that Faith was startled by the touch of a small hand on her arm. She looked down into Jonathan's angular, handsome face. He leaned forward, whispering into her ear.

"Is he truly my papa?"

Faith put her hand across her son's narrow back. She nodded. "Yes, Jonathan, he is," she said, quite softly.

"Why did he leave us?"

"He . . . he is a soldier," whispered Faith, dismayed by the light of animation that came to the boy's green eyes. "More importantly, he is a man of duty, and of honor. Do you know what I mean by that?" Jonathan nodded his head. "Well, my dear, he went on to do what he felt was his duty in this war, and I would not go with him. That is all. You must not blame him, now that he has come, Jonathan.''

Wordlessly, the little boy looked to the chair where Fletcher sat. "Will he stay with us now?" he asked.

"I hope so," said Faith.

Fletcher turned from his conversation with Colton. It was a moment more before the other man's voice dwindled to silence at the sight of Fletcher's distraction.

"Faith," said Fletcher, and his expression was marked by a bitter pain, "I do not want to leave you again. We . . . we cannot let those things which separated us before come between us again. Do you understand my meaning?"

Slowly, Faith nodded her head, feeling three pairs of eyes upon her. As slowly, she turned to face her father. "Will you give us leave, Papa, to speak alone?"

"As you will, my daughter," said Colton, and pushed up from his chair. He took Jonathan by the hand. "Come, boy," he said, "there is something in the garden that I wanted to show you."

"What is it, Gran'pa?"

"Can you not guess?" he teased the boy, as they passed over the threshold into the hallway beyond.

"My chair, Gran'pa? Is it the chair?"

"You will see . . ."

Faith moved quietly to shut the door behind them. She turned her back against it, flattening her palms along the finished wood, and closed her eyes. Her heart beat rapidly within her bosom. She had spent five years of waiting, of berating herself for the fool, of watching her son grow up fatherless, of knowing that a price must be paid for one's beliefs, and then doubting . . . five years of wondering if Fletcher were unharmed . . . of wondering if he loved her still . . . Suddenly, she felt the warmth of a breath passing across her cheek, and she lifted her lids, eyes emerald in the combination of firelight and hazy, filtered sunshine.

"Faith."

"Ah, Fletcher," she said, and wondered at the years that

had etched his face with fine lines about his eyes and mouth. Yet, to Faith, he was more handsome for this than when she had known him before, for each change in the perfection of his countenance only made him more real, defining his character in his visage. "Fletcher," she said again, and touched his lips with her fingertips, the scar on his brow, and was overwhelmed by the time that had been lost.

He bent forward, kissing the place between the fluid sweep of her auburn brows. His mouth was warm, as was his breath. His arms, strong as ever, slipped behind her back, pulling her away from the door, holding her against his chest as he lowered his chin to her hair. His grip was convulsive.

"Faith—"

"I know."

"We can never get it back. The time is gone."

Faith said nothing.

"We were foolish, you and I. I was not mistaken in my duty, nor you in your cause, but we should never—"

"Hush," said Faith, and buried her cheek against his chest, to listen to the pounding of his heart.

"We allowed so much to slip away . . . Jonathan is grown, and quite like you, Faith . . . He doesn't know me. He does not know me."

Faith felt her heart break with his loss. "He will know you now," she said. "We will make certain of that. Already, he accepts you, and I have not allowed him to grow without knowledge of you, as his father. I spoke of you often, to him."

"But when he knows of my occupation, my love? What then? You have not told him that I am a 'redcoat,' have you?"

Faith shook her head against his linen shirt.

"Then, he will either despise me, or flounder in confusion. What is it that we have done? Yet, had he been raised beneath my influence, he might have desired to follow, one day, in my footsteps; and you would have grieved over that, I know." With a sigh, he released her, bringing both hands up to rub at his eyes wearily. "There is no telling what might have been. I am only sorry that we have lost so much time."

"It hurts, very much," admitted Faith, after a moment.

* * *

Night fell, and the four of them settled down to a late supper. Some time during the course of the day, Faith's father had reached an understanding with her husband. The atmosphere was relaxed, and Faith felt content, happy. The fire in the great-room was bright, warming the house that cooled in the absence of autumn's bright sun. Jonathan nodded sleepily over his plate, enjoying the unusual privilege of staying up late, to dine with the adults. Before the meal was concluded however, the boy dozed off, and Fletcher lifted him carefully from his seat, carrying him to bed.

Faith followed behind, to show Fletcher where her son—their son—slept.

"This is his room," said Fletcher quietly, in a strange awe. A sadness, too, was betrayed by his tone.

"Yes," said Faith, as she turned down the quilt, removing the boy's shoes, and breeches, before tucking him in. She bent, kissing Jonathan's brow. Fletcher watched the two of them in silence.

"You have done it, without me," he said. "You have raised him, without me."

"Oh, no, Fletcher," said Faith, drawing him out into the hall. "Not without you. I have considered you, and what you might have done, in all things. I have tried to influence our child on your behalf, as well as mine."

Wordlessly, Fletcher bent and kissed her, on her brow. He took her hand.

"Fletcher?"

"Yes?"

"Now that Cornwallis has surrendered, what will happen to the British troops?"

"As soon as terms are agreed to," answered Fletcher, "most of them will go home."

"And you?" said Faith.

"To England?" he answered, with a slight lift to his voice. Faith peered up at him in the dimness.

"You say that," she said, "as if you are asking me."

"I am," he said. "The war is over. I have seen it through,

to its galling end. It is now for us to decide what we shall do. Or do you no longer wish to do so?''

Faith closed her eyes. "For so long," she whispered, "I was afraid that you would never return to me. Five years is a very long time, Fletcher." The man stirred beside her, in fear of what she was about to say, but Faith brought his hand to her lips, and held it there. "I will go to England," she murmured against his flesh, the ridges of his knuckles, "if you desire it, my heart."

"You would not be happy there," he answered, encircling her shoulders with his arm, "I know that you would not."

"Oh, no," said Faith, against him, "it matters not where we live, as long as I am with you. I should have gone with you, Fletcher, and not allowed you to leave Boston without me. I should have followed my heart in all things, and not abandoned you."

Fletcher tipped his head back and laughed, softly. Yet, he said, soberly, "Did you not have Jonathan to think about? I will not leave here, without you."

"No, Fletcher," said Faith, "you will not."

From below, there came the brisk sound of a summons on the front door, loud, and insistent.

"What the devil—?"

"I don't know," Faith replied, and started forward. "I will go and see."

"No," said Fletcher suddenly, and took her by the arm, holding her back. "Wait." Following his gaze, Faith saw that he was staring down the staircase toward the fanlight above the door. Through the clear panes, Faith could see the flaring, tossing illumination of torches, moving across her father's tended lawn. Unaware of this, John Colton had risen from table, to answer the knocking.

"I am coming, I am coming," he called out in annoyance.

The door was opened to admit William Bliss, and two other men from the village. The torches behind them threw their shadows long across the floor and onto the treads of the stair.

"Mr. Colton," said William. "Good evening."

"Bliss," retorted Faith's father. "What is going on?"

"Mr. Colton," repeated William, "are your daughter and her—husband—on the premises?"

"Naturally," said Colton, without hesitation. "We are only finishing dinner, and they have gone to put the boy to bed. Why? What, precisely, is the meaning of all of this?" he demanded, indicating the two men with William, and the others, outside. He knew them, all of them, by name, but the nature of their appearance on his property had caused him to forego his usual greeting. The color in his cheeks was high with anger.

"I have come—I must—" Bliss faltered then, seeing Faith at the stairhead, with Fletcher close behind. He looked away. "Mr. Colton," he said, "the man who is your son-in-law, and who was introduced as Mr. Fletcher Irons, is, in fact, a British lieutenant, and worse, a British agent of espionage."

This declaration was followed by utter silence, in which the crackling of the torches was as the crumpling of stiff paper, in one's hands. It seemed to fill the hall. Then Faith took a deep breath, and stepped forward, to descend the stair.

"What nonsense—" she began, but was interrupted by Fletcher's hand on her arm.

"William Bliss, this is my home," said her father, drawing himself up, "and I will not tolerate your accusations. Step outside, at once."

Fletcher, sighing wearily, eased past her on the staircase. "What makes you so certain of your facts, Bliss?" he asked, and his voice was marked by what the younger man mistakenly assumed was sarcasm.

"More than two years ago, I came face-to-face on the field of battle with you, Lieutenant. I don't suppose that you have cause to remember me, but I remember you very well. No one bears a scar quite like that one," and he waved a finger in the direction of Fletcher's segmented eyebrow. "I saw you again, months later, in a small town in New York, and you were dressed in finer clothes than your red coat, and pretending to be something other than what you are. But I knew you. Your face is not easily forgotten, not even when under the guise of a heavy beard. Now that you have shaven it, Lieutenant, I know that I am not mistaken.''

A spy, thought Faith. She wanted to tell Fletcher that she had never told anyone.

Outwardly, she remained calm, glaring down at William in feigned disbelief. She swept down the stair behind Fletcher, skirts brushing over the treads as she descended.

''The punishment for espionage in wartime is, as I am certain you know, Lieutenant, nothing less than execution. It is our duty here,'' and Bliss nodded to the other men with him, ''to see that punishment carried out.''

Faith stared down at him, at the fanatical intent in his brown eyes, at the anger, vengeful, blinded by patriotism, and said, slowly, ''Will . . . no . . .'' before she felt her knees buckle beneath her.

Fletcher caught her in his arms as she lost her balance and fell.

Chapter Thirty-five

Through the night, torches flared, and the sound of men's voices was surly and vicious, as they tread heavy over the hard-packed earth. The great shadows of trees were golden-edged, and the sky overhead, star sprayed and black as thickest velvet. Fletcher walked with his hands roped behind his back; his head was bent, and every step jarred his purpled jaw so that the pain shot through, blindingly, to his brain. But it was not broken; he felt certain of that. The flying butt of the musket had done nothing quite so serious; a tooth was loosened, his tongue was split, his flesh was mottled with dark bruising, no more. He could bear it. What he could not bear was the searing memory of Faith's expression of horror when the gun had been brought against him. He had not been allowed to remain around long enough to witness the anger that followed, or he might have had cause to feel somewhat better.

Dawn, he thought. At John Colton's insistence, the execution had been delayed until dawn, and these men seeking revenge rather than justice, Fletcher felt certain, had heeded the man's voice. Now, he had the remainder of the night to consider his life, what he had done with it, and what he was going to lose. There was not much chance of escape, as he was outnumbered by more than thirty-to-one, and bound, besides. He wondered, briefly, if he would be permitted to see Faith again, before the end. Her father's anger at discovering that he had not been told the entire truth concerning Fletcher's occupation might very well preclude that happening.

This is ridiculous, he thought suddenly. Why am I walking along so meekly, a lamb to the slaughter? And he balked, swinging his leg about to catch the man behind him in the knees, felling him with that one blow. The torch toppled to the earth, rolled, and went out in the damp humus. In a fury of motion, he fell on the next man, catching him by surprise, and then the next, but after that, he was caught with his arms pinned back roughly. Someone hit him in the jaw with a closed fist. The star-studded sky spun overhead, and was gone.

Faith gazed down at Jonathan's sleeping countenance. How beautiful you are, she mused; how perfect and beautiful. She ran her fingers through his hair, then across his brow. He winced, and turned his head away, on the pillow.

Slowly, she walked to the window, to stand staring out through the parted curtains at the yard below. They were still there. How could they? These were men she had known her whole life; grown up with; she knew their wives, had helped them in the absence of their husbands, cared for their children; she had harvested their fields for them while they had been away to war. And now they refused to listen to her, to listen to the voice of reason. They had brutally beaten Fletcher, taken him away, to keep him prisoner until the sun's rising. After which, they would hang him. And she was under guard in her own home, so that she might not try to aid the man she loved.

Angrily, she let the curtain fall.

Glancing once more at Jonathan, she left the room, crossing the hall to where her father sat faced toward the fire on the hearth in his own bedchamber. His head was bent, intent on something in his lap. As Faith came forward, skirts whispering, she saw that he held a miniature portrait of her mother folded in his hands.

"Papa," she said.

He set the tiny oil aside, raising his wigless head against the back of the chair; he looked tired. "Sit down, Faith Mary."

Faith did so, on the floor at the hearth. It was not the position she should have taken up, for it made her feel small again, in the way of a child, and moved her toward tears rather than strength. She bit her lip, and lifted her chin. Her green eyes were unblinking.

"You did not tell me," Colton said, at last.

"No," said Faith.

"Did you think that I would not understand?"

"No, I did not. Would you have?" Faith countered, quietly.

"No," he admitted, "I would not have."

"It is revenge that these men want," said Faith. "And what gives them the right to take the life of another man in cold blood?"

"He is a British lieutenant," answered Colton, almost as an echo of her question.

"So? He has freely admitted as much, to you, and them."

"And a spy," added her father. "That is what warrants him his sentence."

"Oh, Papa!" cried Faith, covering her face with her hands, and then she lowered them. "What have we been fighting for, for six years of our lives? Why have men died, in battle after battle? Only so that my husband may be hanged, without due recourse. What point is there in that? The war is over, Papa. And I love him. Do you think that I would love a man who is not good, and kind? He is Jonathan's father, Papa. Do you know—do you know," she said, "that he once saved the life of Elizabeth's husband, Jack? He, too, was imprisoned, and to be hanged. Fletcher arranged his escape, so that he might live.''

John Colton was silent a moment, digesting the news. "Why?" he asked finally. "Why did he do that?"

"For Elizabeth. For her love of Jacques, and her love of me.''

"This," said Colton, "does not make him a good soldier, if he can be swayed to such acts for the sake of love. You must have been a great confusion to him. It would have been better for him had he chosen a different occupation, my daughter.''

"He was a very good soldier," said Faith, reluctantly. "I am neither proud, nor scornful, of that; he is a man of honor, Papa.''

Colton lifted his hand, dropping it gently into Faith's hair. "It is too late, Faith. The young men of this village—of this country!—are a hasty lot. They will do what they will do, in the name of what they believe. In time, there will be men, young men, with sound mind, who will lead them. I know that there was no trial of your husband, Faith, but that which was hastily constructed. Yet, it was not only Bliss who recognized him, but two of the others, also. It is too late to stop them. I am sorry.''

"Sorry!" Faith exclaimed. "Sorry! What good will that do him, or me, or Johnny? None.''

But John Colton merely shook his head, staring in agonized silence at the tears streaming over his daughter's cheeks as she rose, and left the room.

Faith dried the moisture from her skin with the backs of her fingers. She leaned her forehead against the chill surface of the window, gazing out at the intricate shadow of the evergreen that grew against the house. The stars were caught in its thick, needled branches. Long ago, she had climbed down that tree, from the window, on a dare. Long ago . . .

Faith leaned forward, peering down to the earth below. At the far corner of the house, a shadow lounged, half-dozing, hat low, arms propped on the stout barrel of a musket. There was no one else to be seen. Breathing in rapid, shallow gasps, Faith opened the window. The fellow did not so much as glance up. Quickly, Faith divested herself of her hooped underskirt and pannier, tying the dragging length of her gown in a knot above her knees. "Dear God," she whispered, "please help me . . ." Yet, with no clear idea of what she would do once she had escaped the house, she swung her right leg over the sill, and reached out to the nearest branch, grasping it desperately with both hands. And then she swung out, hanging for a moment in the air chillingly before her feet found the lower branch they sought. Her stocking tore. She glanced back, to see if she had been noticed, but the man—young Miller, she thought—was still nodding over his gun.

Making the final drop in relative ease, Faith slipped away quickly into the forest behind. It would be simple enough to find where they held Fletcher, for she doubted that he would be entrusted to the safekeeping of only one man. They would all be there, waiting for the dawn.

It seemed to be well after midnight, though Fletcher could not be certain. The shed in which he had been thrown was damp and dark, smelling of earthiness and livestock. The smoking torches outside did not conceal the odor, nor did they provide more than a small illumination through the cracks in the weathered walls. Several times, he had attacked the door, but it was heavily barred, as he knew it would be. His shoulder was bruised from his attempts at battering it down. Around his wrists, the rope had cut deep. Blood dripped along his fingers.

Sitting on the hay-strewn ground, Fletcher brought his head back against the wall, and swore softly in the darkness.

He rubbed his eyes; smelled the blood on his hands. When first he had been put upon to shed his uniform to commit espionage against Britain's rebellious colonists, he had known what would happen, in the event of war, and his capture as a spy. He had known it, and had expected to accept it, bravely. But he found that he could not. His courage was still strong, yet he held it in reserve for a woman, for a boy, and no longer for the uniform which had clothed him, and which he had served, for so many years.

Sighing, he rolled his head against the splintered wood.

The villagers had built a fire, and were gathered around it, keeping warm as they spoke in sullen, sometimes laughing, voices. As Fletcher listened to them, his anger grew, for he heard Faith's name often, in condemnation. It was a vile injustice they did to her. He knew this, more than anything else. He recalled how she had fought him, and how, even in loving him, she had been steadfast to her country. But, these men would not understand. Once again, Faith would be forced to leave her home. He had heard of the occurrence in Boston from Elizabeth, when he had gone to that town, to Faith's home, and found it in the possession of Jacques Sabot and his wife. When the British had departed, they had left smallpox behind, preventing an immediate entry by the rebel army, but once they had come, and the patriot population had returned to their houses, there had been nothing but misery for Faith: she was castigated by neighbors in verbal assault, her property was damaged, her hopes, he knew, were dashed down, and finally smothered in the earth. She'd had to leave, with Jonathan, Elizabeth told him, for there had been no other choice.

Faith, he thought, where will you go next? We must be together, my love; we must.

In a flurry of furious motion, he rose, and bent double, sliding his arms with great effort along his legs so that he could bring his bound hands before him. After, he stood breathing hard for a moment, listening to the noise outside. There had been no change. These men would not sleep this night.

Stealthily, Fletcher moved to the rear of the building, stepping carefully over objects his boot touched up against. At the back wall, he pressed close, peering through a chink in the planking to the night beyond. Nothing there. Trees, and more trees, reaching back into shadowed blackness. Good.

Dropping to his knees, he began, painfully, to dig. He tasted the iron of blood in his mouth from his tongue, and turned his head aside, to spit reddened saliva into the hay.

"Damn it," he cursed, as his curved fingers moved clumsily through the packed earth. "Damn it."

Suddenly, his ears picked up a new sound, moving just opposite the wall. He ceased his digging with held breath. The sound moved on, yet after a moment, came back again.

"Fletcher?" Spoken so softly, that he almost missed it.

Fletcher bolted upright in shock, pressing his mouth close to the wall. "Faith," he demanded, "what are you doing here?"

"Do you think for one minute," she answered in a barely contained anger, "that I would let them keep me locked up in my own home, knowing—knowing—" and here, her voice broke.

"Hush, my little one," he soothed, through the slatted wood.

"I am getting you out of there, Fletcher," said Faith, recovered. "We—you, Jonathan and I—are leaving here, to-night."

"Is Jonathan there with you?" asked Fletcher in disbelief.

For a moment, Faith said nothing, and then she answered, slowly, "No, he—he is still in his bed." For the first time, she realized the implication of her hasty actions. "We will have to go back for him, Fletcher. I—I am sorry. I did not think . . ."

"No matter," answered Fletcher, hurriedly. "If I find myself free of this place, I will send you back, and you will stay until I send word for you. Understood?"

"Fletcher, no," said Faith.

"Very well, then. Can you dig, without noise? Here, where I tap. As quickly, and soundlessly, as possible. If you are discovered . . . oh, Faith, be careful, I beg of you. I would not risk your endangerment, if I did not—love you so," he trailed off, and bent, to knock on the wall before he began, once again, to claw at the earth.

"Papa," whispered Faith, in confusion. Behind her, Fletcher was just coming over the sill, and he paused, balanced on the ledge. Both of them were dirty, their clothes torn, rent by their race through the woods once they had gone beyond earshot of the men by the fire.

John Colton stood in the center of Faith's bedchamber, clutching his sleepy-eyed grandson to his chest. The boy's head was on his shoulder, his thin, naked legs wrapped about his waist, as he gazed in drowsy bewilderment at the sight of his mother and the man who was his father, climbing through the window.

"It is nearly dawn," said Colton. "They will know soon that you are gone, Lieutenant."

"I am aware of that, sir," said Fletcher. "I plan to leave Faith here with you, and go on, as fast as I am able. I will be no good to her dead. In time, I will call for my family. Soon, God willing."

Colton was silent a moment, and then he nodded. But Faith spoke up quickly, and in a harsh whisper.

"I will not allow you to do that, Fletcher! We go with you, both Jonathan and I. There are some hours yet before dawn; time enough to be away."

"Not," said her father, "if Bliss has already gone into the shed where they were keeping your husband, and has found him gone."

Jonathan blinked, and turned his head.

"We are wasting time, Papa! You know that I will not allow this! Papa, won't you help us?" pleaded Faith. She ran her fingers through her tangled hair and, without waiting for a reply, turned away and yanked the cover from her bed. "Fletcher, take Jonathan to get dressed. I will gather what we need . . . Why won't you go?"

Fletcher shook his head, sadly. "There is no helping it, my love. I must go alone, only for now. Later, soon, I will send for you."

"No," said Faith, and strode past him, to take her son from her father's arms. "Get dressed, Jonathan," she said to him, whispering. "We are going to play a game, in which you must be very quiet, no matter what. Do you understand?" The boy nodded, his small brow creased. "Dress in your warmest clothing, and bring another shirt to me here, and your favorite toy."

"The one that Grandpa made me?" asked the boy.

"Yes," said Faith. "That will do fine. Do not forget your

winter coat. Can you remember all of that? Hurry, dear, do hurry.''

Then, with no further look to either her father or Fletcher, she removed two clean gowns from the armoire, and folded them along with a pair of stockings, a chemise, and an extra blanket. Bending, she tore off the stockings she wore, heedless of the presence of either man, and replaced them, pulling on a pair of sturdy, black boots. In the top drawer of the chest, was a small, tin box. She took it out, and shook it, then opened it to peer at the contents. ''It will have to do, for now. I will write for the remainder of my account, if you will be so good as to have it sent to me, Papa.''

''You will not reconsider the wisdom of your course?'' asked Colton, quietly.

''This is,'' said Faith, ''the wisdom of my course. I love Fletcher; he is my husband. I will stand by him, from now on, in all things. Nothing will make me change my mind.''

''I should have known that,'' said Fletcher.

''As should I,'' answered his father-in-law, gruffly. ''Very well,'' he said, and again, ''Very well. Listen to me. The wagon remains afield, unhitched, where I left it the day before yesterday. You know the place, do you not, Faith? Good.'' He began to pace, thoughtfully. ''It must have been Providence that led me to leave the horses in the pasture. Take the gray mare: she is the most stolid, and trustworthy, though she is not much for speed. Lieutenant—Fletcher,'' he corrected, ''I trust you to take care of my daughter, and of my grandson. You will see that no harm comes to them.''

''Yes, sir,'' said Fletcher, and in the darkness of the room his smoky eyes were luminous.

''You must hurry,'' the man continued. ''And take the river path. It will, of course, be the most obvious, but it is necessary. Hopefully, you will have time to be gone before the search begins. It is possible, also, that there will be no search, for these men will have had the night to consider their actions, and distance may dampen their enthusiasm for—justice. But this, I cannot guarantee. Faith, go now, and take what provision you need, from the kitchens. Quickly.''

As soon as she had gone, the man spoke again. "Fletcher, heed me. I love my daughter very much, and the boy who is your son. Pray, do not disappoint me in your care of them. Prove to me that you are, indeed, a man of faith, and of honor. I would keep them here with me, if I could, but it would break my Faith's heart, and yours. You will go, with my blessing.

"And this," he added. "I will sign over the deed to you, and Faith, of a property which I own in Newcastle. It will be yours, to farm, and to build a life, away from this part of the country that has seen such misery for the two of you. A document must be signed also, by which you will swear never to bear arms against this country again. By this, I will sponsor you, and guarantee your conduct."

"Thank you, sir," said Fletcher. He extended his hand, and the man took it in a firm clasp.

"Now," said John Colton, "I must go and say farewell to my grandson. That is a private matter between he and I. And there is not much time."

The pale sun shone on Faith's red-gold hair, sprinkled here and there with wisps of gray; and into her eyes, so that they glimmered, like glass, and marked the tiny lines beside her mouth and at the places where her lashes met. Fletcher wondered, for a moment, if she had ever looked more beautiful.

Longmeadow was far behind, lost in the fog of morning. Fletcher had listened, time and again, for the sound of pursuit, but there had been none. They had stopped, once, to allow the horse to drink, and to rinse the blood from his own hands, and his battered jaw. He had been shaking with relief, thanking God, Faith's father, and Faith, in turns. Faith, most of all, for the risk she had taken had far exceeded his own. His life, after all, had been forfeit; she had returned it to him.

"Faith," he said.

"Yes?" She seemed to start from a light doze, though in truth, she had only been thinking.

"This is the beginning, at last. All the others," he said, speaking slowly through his stiffening jaw, "were but false starts, and stalls, in our life. Not endings, at all. We will make this work, I promise you. We have let outside influences keep us apart. But no more."

Faith turned her head to look at him, at his dark hair, and the determination of his gray-blue eyes as he squinted in the rising sun. She marked the curve of his mouth, the dark swelling of his jaw, and the crooked smile that tried to break out across his face. She thought of Jonathan, sleeping now in the wagon behind, and wondered about his future, his acceptance of his father, not as a British officer, but as a man. It would work, she decided. Oh, yes, it would work.

Reaching across the seat, Faith laid her hand across Fletcher's, feeling the curve of it, the ridge of bone, the strength of it; the gentleness.

"Our divergent paths have come together at last, my love," she said. "Never shall we part again. That is my promise to you."

And behind them, beneath the mounded quilt in the bed of the wagon, Jonathan rolled in his sleep, and sighed.

GET
LOVESTRUCK!

AND GET STRIKING ROMANCES FROM POPULAR LIBRARY'S BELOVED AUTHORS

Watch for these exciting romances in the months to come:

October 1989
FAITH AND HONOR by Robin Maderich
SHADOW DANCE by Susan Andersen

November 1989
THE GOLDEN DOVE by Jo Ann Wendt
DESTINY'S KISS by Blaine Anderson

December 1989
SAVAGE TIDES by Mary Mayer Holmes
SWEPT AWAY by Julie Tetel

January 1990
TO LOVE A STRANGER by Marjorie Shoebridge
DREAM SONG by Sandra Lee Smith

February 1990
THE HEART'S DISGUISE by Lisa Ann Verge

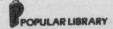

POPULAR LIBRARY

GET LOVESTRUCK!

BUY TWO AND GET ONE FREE!* ORDER YOUR FREE BOOKS HERE...

1) Choose one free title from this list 2) Complete the coupon
3) Send this page and your sales receipt(s) from the books participating in our LOVESTRUCK promotion to the address below
4) Enclose a check or money order for $1.00 to cover postage and handling.

☐ *FOREVER WILD* by Louisa Rawlings
0-445-20170-3 (USA) 0-445-20169-X (Canada)
From the author of *Dreams So Fleeting* and *Stolen Spring* comes an enthralling novel of two passionate loves set in the post-Civil war era.

☐ *A CORAL KISS* by Jayne Ann Krentz
0-445-20336-6 (USA) 0-445-20337-4 (Canada)
A sizzling contemporary romance with a blazing love story.

☐ *SORORITY* by Sheila Schwartz
0-445-20165-7 (USA) 0-445-20166-5 (Canada)
The author of *The Solid Gold Circle* presents a dazzling saga of four women who survive and triumph through the years, their friendships enduring from their college days in the 1950s through maturity.

☐ *THE IRISH BRIDE* by Mary Mayer Holmes
0-445-20171-1 (USA) 0-445-20172-X (Canada)
A dazzling, richly textured historical romance set in Maine in the 1880's, about a spirited red-headed beauty, a rugged frontiersman and a love that knows no bounds. From the author of *The White Raven*.

☐ *SAVAGE HORIZONS* by F. Rosanne Bittner
0-445-20372-2 (USA) 0-445-20373-0 (Canada)
A saga of the wild West centered around the tumultuous life of a half-Cheyenne, half-white man, and his struggle to straddle two conflicting cultures.

☐ *WILD NIGHTS* by Ann Miller
0-445-20347-9 (USA) 0-445-20375-7 (Canada)
The story of two young lovers on a fast-track to fame, fortune—and heartbreak.

☐ *DARK DESIRE* by Virginia Coffman
0-445-20221-1
A spellbinding tale of passion and betrayal set in 19th century England and France.

☐ *SWEET STARFIRE* by Jayne Ann Krentz
0-445-20034-0
This bestselling romance writer has created a passionate, warmly human story of two lovers in the far distant future.

Send to: LOVESTRUCK Promotion
Warner Publishers Services
c/o Arcata Distribution P.O. Box 393 Depew, New York 14043
Name _____

Address _____

City _____ State _____ Zip _____
*Subject to availability. We reserve the right to make a substitution if your book choice is not available.

412